I Wrote this Last Period

I Wrote this Last Period

Kurt Simonsen

iUniverse, Inc.
Bloomington

I Wrote this Last Period

iUniverse books may be ordered through booksellers or by contacting:

iUniverse
1663 Liberty Drive
Bloomington, IN 47403
www.iuniverse.com
1-800-Authors (1-800-288-4677)

ISBN: 978-1-4620-3126-9 (sc)
ISBN: 978-1-4620-3127-6 (ebk)

Printed in the United States of America

iUniverse rev. date: 07/15/2011

Contents

Foreword

By Ramandeep Dhillon and Monica Harrington

Contrary to the title, *I Wrote This Last Period*, we, Honors English III of 2011, have established this piece with the utmost of diligence. We faced many challenges with strenuous hours of labor, but we have overcome and gained much wisdom along the path. As challenges come and go, we grow stronger with every battle won, and learn from every mistake made. Life must also be dealt with the same ferocious attitude to conquer and succeed in achieving what one is truly capable of.

Our stories were indeed not written ten minutes ago in study hall, which is clearly displayed through our creativity, passion, and drive to prove ourselves. Many great writers never get the chance or recognition they deserve, however we will not be ignored in such a way. We are determined to show our worth and attract attention, for we have instilled great time and effort into our writings.

It is important to remember that if one fails to prepare, then prepare to fail. We poured our hearts into our work, not in scribbles on a piece of notebook paper from history class, but from our hopes, dreams, and experiences. The more work one puts into their work, the better the product will turn out, and the larger impression one will leave on a skeptical reader.

As senior year approaches with celerity, we present a taste of our ambitions and unique styles to the whole world. We know we are risking a real deal, for we are amateurs attempting to match the remarkable talent of many before us, but we have no fear. One must burst into the world with confidence and hope for the best, even if they do not know what will occur. Whatever happens, will be for the best and we are sure of that.

Fish Out of Water

By Samantha Chieffalo

—〰ⷧⷨⷩⷪⷫ〰—

The morning sun glistened on the deep blue sea as the serene, rolling waves crashed into the shore. Here, at the waters edge, was the only place where I can find my peace. Being a teenager is stressful enough and the added pressures of being an all-state swimmer only make it worse. Don't get me wrong, I love swimming more than anything in the world because it's the only time where I feel at bay and in control of my life. Swimming is my passion and has allowed for my competitive personality to be brought out. It has taught me so many lessons about how hard work, motivation, and persistence pay off. My mother has always told me that I look so beautiful when I swim because my long blonde hair flows graciously with the current. My body has become so muscular from all the swimming I do that I can't even wear cute bottom up tops because they never fit my shoulders. All the potheads even tease me in school for my green eyes being blood shot from all the chlorine. I'm stuck in the middle between my heart and my head, the two of them playing tug of war with my emotions. I have secrets no one knows, and the decisions I have to make will affect everyone who loves me. No one, not even my mother and father can understand what I am experiencing now and it all started after my 16th birthday.

* * *

Today is finally Friday and my last period class seems never ending. I've been staring at the old analog clock above the door for what feels like hours, but with ever glance the minute hand barely moves.

3

"Ella! Pay attention!" shrieked Ms. Perkins, my English teacher. I quickly looked away from the clock and thought to myself, I only have seven more minutes of this torturous subject verb agreement lesson. Then it'll be time to celebrate my sweet sixteen, the day I've been patiently waiting for since the 3rd grade.

"BEEP!"

Jumping out of my seat I dashed to the door. The hallways swarmed with kids running around chaotically and resembled a stampede of cattle. No one could wait to get out of the prison they call school. When I finally made it through the crowd I ran home eagerly to see if my mom had put up any decorations. The theme of my party was under the sea and my mom and I had worked tirelessly at finding the perfect sand, and seashells to decorate with. There always was something about the ocean that I connected with, and I feel like I could thrive in a world surrounded by water. Walking through my front door I was splashed with the colors of the beautiful tropical fish that we rented for the party. My mom managed to find the perfect fish tank, one that illuminated the scales of the fish in such a manner that they casted of beautiful rays of color. My entire downstairs had been tidal waved in shells and sand and I could not hide the grin that sprawled across my face. This is perfect! It is exactly what I envisioned and my mother couldn't have done a better job in putting it together. I walked upstairs to change into my coral dress and as soon as I reached the top step the doorbell rang. This is it, my party has officially started and I can't wait to have some fun!

After getting all-glamorous for my guests I walked out to the back to see a beautiful clam bake all set up. All of my closest friends arrived and stood around a picnic table covered in any type of seafood a person could imagine. There were steamers, mussels, lobsters, and crabs and no one was shy in grabbing a huge plate full. While filling my plate up with some mussels my crush, Gil Stern, wandered over to my side. Gil is as dreamy as they came with his ocean blue eyes and dark brown tousled hair. His teeth are perfect, with each tooth as white as sugar and perfectly aligned in his mouth. I can feel his eyes on me and I pretend not to notice despite the fact that I desperately want to look longingly at him. He is my perfect guy and ever since we were five years old I have wished I were his perfect girl. Suddenly I snapped back into reality due to a tap on my shoulder.

Gil offered me a smile and said, "Great party Ella. Your house is beautiful!"

The fact that he spoke to me surprised me so much so that I was unable to utter any words.

"Oh thanks, I'm glad you could come," I said. I took a moment and thought, is that really all I can say 'glad you could come'? I'm pathetic. No wonder he hasn't paid any attention to me up until now. As our short conversation ceased I started to walk away,

"Wait Ella," he said, "why don't we go down to the beach to eat this?" I couldn't have been more overjoyed at the thought of eating my favorite food, in my favorite place, with my favorite boy. On our way down to the shore Gil kept asking me questions like he was interested in getting to know me; our conversation never got awkward. He's so down to earth and unlike any jock at our high school. We spent hours down at that beach talking about everything from our fears to our quirks. When it started getting dark Gil walked me back up to my party but before making it inside he made sure to mention that he really wanted to see me again. We hugged goodbye and as he made it halfway down the street he turned around and screamed,

"I forgot to give you your birthday present!" I watched him rush back and as he approached he pulled me in close and kissed my lips so gently. As we pulled apart a grin lay across his face and he turned and made his way home. My party was such a success and I couldn't have asked for anything better. When the last guests trickled out I made my way up to my room and turned on my beach waves CD. The only way I was able to fall asleep at night was by listening to the soothing sounds of the ocean. As I fell into my down comforter I thought about how perfect life was. Everything I wanted is working out for me, and as I thought more and more about it I drifted away into a deep sleep.

"BEEP! BEEP! BEEP!" It's 5 AM and time for me to get up and get ready for swim practice. The sound of my alarm reverberated in my head and as I went to shut it off the touch of my hand electrifies it. Dazed and confused I curiously look around to see if I spilt a glass of water. With no water to be seen I conclude that a fuse must've blown and made my way downstairs to the refrigerator. I pulled out a cartoon of Florida's Natural orange juice and take a nice healthy swig. When I reach in to put the orange juice back it didn't come off my hand. The cartoon feels like it is super-glued to my palm and nearly impossible to force off. Grabbing any utensil I can find in the kitchen I try to remove the cartoon, but hardly anything can get it lose. Finally, I decide to run my hand under some cold water and within seconds the cartoon releases from my hand. The whole situation is so confusing and I can't come up with a logical explanation for what has just happened. While washing my hands I notice that they are covered in reflective iridescent scales. I scream at the top of my lungs and my mom comes rushing down the stairs,

"What honey, what's wrong, is everything okay?"

"No mom," I stutter, "there are scales all over my hands and I'm electrocuting alarm clocks!" She looks down at my hands with fearful eyes. As she yells for my dad the scales on my hands disappear. It had been the strangest morning and I had a feeling it was only the beginning. I had missed swim practice at this point and was almost late for school, but before leaving, my mother urged me to call her if any more scales showed up on my body during the day. Leaving my house I knew exactly who I needed to go see about this strange phenomenon that overcame me in the morning.

Arriving at school I'm terrified. I couldn't let the other kids see who I am morphing into because not even I knew. I needed to find Ms. Berkley, and fast because she could hold the answers to my dilemma. Ms. Berkley was a biology major who specialized in the field of marine bio. She is a slender tall woman with red curly hair and very small brown eyes that squint when she says something important. Everyone at school thinks she's a wack job because she always rants to her classes about how mermaids and lochness monsters actually exist. She claims she has actual research to back up her radical ideas but nobody ever wants to listen, except for today. Today was my day to listen to Ms. Berkley talk about mystical underwater sea creatures because I needed explanations. Who else in this school could try to substantiate the fact that a human was turning into a sea creature? No one but Ms. Berkley. When I walked in Ms. Berkley looked at me with a spirited face,

"Why hello Ella! I haven't seen you wandering these hallways since freshman year! How are you darling?"

"Not so great Ms. Berkley which is kind of why I came to see you today," I answered. She looked at me in a strange manner and then proceeded to make her way across the classroom to my side.

"Well what's bothering you dear?" she asked.

"I've been experiencing some strange, out of this world symptoms which started this morning. I was hoping maybe you could help me figure out what's wrong." I responded.

"Well honey I have a biology degree but that does not mean I'm a doctor or know anything about anatomy for that matter."

"I know, but a doctor can't help me with this problem. Only someone who knows a great deal about sea creatures can." The look of confusion that was previously displayed across her face vanished as excitement projects from her eyes. At this moment I knew I confided in the right person because she is going to find a logical explanation for this phenomenon one way or another. As I stood there Ms. Berkley inspected my body and asked me what had happened in the morning. I explained to her that I electrocuted electronics and that objects stuck to my hands but before I could finish my sentence Ms. Berkley asks if I saw scales anywhere on my body.

"How did you know?!" I asked.

"I read a case once in a psychology book about how a patient was admitted into a psych ward because she thought she was turning into a mermaid. Her friends and family believed she was a schizophrenic because she had crazy "delusions" where she believed she was developing scales. It turns out in the middle of the night one of the nurses witnessed the girl's leg's morphing together and turning into a tail. They quickly brought her to the ocean and she was never to be seen or heard from again. She displayed the exact same symptoms as you Ella!" she said.

"So you're saying—"

But before I got the words out Ms. Berkley darts to the back of her bio lab and starts pulling out all sorts of books and equipment. For the rest of the day Ms. Berkley and I sit in the back of the classroom running all sorts of tests and doing all kinds of research and our results showed a lot. The six hours of experimentation paid off because by the end of the school day I knew all kinds of new things about my new self.

On my way home from school I thought about how I should break the news to my parents. I mean how exactly do you tell your parents that you're turning into a mermaid? Most people don't even believe that they truly exist! I can't even believe it myself, but I knew Ms. Berkley was right when she came to her conclusion. We had run so many tests and they all pointed to exactly that! We learned I could climb walls, generate electricity, talk to fish, and swim extremely fast. Ms. Berkley recommended that I show my parents instead of telling them because it would help them to accept who I truly am. So when I walked through the door I turned and climbed up my living room wall. My mother came rushing in from all the noise and saw me hanging on the ceiling and fainted. This isn't going according to plan and it appears to be harder to break the news then I thought. While still hanging on the wall Gil walks in from my kitchen. I forgot we made plans to study for our English test so the shock of seeing him causes me to fall from the wall onto him.

"What is going on?" Gil shouts.

"I'm sorry, I'm just trying to kill a fly that was up really high on the wall," I said.

"No you weren't Ella. Don't lie to me. I watched you climb that wall! What are you?" My stomach felt like it had been punched. Now the boy I have started caring so deeply about is going to think I am some freak of nature and never talk to me again. My mother arose and looks at me with crazy eyes.

"Was I just dreaming or did you just climb that wall?" she asks. I knew it was time; I just needed to tell them. I called everyone to the living room to explain what they've just witnessed.

"Mom, Dad, Gil . . . I'm a mermaid. And I know this is going to be hard for you guys to believe but it's really happening to me. All the weirdness that we experienced this morning happened for a reason. I'm changing into who I'm meant to be and I want you guys to embrace it with me because in a month or two I will sprout a tail and be forced to live a life away from you in the ocean."

A huge weight has been lifted off my shoulders and I know that I can count on these guys to be there for me through everything that I am about to experience.

"Honey, we'll love you no matter what and the fact that you're turning into a mermaid doesn't change that. We love you unconditionally and we've always known you've had a passion for the sea, we just didn't realize that you were actually meant to be in the sea," said my mom. Everything just seemed so perfect. My secret is out, and I still felt loved. Looking over at Gil I could tell he was still uneasy about the whole situation. I grabbed his hand and dragged him down to our favorite place, the beach.

"Gil are you okay with this?" I asked.

"Ella, there is something I need to show you." Gil got up from the sand we sat on and walked over towards the calming waves. As I watched him I couldn't fathom what he wanted to show me from the ocean. Slowly he submerges his entire body under the sea and allows it to be tousled around by the strong undertow. Afraid that he may be drowning I run over to the shore only to await the sight of someone else like me.

"This is what I have wanted to show you for so long Ella." Gil says as he splashes me with his beautiful indigo tail.

"You're a mermaid too?" I ask.

"The proper term is merman, but yes I am." I couldn't believe my eyes. I didn't feel so alone in this strange situation anymore, not only did I have my family, but I also had Gil. So many questions poured in my mind and I needed answers.

"How long have you been like this? And why can you turn into a mermaid whenever you please? I ask.

"My transformation began after my 10th birthday. Don't you remember when I moved for those 5 years? My mother told everyone I was living with my aunt, but I was really out in the sea. As a merman when you turn 16 it is your mission to find your soul mate. One day I watched you practice swimming at the beach and ever since I hadn't been able to stop thinking of anything or anyone else but you. I came and watched you all the time. That's when I knew you were my soul mate. So I went to our king and asked him to grant me with a year on land so I could be with you and so you could fall for me." Everything Gil said made sense. I really don't remember seeing him after 5th grade up until this year. Maybe he is right. Maybe we are soul mates. But what does that mean for me? Am I supposed to drop my whole life and family so I can swim away with the man of my dreams?

"I am scared Gil," I said.

"I know you are Ella, that's why you need to come with me. In a few days your legs will become connected and layer after layer of shimmery scales will encompass your bottom half. Soon after your fins will sprout out of your feet and you will need water. If you choose to satisfy your need for water you will forever be a mermaid, but if you choose to go without water you will remain a human. I can make you so happy; you'll love everything about ocean."

Conflicting thoughts take over my mind as I sit and worry about my future. My heart and my head are in two completely different places and both will not surrender. The life I have created is on land. Everything I know is on the surface and everything below is unknown. Gil is an important part of my life, but I know what I must do. The next few days flew by and the decision I did not want to make is quickly approaching. While lying in bed a strange sensation came over my body. I flipped off my covers and glanced down at the body part I had previously known as legs. Now they glowed from the scales and no longer remained separate. I called Gil and he rushed to the house to bring me down to the beach. As soon as he arrived he threw me over his shoulder and carried me down to the beach with my mother and father following. Once there I lay in a bed of warm sand and prepare for the next step of my transformation. Gil sits alongside me holding my hand so tightly in hopes that I will never let go. Before I know it my feet vanish as turquoise fins replace them. It is decision time. The shore has always been the place where I find my peace. All elements of the ocean soothe my soul and it's a place where I want to stay and be enriched.

"Mom, Dad, I love you both," I said. And with those final words, Gil and I dove into our home.

Buzzer Beater

By Matt Mason

—ᴥᴥ◦◦᠑᠊᠍᠑ᴥᴥ—

It seemed like everything was going our way and we had the momentum as Scott grabbed the rebound and dribbled up the court. I tore down the court rapidly with ten seconds left on the clock ready for the pass. But that pass never came. I was wide open in the corner but Scott never looked my way. He took it himself and never got a good shot off. We lost our first game by two points and as I walked off the court, I gave a menacing glare in Scott's direction. I would make sure that never happened again.

I'm a baller. It's my game and I'm good. I have started on varsity since my freshman year. So has Scott. We have had many colleges come watch us this year and there is a surge of rivalry and jealousy between us. The competition is huge, especially between us. Word has spread that we are going to get full ride scholarships to Division 1 schools and I need to uphold my expectations. I don't know about him, but to me, basketball is serious stuff. It's more important than school, family, and friends. To me, basketball is life.

When I'm dribbling up the court I am in a totally different world. I'm in the zone when playing and nobody can stop me. I can see plays before they happen. I know where everyone is on the court, when they are cutting to the basket, or when someone is in position to shoot. It's like I'm a mind reader. I'm a playmaker and always one step ahead of others. I understand basketball better than anything else, like the back of my hand. Basketball is my game and it will remain that way forever.

I'm 6'4 and I have made the All-State and All-American teams every year. Scott has been named "Defensive Player of the Year" for the past four years but there is no question that I am a much better player. Everyone knows that I'm more experienced, know and understand the game better, and am just an all around better player than he is but he won't admit it. Scott is too cocky. I think he is more jealous of me than actually hating me, but Scott takes his anger out on me in practice. He is like a raging bull in a rodeo trying as hard as he can to take me out for the season. I am more of a team player, while he is all about his numbers. I have won a couple of games this year on last second buzzer beaters, but unlike Scott, I will pass the ball off if I don't have a shot. He will do whatever it takes to rack up points and will occasionally throw up shots even if there is no way he will make them.

I guess that's why I got the nickname MJ. Everyone agrees that my playing style is like his. I'm clutch, one step ahead of everyone on the court, and can take over the game by setting the tempo just like Michael Jordon.

Our team has good ball movement and great teamwork. Every year we are state contenders but this year we have a chance to go all the way. All of us have been on the same team since we were in middle school, except for Scott. He transferred from another school because his dad got a new job. I heard that Scott was the star player of his old team and was used to doing everything alone. It's different here. We all play different roles on the team and contribute in different ways.

Swish! Another basket made and we had another win under our belts. We shook hands with the other team as we ran into the locker room to celebrate. It was the middle of the season and we were 8—1. After starting off the season slowly with a loss, we had the best record in our division. The games haven't even been close, but our easy schedule was coming to an end. Our team is good. We are too good, too powerful, too controlling. We have controlled the tempo of the game without letting any team in it. We have annihilated every team that has blocked our path. Me, Scott, and the rest of the team were going to have to step our game up to the next level if we wanted to make a run at the championship. The pressure had increased and so did the competition. The road to finish out the schedule was going to be tough.

We went on to win our next two games in the fourth quarter but the following game was one to forget. We were playing our high school rivals across town who were our arch enemies. The game was going back and forth. We would score, and then they would retaliate with another basket. If we stopped them on defense and went on a small run, they would creep their way back into it.

I was outstanding, making incredible passes and looking for the open man. They were double teaming me but they couldn't stop my intensity. I made my team look great, but Scott was doing the complete opposite.

Our rivals were big, powerful, and dominant but we were too fast for them. Scott wasn't getting exceptional position and as a result, he was faltering. He was playing horribly while I had my "A" game on. Scott wasn't grabbing rebounds, or averaging anywhere near his six blocks per game. Instead, he was just throwing up shots this way and that. By the time halftime rolled around, he was sitting on the bench.

Scott soon came back in to start the second half. Although he was being shut down and playing horribly, without him in the starting rotation, we didn't stand a chance.

We started falling behind and the game seemed to be out of reach. Putting Scott in was our only hope. After promising coach that he was going to get his head into the game and start playing hard, Scott was back in. Scott finally managed to put a body on the big man for the first time in the game and then did the dirtiest play I ever saw from him. Scott backed him down, spun, and elbowed the giant square in the face as if he were aiming for a bulls eye. The floor boards of the gym rattled and it felt like an earthquake erupted as the big man fell hard to the floor face first. Scott was ejected from the game and the big man was rushed to the hospital with a concussion. Scott was charged with a technical foul and coach was furious. His foolish play took us right out of the game and, in a couple of minutes, they had a ten point lead. Before we knew it, the buzzer sounded and we had lost our second game of the season.

The crowd stormed the court as my team meandered to the locker room with our heads slumped. There was dead silence in the locker room and soon everyone left for the bus; except for me and Scott. I was disappointed and full of rage as my head rested in my hands. I was pissed at Scott who single handedly lost the game for us and ruined our undefeated season.

"Are you coming? The bus is going to leave without us," Scott said as I gave him a menacing glare.

"The bus is going to leave without us? That's what you have to say to me after today's loss?" I was full of anger and frustration, rage, and the hate for Scott made me explode. I couldn't control my emotions and I shot up like a rocket and got right in his face.

"We had a chance to go undefeated and you let the team down. You single handedly lost both games for us and ruined our chances of having a perfect season!" I yelled in his face as I gave him a hard, forceful shove into the lockers.

"Calm down. Why are you so excited? It's just a game." Scott squeaked in a scared, nervous voice.

"No it's not just a game! Don't you get it, Scott? This was the biggest game of the year. Not only are they a squad full of stars and talent, but they are our cross town rivals. This is our whole season. This is what we play for! This game passes and then we focus on states. You are a ball hog! You are all about yourself and your stats! If we are going to compete for the championship, we need to play like a team and we need you to be part of it. You played like a scrub today!" I was in his face screaming and was all over him. I was furious and going ballistic. Then, suddenly, without warning, I punched him square in his face. It happened so fast that he didn't even have time to react. I started walking towards the door, of the locker room and when I arrived at the door I turned around and yelled,

"Either change your ways fast or don't even bother showing up to practice!" At that moment, coach walked in. It was a bad time for him to walk in and I dashed out of the locker room. To my surprise, he didn't yell, or even scream. He just spoke to me in a calm, simple voice.

"Get on the bus. We'll talk about this tomorrow at practice."

That night I didn't sleep well, as I was nervous about what the coach was going to say at practice the next day. Everyone was there except for coach so we decided to just shoot around until he came. You could hear a pin drop in the gym that afternoon, because other than the sound of basketballs bouncing, no one said a word. Coach came in and brought us to mid-court and told us to take a knee.

"I'm very disappointed in our performance yesterday and extremely disappointed in some of you," Coach said as he gave me a death stare that sent chills through my body. Everyone started to point at Scott and Coach began his speech again. "There is no need to point any fingers. You two know who you are. We are a team and we need to play together. We have great ball movement when we work together on the court but that only gets us so far. Yesterday, we had great ball movement but we dug ourselves an enormous hole that we couldn't get out of. That can't happen anymore. We are a team that's good but to become great, we need to have trust in each other, and lead by example. We were able to get past the first part of the season but now our schedule is getting harder. We need to prove again that we are state contenders and we can beat the elite of the elite in our conference. I want you guys to look for that extra pass instead of throwing up the ball when you don't have the shot. This goes for driving to the basket when nothing is there because someone is bound to get open. Don't force the ball but make crisp, sharp passes that will result in points for us and not for them. Scott and MJ, you guys are our leaders on and off the court and I expect you two to act like leaders and settle your differences fast. The quicker you guys resolve your problems, the better we will play." As he dismissed us to start practice, he pulled Scott and I to the side and said with a grin,

"You know we can have two stars on our team, not just one. Start playing together!"

That practice all we did was passing drills and they transferred into our games. We were passing well and playing the best ball of the year. We were looking forward to playing and that little pep talk by coach turned our season around. Scott was still himself but he was getting better. He was slowly changing. He was coming around and he started becoming apart of the team.

Those were the only losses of the season and we were on fire. We rolled right through into the state championship. It was time to play ball and become state champions; our ultimate goal.

It was game time and we were pumped. The adrenaline rushed through our bodies as we got ready for the tip. As the game started, the thoughts of college scouts watching us were washed away and thrown into the back of our minds. We were here to play and that's what we were focused on.

Scott took the tip for us and as we were walking onto the court, he came up to me and said,

"Look, I don't like the style we play here and I'm playing to impress the college scouts today. My numbers have been lower since our second loss and I want them to see my full potential." He didn't even wait for my answer. Instead, he ran off to take the tip leaving me standing still with my mouth wide open and frozen in disbelief.

The whistle blew, Scott took the tip, and the game was under way. I couldn't believe it! Scott reverted back to his old self again! He was not playing team ball or passing to anyone.

It felt like a flashback to the first game we lost this season. Scott was losing the game for us and was eventually pulled from the game when we were down by a dozen. With a team effort, we were trying to inch our way back into the game. I was playing really well and was able to create opportunity by spreading the floor. Our ball movement was fantastic and I was doing everything I could to help keep our team in it. But our opponents were doing everything a little bit better and we weren't able to make much of a dent in their lead. By time the second quarter ended, we were only down by six and finished the half on a 6—0 run.

There was still a lot of game to play and we wanted to come out strong for the second half. The tides changed and we had the momentum going into the third quarter. Scott was back in and they were double teaming me, which left Scott open for a couple of easy buckets down low. I hit a couple of threes and our team was keeping it close. Although I already racked up over twenty points, I was creating plays that not even NBA players could stop. We were doing everything right and as the fourth quarter started, we took the lead and we were up by one. It was neck and neck through the entire second half, and it was anyone's game.

Our adrenaline was pumping hard as our play intensified. Our confidence was high, as everyone was contributing; not just one particular player. The lead continued to oscillate back and forth. I was in the zone. It was close going into the final four minutes of the game.

We stopped them on their next possession and when we got the ball back, I lobbed a pass over the defender to our big man. Scott caught the ball, put a body on his defender, laid it up, and with that, we were up by two. They called a timeout, made a play, and hoped it was successful. We were in a tight press and somehow they managed to get a shot off in the lane with 3.5 seconds left on the clock. That shot tied it up and Coach quickly called a timeout to stop the clock. We knew our play. We practiced it all the time. We understood this play inside and out. It was up to us to seal the deal.

I was nervous as I picked up the ball to inbound it. The whistle blew and the clock was ticking down. Scott flashed to the foul line. I passed him the ball with some zip. He turned around and I sprinted up court. I caught the pass near the sideline right beyond half court. I quickly dribbled to the top of the key. Time was winding down and I didn't have much time. We were only down by one point and I had the open shot. My mind was whizzing. I set up to take the shot but out of the corner of my eye, I saw Scott cutting to the basket. In an instant, I passed the ball! Scott caught it with one second left and made an easy lay up as time expired.

We won the game and everyone celebrated. The crowd stormed the court and carried Scott off. As Scott was carried off the court, I looked on in the distance. We won the state championship! We finally achieved our goal after a long, hard season. As I looked into the distance, my anxiety was growing and building up inside of me. It was time to celebrate, and I sprinted into the locker room to participate in the celebration.

Through all the chaos and drama through the season, we had reached our goal! Everyone was going ecstatic; celebrating, cheering, and glad that we ended our season on a high note in the most dramatic finish possible. We were excited and couldn't be happier!

As I sat on the bench in the locker room watching everyone celebrate, Scott came up to me and simply said "nice pass."

Dream Come True

By Matthew Ederle

It all started when he was around the age of four. He sat on the lap of his uncle, staring intensely at the television screen. The New York Yankees were playing against the Boston Red Sox that fine, fall afternoon. It was a perfect day for baseball. As the youngster watched each Yankee player run on and off the field, hustle for every baseball, and have the time of his life, he knew that, when he grew up, he had to be a Yankee.

Young Andrew Thomson was a die-hard Yankee fan ever since he was born. The one thing that he loved more than the Yankees was the actual game of baseball. There was nothing he could compare it to. He loved the game of baseball with all of his heart. He had never seen something so beautiful. The look of the uniforms, the cheers of the fans, the thrill of the game, it was all perfection to him.

Andrew's father loved him very much and did everything he could do to make him happy. At every store that they went to Andrew wanted a ball. He would cry and cry and cry until he got that ball. He would cry forever if he had to. Eventually his father would give in and buy the baseball, even if it killed him to do so. Andrew had more baseballs than he could ever dream of. He had more baseballs to play with than any other kid in the world, but something was missing. He needed something to catch them with; he needed a glove.

Not just any glove, it had to be top of the line, the finest leather, the most perfect pocket and size, and it had to look good, of course. As soon as Andrew got his glove he was the happiest kid alive. Everyday after school, rain or shine, he would play catch with his dad until the sun came down. The front yard became his very own

Yankee Stadium. His dad would act as an announcer and give a play-by-play analysis of Andrew's actions.

"It's a fly ball to Thomson and he makes the catch, oh my goodness I have never seen that good of a catch in all my days!"

"It's a hard hit ball to Thomson, Thomson dives and he makes the catch! The crowd goes wild. What a miraculous catch by Thomson!"

Every time Andrew's dad cheered for him and praised his efforts, Andrew became more and more motivated. He started to throw harder, run faster, and give more effort each and every day.

When summer came around Andrew's father bought him a bat. Andrew was now around the age of 6 and was now strong enough to swing a baseball bat. Every summer day his dad took him out on his boat to Cockonoe Island for a little batting practice.

Andrew's father was a boat fanatic. He grew up with boats his whole life. He played with boats, he raced them, studied them in college, and he even worked with them after he got out of college. Andrew's dad loved boats just as much as Andrew loved baseball; the only thing he loved more than his boats was his son Andrew.

Andrew Thomson was no ordinary kid; therefore this was no ordinary batting practice. There was no field, no fielders to shag balls, and no baseballs to be caught. All there was was a kid who loved the game of baseball with a bat in his hands, and a dedicated father with an unlimited amount of rocks to throw at his child. Andrew would face towards the open sea while his father would stand either right next to him or right in front of him and chuck rocks at him all day. The sun hitting off the clear blue water supplied the perfect spotlight for Andrew, the nearby and passing boats and even the animals indigenous to Cockonoe Island made the perfect crowd, and the smiles and laughs baseball brought to Andrew Thomson made it the perfect day.

When Andrew grasped the bat in his hands, he felt empowered. Everything went motionless around him; it was as if time stopped. Nothing else mattered. The only thing that was on his mind was he hitting that rock as far and as hard as he could. He would hit all sorts of rocks, big rocks small rocks, fat rocks, skinny rocks. It didn't matter to Andrew, they were all baseballs to him. He would start off easy with the bigger and more round rocks. After he was a master at hitting those he would move to the more difficult skinnier and smaller rocks. Eventually he would be hitting the tiniest rocks on the beach, he would even hit grains of sand that not even the well-trained eye could see. Andrew and his father, and anyone closest enough to hear the "Swoosh" sound the bat made when Andrew swung it, knew he was hitting the sand grains, even if they couldn't see it. They heard the "Ping" from the bat when he made contact. The ping was music to his ears. It was like Mozart to him. Such a beautiful sound, it was a sound that you got addicted to, a sound that fed your soul, it was a true melody.

All of this batting practice made Andrew the best hitter in town. His hand eye coordination was inhuman. He never missed a ball. He caught everything he could reach and hit everything that was a strike. He had a great eye and everyone knew it.

Andrew went through more bats in one summer than most baseball players would go through in their entire lives. He hit so many rocks that he would put cracks and dents into his bats. Eventually those cracks and dents turned into broken bats. Bats would snap in half like it was nothing when Andrew was hitting on Cockonoe Island. Every bat that he broke, every rock he hit, every drop of sweat that dropped from his face; made Andrew a better ball player. He became the best hitter in the league in just one summer. Pitchers all over the state feared him, even those older then him.

As years went on Andrew grew stronger, ran faster, and his knowledge of the game increased. He became a better ball player with experience. He made the all star his first year of little league. He was the best player on the team by far. When players voted for the captain of the team it wasn't even a competition, Andrew Thomson won unanimously. That all-star season was a breakout season for him, even though it was his first year. He carried the team to the World Series championship game and won the game for them with a walk off grand slam. He never made an out. He hit 1000. He had 36 hrs, 127 RBIs, 43 stolen bases, and 83 walks. Pitchers were scared of him, who wouldn't be? He was an absolute monster, beastlike.

Years of dominance in little league forced coaches to move him up to the next level, 3 years early. He was 11 years old and was playing with kids twice his size and 3 or 4 years older than him, but he was not intimidated. He welcomed the challenge. He wanted to do anything that could make him better. Andrew made the all-star team, as expected. He had a great year, not as great as his little league days, but still phenomenal. He started at third base for the all-star team. He was as defensively sound as he was offensively. He never made an error. He made every play. He was exceptionally fluent with every move he made. Everything was smooth. Each throw he made was spot on and every ground ball was fielded with finesse. His plays at third sure were a thing of beauty; he made his father proud.

Andrew thought high school baseball was going to be a breeze for him. He was the fastest, strongest, and best player on the team, but he still had a lot to learn. About half way through the season Andrew's team played their cross-town rivals. In order to guarantee a victory, Andrew's coach made him pitch that day. It was a little bit foggy on the field, hard to see. The air was cold and damp, not great weather conditions to play a baseball game in, but this did not stop Andrew from getting on the mound and pitching his heart out. It was a home game for Andrew and his team, so they took the field first. When the first batter stepped up to the plate a feeling of intensity went over the crowd, they knew they were about to witness greatness. Andrew struck the first batter out in three pitches, 3 straight fastballs. The sound of the ball releasing from his hand was pure power, the sizzle sound the ball made as it traveled toward the catcher struck fear into the opposing team's hearts. When the ball hit the catcher's mitt, which was in what seemed like a blink of an eye, birds fled from the trees near by because they thought it was a gunshot, but no, it was only Andrew.

He struck out the side for the next 3 innings. When the fourth came tumbling along, something changed. When he went out to the mound to take his warm-up pitches before the start of the new inning, everything seemed normal, but it wasn't. He still had a flamethrower for an arm and all the confidence in the world, but something was different. The rival team did not look frightened or disturbed, scared or threatened; instead they all had a smirk on their faces. It was as if they figured out how to hit Andrew, but it didn't matter because Andrew's team was up 13 runs, no one could come back from that. The first batter of the inning came up to bat, he repositioned his helmet, knocked the dirt off his cleats, spit out the leftover sunflower seeds in his mouth, and looked over for the signs from the third base coach. All preparation to get struck out by Andrew again, or so everyone thought.

Andrew gave up 18 hits that inning. He walked 6 batters and blew his team's league. He let up 15 runs, all earned. Andrew had failed his team, and failed himself. He was taken out of the game that inning. On his was to the dugout he kicked the dirt, pouted in his steps, and slurred profanity underneath his breath. It wasn't until he reached the dugout that he would unleash his true emotions.

When Andrew reached the dugout he threw his glove at the bench knocking over the water cooler and spilling water and ice all over his teammates bags and equipment. He started cursing loud enough for everyone to hear, even the scouts near the left field fence could hear him, and he was in the first base dugout. He started throwing equipment all over the place, helmets, gloves, and bats, even his own teammates. Anything that got in his way was dealt with.

His teammates and friends tried to calm him down, but it was no use. Andrew just pushed them out of the way and continued on his little temper tantrum. Andrew's "outbursts" lasted for a little over 10 minutes. He finally cooled down after the umpires threw him out of the game and he was removed from the dugout and was driving home in his father's car because he wasn't allowed to stay and watch the game. This was the worst day of Andrew's life. He lost his team the game, he acted completely juvenile in front of his family, friends, coaches, and multiple scouts, and above all, he let himself down.

The look on Andrews father's face when he got home from the game was devastating. It struck a shiver down Andrew's spine.

Andrew's father sat him down and said something that stuck with Andrew for the rest of his life, he said,

"Son, I am not mad and I am not upset with your performance today. You played your heart out and for that I am proud, but your behavior on the field, and in the dugout was unacceptable. You not only embarrassed yourself but you embarrassed me. Once again I am not mad or upset with you, I am just disappointed."

Disappointed, that word echoed in Andrew's head for the next minute. He didn't understand what his father meant, but he was certain that he would never allow his father to be disappointed in him again.

Andrew had never lost at anything in his entire life, therefore he had never learned anything about the real game of baseball, and baseball has a lot to offer. You don't learn anything from winning, but you learn everything from losing. You learn who you truly are, you learn how to become better, how to improve, you learn how to cope with your emotions, and lastly you learn that nothing is impossible. No one would have guessed that Andrew would of blown that game for his team, but he did. Andrew learned that he has the worst attitude out of all the people he knows, and he has 3000 friends on facebook. He learned that he allows his emotions to get the best of him. He lets them fuel his fire and put it out. He cannot control his emotions and if he wants to continue with his baseball career, that's going to have to change.

Andrew was suspended for the next two games of the season. After his suspension had concluded he returned to the team and apologized for his actions.

"Guys, I'm sorry for what I did. I let my emotions get the best of me and I promise it will never happen again. More importantly I'm sorry that I failed you, you guys deserve better and I promise that too will never happen again."

After Andrew's apology he was greeted with hugs from all his teammates and coaches. They all forgave him and were surprisingly not mad at him. They all knew how important baseball was to Andrew and they knew losing was not an option for him. They all thought that it showed his love for the game and his compassion toward it.

When Andrew stepped back onto the field the next day at practice he felt strange, as if he didn't belong. It wasn't because of his teammates or coaches, but it was this feeling inside of him. He had trouble catching and throwing a baseball, and even more trouble hitting. He was no longer his usual self. He had lost all confidence in himself and was no longer the ballplayer he used to be. It was like the baseball gods had struck down on Andrew and stripped him of his gift he was once blessed with long ago.

Andrew Thomson was left dazed and confused after that miserable practice so he went to the person he could trust most in the world, his dad. Andrew asked his father a barrage of questions. He asked him why he wasn't playing well, what was this feeling inside of him, and most importantly, how could he get back to the old Andrew everyone knew and loved.

Andrew's father sat his son down and told him,

"Son, the old Andrew is dead and gone, and he is never coming back. You have an opportunity now to be a better ballplayer, a better teammate, and most importantly, a better person. Don't let this chance pass you by, it's a once in a life time opportunity."

Andrew was left in shock after hearing this. He was filled with excitement, but he wasn't able to comprehend what his father said, "What opportunity? What chance? I'm playing awful baseball right now, how can I become a better ballplayer, even a better person for that matter?"

Andrew was flabbergasted; he was so baffled that he could barely get any sleep. He ended up taking one of his dad's old sleeping pills in order to fall asleep. After he took the pill, he knocked out as soon as his head hit the pillow. He slept like a baby, it was his best night of sleep in years, and he was going to need his rest because tomorrow he had a game against the team that forced him to change who he was, his cross town rivals.

Andrew's day at school went by at a ridiculously slow pace. He had three tests he didn't study for and a presentation in AP English that he was unprepared for, he thought he would just improvise. After the school day was over Andrew was able to breath a sigh of release, but he quickly inhaled because he realized his day wasn't over. He still had unfinished business to attend to.

Andrew got on the bus to go to his team's game. The game was away this time so they had to take a bus. The bus was absolutely silent. All you could hear was the sound of the player's headphones playing music into their ears.

When the team arrived at the field, the cheers from the opposing teams fans filled the air. Warm-ups went quick for Andrew. He did his stretching, calisthenics, and warm-up throws relatively quick, compared to his teammates. Andrew was not pitching today so he wasn't worried as much, but he was still nervous. The opposing team had the best pitcher in the league pitching today Bryce Johnson. Bryce was a big guy. He was a man amongst boys at 6'4" and 215 lbs. He was a monster, probably better than Andrew, but no one knew for sure. No one ever compared the two.

Andrew's team was up first and he batted third in the line up. The two batters before him both stuck out on 3 pitches each, not a good sign for Andrew. Andrew despite his anxiety, still walked out into the righty batter's box spit onto the infield grass with confidence, tapped home plate twice with his bat for good luck, and dug in, ready to hit without a flicker of fear in his eyes. Bryce smirked at Andrew and gripped the ball tightly in his glove, wound up, and let it fly.

The ball hit Andrew right in his head, more specifically his temple. The ball smashed his helmet to pieces and broke right through the padding and struck Andrew's head with authority. The pitch was a 96 mph fastball, verified by tree scouts with radar guns. There has never been that much blood on a baseball field before. Andrew instantly blacked out when the ball collided with his skull. The last thing he could remember was hearing people in the parking lot talking about how Andrew Thomson's father was just diagnosed with cancer.

Steven woke up in the hospital on a rainy summer morning. He was woken by the sound of an old lady's raspy voice over the intercom. She called for a certain doctor in the surgery room; Steven couldn't make out the name, he was still a little bit drowsy. Steven couldn't remember who he was or where he was. He called for help as soon as he could gather enough strength to speak.

A nurse rushed in when Steven called. The nurse was female; pale skin, blonde hair, greenish blue eyes, and a nice smile. She seemed extremely nice and spoke with a very gentle and soft voice.

The nurse introduced herself as Sarah. Sarah began to explain what the situation was. She told Steven his name and who he was and explained why he couldn't remember anything. Steven had pancreatic cancer and on top of that he also had a mild case of Alzheimer's. He would forget who he was every now and again. When he heard the news it brought a tear to his eye. He asked how long he had to live and the nurse said with a saddened look on her face, "Not much longer, you probably won't make it through the night. You told your son not to come visit you to leave you be. You said he had more important things to do." Steven was shocked with his decision. His only son wouldn't come see his father on his death bed because he had more important things to do? What could be more important than his dad?

Steven was so caught up in the moment that he didn't realize that he didn't know who his son was, so he asked, "Who is my son, what is his name?" The nurse then explained that his son was Andrew Thomson. She explained that he is a very talented baseball player that you loved very much, more than anything in the world. You told him to follow his dream of becoming a professional baseball player, and hopefully one day become a New York Yankee.

It all came back to him now. The buying of the baseballs, hitting rocks on Cockonoe Island, the countless hours of hard work and dedication the both of them put into Andrew's baseball career, and most importantly, all the fun and good memories the two of them shared.

Steven Thomson, Andrew's father, began to reminisce about his son and how amazing he was, not only as a ballplayer, but also as an individual. He remembers the one thing he wanted most in the world; he wanted his son to be happy. The smile on his son's face and the joy in his eyes were more valuable to Steven than all the money in the world. He wanted to see his son's dream come true; he wanted him to be happy.

After hearing him babble on about his son, the nurse recommended he turn the television on, so he did. She recommended a few channels to watch but put a lot of emphasis on channel 36, sports center. Steven immediately turned to sports center and read in the highlights on the left side of the screen, "Thomson goes pro, and in Yankee fashion". The sportscaster begins to talk about how spectacular Andrew Thomson is, his son. They proceed to show an interview with Andrew. He's all grown up now, around the age of 24. He talks about how thankful he is to become a New York Yankee and how baseball has taught him so much. He explains how baseball teaches you about life, and how to live it. The last thing he says is that he is most thankful for his dad, Steven Thomson.

"If it wasn't for him, I would never be in the position I am in today, and I would never be the person I am nowadays. I love him with all my heart and even though it kills me not to be with him right now in the hospital, I know he knows I will always be with him, in his heart. And he will always be with me, in my baseball, in my life, and also in my own heart. I love you dad, get better soon, I dedicate everything I do from now on to you. Thank you for always being there for me, and thanks for making my dream your top priority and making it possible."

Andrew then looked directly into the camera, as if he knew his dad was watching and said with tears running down his cheeks, "I love you dad."

When Steven heard this his heart skipped a beat. Never in his life has he ever felt so happy and proud. The tears of fear and sadness on his face turned into tears of joy and glee. He saw his sons dream come true, therefore his dream come true. He wanted his son to be happy; he wanted his son's dream to come true. That was his dream.

Steven then turned the television off and closed his eyes. He spoke with a very soft yet powerful voice, "It's a dream come true". He then died, right then and there. He died as a proud father, and because of his son, a happy man.

Dance

By Sarah Vargas

—⁓⁓∘ᘓᗢᘓᗢᘓᘓ∘ᘉ⁓—

"One, two, three, four, five, six, seven, eight. Two, two, three, four, five, six, seven, eight," Alice counted the beats along to the song. As the music played, it flowed through her ears and into her soul. She let the song consume her and take control of her body. Alice began to dance. The movements were exact and on count. Along with the rhythm, her body swayed. Her routine: a mixture of both fast and slow actions. Whatever it was, it was beautiful and it was her passion. There wasn't a care in the world that could disrupt her peaceful, relaxed mindset.

When the song ended, Alice took off her dance shoes. These shoes were the definition of commitment. Many years of dancing had caused the beige color to fade into a dull gray. Every crease and every rip had a story embedded in it. Even the slightest glance at these shoes brought a wave of warm memories to Alice. She wouldn't replace them for the world. Alice placed them and the rest of her stuff into her duffle bag and left the room.

"Oh! Hello Alice. I didn't think you were still here," said Mrs. Damon. Mrs. Damon was the owner and one of the instructors at the dance studio. She was an older woman of twenty-eight. Her face looked worn out today, probably due to the lack of sleep from the previous night. The long hours she's put in to teach extra classes, in order to make her monthly rent, had been adding stress to her life. Other than that, Mrs. Damon was a nice-looking, tall, petite woman. Her long blonde hair was always tied back into a ponytail and you almost never saw her without a cup of coffee. She was about to close up when she caught Alice emerging from the doorway.

"Sorry Mrs. Damon. I just got so caught up in the music that I lost my sense of time. You know me, it's like I'm in my own little world," she smiled.

"That's okay. Hurry up now," she motioned Alice towards the exit, "You can come back tomorrow and spend the whole day if that is what you wish."

Alice could not have been happier. Her eyes lit up like a star in the night sky. She wasn't sure of much in her life but dancing was the one thing that made her feel complete.

The next morning Alice woke up with a smile on her face. "Today is going to be a great day," she thought to herself. Alice could hardly keep still in school. Her excitement of what was soon come was overwhelming, not to mention distracting, to her studies. She didn't mind though; everything was second place when it came to dancing. As soon as the dismissal bell rang, Alice rushed out of class faster than imaginable. She skipped joyfully to her car and drove to the studio.

Upon entering, Alice was approached by Mrs. Damon.

"Can I talk to you for a bit before you go off and do your own thing?" Mrs. Damon asked with a smile on her face.

"Yeah sure," Alice replied innocently. She honestly had no clue what Mrs. Damon wanted to talk about. She hoped she wasn't in trouble.

"Dancing is important to you, right? I have seen you here almost every day, surely it means a lot to you. What I wanted to talk to you about was how dancing affects your life. I want to hear you tell me how it feels. Don't be shy," Mrs. Damon said. Her tone was soft and gave off a friendly appearance.

Alice opened her mouth to say something but hesitated and stopped. She took a moment to ponder her answer. She knew how it felt but could not explain it. Dance was all she knew. Growing up on welfare in a single parent home did not create as many opportunities with hobbies as she would have liked. Nevertheless, if her life was any different, she wouldn't be the same person she was today.

When Alice felt like she collectively organized her thoughts, she spoke.

"To me, dancing is something hard to explain. The way it makes me feel is beyond words. When I'm dancing, I forget all the problems I face every day and just lose myself in the music. I get to escape my reality and do something that I enjoy." Alice paused to think of the right way to explain herself. "I feel like I'm in heaven dancing from cloud to cloud to the sweet angelic melody coming from all directions of the sky. Happiness just overflows me and I find myself in such bliss. Dancing is and will always be my passion. I could never see myself without it."

Alice was not completely satisfied with her answer. She felt like there was so much more to say but her mind couldn't construct her thoughts into sentences. Mrs. Damon could see this and spared Alice the trouble by asking another question.

"I'm glad to hear that. You remind me of myself when I was your age. Anyways, there's a competition coming up. Do you think you'd want to compete as my pupil?" said Mrs. Damon with the slightest hint of excitement.

"Oh my gosh! Oh Mrs. Damon, it would make me happier than anything in the world!" Alice jumped up and down with joy.

"But you know this is going to be a lot of work. You're going to have to put in long hours and more effort than you normally would in order to perfect the new routine I am going to teach you. After a while you may even start to think you hate me. Nevertheless, strict training is what it will take if you want to have a shot at winning. I hope you can understand that," Mrs. Damon spoke slowly in an attempt to calm Alice down.

"I already spend many hours here. I practically live here! I can't wait to start practicing."

And practice she did. As the weeks went by, Alice's talent and skill increased. Her moves were precise and accurate. Every step she took was in step with the tempo of each song. Alice was on top of her game; nothing could stir up her doubt.

Three months had gone by since that day in the studio. The competition was coming up in a week. Alice and Mrs. Damon knew hell week was about to begin. The hours in the studio became long and tedious. Her body ached from the constant strain it was under.

Alice came home exhausted every night, yet she returned each and every day after school. Her commitment was almost as great as her passion.

If Alice didn't love to dance, she might have quit after the first two weeks. But it was because of her love that she stayed. Even when she twisted her ankle and sprained a ligament, she got back out there and practiced into the late hours of the night. When faced with sickness or headaches, she still looked forward to practice. Dancing was her form of healing. It was something that would always be there for her. She relied on it.

The day before the competition Alice began to get nervous. She usually wasn't one to get nervous; however, today was somehow different. Her nerves were getting the best of her and affecting her performances during practice.

"Is everything okay, Alice? You were off by a whole count for more than half of that song," Mrs. Damon asked with great concern.

Alice shook her head and said, "I don't know. I was fine before, but the more I think about the competition tomorrow the more I feel like I'm not ready and that I need so much more practice."

Mrs. Damon sighed. "Oh Alice, don't worry. Those are just the before-competition—jitters getting to you. You know you can do this. We've both worked hard for this. You have shown so much growth in both skill and maturity. You know you're ready for this. Don't give up now."

"I just don't know. I don't want to let myself down if I don't perform well, but I also don't want to give up and regret not taking this chance," Alice said.

"Alice."

"Yes?"

Mrs. Damon looked at Alice for a good minute. Her long pause was making Alice uncomfortable, though she failed to notice. She wanted to make sure the next words out of her mouth would not be the wrong ones.

Finally she spoke, "If you give up now, I know for certain you're going to look back at this moment and wish you took this chance. I don't want you to feel like all you did was a waste. Although it didn't hurt to become better, you shouldn't feel like all the long hours were for nothing. You deserve this. The competition should not be scary to you; it should be seen as your reward for all the effort you put in for it. That's how you should think of tomorrow as something you want to do. This is your passion."

Alice's personality flipped completely. Hearing the inspiring words of Mrs. Damon gave Alice a new found confidence. Nothing could get in her way now.

"You're completely right. I deserve this. I am going to walk into that studio tomorrow and dance like I've been doing every day. I am going to embrace the music and let it guide my movements. The music and I will be one," Alice said, "I'm going to give it my all."

The next morning Alice arrived at the competition. Her dance shoes tied tight.

Reflections

By Emily Kopas

—⸙⸙⸙—

I remember like it was yesterday. Hugging me so tightly against her soft warm skin to a point where I could barely sneak in a breath; I remember feeling the greatest affection and emotions I had ever experienced. It is the simplicity of this picture that makes the photo so special to me. It is of me and my best friend; the person who was there for me at every step I took, the person who I could tell everything to, and always be assured everything would be okay.

Right now I am in deep need to hear this voice of my mother again. The attic, full of junk my mother loved to buy, made the loft feel as if I were in her presence and had been reunited with her again. I was cleaning and giving away all of the mementos my mother had cherished when she was alive, when I came across this photograph of my mom and me. The picture was from when I won first place in my second swim race. Swimming, a passion my mom and I always had shared, brought upon so many exultant memories I have of her.

There is nothing better than the feeling of being loved and admired by your mother. These emotions were expressed in this photo. At every race my mom was there to cheer me on as well as throughout my life. Not a moment went by when she hadn't supported me, which I believe made me the mom I am today.

When the day arrived when I watched her grasp for that last breath of air, a feeling of relief came over me knowing that she was no longer going to suffer from this unrelenting disease known as cancer. This caused a flood of emotions to run through my soul and mind. Even though I knew that her presence would no longer be with me to share memories, the relief of knowing that I no longer had to deal with the uncertainties and personal anxieties gave me a mixed bag of emotions, both happy and sad.

I lost my mom two years ago today, and not a day goes by without thinking about her. I feel as if someone ripped my heart right out of my chest. She had just come over to congratulate me on my third child I planned to have in May, when my life drastically changed for the worst in a blink of an eye.

*   *   *

"Congratulations, Mary I love you so very much," were the last words I heard my mom say. My mom had come over for my annual birthday dinner and she brought her famous chocolate chunk mouse cake she had made for every birthday I had since I was five. My husband and I told her the news of our expecting child. The joy my mom expressed in her endless smile brought tears to my eyes. My oldest daughter and I walked her out to her car but right before she left she had given me a shiny gold locket that she always wore on her neck. It read, "A mother and daughter are special you know. They are friends of the heart wherever they go. They like to share secrets and life's simple pleasures. Memories of home are their greatest treasures."

She gave me a tight squeeze much like the one she gave me in the photo and was off. As my family and I went on our usual nightly routines, I got a phone call from the Los Angeles Police Department.

"Is Mary Jones there?" From the serious and deep tone of the officer I knew something was wrong.

"Mrs. Jones, your mother has had a bad accident," he said. After hearing these words everything became a complete blur.

"Mommy is everything okay, are you sad?" asked my daughter Grace, as I hung up the phone. Grace, my eight year old daughter, sensed my anxiety and concern. I told her everything was fine and sent her to bed. I felt as if I needed to deal with this emergency on my own. I didn't want to worry my family. My husband's mom was recently put in a nursing home and I knew he had struggled emotionally. I did not want to burden him with this new tragedy. That night I told my husband, Jay, that I was going to take a drive. I drove around the neighborhood frequently to

clear my mind. When I arrived at the hospital, the volunteer working at the information desk, told me my mom was in intensive care on the 9th floor. When I got to the floor I went straight towards the nurse's desk.

"Your mother has been in a very serious accident," the nurse explained. I asked if I could see her and I was told the doctor wanted to speak to me first. I tried my best to stay calm and to breathe, but I just couldn't. I knew the outcome would not be good. I began to fall apart, I felt my face get hot, and the tears started rolling down my cheeks as I saw the doctor walking towards me.

Seven hundred and thirty days later, I haven't stopped thinking about my mom. Every day since my last birthday with my mother, I think about what if I had brought my mom home the night of her accident. Would my best friend still be living out her dream in our house, helping me raise my children? As I am going through all of these pictures of my childhood which my mother has stored in her attic, I realize she would be disappointed in me. She would not want me to dwell on the past but to move forward and continue to live life to its fullest. My mom always told me that life is too short to worry and to not dwell on the past. However, I cannot seem to overcome the profound feeling I suffered when the doctor had informed me that the end of the road was approaching for my mom.

* * *

Dr. Paul told me, "Your mother is in critical condition, Mrs. Jones. The impact of the car that slammed into her has caused her right lung to collapse." I didn't need to hear anymore. I knew that the cancer my mom had been fighting for the past six months did not give her a chance to win this new battle. She was just too weak. The doctor let me know that it was only a matter of time. He said that we could put her on a respirator to keep her with us a little longer. At this time I knew I needed my family with me. I tried to be strong and handle this on my own but I just couldn't bear the pain any longer. My eyes blurred as the tears streamed down my cheeks.

Reflecting back on the emotions I experienced on this day, December 28th, 2008, I remember the feeling of failure and lack of strength. I had to face the loss of personal control and the inability to save my mother's life. I felt as if I should have been able to cope with my mother's death on my own; to prevent my family from having to endure the harsh realities of fatality that I had been dealing with. Looking at the picture of my Mom, Dad, and me in Florida during happier times as we shared wonderful family memories together, I realize the importance of the family unit to support and guide you through these tough and unsettling times.

*   *   *

My husband arrived at the hospital fifteen minutes after I called him. He gave me a hug and reassured me that everything will be okay.

"I just don't know what to do, I love my mom dearly and hate to see her leave us but at the same time I do not want her to suffer," I explained to Jay as we were walking to my mother's room. I took my mom's cold, frail, and lifeless hand. It was once smooth and soft, and held my hand whenever there was a problem that I couldn't handle. This was the hand that was strong enough to shovel the winter snows back when the snowfalls were four feet deep, filled our garden with beautiful flower beds, and tended to its needs all summer long. This was also the hand that held my new born children and cared for them for the first years of their lives. Now it was the hand that had its life drained from it. It was thin, white, weak and fragile; the nail beds were even white instead of pink. Her life was slowly slipping away and I had no control over what was happening.

"How can I keep this lifeless body going when it wants to slip away from the pain and suffering it is enduring, just for my selfish desires to preserve a past that is slowly slipping from my grasp," I asked myself. "I am not being fair to the women, my mother, and the grandmother who has done her job here on earth and is looking for the peace and tranquility in a life here after. God give me the strength to make a fair decision for my mother." As I gently twisted my locket on the long chain around my neck in my hand, it clicked open and I once again read the words, "A mother and daughter are special you know. They are friends of the heart wherever they go. They like to share secrets and life's simple

pleasures. Memories of home are their greatest treasures". These words, given to me in a necklace by my mother, helped me make my final decision as I realized my mother and I will always be, "together where ever we may go."

As I spoke to my mom in a soft shaky voice, I told her, "It is time mom for you to enjoy peace and rest, which you have earned so much of. I have decided to let you go back to your creator and end this pain." After I said these words, a tear ran down the left side of her soft, pale, white cheek. I knew this was her way of telling me she had been listening to every word I said. I then felt her heavy, weak, fingers start to flex using up all the strength she had left, to wrap her fingers around my hand as she had done so many times before. It was then when I saw her chest heave forward and then her body slowly fell back into the sheets. I knew she was finally at rest.

So many emotions and memories flooded my mind as I cleaned up my mother's attic. Spending the time to reflect upon all the memories and feelings I have had since my mother had passed, had allowed me to come to peace with myself. My mother was my companion and friend. I never realized the impact she had made on me as a woman, a wife, and a mother. Growing up I would argue and disagree with many of my mother's ideas about life. Now, as I look back and examine the last few years, I see the journey my mother has lead me on has brought me into a new appreciation for my family.

As I turned the last box in the attic over to make sure I went through all its contents, an envelope descended through the air and onto the floor below. When I picked it up, the content was thick and bulging. It was addressed to my parents. The return address was The Catholic Charities Orphanage. As I opened up the envelope and read through its pages, I came to the realization that I was adopted as an infant.

"Why hadn't Mom and Dad ever told me," I asked myself. My mom and I never kept secrets from each other. Confusion began to overtake me. My mom and I shared everything with each other. My parents raised and treated me as a person they cherished and loved, yet I was never their genetic offspring.

Although the discovery of this letter had caught me by surprise I realize the unselfish and unconditional love that my parents had given me. They took me in as an infant and made me a part of their family. They were there for me when I took my first step, said my first word, road my first bike without training wheels, graduated from high school and college, walked me down the aisle, and most importantly, my parents loved me for who I am. My eyes welled with tears.

My connection and love for my mom has grown even now in her death. My reflection on the memories in the attic, in the boxes, in this letter, and in my locket, has created a powerful bond between my mother and me which shall never be broken.

The Cage

By Kathleen Gill

—〰〰✦✦✦〰〰—

I haven't seen daylight in five years. Not directly, at least. I've seen the small lines of light on the floor, as the sun shines through the tiny, barred window across the hall near the ceiling, but I don't think that really counts. All these years, I have been locked up in my room, if you can call it that. It's more like a cage. There is a hole in the door for the tasteless food he shoves through twice a day, and there's a toilet in the corner, but other than that, it's empty. I sleep curled up in the middle of the floor, my matted dirty blonde hair acting as a pillow between my head and the cement. The cold metal bars separating me from the hallway, hinder any chance of escape. He tells me that this is for my own good and that he doesn't want me getting hurt. He says it's safer to be here, and living out there in the world is overrated. Some days, I believe him. Others, however, I manage to find hope. Today is one of those days.

My name is Trista Cooper. When I was a younger, I had a great life. My family was supportive, I had a few close friends who really cared about me, and I was in the top of my class at school. As I got older, I became distanced from everything in my life. My friends stopped talking to me, my grades fell, and I was constantly arguing with my parents and younger siblings. I developed paranoia, feeling as if someone was watching me everywhere I went and hearing whispering when I was alone. I tried telling my parents, but they said it was just my imagination. It wasn't.

When I was thirteen, I saw him for the first time. I was home alone, and as I was walking down the stairs from my bedroom to the kitchen, I glanced out the window into my yard. In between the two trees in the center of the lawn stood a man dressed in black. I sprinted back up the stairs and dove under the covers of my bed, but then the whispering began. However, instead of going away after a few minutes, it only intensified. I couldn't make out what the voice was saying, even as it grew louder and louder. I heard footsteps coming up the creaky stairs and the doorknob turning. Trembling, I slowly pulled the bed sheets off my head, but before I could see anything, he jammed a hood over my head to obstruct my vision, dragged me down the stairs, and pulled me out the front door. He threw me in the trunk of a van and started driving. At some point, I fell asleep, and when I awoke, I was in this prison, and I've been here ever since.

I still don't know much about the man who brought me here, other than the basics. His name is Eric, he has dark, shaggy hair that falls in his eyes, and he always dresses in black. He rarely talks, but when he does, it's usually because he's angry or frustrated with me. Unless he's bringing me food or the television, he just acts like I'm not even here. Every day around noon, he pulls up an old TV outside my cell so I can watch it. It only has one channel, but it's nicer to look at than my usual surroundings. The show he lets me watch isn't really a show at all; it's actually footage from the outside world. I see everything that goes on out there: friends laughing together; parents looking at their children, eyes filled with love and amazement; students being filled with knowledge. Once, I saw my family. They were walking the dogs at the park, and they looked happy. Eric told me that it wasn't really my family, but his sly smile told me that he was lying. I'm pretty sure that he only brings me the TV to remind me of what I'm missing. It makes sure that I don't get too comfortable here, that I can't convince myself that it's not that bad here.

I like to follow a routine to achieve some sense of normalcy. I wake up when Eric turns on the dull fluorescent lights and slides in my breakfast, a bowl of cold, bland oatmeal, a piece of stale bread, and a small cup of water. He must fortify the oatmeal with nutrients missing from my diet, like protein and vitamin C, because if he didn't, I would've died from malnutrition by now. After finishing breakfast, I like to pace the six- or seven-step length of my cell and write a story. I can't actually write it down, since he won't give me a pen or paper, but I use my imagination. I have a couple of different situations that I rotate, like where I would be today if I had never been brought here, what I would do if hr set me free today, things along those lines. My stories always have happy endings.

I try to finish my story as Eric wheels up the TV around midday. I used to look forward to the TV; it was a window to the outside world. It let me see what was happening out there, from wars and natural disasters to school plays and birthday parties. Celebrations were my favorite scenes to watch; now I dread them. The onslaught of smiles hits me like a punch in the gut, laughter is the stab of a knife, and hugs and kisses deliver the final blow. If I'm lucky, they show a poverty stricken orphan from a third world country, a widow at her husband's funeral, a homeless man sleeping on the sidewalk, or something like that. When I look into the eyes of a victim, I see the same bars that are keeping me locked up in here.

After he is satisfied that I am up-to-date with everything that is going on out there, he drags away the television and I lie down to take a nap. Even though there is no way for me to exert myself in here, I'm always tired. The exhaustion always hits late afternoon, and Eric lets me sleep until he brings me dinner, which consists of a piece of dry bread, a lump of unidentifiable meat, and some water. After eating, I curl up on the floor, hoping I can fall back asleep before the next day begins.

This morning, however, I wake up feeling well-rested for the first time in months. I actually feel like getting up and moving around, rather than following my same old routine. In fact, it is rather exciting to have the desire to do something new. Eric must have noticed that I seemed different, because when he brings over my breakfast, he pauses before sliding it to me.

"What's going on?" he asks.

"Nothing. I just feel . . . good," I reply.

Even though he kidnapped me and has kept me here for five years, it is easier to be civil towards him, the only human contact I have. He raised his eyebrow and sat in the chair across the hall from my cell. He sits there all day, just watching me, occasionally tilting his head to the side, especially when I smile at him. This euphoria is making me do strange things like that. He wheels up the TV and the first thing on the screen is a girls' soccer team celebrating a win. It's weird, but rather than making me miss that kind of enthusiasm, the scene cheers me up even more. Instead of feeling defeated, I am reminded of what it felt like to accomplish something, and I actually begin to feel happy for them. Another scene brings this newfound kind of empathy to my attention. A devastating earthquake hit parts of Asia, and when I see the faces of those injured or homeless because of it, I still feel their pain, but it's a new kind of feeling. I wish I could help them. I've never thought about helping them before.

Once Eric takes away the TV, I skip my nap. I am just too invigorated to lie down. I spend the extra time exploring this new feeling. It seems familiar. I think it is hope. Not just wishing to get out of here, but believing that I can and will. Gazing out into the hall, I see that Eric is eying me suspiciously. He must see the optimism in my formerly vacant eyes. A little while later, he brings me food and lets me finish every crumb of bread and drop of water. As I curled up on the floor to try to sleep, I was shocked to find that when I laid my head down, my eyes were actually closing on their own. The insomnia seemed to have left.

Over the next few days, my outlook on life continued to improve. I was now laughing along with the joyful people on the television, especially now that I saw them more often than the disasters and sadness. I had not felt happiness like that in years. Eric had even been affected by this cheer. Yesterday, he wore a pair of blue jeans with a t-shirt instead of his usual gloomy getup. Today, he wore khakis with a green polo as he carried up my plate of breakfast. I reached down to start eating, but I froze.

"What is this?"

In place of my cold oatmeal is a stack of steaming, freshly-made pancakes smothered in butter and syrup. On the side are two greasy sausages and a glass of orange juice. Eric just looked at me and shrugged. I took time to savor each bite I took, and it was worth it. Everything was delicious! Throughout the day, whenever I looked across to Eric, he gave me a look like he knows something I don't know. When it's time for my dinner, however, instead of bringing my plate, he walked over empty-handed. He slowly reached into his pocket and slipped out a key. I eyed him as he unlocked the door, never taking his eyes off me.

"I think you're ready," he tells me. These words stirred something deep inside of me, a memory from years ago. He said these words once before, but as he led me down the long, gradually lightening hallway, he must have changed his mind because he turned and shoved me back to my cell. This time, I begin making bargains with myself; if he lets me go, I'll get a job and donate half my salary to charity, I'll volunteer at local soup kitchens and animal shelters, I'll take time every day to express to those nearest to me how much they mean to me. Making my way down the hall, I stared at the lights on the ceiling to adjust my eyes to the light waiting for me on the outside. As we reached the door at the very end, Eric looked at me.

"I truly hope you make it," he whispers, so softly that I almost don't hear it. He turns and unlocks the door. I nod once, and step outside.

Eric took me a few steps to a black van with tinted windows, which I am grateful for because I felt blinded by the sunlight I've missed for so long. He gestured to a bench in the back, and I sat there for the painfully long trip back home. I fell asleep, and woke up in a field of grass. This was my yard. I realized this instantly and sprinted to the front door of the house, bursting inside like water through a broken dam.

Sitting at the kitchen counter was my mother, doing her New York Times crossword puzzle. She looked up, startled, and froze for just a second before realizing who it was. I was almost tackled to the ground by this tiny woman, who was sobbing. Within seconds, my father and younger brother and sister appeared in the doorway. For over an hour, our reunion was full of hugging and crying before anyone said a word. My sister, Amy, was the first to speak up.

"Explain." She never had the patience for incessant questions, and apparently she had not changed a bit.

I took a deep breath and started from the beginning, skipping over minor details like seeing them on the TV, in order to spare my mother from any unnecessary pain or guilt. I talked for hours, emphasizing how much I missed them all. Then, my brother asked,

"So who is the guy who did this?" Nick's fists are clenched so tightly his knuckles are white.

"Well, he-" I paused, confounded. I can remember everything I did while I was gone, from what I ate to what I watched on the TV on any given day. The one thing I can't recall, however, is the man. Other than knowing that he existed, I have no memory of him. No memory of his face, personality, or even name. I explained this to my family as best I could, and it still didn't stop my father from calling the police to report my return, and immediately started yelling on the phone about their incompetence. My mother gave me one more hug before rushing into the kitchen to cook up a feast. Nick and Amy settled on either side of me on the couch, watching a clichéd sitcom about "real" teenage problems. In this episode, the older sister and younger sister are fighting over the same guy, but they realize he's not worth all the trouble and they reconcile. As they're hugging, I sighed. I missed this show.

Six months later, I was being home-schooled to catch up on all the school I had missed. I had reconnected with some old friends, but our connection wasn't quite the same. There was still no word on the man who kidnapped me, but my dad was always sure to keep the cops working on it. He, along with the rest of my family, reminded me every day how much I was missed. I've kept the promises I made myself; I volunteer once a week at the soup kitchen serving bowls of chicken noodle soup to the less fortunate, and twice a month, I help scrub cages and walk the dogs at the animal shelter. I don't have time for a job with all of my school work, but I told my mom to donate my salary to the charity of her choice. I spend as much time as I can with my family. Just being around them is enough to keep me going.

One morning, as I walked into the kitchen for breakfast, I caught a glimpse of a figure outside the window, but as I looked back outside, no one was there. I smiled at my mom as she served up pancakes and bacon, but there was a nagging feeling in the back of my mind. Trying to ignore it, I thanked my mother again for making breakfast.

"This food looks great. You can't believe how much I missed your cooking when I was gone."

She just looked at me, smiling and probably thinking of how she would do anything to show how much I meant to her. After I finished eating, I started walking back upstairs to my room, but froze. This time, it's unmistakable. There was a man standing behind one of the trees in the yard, peering out at me. I jogged up the stairs, shaking my head.

"Bye, honey! I'm going grocery shopping, so I'll be out for a few hours. Your dad took your brother and sister to the mall earlier and they should be home by three."

The door slammed and I slide under the covers. That's when the whispering started.

Unnoticed Reality

By Jennie Deering

January 7, 2010

The bright light from morning hit him like a slap in the face as he rolled over to look at the clock; it read 6:00 AM.

"Well at least it's later than yesterday," said Sam.

He was never able to sleep for more than 4 or 5 hours a night, since his wife Martha had moved from their bedroom and into on the guest room. She claimed Sam's tendency to snore was the culprit, but he though otherwise. As he began to get out of bed he noticed the slowness of his movements, like a boulder was constantly sitting on top of his shoulders. He reached for his glasses on the nightstand and made his way downstairs to start his daily routine. As he walked down the stairs he heard Martha rummaging around in the kitchen, while scents of freshly brewing coffee filled his nose, making his stomach roar with excitement.

"Good morning Sam, how did you sleep?"

Sam was already sitting at the table patiently waiting for his coffee.

"Not good," he took a deep breath, "when are you moving back to our bedroom?"

Martha paused and looked at Sam with curiosity then said, "When you fix that snoring problem."

May 2, 1968, besides the birth of his children, this was Sam's greatest day of his life. It was the day he married the women of his dreams. From the first time he saw her Sam knew it was the woman he was going to spend the rest of his life with, but what had happened? The butterflies in his stomach and skip in his step had somehow faded away over the years. Lovers now turned strangers living under the same roof. He still loved her unconditionally but now longer could they reminisce or make one another laugh. There was a constant uneasiness that filled their household day by day. Martha's voice crowded his hears as he came back into consciousness.

"I have a doctor's appointment at 3:00 PM in Norwalk, so I have to take the car."

"That's fine I was going to finish that painting I was working on or take a nap anyway."

They sat there in silence until Sam started to become impatient. His constant frustration and bursts of anger was a normal occurrence for Martha. But out of all the fights and harsh exchanged words neither one had ever apologized.

"Martha, where's my goddamn coffee?"

"It's coming Sam, I'm making your eggs for you right now."

"That can wait, you know I like my coffee first thing in the morning." Sam slammed his fists on the table when he saw Martha not following his instructions, "Jesus Christ you can't do anything right!"

He stood up, and like a rag doll, pushed Martha out of his way, grabbed his coffee off of the counter, and sat back down. You could see in Martha's stoic expression the hurt she felt as she handed Sam his plate. She finished making his eggs and slammed the pan on the table. Without saying a word she left the kitchen and Sam to eat his meal alone.

The day continued as the couple did not speak, going about their own business and keeping to themselves. Then, with no goodbye, Martha left for her doctor's appointment. After a rough night of sleep Sam decided to take a well needed nap. He went through the living room looking at old family pictures as he passed. He stopped at the mantle over the fireplace to look at their wedding picture. They were so young, only 22 years old, but at the time they both new this is exactly what they had wanted to do.

"She was so beautiful . . . she still *is* beautiful," Sam thought to himself apologetically.

He lay down on the worn out black leather couch filled with tears and scratches. Like Sam, it had been through three children, two dogs, and a cat but all of that was gone now. He looked up at the white ceiling and wondered how his life had come to this. He thought the butterflies in his stomach for Martha would last forever and he would never have to be by himself. But as Sam watched the sun beginning to fade he realized that was exactly what was happening.

"Sam wake up, dinner's ready . . . Sam; Sam WAKE UP!"
"I'm up Martha; I was just resting my eyes."
"Well you've done enough of that. It's already 7:30 PM Sam."
"Okay I'm getting up. I'm coming, I'm coming."

Sam and Martha both sat down at the dinner table but as he started to eat he noticed Martha sitting across, staring at him. She sat their poised, with the look of determination and struggle on her face. He stared back at her curiously, beginning to get aggravated at her blank stare.

"What the hell is your problem?"
"I've been feeling very weak lately, that's why I scheduled an appointment."
"So what? I'm sure the doctor told you it was nothing."
Sam looked down at his plate and continued to eat. When he didn't get a response from Martha he said,
"Well? Are you going to stare at me all night like that? I don't see the problem Martha; you're just overreacting like you always do."

Martha remained silent as her husband refused to listen as she pleaded with her eyes for him to look up at her. Finally Martha spoke,
"I have cancer Sam." Sam paused for a moment, then put his fork down and looked up at Martha. His face filled with disbelief and terror as he had just woke up from a nightmare.

"How do you know this?"

"The doctor did some tests, so I waited there for the results. That's when he told me."

Sam continued to stare at Martha until the doorbell broke their silence. It was their youngest son Max. He was the only child who had stayed in Connecticut as the oldest Sarah, moved to California to pursue a singing career, while the middle child Joseph, moved down to Virginia to be with his college sweetheart.

"Hey mom, dad . . ." He gave each of his parents a warm embracing hug.

"Mom you called; what's up, you sounded worried on the phone?"

Martha stood there, silently looking at her son. Tears filled her eyes as she began to speak,

"Max, I went to the doctor today and . . ." She began to break down and fell into the arms of her son, "I found out I have Leukemia."

Max hugged his mom as she shook from crying, while Sam sat at the table in disbelief, staring at his inconsolable wife.

May, 2011—Four Months Later

As Sam walked down the stairs to the kitchen all he heard was the wail of the wind against the house. He didn't smell coffee or hear any movement in the kitchen. Martha had been well along in her chemo treatment but her doctor became worried when they only saw her cancer continuing to grow throughout her body.

Sam yelled up to Martha, "Martha where the hell are you? I need my coffee now!"

She slowly walked down the steps into the kitchen with a pale face that carried an innocent expression of desperation. Without a word Martha began making his coffee. Even with the constant trips to the hospital and being in and out of various doctors; as Martha's cancer got worse so did Sam's anger. The only way for him to take out his aggression was on the person that needed him the most. As Martha made the coffee with her back turned to Sam she said,

"I have chemo today."

"Alright well I'm still working on my painting so you can drive yourself. It's not far anyway."

Martha held back her tears as she handed Sam his coffee. She left the kitchen and as she walked up the steps she thought to herself,

"This isn't the man I fell in love with."

As Sam sat at the kitchen table he heard a sudden, *THUD THUD THUD*. Sam ran to the bottom of the staircase to find Martha lying on the floor not moving, with blood starting to surround her head. He checked her pulse and gave her CPR but she seemed to be unconscious. He rushed to the phone and called 911. So many thoughts ran through his head at once.

"This is my fault. She doesn't deserve any of this."

Sam blamed his actions for Martha's fall. It was time to put his emotions aside and finally help his wife.

When the ambulance got there they found Sam sitting at the bottom of the stairs holding and gently rocking Martha in his arms as he cried softly and held her bleeding head with a towel. On the ride to the hospital as the EMT's checked her status, Sam was next to Martha holding her hand and whispering in her ear,

"It's going to be okay baby. Hang in there for me. Please stay with me; I know you can do this. You are so strong, please . . ."

Sam paced in the waiting room while Martha went into immediate surgery for the wound to her head. He had already called all his children and they would be flying in soon to wait with their father. After three hours the doctor came out to talk to Sam and Max, who had arrived shortly after his father called.

"Hello Sir, I'm Dr. Stanford."

"Hi doctor. How is my wife? Is she alive? Oh God please tell me she's alive."

"She is alive Sir, but she lost almost three pints of blood and she is having a very hard time breathing on her own, so we put her on a respirator."

After getting no response from Sam, Dr. Stanford continued, "Let me explain this to you Mr. Jacobs,"

Sam interrupted him, "Sam, just call me Sam."

"Okay Sam, since she has had chemo treatment for the past four months her white blood cell count was already at an extreme low. These white blood cells are extremely important because they help the body and immune system fight infection. Because of the low count from chemo your wife does not have the strength to fight this fall."

Sam stared at him silently in a trance, detached from the real world. Then he spoke,

"How much longer does my wife have?"

The doctor sighed and said, "She has only a few days to live. I'm truly sorry Sam. If there is anything I can do for you please, let me know. You can see her now if you wish. I'll show you to the room."

Sam and Max followed Dr. Stanford into Martha's room. She lied there helplessly with her eyes closed and chest moving fiercely from trying to breathe, while wires and machines were attached to her. Martha, once such a strong woman, now looked defeated as she lied in the hospital bed. Sam sat down next to her, laid his head against the side of the bed, and wept. All of his emotions came breaking through as he cried for his wife and prayed for her good health.

Day after day Sam stayed next to Martha moving only occasionally to let the nurses check her pulse and feed her. Their kids had all come to the hospital and took turns coming to visit their mother. For the first time in years the entire family was together again. Martha opened her eyes every so often to look at her family and could make out a weak smile. The third day of her stay at the hospital came and Sam knew he did not have much longer with his wife. Around dinner time the children went to get food from the cafeteria, while Sam stayed with Martha. As he sat there looking at his wife she opened her eyes and stared back. Sam knew it was time to tell her what he had been feeling for so long.

"I'm sorry Martha. This is my fault. All my yelling and demands has made you sick and if I never called you to get me coffee this would not have happened. We wouldn't be here right now," he paused, feeling choked up, and began to cry, "I love you with all my heart Martha. You are my life, my world, and my other half. I'm in love with you and I always will be."

Sam held Martha's hand as he put his head down and cried. Then Martha spoke with a soft and weak voice as she struggled to say her words,

"This isn't your fault Sammy. It's my time to go and I'm okay with that," she stopped to cough. After catching her breath she looked back at her husband and continued,

"Neither one of us were at fault. Apologizing doesn't always mean you're wrong or right, it means that you value your relationship more than your ego. Your apology means more to me than anything else. I love you too Sam and I always will. I forgive you."

Sam rose from his chair and hugged Martha. The couple grasped one another like they would never let go as they both cried in each others arms. Martha's monitor began beeping as Martha went into unconsciousness. Nurses and doctors rushed in as Sam stood there helplessly. After a few minutes the doctors told Sam she was gone. He scanned the doctor's face looking for answers but Dr. Stanford simply shook his head. Martha had passed away.

A Journey for Fame
on the High Seas

By Haasim Vahora

~~~⚬⚬⚬⚬~~~

The salty mist splashed my face as the nauseating smell of the sea finally escaped me. The sun was beating down upon us with its unforgiving rays and intense heat. The screeching of the gulls as they capture their meals and the loud whooshing of the water as it crashes against the bow, sending up sprays of mist and water. The burly smell of a ten hardened men, all sweating from dawn until dusk, to keep us moving was overwhelming. The long wooden rails, carved with such delicacy that it shames me to see it so susceptible to the elements. Carved out on these ancient beauties, were the markings of great sailors, with the final one being "JB". The spot under it was reserved for the rightful owner, but transition of property did not go as planned, therefore it is empty. From my view everything was so exhilarating, as when I was younger. The pristine water rushing under me, and the suns glimmering rays bouncing off the surface of the clear and light liquid; it gave such depth that, at a glance, you would be lost for ages before returning to reality. I reared through the sea like a plow, splitting the sea in half, as I went crushing anything unlucky enough to come in my way. The vastness of my playground is almost overwhelming. From every direction there stretched a long and blue horizon that slowly turned turquoise as the day withered on. My sides were aching for a break, although I was built harder than stone. Along side of me stuck disgusting creatures that have decided to take advantage of my hospitality. Dirtying and tainting my beautiful wooden shell with their disgusting bodies. Hopefully the sailors will do something, not just push around the muck on top of me. The wind is life like this time of the year, tickling my sides and providing me with the cool, long lasting sensation needed to relieve my burning body.

As the day presses on, the darker clouds roll in, and the men and I prepare for the oncoming chaos. The sea starts growing restless as darkness is rolling in from the horizon. A long, dark shadow can be seen edging closer and closer, engulfing all in its way. The wind starts changing from that nice gentle breeze to a much coarser, harsh, and intense gale. Suddenly, a loud rumble can be heard from above, surrounding me and vibrating through my boards. A flash of light can be seen filling the sky with terrifying yellow light that can shatter me in pieces. One . . . two . . . three . . . the rumbles of the clouds signal the rain as it beats down upon my mast and sail. The mixture of wind and rain is now prevalent. As we delve deeper into the storm, I face the brutality of Mother Nature. The torrents are now swirling all around me, as they try to deter me off my course. Dodging tsunami sized waves and navigating through whirlpools, Black Beard is a technical genius until he exercises his more ambitious side. Up ahead, hidden in the chaotic storm raging around us, laid a monster waiting to emerge. Its fangs are at the bottom of the torrent, and its arms can wrap around hundreds of ships and drag them underneath. As the arms of the whirlpool kept on stretching farther and farther, they soon seemed to cover the width of the entire world. Black Beard knew this of course, as he sailed me into the mouth of this beast.

While his confidence was unwavering, the crew's was not but they dared not to question his decision. As I broke though the inner rim of the pool I was over taken by the current. So strong was it that my rudder almost snapped. Black Beard let go of the captains' wheel and let it spin with my shifting rudder and allowed the storm to take us straight into its center. For a moment, the world stopped and everything was at peace. No sound came from the crew as they stared in awe as the swirling whirlpool guzzled us up. The center was only a little ways away and I could already see through the dark depths of the center vacuum. The walls of water cycling downward and all the debris and water going with it, into the bottom of the ocean, forever lost. Leading into a deep treasure trove of lost ships and valuables, dead men and rum, the cyclone plagued this part of the sea for ages. To gain dominance it would surely mean fame and fortune; something Black Beard is intent upon obtaining.

At the last moment as all seemed to be lost and on the very jaws of the dark blue monstrosity, Black Beard quickly took hold of the captain's wheel and with all his might tugged it to one side. As soon as he hit the ground and the wheel wouldn't budge any further, I, almost simultaneously, flipped around from going into a nose dive. The momentum of my haul seemed to throw me away from the center, evading capture. Ripping a path through the all engulfing water and going backwards with no way of seeing or hearing, I relied upon the jeers of the men to guide myself. As I reached the edge of the mouth, the storm raging around us began to subside. The pelting rain drops ceased to impale my dense wooden frame and I had finally gained control of my rudder, now that there was not much current to ride against. As the clouds uncovered the once blanketed sun, and the sun started dipping down into its yellow pool, the sea was as quiet as ever. No wind ripping across my boards, no waves crashing against my stern and bow, and no noises to disturb the peace. While the sailors celebrated their triumphs, they failed to take notice of the black sails billowing up ahead in the distance.

The creaking of my boards was never as apparent as during this night. The night garbed me in black concealing our true identity from the pursuers. The once jolly, gay, and rough housing men that were carousing only hours before were now quiet as I'm steered into the vast darkness, unable to hide but only to camouflage.

The ship with black flags had bluish green boards, so worn from mildew and moisture that not a spot of the original brown boarding could be seen except on the mast. The starboard and port side were decorated with an assortment of seaweed and grime that showed the wisdom and years the vessel had spent in the water. Holes and worn repairs littered the surface that opened every now and then from the impact of the water against the stern. The captain was a taut man with scars running along both his eyes, encircling his mouth in an awkward oval that ended where the unfading red lines met.

His eyes were dyed in blood with ambition set in them, the kind of starved ambition with no end, and to be the most dominant. The foolish men have yet to realize the true danger of being at sea, but in a moment they shall see.

A large crack resounded through the air as a cannon ball went flying from the black sails ship into me. A sharp pain struck at my rear and a load of cargo eased out of my end, plummeting it into the ocean. The ship seemed to have outmaneuvered me in the cover of the night and I was unable to avoid the deadly metal rock. From there on the only thing that could be seen were the red explosions emerging from the cannon's openings and the burst of light that emitted for a second. In the darkness, neither the size nor the object being thrown at you can be seen. All you hear are the roar of the cannons and the spilt second hiss of the projectiles whizzing by you, sometimes less than a foot away. The contact being made with the other ship is more noticeable, as I hear it bellow loud moans of pain in response to the holes being places within its hull. More and more gunshot holes are escaping through my boards, bouncing around inside of me, puncturing the flesh of the men commanding me, and releasing their red liquids over my deck. The bloody fight continues as I swerved around my pursuers in an effort to attack their tail side. On a count of three the battle hardened sailors fired a bombardment of ion shackles and balls, both to target their rear most holds and their mast, in an effort to tear down it down. As the balls burst through the rear of the boat, a huge explosion overtook the ships cargo hold. The explosion was large enough to engulf the lower levels in flames, but only seemed to cover the lower bilging rooms where the water was already being displaced. Having taken this moment of weakness and turning it into an advantage, the ship turned twice as it seemed to be heading straight into our port side, and a set of guns were revealed in the forefront of the ship. These guns shot endless rounds of what seemed to be oil covered cannon balls. Every single one pierces me, two on deck wiping out the captains room and another one at my mast, rendering it useless for the time being. Punching hole after hole, I yelped with pain as I began falling apart, first my side was exposed and sooner, my starboard side began opening. As the ship rocked back and forth it became even more difficult to fire the mobile cannons. From above, the captain made one final attempt to overwhelm the opposing ship, by going head long into it. The plan worked successfully as we were not on a collision course with one another. While the black sailed ship prepared its forward cannons, Black Beard swiveled my rudder to the side at a 35 degree angle causing a slight turn in my direction. Now as the ship ahead of us fired cannons into the open sea, we could run along side of it and openly blow them to planks and nails. As proposed, the ship had nothing to do but yelp in pain as my blood bathed cannons seeked revenge in its feeble wooden hull. As all my anger and spite poured into the gun powder being used, it threw my unrelenting load of fury at my nemesis, opening it up to the full moons reflecting light. Both of us now mutilated, completely destroyed on both sides, and little to no cargo or supplies to sustain us in the after math. The one and final deciding factor of the duel would have to be combat between the sailors.

Black Beard reared me against the black sailed ship in an attempt to commandeer it. He swung on to the ships deck along with 4 other sailors. As the sun started to rise up in the distance, feint outlines of the pirates were becoming noticeable with the deep ringing of swords clashing against one another and rattling the air. The morning sun was gleaming of the metallic strips as they made contact with one another. One pirate can be seen ducking and from the deep slash that was opposed upon him, with a mighty swing of his own, he cut a rib from his enemy. Another drops dead as some of the pirates pull out muskets from the armory rooms and try to take aim during the brawl. Gun shots now entered the fray and the smaller rocks now zipping through the air. As the men kept on exchanging sides, there was fighting on me as well, but the original pirate that had left to man the captains wheel, was punctured in the heart, leaving me unattended. As the suns first ray of light started to emerge onto the sea, both me and the other ship could be visibly seen heading toward one another. No one could stop either of us while Black Beard and the scar faced captain fought in an epic duel for their lives. As I try to rear around and turn in any direction, I forget that im restricted to only what the pirates allow me to do. As we neared one another, the pirates began to realize their neglect and rushed to fix our course once again but it was too late. Both of our masts collided and buckled, tearing them down in an instant, and sending my bow straight into the black ship's side. My bow was completely torn off and I could no longer sense it. I was left feeling like something was missing. Pained seared through me as we continued to collided and merge with the ship. The opposing ship soon split in 2 and was now sinking from both ends. As the same began happened to me, I began to tip over. I caught a glimpse at the pirates jumping into sea, abandoning all hope of survival, and trying to escape the destruction they brought upon me.

Sunset Stallion

By Monica Harrington

—◦◦◦◦◦—

Where was he? It was 5 o'clock on a Friday afternoon and he was late. Just then she caught a glimpse of the top of his head over the hill. His brown hair glimmering against the descending sun, which made her hand come up to shield her eyes. She sighed with relief and stood at the barn entrance tapping her foot impatiently as their mother often did when they arrived home past their curfew.

"Cutting it kinda close, don't you think?" She asked as he approached with his favorite baseball T-shirt and his hands in his pockets. Then she softened and smiled in a way that forgave without words.

"Why were you so worried? You know I'd never miss it for the world." He put his arm around her shoulder and they walked into the barn to get ready for their weekly ride.

Every Friday since they were little, Lisa and Mark would go riding through the charming fields of their small ranch in West Des Moines, Iowa. Lisa was 17 and her 19-year-old brother was her mentor and eternal best friend. She could tell him anything and he could talk away any of her problems with comforting words that seemed to just roll off his tongue.

Once they were inside, Lisa collected her long, wavy hair in a neat ponytail as she always did and positioned her mother's old riding helmet snuggly onto her head. She walked over to her chestnut mare and brushed his perfect mane, while Mark slipped on his worn boots and clipped on his own helmet.

"All set," He said and led his pure black stallion out the back with Lisa not far behind.

They both mounted and hesitated a moment, neither one wanting to be the first to advance and conclude the evening. They would not voice their feelings but they knew why this particular ride would be more special than either of them could ever imagine.

Finally, after seconds that seemed like hours, they set off leaving a dust trail in their wake. At that point it was the familiar casual Friday evening, filled with conversation and laughter that seemed to dance on the wind and tickle the clouds. The sun's rays ignited the stallion's slick coat with colors more magnificent than Lisa's eyes had ever beheld. It was almost as though he belonged in the sky. There was nothing Lisa enjoyed more than spending time with her brother.

After about an hour had passed they headed in the direction of the barn, more slowly this time. Eventually they acknowledged that the sun would soon bid farewell and they would have to get back before it disappeared. When they arrived at the entrance they paused for a short time to breathe in this moment and engrave it in their minds; the sounds of blue birds flying freely above and the steady gentle breathing of the horses against them. Then, as if to officially end the lifelong escapade, they glanced back one last time at the setting sun. It painted the clouds with the perfect blend of colors that only nature could create.

"Well this is it," Mark said solemnly his eyes still fixated overhead. "It's the end of an era. This has been our special tradition practically our whole lives. There is no one else in the world I would rather spend my Fridays with."

"Mark?" Now he turned and looked straight into her eyes. "Thank you, for everything."

He could not help but smile at this as a single tear crept down her delicate cheek. He nodded his head towards the barn and she followed willingly.

They took their time putting away their gear and getting the horses settled. When they were finished they secured the gate and headed for home.

"Hey," Mark said brushing away a lingering tear from Lisa's cheek, "I'll write to ya every day, I promise. I'll tell you everything that's goin' on and I expect the same from you. Don't you dare leave me hangin'."

"Oh, I know," She answered, "but the war is so far away and it won't be the same as talking to you face to face. I'll miss all your reactions and the sound of your laugh."

"Awww," He said nonchalantly and gave her a squeeze. "C'mon I'll race you home just like old times."

This made Lisa perk up as he had knew it would and they sprinted neck and neck all the way to their front porch. Once inside, Mark, Lisa, and their parents had Mark's favorite meal, chicken parmesan, and then collapsed exhausted on their beds, where they stayed until early the next morning.

Lisa was woken by a tapping on her shoulder and a whisper in her ear.

"Get up and get dressed." Her mother was very choked up but she was a strong woman. "Mark is getting ready to leave and he needs you right now."

Lisa leapt out of bed in her pajamas and ran downstairs to the front door where Mark was patiently waiting for her. They stood there for a few seconds and then she ran into his arms in a mess of tears. How could he be so strong when he was about to go halfway across the world in Iraq to risk his life? But then it became too much for him and she could feel his chest move faster and hear his labored breathing.

"I'll miss you so much," he managed, burying his face in her hair. "I will always be here for you." He cupped her face in his hands and looked right into her eyes. "You may not see me but I have always looked out for you and I'm not about to stop now."

He said his final goodbyes and walked to his car, but before he vanished behind the windshield he took one more long look at his family. He took in every last detail creating a mental picture to carry with him at all times.

*   *   *

Every day after school Lisa would fetch the mail and every other day without fail there would be a letter from Mark. He wrote of the weather and the people he had met. He would say how much he missed her and how he was fighting for them. The letters gave her hope and got her through the tough times without him.

Every night after receiving a letter, she would write back and tell him about school and the family. She told him she was praying for him and that she thought he was the bravest person in the whole world. Most importantly, she let him know that every Friday she went to the stables to watch the sunset. He informed her that he also gazed at the sun as it receded and that it would always be their connection across the world.

A year later, she got the mail as usual and flipped through for Mark's letter. She flipped through again, nothing. She went out to see if she had dropped it or left it in the mailbox with no luck. The next day was the same and Lisa began to feel uneasy.

"He is fighting a war sweetheart," her mother assured her, "you can't expect him to have so much free time. Give him a couple more days."

Five days passed with no word from him. Friday came along and Lisa went to the barn as was her routine and sat with eyes to the sky in anticipation. The light through the clouds danced along in the usual way at first but then started to reveal a pattern Lisa had only seen once before. The stallion appeared on the horizon accompanied by the same majestic colors that she had noticed after that last ride. It was his spirit reassuring her that he was still there looking out for her.

After weeks of no communication with Mark, Lisa's friends and teachers started treating her extra nicely.

"I'm so sorry about your brother Lisa." Her art teacher said to her one day.

To which Lisa replied, "Why? He is fine."

"Right." Her teacher just nodded sympathetically like there was some secret they shared and took her hand. "I can only imagine what you are going through with the loss of your brother but remember you always have friends you can go to."

Lisa had smiled politely and brushed off the comment because there was no doubt in her mind that Mark was all right. Why couldn't anyone see that?

Today was Friday. She found her mom in the kitchen and the house smelled deliciously of meatball marinara sauce. She walked in and dropped her bag on the floor.

"Hi, mom. How was your day?" She said cheerfully. Her mother however did not respond. "Mom." She tried again, "Mom? You okay?"

Her mother turned to her with fresh tears on her face.

"Honey," She took her hands and continued, "I think it's better if you accept that maybe Mark is not coming back." Lisa recoiled her hands and stepped back in disbelief.

"How can you say that? Don't you feel him?" She tried to keep her voice down but something inside of her just wanted to scream.

"It's just that he used to send letters every day Lisa. What happened to that? It isn't like him. I'm just saying it's a possibility." But her eyes said otherwise. She truly believed he was gone.

Lisa shook her head and ran out of the kitchen straight through the front door with her mother calling after her. She ran faster than she knew was possible until she reached the barn. She swung the doors open and wiped the tears from her eyes before they had the chance to proceed down her face. How could she let them get to her? She knew he was there. He promised and he never broke a promise.

She sat down out of breath and caught a glimpse of something in the corner of one of the stalls. It was Mark's favorite old baseball T-shirt. She smiled, put it on, and closed her eyes. She took a deep breath and was almost overwhelmed by the memories that flowed into her mind. When she opened her eyes she squinted as the sun beat down on her. She waited for the stallion to appear and drift away taking all her doubts along with it, but it never came.

The sun came and went without any color or sign of joy. The grey shirt was quickly becoming darker as her eyes emptied their contents. She buried her head in her hands and sobbed weakly. Her only hope had vanished beneath the horizon and for the first time in her life she felt alone.

She drowned out all other sounds with her weeping but though her vision was blurry the colors were still visible. She stopped for a moment and looked up puzzled. The sun was rising again. This time with colors twirling and leaping and skipping across the entire sky.

The crinkling of grass behind her startled her and she jumped up and turned around. But when she saw him she almost had to sit back down. Mark stood in the doorway crying openly upon seeing his sister's face again. He dropped his bags and they ran to hug each other. They embraced as though they would never let go and Lisa felt more loved than she ever had before.

Through bouts of tears he managed to say, "What were you worried about. You know I'd never miss it for the world."

He took his army jacket off and wrapped it around her. She stole a peek in the inside pocket where she pulled out a thick bundle of envelopes. She examined them and gave a small sigh and felt the water works building up again. They were all of the letters she had written to him. He had received and kept safe as his most prized possessions, even as he explained, when he was in action and couldn't write to her he never stopped thinking about her. He said he always kept them close to his heart because she was what he was fighting for and it was she who brought him home.

Goodbye Is Never Forever

By Taylor Greene

I closed my eyes, breathing deeply; I stared back, back into the recesses of my mind where it's locked up tighter than a safe, more than 5 miles thick and 2 inches wide so I don't have to deal with it, hidden behind happy memories and false pretences.

I never really understood why people wrote journals, poems and stuff like that. I let most of all my thoughts out without a problem, whether you wanted to hear it or not it was coming out; if it was on purpose or by accident I never truly knew. Maybe that's why I ended up having to do this, I wonder if it could've been avoided somehow . . . if it all could've been avoided in the long run . . .

*   *   *

"JEN," I heard someone scream as I was about to grab my bag out of my car. I spun around just in time to see the bright yellow object blurring toward me. I laughed as I held out my hand in the universal symbol for stop and she skidded to a stop in front of me.

"I missed you too, buttercup." I shook my head at the girl bouncing in her place to hug me. Lynn Jacobs was the most hyper girl I have ever met. As my best friend, and almost sister, she was obligated to do this, even if she saw me every day. I guess she had a reason this time. It was the longest we've been away from each other in six years. Lynn moved next door to me in the summer before sixth grade, great timing for her but then again she always had great timing with that type of stuff.

I couldn't stop laughing at this girl, 5'2, black and purple hair glimmering blond and red in streaks where the sun hit. The frustration in her chocolate lab, puppy eyes made me laugh harder. When I went to Jersey these past weeks I missed doing this routine of being difficult just to be a pain to her. I shook my head to get off the subject.

I knew it wasn't the time to tell her yet. Lynn had such a good heart . . . she wouldn't be able to handle it . . .

"Jenna Winters, you better hug me before I tackle you," she warned. I looked around and saw, as luck had it, I parked right next to the football field. We didn't want another repeat of the last time we played street hockey. I saw a gleam in her eyes as she picked up on my thoughts. I shot her a *bring it on* smirk as I took a step back to shut my door and she jumped at me.

"Gotta catch me first," I called as I took off. My red flip-flops long forgotten on the curb near my car. Carefree thoughts and memories swarmed me as I ran, happy to be home, to be past it all. The Connecticut sun shining on my wavy brown hair as it blew back in the wind was perfection.

I remember thinking back to when we were in sixth grade and Jake told me we shouldn't wear shoes; that we should get everyone to take their shoes off and walk around school like we did during the summer, daring and unafraid, heads up and shoulders back. We took on the world, a very clear thing I remember, when I first mimicked the walk that felt like I was a duck . . .

I wasn't paying attention, maybe that's part of the problem, I tripped with the force of Lynn, at least that's what I thought till I realized, Lynn wasn't this heavy. She was only 110 pounds soaking wet. Plus she was 2 inches shorter than me, or 1 ½ as she likes to always correct. This kid was at least 6'2, shaggy hair, that was the color of cherry wood, reddish brown, pretty nice build but his body weight packs a punch. I wasn't really sure what happened or how we had hit each other. It was a tangled mess of arms and legs. I had turf burn on my leg and elbow, and a bunch of tiny, annoying tar pieces in my shorts and all over my tank top.

Some how time stood still and life was complete . . . I'm not sure how . . . but it was.

Some how he ended up only half way on top of me, so it seemed like he was holding on to me. He finally opened his eyes, blinked a few times bewildered, then raised an eyebrow and smirked . . . he looked familiar, I just couldn't put my finger on it, but then as the smirk faded wonder took its place, his clear gray eyes widening. I guess I was a sight to see, my hair everywhere with the sun hitting it, making it tint red. My eyes though normally blue-green, change with my mood, going from black to black-blue, blue to blue-green, and then bright green to green-black. The cycle continued forever along with my "witches mark" in my right eye that seemed to allow me to feel when things were coming, good or bad. Jake was only able to feel emotions in the room, meanwhile I could manipulate them. Tears welled up in my eyes—Jake—I started to sniffle.

"I'm sorry! Did I hurt you?" He asked all flustered. It made me smile and I shook my head no. He looked startled again and I forgot I didn't know him as I reached my head up to smooth out the wrinkles between his eyebrows. The ring and bracelet on my left arm gleaming as he reached up to tuck my hair behind my ear.

"Why does he get a hug first?" Lynn's voice broke through the bubble around us "you don't even know him yet," she pouted.

"LYNN!" The boy spoke, a light blush on his face as he let go and we sat up. I started to giggle, it was so cute, and I couldn't help myself. Lynn just tackled me again making me laugh in gasps of air. But I was missing something, how did this boy know Lynn? I looked more closely at him, skin kissed from being in the sun all summer and an easy-going smile. He had a scar through his left eyebrow straight down making him look slightly dangerous than a second ago.

Then Lynn said "Jen meet Max, Max this is Jen."

"OHHH," we said at the same time. I heard a lot about him from the way Lynn was always talking about him. I started to develop a crush over him actually about four years before.

"So your Max huh?" I dimpled "It's nice to meet you. Lynn talks about you all the time," I giggled the last part hoping I wasn't too obvious.

"Yep, the one and only," he smiled. "Lynn's favorite cousin and you're her clumsy best friend," I blushed. "It's nice to meet you too, Jen," He laughed. His laugh made my heart pound, but then I realized we were sitting in the middle of the football field and school was about to start.

"Oh god! Come on guys." I got up and grabbed their hands, felling a tug in my heart. Somehow I knew he'd fit in here . . . with us.

Time goes by; this one poem by Sri Chinmoy still sticks with me. I journeyed into time,
I journeyed into space, I journeyed into skies, I failed to see His Face. It seemed appropriate for some reason.

$$*\qquad*\qquad*$$

The door slammed behind us as Lynn and I ran though the apartment. The bags on our arms barely holding us back as we ran to his room. Luke Crowe, Lynn's boyfriend, crashed against the just closed, and locked door.

"Guy's this isn't funny" he yelled.

"To you," Lynn giggled back. He won't stay mad at her. She just smiles and he melts. We snuck over to the middle of the room and started going though the bags. Max lived with Me, Lynn, and Luke since we went to college three years ago. He quickly became my best friend and the three of us were inseparable, till Lynn met Luke our second year. That was when things got a little more complicated, splitting us all into pairs of two. Max and I started dating that year, I mean I've been in love with him since the second semester our senior year, when he found out everything that happened the summer right before I met him. I rememb-

"Jen, hurry up!" I heard impatiently snapped and I turned to glare at Lynn.

"What", she asked. "He's only gonna be gone for two hours, if that," she stated and grabbed the black lights out of the bag as I grabbed the feathers and rose petals in every color to make the room look crazy. Max is very temperamental about his room so we made it a payback joke with lipstick on the mirror and pictures left everywhere, candid's of us taking the photos and leaving them everywhere. It was so fun and I knew he wouldn't stay mad at us, this wasn't the worst thing we've ever done and he's done worse to the both of us. We teased him with pictures in the hall to his room so he'd pick them up. Lynn and Luke went on a date so I hid in the closet till he came through the door. I jumped out and got a picture of his face for Lynn then ran down the hall laughing hysterically. He chased me cracking up at our antics, while trying to get the camera and tickle me, but I was just trying not to fall more than I already was.

"Oh, babe," I heard him whisper as he caught me and tackled us on to the couch, "You shouldn't of done that," then proceeded to tickle me till I couldn't breathe. We were asleep like that when Lynn and Luke got home.

*   *   *

Three years after that, we all bought separate apartments me in max next door to Lynn and Luke. Lynn and Luke got married and we're expecting a baby. She was six months, a huge hassle to deal with but I was so excited to be an aunt.

Maybe things aren't always meant to be. A life has to be taken for a life to be given . . . . It's the way of the world

Max wanted us to go see Jake down in Jersey. Lynn agreed whole heartedly saying max will help me through whatever my problem was that she still wasn't told about that summer.

I never told Lynn why Jake and I don't talk any more. She would be broken; after all . . . . Jake was like her brother too.

I'm not sure why I agreed but as soon as I got on the plane I tried to block out the memories. I didn't understand why Max wanted to go so badly, why he was so persistent about us spending the month with my brother in that god forsaken place. Even though I was upset with him. I put my face in his neck and cried softly, seeking the only comfort I could.

When we got to the airport, Jake looked at me with fear in his blue eye. He seemed so haunted, less happy than he use to be when we use to talk every day. He's only an year older than me, not even only about 10 months, but he seemed like four or five by the way his body slumped.

I wish I knew what I did now. Maybe I wouldn't have taken so long to forgive him for not believing me, I knew he never meant to let anything like that happen to me. It was never meant to happen anyways.

Something happened once I saw him though, I was planning on being distant. It was if a dam broke in me and I started to run. I ran like I did when I had a bad dream and wanted him to give me hope that even if things aren't always great, I have people who will protect and support me. I ran like I needed to be little again, straight into his arms, as we started to cry and he apologized profusely. My heart lifted as he put me down.

"I missed you, Rain," he smiled while wiping my tears away.

"Not as much as I missed you, cloud," I responded using our parents nicknames for us. They always made us feel weird but today it was comfort it felt like home. The names were Native American, just shortened. Mine was dances with rain and Jakes was rolls with clouds. Don't ask me why, to be honest, I don't know what they were thinking. I grabbed Max's hand and introduced them. They hit it off perfectly and I was happy again, everything seemed perfect in that moment.

Now as I think back I wonder if he knew, if he realized subconsciously and just had to get everything in order before the end came. They say people know, that they start saying their goodbyes right before . . .

*　　*　　*

I was crying and screaming in my sleep, I could tell I just couldn't wake up. The memories came fast and hard, seeing as I was in the same bed, maybe that's how I knew it was dreaming. The flashes came faster. The ones of all of us laughing and Jake giving me safe drinks. Jake disappearing into the crowd and his friend appearing.

I remembered Jake saying he trusted this guy, named Allan and that he would take care of me so I trusted him . . . you know what they say, listen to your gut, right? . . . . Well right then my gut was telling me get away . . . and fast.

The night got fuzzy after that, everything coming in random pictures and noises. I remember water or what I thought was water being given to me and then randomly colored drinks. I remembered being brought upstairs and I swear I saw Jake following but when I got to the room it was locked as soon as it shut behind us. I can still hear the click in my mind as I tell the story. It's funny now, how it didn't connect in my mind till he blocked the door. I had a passing thought of maybe he didn't want anyone to bother me . . . . I was only partially right in that assessment. He walked over and I told him "you can get out now," with a snotty attitude and a push to his chest toward the door. He smacked me hard, so hard I tasted blood . . . . then the real pain started.

I'm gonna spare you the details but yes, Allan, my brothers trusted friend, raped me. However, when he was done with me I guess he told Jake that I was freaking out and that I kept rambling about Allan raping me and hurting me. He told Jake he should just help me in the morning, explain that it was all just a bad dream. Needless to say, when I told Jake he ignored my whole plea for help and told me that I had too much to drink, that I'd be fine. We haven't spoken since that day, till Max had me come down to see him. I'm glad he did though. I got to reconnect with my brother, there was no hard feelings. That was until he mentioned to me that he had told Lynn.

When I heard that I flipped out. She was 7 months pregnant at that point and so hormonal that even I was scared to be around her half the time. She was coming down that day and I was nervous as anything, sweating like a sinner in church. We went to go get her from the airport, and as she waddled up to hug me, I knew it was all ok.

I remembered the look of sadness in her eyes. Its burned in my head, just like the sound of metal . . . .

She scolded me for 10 minutes. Then continued on to all of us for thirty while she ranted and raved about Jake's stupidity. She spoke of my weird habit of not caring for myself, and Max's quietly kept secret. Everything got fixed within the next few days and we were having fun again like the old days, then she had to get back home.

We almost missed the time too. That's one thing I feel really guilty about. If I kept my mouth shut none of it would've happened. By chance I looked up at the clock and told her if she didn't hurry up Luke would leave her. Laughing she told me that would never happen and I agreed wholeheartedly. She grabbed her stuff, kissed Max and I on the cheek, and ran out the door

Max and I were going for a walk, it was beautiful out so we wanted to go to the beach alone for a while. My brother had been with us constantly for the last few weeks so we had no privacy.

The last image I have of them was Jake standing at the car, door open head on his arms that were resting on the roof of the car, laughing in his blue hoodie, shorts falling off his hips, brown curls going everywhich way, sunglasses on and dimples out in full force. Lynn had a beautiful smile on her face as she yelled for Jake to hold his horses making us giggle while she walked backwards blowing us a kiss. I wish I had a real picture to show all the angelicness of my pregnant best friend and brother. As they drove away they screamed, "Love you!!" out the car windows.

*   *   *

About twenty minutes later I called them to see how the ride was going. When Lynn picked up she was happy, saying the baby was moving around. So I told her how Max proposed and we were going get married. She screamed and told my brother, who I'm pretty sure I heard say, "I know. I know woman now stop bouncing". I couldn't keep from laughing. Everything was the way it should be. It was perfect.

But nothing ever stays perfect for long . . .

The sound of screeching tires made me flinch and then I heard Lynn scream. Tears started to stream down my face once I heard the banging of metal over and over, then one final bang of metal on metal. I screamed their names, but I didn't get an answer. I ran to Max who had just walked into the room, and tried to explain what I had heard. I remember her telling me they were near the airport. We raced down the highway but when we got there it was too late. It was already a fatal crash with no survivors in either car. That was the worst moment of my life. My best friend and my brother were gone. I wasn't going to be an aunt and Luke would most likely never be a father. We all fell into a black hole together.

*   *   *

"So as I stand in front of you here, I want you to think that if it were you in this situation, would you try to find closure? Try to say goodbye as best as you can? Problem is, I don't want to say goodbye. Lynn you're the single most amazing person in my life, a bright star that would shine all the time. Jake you were the best older brother you could be and I know we should've had more time together. I wish both of you were still here but there was another plan for all of us. I love you both with all my heart and miss you so badly, but this isn't goodbye. Take care of each other up there and watch out for everyone down here. We'll see you soon"

I looked back at the crowd finally and saw so many different looks. I found Luke and Max and they both smiled at me. I walked toward my family, tears streaming down my face. I knew it would be okay though. Just because of what Lynn had said that had scared me when she was leaving the house that morning. "I'll be seeing you soon Jen. You know, goodbye's never forever."

The Unexpected

By Donny Faretta

The bracelet wrapped itself around Jane's wrist perfectly as her face lit up with excitement. The elegance of the restaurant around them added to the aura of the moment. The teardrop flowing down her left cheekbone forced Jack to grin because he knew that he was winning her over. Jack examined all of Jane's movements and expressions as he realized how great she looked that evening. Her gentle brown hair and soft hazel eyes reflected her personality and attitude. Jack glanced over at the bracelet and decided it was the best present he could have gotten for her. He knew that he did not have enough money for something too extravagant, but he could go out of his way to do something nice for her this time.

Jane quickly shouted with a burst of energy, "Jack! You didn't have to do this!"

While he stepped closer to her, the light above his head revealed the overgrown brown beard surrounding his chin. The illumination showed his disheveled dark brown hair and cavernous blue eyes.

He responded, "No problem. I just thought that I would get you a little gift for the occasion. I know it probably isn't what you're used to."

She looked up with a confused gaze at him and said, "What do you mean this isn't what I'm used to? I love this bracelet. Just because I grew up in a wealthy family doesn't mean I only like diamonds and gemstones."

Jack apologized for his assumption while they threw on their jackets and exited the restaurant. He wanted to act as normal as possible, so that he did not upset her any further. The fights had been escalating the past weeks and he wanted to suppress them.

During the night, Jane was fast asleep in their one bedroom apartment, while Jack snuck into the dimmed kitchen. He rummaged through the dark wooden drawers for papers he needed. The papers seemed to have vanished into thin air, but then he discovered them hiding under a stack of credit card bills that he had yet to pay off. His vital documents descended into a paper shredder and disappeared forever.

The next morning Jane woke up and crept onto the filthy yellow carpet with her slippers on. The lights around the house were still on and she was suspicious. Usually, Jack would leave the house and make sure to turn off all the lights. She turned into the kitchen and saw Jack sitting at the counter on their wooden stool.

Startled at the sight of Jack, Jane said, "What are you still doing home? Shouldn't you be at work?"

He muttered, "I didn't get a lot of sleep last night. I was thinking about things too much." She continued interrogating him, "What were you thinking about so much that you couldn't sleep?"

He lied and said, "Oh, you know the usual. Just thinking about how much I love you."

She lowered her eyebrows and replied, "Yeah right. That's the worst lie I've ever heard in my life."

She let out an explosion of laughter at just the thought of his response. The paranoia set in when he began to think that she was on to him. Sweat slid down the center of his forehead as he considered all the answers that would seem normal to her. She began making breakfast for herself as her doubts seemed to rise about the validity of his story.

He said, "Well, um, I was just having trouble sleeping. You know how that happens sometimes."

She opened the garbage can to throw out her oatmeal box as he spoke and noticed a large amount of shredded paper sinking to the bottom. As Jack saw her open the garbage can, he worried that she would be shocked by an unexpected discovery.

Then she said, "Why are all of these papers in here? They weren't in here last night when I went to sleep."

He replied, "Oh yeah, I was just cleaning out some of our old useless mail. We had too many papers lying around that we didn't need any more."

As he spoke, his anxiety grew by the second. He didn't think his story was acceptable and did not want to do anything that could jeopardize his plan. He needed to execute everything to perfection if it was to go over the way he envisioned it.

She responded, "All right. I may be wrong, but I think you've been acting stranger than usual lately. The sleeping problems, the tone of your voice when I ask you specific questions; you just don't seem like the regular Jack that I know and love."

Thoughts raced through Jack's mind as he realized his plan would soon be ruined if he did not act quickly. He had to put it into action within the next day and he knew it for sure now.

He said, "That just sounds like you're making things up. I'm the same old Jack that you know and love. I'm going to the store to pick up some groceries. See you in a little bit."

He rushed to the store to get away from Jane as quickly as possible. He hurried into the nearest Wal-Mart and found what he was looking for. The blade was a little longer than what he wanted, but it would have to do. Also, the baseball bat was a little expensive, but he knew that he needed it to get the job done right.

He entered his apartment later that evening to a distraught Jane. He could not figure out why she was acting this way. Questions raised in his mind about what she was thinking or what she might have been concerned about.

Jack said, "Hey, what's going on? Why do you look so worried?"

Jane replied, "I've been thinking since you left and things aren't the same anymore. You continue to hide information from me and I know it. A relationship can't survive like this and I feel like we have to be more open with each other."

Jack responded, "What do you mean? I've been telling you everything and I don't know why you are freaking out. I think you've been overreacting to everything I've been saying lately. Just get yourself together for your birthday tomorrow. It's going to be a long day."

Jane said, "Okay. I'll try to get over it I guess, but there's something not right. I just can't put my finger on it."

Jack said goodnight while he plotted the events to come the next day. He was scared to finally put it in to action because he didn't know how he would follow through with it. She had become more suspicious than he would have liked, so he had to be extra cautious. He crept out into the hallway as the darkness fell upon the apartment. He turned on the closet light and took out his Wal-Mart bag. The contents were still wrapped up, so he had to get them ready for the next evening. He carefully placed the knife into their kitchen drawer and hid the bat under their bed.

The morning came fast while Jack and Jane were startled by Jane's alarm at 8 A.M. Jane wanted to go to the mall for her birthday and Jack was happy that she was going. He knew that it would give him a good amount of time to put everything in order. He made sure Jane left for the mall before he got out the items which he needed to carry out his plan. As time flew by, Jack uneasily awaited her return, so that he could give her an unexpected shock. He turned off the lights when he saw her car turn into the parking garage out of their small window. She arrived at about 2 P.M. to a mysteriously empty apartment while Jack was strategically hiding behind the couch in their living room.

Jack jumped up from behind the couch with excitement as he screamed, "Surprise!"

The rest of the guests followed him with a huge shout saying, "Surprise!"

Jane was shocked at the number of people in her apartment that came for a surprise birthday party. Jack quickly brought out the cake and put it on their living room table. After she blew out the candles, he took out the newly purchased knife and cut through the cake. He handed everyone a piece of cake while he set up the piñata for Jane. Then, he went into their bedroom and got out the baseball bat which he placed in Jane's hands.

He told her, "All right. Now, I am going to blindfold you and spin you three times. Just swing away at the piñata. It's going to be right in front of you. Also, try to not to hit anyone."

She laughed at him and struck the piñata with all her force. The piñata ripped open and a necklace fell to the ground. It matched the bracelet he had gotten for her a few days earlier.

She was amazed at the silver necklace with a small heart at the end of it and said, "Jack, you have really outdone yourself. I was so worried that you were hiding something bad from me, but now I realize what you've been doing all along. Wait a second, so what were those papers that you shredded and looked so stressed about?"

He smiled and said, "It was the leftover invitations that I didn't want you to see. I didn't want to ruin the surprise for you."

They laughed about it and Jane realized how her mind was playing tricks on her the whole time. She learned to expect the unexpected.

The Old Man's Scorn

By Raman Dhillon

Daniel sat silently at his computer. He started to type a message but quickly deleted it. He shouldn't send it. It wouldn't make a difference. Nothing will help. While he is there alone in the darkness of the room with the blinds snapped shut and the luminous screen acting as the only light source, someone ambles towards his door. Daniel can hear the swift but sly footsteps. He tries to remain absolutely still, for if the stranger detects movement, Daniel will have to answer the door.

Daniel, a 30-year-old man, has been unemployed for the past year. His field of work was in electronics. He has two girls and one son. He is separated from his wife, but lives within a ten minute driving range for easy communication with his kids. His hobbies include fishing and cooking.

Both Daniel and the stranger at the door play the game for as long as they can. They are both waiting for the other to make a move. Daniel wishes the stranger would go away, but the stranger is adamant and stays firm.

The stranger is none other than Daniel's landlord. He is a constant pest. Even though Daniel pays his rent on time with the full amount, the landlord refuses to leave him alone. His landlord knows Daniel has the money to pay but still is on top of him by repeatedly asking about his job and unemployment situation, his kids and his divorce with his wife, and the fact that he lives alone. The old man simply likes to put him down because he has power—for Daniel has to stay in that apartment because he will otherwise have to move far away from his ex-wife and kids; thus cutting off his access to connecting with his children.

Although the old man is not content, for he believes Daniel is in his apartment, he starts to turn. As he begins to walk away, he has a gnawing feeling that he should find out for sure. He turns back around and knocks on the door. Daniel's heart sinks. He was sure that he could outplay the master. But no, this could never be done. However, Daniel was not about to let his chance of peace go this time. He was not going to let the old man ruin another morning for him.

The landlord knocked on the door with his blistered knuckles. Daniel understood that it was time. He dragged his feet, which suddenly felt numb with apprehension, to the front door. He stood there for a while, attempting to clear his head of the numerous thoughts reverberating throughout. Finally, he gave up and turned the knob to open the door.

"Good morning, Dan. Today is such a fine day, don't you think?" said the old man.

"Hello, Mr. McConnelly. Yes, well I guess it is. What brings you here?" he asked sarcastically.

"Well, I was just on my morning walk when I noticed you were home and thought that I should drop by to remind you that your rent is due next week. For I know that your mind tends to wander with all your ventures with your ex, children, and your job . . . Oh yeah, that actually reminds me—did you find any work yet? I'm just prying to keep notice about your financial situation because I need your rent money, you know?"

Daniel glared at the old man. Once again, Mr. McConnelly had begun to decry Daniel's personal life; never ceasing to find the time to nettle.

Daniel responded with, "No, Mr. McConnelly, but I am continuing my search and hope that a position will open up for me soon. However, don't you worry about the rent, I am more than capable of handling my affairs."

The old man simply smiled. Though that might have seemed like a positive sign for some, for Daniel it meant more floundering on his part.

"Well, I see that you are optimistic, which is good, mind you. Fortunately, I have no such worries as my children are securely settled in their own homes, while Martha and I can relax with relief. However, having to come here and practically beg money out of you so you can live under my roof is a hassle. Again I don't mind much because you are my dear late friend's grandson, thus I have allowed you to stay for so long with the utmost magnanimity."

With these words, Daniel flared with disgust. He deplored the comments of his landlord because Mr. McConnelly's complaints were absolutely ludicrous. Daniel was appalled by such lies because he was a decent guy who had never been questioned by anyone in his life, other than this Mr. McConnelly.

Seething with rage, Daniel established his final statement on the matter after growing weary of this recurring conflict.

Daniel then said, "Mr. McConnelly, you express my presence as an inconvenience for you, thus I have a solution to relieve you of this fact. I have decided move out. I already paid you one month's deposit when I first moved in, and I will move as soon as I find another suitable apartment. Thank you for all your assistance, I really appreciate it."

Mr. McConnelly, stupefied, looked at Daniel. He was taken back with Daniel's rash decision. He did not understand; he could never have fathomed that Daniel would announce his leave in such a manner. Mr. McConnelly continued to process through this new development when . . .

"Now if you don't mind, Mr. McConnelly, I have much to do today and must be on my way if you would just . . ." says Daniel, nudging the landlord out the door.

Dumbfounded, Mr. McConnelly stumbled onto the front steps. He did not know Daniel to be such an aggressive fellow. He was always pleasant and respectful, however today Daniel was acting strangely.

As Daniel brushed past him, the landlord remained deep in thought. As Daniel got into his car to leave, Mr. McConnelly was still on his steps. After some time, Mr. McConnelly began to walk home, not paying attention at all to where he was headed. In this lost state, he reached his destination. He sat down in his armchair situated in the study and reached for a book on a table nearby. He began to flip through it and soon fell into a restless slumber.

Mrs. McConnelly saw her husband and shook her head in disappointment. She had known him to have a callous nature, but she had learned to live with his ways. However, now, as she saw him commit such an injustice to Daniel, she could no longer stay silent.

She must speak to him in the morning, she thought to herself.

*　　*　　*

The following day, Mr. McConnelly left the house without a word. As he walked by Daniel's place, to see boxes piled high in the living room through the open blinds. Mr. McConnelly rushes to Daniel's door. He could not believe that Daniel was already preparing to leave.

Mr. McConnelly thought to himself as he approached Daniel's door.

Surely, he couldn't have found an apartment already?! I cannot afford to lose this young man. I must not let him go! I have, no, I will stop him.

As Daniel let the old man come inside, Mr. McConnelly immediately began to bargain with him.

He has to stop Daniel from leaving. After his retirement, he gained a multitude of time on his hands with nothing much to do. Now with all of his responsibilities done and over with, he needs someone to constantly bother and to spice up life a little bit. He requires someone in life to vent upon.

In the attempt to halt Daniel's departure, Mr. McConnelly made a staggering offer to Daniel. He persuaded Daniel to stay by claiming that Daniel should stay for his children, for if he moved far away, it would become difficult for the family to stay united. The old man enticed Daniel more through declaring that Daniel could stay for free. The landlord trapped Daniel and convinced him to remain.

*　　*　　*

For a while, the landlord stopped pestering Daniel. However, bad habits do not go away easily. After some time, the landlord began to criticize Daniel once again. He complained about the lawn not being kept properly, a broken window that some kids accidentally launched a baseball into, and garbage being rummaged through by some raccoons. Then, he finally settled on one major issue: Daniel's dog. He claimed that Daniel's pet keeps his wife and him up at night, ruining precious sleep time.

Mr. McConnelly started this problem because he gained joy from other's misery. He realizes that the dog is a weak spot for Daniel because he is lonely and the dog is the only comfort that supports Daniel through his solitude.

Daniel, on the other hand, did not know what to do. Before, when he tried to move, the old man had prevented him from accomplishing this task. But, now the old man was back to his old ways of denouncing him. Mr. McConnelly even placed an ultimatum of either getting rid of his beloved pet or moving out. Daniel could not even think of moving away from his current apartment because the only available one in the area was three hours away from his children. He was in quite a predicament. Should he keep Tiger and be forced to move out, or will he have to give him up for his family?

*　　*　　*

After a couple of weeks of arguments and intransigent foothold on part of both parties, Mrs. McConnelly was seen strolling around when three street dogs startle her. The savage beasts look hungrily at the feeble old lady. However, she recognized their stare and began to run. She ducked into a dark alley, but as soon as she entered, she realized that she jumped from the frying pan into the fire. She was halted in her path as she saw a man dressed in black. It was a robber and it was apparent he had a knife. She clutched the item she had in her arms, and closed her eyes waiting for an attack. However, as

85

he approached her, Daniel's dog, Tiger, had also arrived at the scene. The robber did not care about the dog, thus he leaped forward to grab the old lady's possessions. Tiger, on the other hand, barked at him aggressively. The robber jumped back. He eyed the dog looking for a moment to make his move. However, that was a terrible choice. The robber soon grew tired and Mrs. McConnelly had now opened her eyes. She realizes that the robber did not steal anything from her. Then suddenly, the robber attempted again and this time the dog did not give him another chance. He lunged forward, snarling at the robber. The robber pondered his costs and benefits, if he continued, and choose to run away instead. Tiger had scared him away and in the effort saved Mrs. McConnelly's life.

*   *   *

The next day the dog was found dead because Mr. McConnelly had poisoned a biscuit and gave it to the dog as a treat. He killed the savior because of all of his hatred. He could never let that go . . .

*   *   *

The item Mrs. McConnelly was holding onto so dearly was the same photo album Mr. McConnelly was flipping through before. Mrs. McConnelly had gone into town to have the old album restored. Hence Daniel's dog had protected Mr. McConnelly most prized possession—his memories over the years displaying his triumphs and unique moments. But, Mr. McConnelly had given the dog such a prize for this accomplishment that no one would ever forget.

When Daniel found out what had happened, he could no longer bear the sight of Mr. McConnelly. He desired to sue Mr. McConnelly. However, going to court and hiring a lawyer to convict a dog murderer would have been too much for him. Therefore, he decided to move anywhere as long as it was away from the evil old man.

Mrs. McConnelly did not know how to react to her husband's cruel action. She could not leave him now for all the years she had already spent with the man, but she knew that she could never forgive him wholeheartedly. However, she also knew that she must do something to make amends for such evil intentions of her husband. She decided to meet Daniel one last time before he left.

As she caught Daniel leaving from the apartment, she could not dare meet his eyes for she could not bear the sight of the poor, harassed young man. She asked for his forgiveness and the polite young man accepted it, of course. They exchanged goodbyes and well wishes. Mrs. McConnelly then motioned for one of her granddaughters to come around back. As Daniel turned around, the little girl presented him with a small puppy.

'Till Forever

By Ashely Balunek

—⁓⊶⊰⊱⊶⊷⊰⊱⊶⊷⁓—

Sweat drips from his forehead, adrenaline rushes through his body. The last eight seconds meant everything for the team and for his future, but not so much for him. As the leather ball was in his grasp, he used all the power that he had left and threw a twenty-seven yard pass. The half of a second it took for his teammate to successfully receive the ball felt like years to all that were viewing this marvelous moment.

TOUCHDOWN.

The Jefferson Jaguars had just won their first state title in 20 years. Derrick Middleton was a hero. He took little notice of the hundreds of excited fans running toward the center of the field to congratulate him. Running toward him, pushing and shoving the crowd around him was a short old man. He was probably in his mid 60's. With his grey hair and glasses, it was hard to tell if he was really that old or if he just looked old.

"Are you Derrick Middleton?"

"Yes sir."

"My name is Mark Tang. I am on the board of representatives for the North Carolina Tar Heels. After your performance today there is not a doubt in my mind that I will sign you to play for us right this very moment. Full ride and all."

This was the greatest moment of his life, yet something told him that he was not content. He accepted the invitation to go to the college any high school football player would dream of playing for. He shook the hand of Mark Tang, paying no attention to what he was doing. He shifted his head to the left, no longer staring Mark in the eyes. He was looking for something, someone. Scoping the hundreds of people in the crowd, he found what he was looking for. It was her.

In his mind, everything went silent. He could no longer hear the roaring crowd or the hundreds of conversations going on around him. He only saw her, the girl of his dreams. She was what you would call "the girl next door." She was different from any other girl he had ever met, and he loved that about her. The only thing was, she had no idea that he had secretly admired her for years now. She was walking toward him. He could feel his palms start to sweat and his heart begin to beat faster by the second. He became more nervous than he was during the actual game.

She was not but five feet from him. He noticed her brown hair with those cute loose curls, and her green eyes that could be mistaken for blue when in the right light. And that smile that made him, the number one jock at Jefferson, feel weak at the knees. She was standing right in front of him.

"Congratulations, you were amazing."

Keep your cool man; you can do this. Say something back. Say it. You can do it.

"Sarah, I need to tell you something . . . I, well, I lo-"

In mid sentence, he froze. What he just saw would hurt him for the rest of his life. His best friend, Mitch, the wide receiver, had just come up behind Sarah. He had spun her around and kissed her. Mitch knew how Derrick felt about her. Derrick watched as Sarah began to talk again.

"I'm sorry Derrick, what were you saying?"

He could not help but notice that she was not paying the slightest attention to him, but only to his so called best friend.

"Oh its nothing really, I just wanted to thank you for supporting the team and cheering us on."

She looked at him with that look that he always admired about her. She was not smiling, but you could see the smile in her eyes. He figured she would just nod her head and respond with a "no problem!" or a "you're welcome," but instead she switched her attention to Mitch who would not let her go.

It had been exactly eight months since the big game. School seemed to fly by; senior year was, in fact, over and summer was coming to an end. Derrick had officially signed with the Tar Heels and was getting ready to leave in two short days. Sarah and Mitch were still together even though Derrick could not even remember when they ever started seeing each other. It seemed as though it happened overnight, like some weird dream; but in this case, the dream continued on into reality.

"Are you ready to make me proud up there in North Carolina?"

"Of course, Dad. When would I ever let you down?"

"You never have son, and you never will. No matter what happens, I will always be proud of you."

Derrick was in the middle of packing for college. With clothes and suitcases scattered all over the floor of his small, ten by thirteen foot bedroom, it was hard for him to keep track of exactly what he was doing. His father, standing at the door, walked into the mess of a room.

The sound of breaking glass was heard underneath his father's left foot. He leaned over to see what he had stepped on, lifting up shirts and boxers in order to see the floor.

"Who's this pretty girl? Isn't that you're friend, what's her name? S something . . . Sarah?"

"Let me see that," Derrick replied.

It was from before the big game. He had seen Sarah just before he walked into the locker room to get suited up. She had yelled his name from across the hall, demanding he take a "before the big game" photo with his number one fan.

"I remember her being around at those games; do you still keep in touch with her? She's a very nice girl."

"I'd rather not talk about it Dad, let me just finish packing."

"Oh, I see. Well if you don't want to talk about anything that's fine, but just a little piece of advice, if you want something bad enough, you'll fight for it. Just remember that son."

The night before heading off to college, Mitch was throwing an end-of-the-summer bash. Everyone who's anyone was there.

Derrick walked in the front door and automatically started getting "yo, dude wassup's?' and "hey Derrick's" from his hundreds of his drunk peers. He was in no mood to drink, and he knew that the next day was going to be a long day, going to college and all. He felt a tap on his right shoulder, it was Mitch. Not sober, to say the least. Derrick turned around and could immediately smell the alcohol on his breath. He had had a little too much vodka, and his breath reeked of cigarettes.

"Mitch what are you doing? You don't smoke, and you never drink this much."

"Just having fun man, lighten up. I can do whatever the hell I want," said Mitch.

Sarah walked up behind Mitch. Wearing a light blue spaghetti strap dress that went to her knees and her hair pulled back in her soft pony tail with loose curls hanging by the side of her face, she looked beautiful.

"Mitch, I really think you've had enough. You're starting to worry me," said Sarah. Mitch had no verbal response, but instead he quickly turned around and slapped Sarah on the side of the face, leaving five red finger prints molded into her skin.

Derrick grabbed Mitch and pinned him to the wall. Mitch was strong, but Derrick was stronger. He grabbed the collar of his shirt, twisting it, making it harder for Mitch to breathe.

"If you ever touch her again, there will be a problem. I don't care how drunk you are, no one, I mean no one, has the right to hit her. Go take a walk and straighten yourself out. We don't need you here if you are going to act this way."

Derrick shoved him out the front door, closing it behind him. Quickly looking back at Sarah, he could not help but to hold her in his arms and tell her she was okay. Tears ran down her face, and that smile she always had was gone. With her head tucked under his arm, he held her tight, never wanting to let go.

"It's going to be okay Sarah, I promise."

With tears rolling down her cheeks, she struggled to speak, breathing hard and fast.

"He's changed; he's not the same person he was. Everything I do is wrong to him. He's never hit me before, I swear, but I—I can't do this anymore."

"I understand," replied Derrick.

"Derrick. I don't mean to bother you but . . ."

"Yes?"

"Would you mind walking me home?"

It was 11:00 p.m. when Derrick took Sarah home. Since she only lived two streets away, it was not a far walk at all. It was a warm summer night with the stars shining brightly and the crickets chirping. He knew that this was the only time he would have to tell her his true feelings. Regardless of the state she was in, he had to do it. He was leaving tomorrow; it was now or never. He looked over at her, walking slowly, still sniffling here and there from crying. He tried not to stare, but he couldn't help it. The reflection of the moonlight was on her face, making her look so innocent, so helpless, but yet so beautiful. He stuck out his hand, gesturing for her to take it. She did not hesitate. As her hand slid into his, they interlocked fingers and kept walking. He knew this felt right.

He began to speak, not exactly knowing what he was saying. "I'm sorry about Mitch, I've known him for a long time, and I've never seen him act that way. No one deserves that, especially not you."

"Things have been shaky for a while now. To be honest, I'm glad this happened; now I have a reason to end it. We weren't going anywhere, and I knew I had to stop things soon. Thank you so much for sticking up for me. You're a great guy Derrick, I hope you know that," she said.

She started tearing up again. Embarrassed, she continued, "Sorry you have to see me this way."

He felt his palms begin to sweat as they held tightly onto hers. He felt weak at the knees; an explosion of words began to pour out of his mouth as he stared her gently in the eyes.

"I love you, and I always have. I'm not trying to sound like I'm obsessed, but there has just always been something about you that I admire. And I know that I will always admire you. You are perfect in every way, and seeing you with Mitch broke my heart. I know this is a lot for you to hear all at once. I'm actually surprised that, I, the high school jock, am telling you all this."

She said nothing for what felt like an eternity but in reality was about five seconds. His heart was beating fast, so fast he had trouble counting his heartbeats. They were steps away from her front door. Thinking he just ruined any chance he ever had with her, he removed his hand from her grip and began to say the word goodbye.

Right as the word goodbye was about to roll off the tip of his tongue, Sarah grabbed him. She passionately brought her lips towards his. The kiss felt so real, so right. It was like a fairytale ending. She pulled away and stared at him with that face that he loved, the smile that was told through her eyes. She whispered the word "goodbye," and went inside the house, quietly closing the front door behind her.

There was not a day that went by that Derrick didn't think about that kiss. It seemed as though it happened yesterday, but fifty-four days ago was definitely not yesterday. He assumed that Sarah was having the time of her life learning new things and making new friends up at Georgetown. He came to the conclusion that she had completely forgot about him. Heartbroken, he was at UNC, living his dream playing football. The team was undefeated, and the next day was the big game. The semi-final game was tomorrow. The game that determined which two teams would be competing in the final winner-takes-all game of the Rose Bowl. Boston College was a tough team to beat, but with the tens of thousands of fans that were coming to the game, he was sure he would be able to get his adrenaline going to play his best.

The clock was ticking and the seconds began spiraling downward as the fourth quarter flew by. There were two minutes remaining in the fourth quarter and UNC was down by one touchdown. Having possession of the ball, Derrick knew he had to take one for the team and give it all he had, emotions aside.

"Ready, set, hike!"

This was it. Derrick did what he does best; he threw the football to his teammate thirty-four yards away.

BOOM.

Out of nowhere, Derrick felt pain like no other. He had been tackled, tackled hard. His knee felt as though it was no longer connected to his leg. That is the last thing he remembered, the rest was a blur to him.

"Derrick, Derrick."

The bright lights of the hospital room took a while for his eyes to adjust to. Not fully knowing where he was or how he got there, he quickly realized he was not at UNC anymore.

As his eyes adjusted to the light, he focused on his other sense, hearing. He heard a female voice saying his name. He turned his head to the right, slowly and painfully. Was this a dream? Was Sarah really standing next to his bedside?

"Wake up, Derrick, wake up," she said sweetly.

She was wearing his jersey, the old number 16, his high school number and now his college one. Her hair was down, and she had black eye paint under her eyes and pom poms hanging out of the brown leather purse that sat on her left shoulder.

She began to speak, "Derrick, are you okay? You had me worried sick."

"What happened? I don't remember a thing. Wait, how are you here? Where did you come from? What is going on?" he replied.

"I was at the game, cheering you on. You were doing amazingly. I was hoping to surprise you after the game, but I guess this will have to do. Who knew you were going to end up here afterwards. You're knee is dislocated, but other than that I am sure you're going to be just fine," she said.

Before Derrick could respond, she started talking again. She was talking a mile a minute, as if she had so much to say and no time to say it.

"Truth is, I came here not only to cheer you on, but to tell you something. I haven't been able to stop thinking about you. Actually, I don't want to ever stop thinking about you. Is it too soon to say that I love you? I know we've only been friends for a while and nothing more, but I feel a spark."

Derrick didn't say a word. He smiled from ear to ear, and suddenly all his pain was gone. All he managed to say was, "Come here."

He kissed her as if the world was going to end and he would never be able to kiss her again. The love of his life was just standing in front of him announcing her love for him. How could anything go wrong? It couldn't. This was what he always dreamed of and more.

After a week of being in the hospital, Derrick found himself sitting on the sidelines watching his teammates play in the championship game. As much as he wanted to play in this game, he found that he was just as happy knowing that Sarah was there to support him no matter what. He turned around to see her cheering in the stands, smiling back at him. That look on her face would never get old. She was his, no matter what happened. That is exactly how he wanted things to be. She was his number one fan, and he would always be hers.

A Life Changing Mistake

By Catalina Carvajal

—◦◦◦◦◦◦◦◦◦—

Shane asked himself, "Where am I going?" every morning when he got up. With a feeling of despair, he put on his bracelet that his mother had given to him as a little boy. Shane was eighteen-years-old and about to face the most difficult challenge of his life. He went to school, high school that is, and his senior year was coming to an end. Having been in a relationship for over a year, he definitely had someone in which he could confide. Little did Shane know that his life was about to completely change. He lived with his father, who is very supportive. His mother had died a couple of years ago from alcohol poisoning, right after giving him his bracelet. Shane felt alone in the world, though he had great friends and a supporting father.

One night before entering college, Shane decided to go out to a party in the valley. The valley is known as "Sin City" here in Virginia. Shane wasn't the type of person to be on his own when it came to going to parties. He wasn't the most social person, so it was strange that Shane had gone out by himself that day. The morning after, Shane couldn't remember a thing. He had quite the night because he woke up with a terrible headache and felt very flimsy.

"Where were you all night?" asked his father. Shane could only shrug his shoulders. He had gone out to get away from his problems, which wasn't the best idea.

Two months passed and Shane was already starting his new beginning in college. Shane still asked himself, "Where am I going?" He was having trouble adjusting to living on his own, and it was evident that he had trouble managing his grades. Not only was Shane experiencing many troubles, but he no longer had that relationship he had in high school. With everything that was going on in his life, many of his friends found themselves separating or simply just living the college life. Shane was having more trouble than any of the close friends he had. Considering his mother had died from alcohol poisoning, Shane had been exposed to alcohol much more, even if he had not wanted it. Every weekend he went out, he went out to get intoxicated. The people around him eventually got worried and wanted him to get help. Though they wished the best for Shane, it was only him who could make any type of change. Like most people experiencing a problem, Shane didn't want to accept that he had an issue.

Some time passed, and Shane was now in his second semester of freshman year in college. To his surprise, he received an anonymous phone call one rainy afternoon.

"Hello," Shane answered.

"Is this Shane Cane?" responded a girl in a shrill voice.

"Yes it is. What may I help you with?" Shane asked.

"Listen, I don't want you to get worried or nervous, but we need to have a serious talk. My name is Sara, and I was with you that one night you decided to go out on your own."

There was silence, and Shane didn't respond.

"Hello, are you there?" Sara asked desperately.

"Yes, yeah I'm here. Um . . . what is it?" Shane replied hesitantly.

"This might scare you a little . . . it did for me, but I've been pregnant for the passed five months. I didn't want to scare you or anything, but you are the father."

There was yet again more silence as Shane breathed heavily into the phone. Not a word came out his mouth until he finally said, "I know."

Right then, Sara hung up, and Shane was left on the phone. Though Sara sounded calm, her immediate reaction was to disconnect him from the phone, the way she hoped she could take Shane out of her world. He knew what he had done; he realized what he had done because the night they were together, he hadn't brought protection. Shane had been going about his life knowing that he had gotten a girl pregnant, and did little to nothing to help the situation. It was now obvious that Shane had to do something about what he had done. He called Sara until she finally answered, and they agreed to see each other the following day.

Nothing was ever mentioned to anyone about what happened that afternoon with Shane and Sara. All anyone knew was that Shane was soon to be a father. To his surprise, he didn't feel as lonely as he had before, and somehow he knew what he wanted to do with his life. It seemed as though this mistake was altering his life for the better. As time progressed, Shane's life began to improve, and his father knew that more than anyone else. Since Shane's father was so supportive, he didn't want him to drop out of school. Having this baby was possibly the best thing that could have happened to Shane. On the other hand, Sara wasn't so happy. Though she wanted to keep her child, she didn't know how to cope with being a mother at such a young age. Considering Shane and Sara were seeing each other as much as they were, they started a relationship. They didn't want to start the baby's life without a steady environment, and to their surprise, their bond grew much more than they had originally expected. Shane went from being a complete disaster to having someone that meant the world to him. He was probably getting the most benefits out of the pregnancy.

It was May, and the baby was soon to be born. The baby was going to be a girl, and everyone was very eager to see her. Shane and Sara were probably the most anxious ones, but Sara was especially scared. During the pregnancy, Sara had been experiencing problems with her blood pressure. There would be days where Sara couldn't even get out of bed because of her weariness, and other days where she felt completely fine. She thought this was simply because of the pregnancy until the day the baby came. On a very rainy day in May, Sara went into the delivery room and was ready to give birth. Everything that could go wrong seemed to go wrong on that day. Shane was late because he had been stuck in traffic, and Sara was alone. Her doctor had been helping throughout the whole process, but there was only so much he could do for her. Unfortunately, there were many problems with the delivery. Though Sara felt as though she was doing fine, the baby was not. Due to Sara's high blood pressure, the baby was born, and Sara let out a breath of relief, until the doctor came back in *without the baby.*

Before the doctor could say anything to Sara and Shane, Shane asked for his baby. The doctor responded, "You see Shane, we didn't forecast this problem, but well, your baby girl didn't make it."

Months passed and neither Shane nor Sara could get over it. Most people got closer to Shane because of what had occurred, but others were too frightened and distanced themselves. Either way, Shane had begun to grow even closer with Sara. It befuddled Shane's mind that he could have gotten so close to someone by a simple mistake.

Shane's father was scared that he might start doing what he had done earlier, so he told Sara to make sure he wouldn't do anything he would regret. Sara promised him that she would do her best to keep Shane out of any problems.

Sara succeeded in keeping Shane out of trouble. Shane continued going to school. He realized what was important in his life, and what he wanted to do. Shane dedicated himself to school, and still had time for Sara. He wanted to become a maternity doctor to help other people and eventually marry Sara. It was unfortunate that it took the death of his own child to realize what he wanted, but at least now he knew. Shane thanked Sara for everything she had done, and for everything they had gone through together.

But most importantly, Shane thanked his father; that even through all his faults, he never given up on him.

Enough

By Derick Edwards

Leo Davies had it all: he was the "A" guy of every girl's dreams; captain of the football team, captain of the lacrosse team, and even a straight student. On his way to school one morning, Leo noticed the sunrise just peeking behind the mountain. He brushed his neck and straightened out the slight crease in his green and white patterned varsity jacket. As he walked into school, he gave a quick glimpse to the girl he just finished sending a text to. He tried not to stare for too long, knowing he couldn't let anyone else suspect what he had just been doing.

As he walked through the halls, he noticed his hand getting tired from shaking and slapping the already sweaty palms of his peers. Leo shut his locker and entered his class. He quickly got distracted and started staring at the cracks on the walls and pointing out different smudges of vandalism. He occasionally tuned in and out, listening to his teacher ramble on about how his weekend, something Leo saw as completely irrelevant to the class.

His thoughts quickly switched to his father. Leo and his father had a relationship like no other. Not only was he his best friend, but he was also his mentor. Both of them alone could brighten up a whole room. Though they had a close relationship, Leo knew that when it came to reprimanding, his father was the first to do it whenever he thought it was necessary. He then thought of the rumbling car and dirt spotted window which he had been focusing on the night before as his dad lectured him.

"Son, in today's world everything revolves around money. I had it rough when I was your age, but you on the other hand, you have everything that you could possibly need to succeed. Everyday you're getting closer! You're so close, I feel like you're right there, about to finish."

"Yeah, I'm focused, Dad, don't worry. I'm going to do this for you."

"Well I hope so because everyone's counting on you, especially me. You know you're all I've got. Right now I feel like I'm living my life through you, you know?"

Just the mordant thought of letting his father down made his stomach twist and turn.

"This world isn't fair. You know I'm struggling to supply your mother with the sufficient money to provide for you," his father said truthfully. "Do you want to end up like me?"

Leo had noticed the tremble in his father's voice, no matter how much he tried to hide it. The tiny particles of saliva from his father's mouth and distinctive emphasis of his hard spoken words showed Leo how meaningful his father meant them to be.

Sympathy ran through Leo's body as he met his dad's gaze. Speechless, he nodded his head up and down, hinting to his dad that he knew exactly where he was coming from.

The bell's sudden ring snapped Leo out of his trance. He looked over at the calendar and suddenly realized that he had the biggest game of the year later that afternoon. As an "almost" professional athlete, Leo was fast to regain his composure, despite how unprepared he felt. After all, all the pressure was on him; he was an all-state player, and everyone was counting on him to bring home the win.

After his math class, he aimlessly walked through the halls period after period in order to just get through his classes. The only thing he noticed while walking through the crowded halls was the chatter about the anticipated game. By the end of the day, it was obvious he was getting a little edgy.

Finally it was game time. Leo sat as his locker, staring into space with the sound of blasting music running through his ears. The stench of body odor and over used pads filled the air. His eyes wandered around the room and came in contact with his coach. He looked at Leo as if he had important news to give him but only proceeded with a slight fist pump.

As if it was a quick reaction to his notion, Leo put on his solid steel helmet and began to run out of the tunnel grasping the hand of his best friend, Shabaz. He felt the roar of the crowd in his chest when he stepped foot on the field.

"I have to win this game for them, I just have too," Leo said to himself out loud just before kickoff.

The ball belted throughout the air, twirling around like a kite against the wind. Landing in Leo's hands, he began to run, grasping it firmly. His feet moved swiftly, barely touching the ground. As he was running down the sideline of the field, the crowd started getting louder, anticipating his touchdown.

Then, everything momentarily stopped. The thud of the helmets broke through the noise of the crowd. The crowd sporadically stopped. Leo lay on the ground, motionless, like an un-rippled pond. His father immediately ran onto the field, with the grace of a football player himself. By the time he got there, Leo showed slight, almost unnoticeable signs of consciousness.

"Son, are you alright? Please Lord, tell me you're okay!"

"Yeah, Pops, I'm fine. Let me play," Leo said, barely audible.

His father let out a sigh of relief.

"I have to play Dad, let me play; I want to win it for you, and for everyone else. Please, you have to let me play."

Leo took all his remaining strength and staggered across the field, receiving a standing ovation from the crowd which viscously clapped for their best player. For the rest of the game, Leo watched at the edge of the bench in despair as his team attempted to win. All Leo could do was glimpse at the field, holding his breath every second of the game.

The next day, as his math teacher slapped a test on his solid, dark silver desk, the sharp clap quickly reminded Leo he still had school. He looked at the test, which had a 70% written in red pen at the top, and remembered the words his father had told him just a few days ago. Leo's teacher gave him a look of concern. Millions of negative thoughts began to race through his head like scurrying squirrels.

What if he didn't keep his grades up? What if he didn't do well on his next SAT exam? Leo's palms began to drip fluids on his desk. Sliding his hand off where it had been resting on the desk, he could see the thick hand print left there. His heart began to pump a tad bit faster, increasing as he thought about it more and more. Raising his shaking arm, he politely asked to use the lavatory. Feeling the different crumbs of food on his shoes, he looked down ignoring all the greeting and handshakes offered to him. The smell of transmission fluid ran through his nose on his walk to the bathroom as he walked past the Auto-Mechanics class. Strange blurs of different colleges, his mother, his friends, and lacrosse all flashed through his head. He reached for the rusted bathroom stall handle and tugged. The strong stench of urine reeked, but didn't disturb him. Sitting down on the toilet seat, Leo took a long sigh as he looked up at the ceiling. Diving his face into the cracks of his hands, he began to cry. Bottled emotions burst out like a jack-in-the-box. The salty water from his tears slipped past his lips. The person who gave a billion hugs a day was desperately in need of just one.

The Coin

By Emma Vita

———⁓⦿⦿⦿⁓———

I wiped my eyes, saw the red lights come on in front of me, and slammed on the brakes, screeching to a halt. My tears had begun to pick up and made driving on this busy highway difficult and increasingly dangerous. My heart grew more and more torn. I needed to decide between two choices. Both which would affect my life completely, each in a totally different way. I had no idea who I would choose. My heart ached even more at the thought of eventually having to make a decision and be strong enough to follow through with whatever choice I made. I wished someone else could just choose for me, and with that an idea came to mind.

"What if I flipped a coin?"

But I didn't have a coin. After driving about a mile further, I became so desperate that I pulled off the highway to find one. I exited off the ramp and spotted a "Park and Ride" lot. Completely empty, I took the parking spot in the exact middle of it. I had tried to slow down my crying in order to see the road on the highway, but now that I was parked safely all alone, I didn't have anything to worry about. After taking one last look around, to make sure I wouldn't be seen, I broke down. Unable to control my heaving, I rested my head on my hands which sat on the top of the steering wheel. My tears dripped onto my hands and cheeks. I lifted my head and looked into the rearview mirror.

"Why does this have to be so hard? I just want to know the right thing to do," I said to the red eyes that stared back at me through the mirror. My eyelashes were no longer black from my make-up, but from being soaked from my tears. My make-up was running all down my face, making me look even more hopeless. I grabbed a tissue from the glove compartment to clean myself up, but realized it was no use. I was nowhere near done crying yet. When I would be done, I did not know.

"Oh right. The coin."

I took a deep breath and opened the car door. As I went to put my foot down, I saw it. A shiny, copper penny, heads up. I laughed and shook my head, surprised at how easy it had been. I leaned over, picked it up, and rubbed my thumb back and forth over it, impressed by its perfection. I wondered how it had sat in this parking lot for however long, without being tarnished or scratched. I flipped it over to further study it, but then . . . wait.

"What's this?"

I flipped it over again and again to make sure I was seeing alright. Both sides were heads. The back was not tails.

"No way."

Is this penny always lucky or simply just a defect? Then I realized that this penny would be no use to me. I had to find another one. I needed a penny to make a decision. If both sides were the same, I wouldn't be able to tell what it had chosen for me. I considered trying to search for another one, but knew that finding one wouldn't be as easy as coming across this one had been. I needed something that could make a mark on one side of my penny. Maybe if I could find a sharpie. There was one in the center console. I took it out and scribbled all over one of the sides.

I sighed and muttered, "Here we go."

I put the coin in the palm of my hand and through it into the air. As I watched the coin flip from copper to black, I pictured his face instead of Abraham Lincoln's. The copper color of the penny reminded me of his light brown hair and hazel eyes; his hair that always smelt like sea salt from the water he swam in every morning. Each day after his swim, he would climb back into bed, and I would wake up to the smell of his hair and his sweet eyes that made me smile as soon as mine opened. Then I thought of how hard it had been to leave him and go back home. My chest started to swell up again. My fiancé had found out where I was and what had happened and demanded that I return to him. The color of the penny also made me think of the dark liquor my fiancé always kept in his office. I hated smelling the rum on his breath. He would lie to me, telling me he hadn't been drinking. I knew where he kept his stash, so I could see when bottles went missing. It was better to pretend I believed him then to argue, which was what we always did. His drinking only made it worse.

I decided that the sharpie side meant I would turn around and go back to where I was being forced to drive away from. If it landed on Abe Lincoln's side, I would continue on my way, back to my fiancé.

The coin hit the ceiling of the car and plummeted back down, straight into my open cup of coffee.

"Oh! Sh . . ."

Before I could complete the rest of the word, I looked down into the cup and saw the coin floating. I ignored the fact that the circular piece of copper was actually floating at the top of the liquid, and saw that it was heads side up. My heart sank. It had decided that I had to continue back home. I picked up the penny out of the cup and gave it a dirty look before tears began to flow again. I threw the penny at my windshield in anger. It hit the glass, then fell to the dashboard and started to spin. I watched it and noticed that I couldn't see any black on the coin as it spun. I swiped the penny back into my hand. There was no longer any sharpie left on the back. I didn't think it could have happened so quickly, but the coffee must have washed the sharpie right off. Then I smiled. This gave me hope. The coin flip wasn't valid because I couldn't be sure which side had really been facing up. I smiled, realizing that I had to re-do it.

I needed something else to mark the coin with. I rummaged through my make-up bag and found a bottle of pink nail polish. I was sure that coffee would have trouble taking this off. I painted over the back side and looked down at my cup of coffee which had caused all the trouble. I thought it would be safer to step outside to avoid the coffee all together. I opened my door all the way. Once again, I threw the coin into the air.

Seeing the pink appear and reappear as the penny flipped through the air, I remembered the pink dress I had worn on my fiancé's and my first date. I remembered how much he had talked about himself and how I barely managed to get a word in. But he was charming and my parents had been impressed by him, so we had gone on a second date. The pink also reminded me of the sunset I had shared the night before with the man I was being forced to leave behind. Lying on a blanket with him and watching the sun go down was much better than any five star dinner my fiancé could pay for.

The coin hit the asphalt and started to spin as it had done before. It seemed to spin forever. I thought nothing of it at first because of the way everything seemed to happen in slow motion lately.

But it just wouldn't stop. It kept spinning and spinning. Finally, I went to lean down and pick it up, and then it stopped abruptly, balanced perfectly on its side. It had to have been the perfect circumstances, or maybe something more was going on, for it to stay that way. Frustrated, I picked up the coin and threw it once again. It flew through the air and pinged off a sign that read: "South". I had been on my way back north, back to my fiancé. I realized the direction I wanted to go.

From the penny, I got a sign, and now I realized what I wanted. I understood what I had been hoping for this whole time. I didn't care about going back to my fiancé. I had only been on my way back because I thought it was the right thing to do. I was in love with my best friend who I had given up years ago for my fiancé. On this visit, I had returned to my hometown to see him and discovered that I had been hiding my true feelings for him for years. I knew what I wanted now. I didn't need the coin to decide for me because I had decided for myself each time the coin had been in the air.

Using my sharpie, on the back of an old receipt I wrote: "In life when you face choices, just toss a coin. Not because it settles the question, but while the coin is in the air, you'll know what your heart is hoping for." I ran to the spot where I had seen the coin land. I picked it up and placed it right back beside my car where I had found it and on top of the note I had made. I left it there so that maybe another traveler could use it and eventually understand its magic and learn what I had. I knew I didn't need it anymore. I jumped back into the car and followed the sign back south.

The Monster

By Jenn Roginski

—⁓∿∘⊶⊷ʘ⊶⊶∘∿⁓—

My life was never perfect, nor do I expect it to ever become anything close to that. This life will never be a good life. A long time ago I gave up on hoping for something better. Some people think it's a bad thing or that I'm depressed or something. I really do not think it's either of those. It is easier to have no expectations for me because that way I will never be disappointed. Shakespeare said it best with, "Expectation is the root of all heartache."

For being alive for only 17 years, I've had my fair share of disappointments. My Daddy blames all my problems on my mother. If there's not enough money to pay all the bills, it is always because that damn woman left us 11 years ago. Even if he just drops a pen it's somehow all her fault.

I don't remember much about my mother. Her voice has vanished from my memories, and I only know what she looks like from two photographs I have managed to save of her. Daddy doesn't like to talk about her, and I know better than to ask. I'm sure you think this would upset me, but it doesn't. I have absolutely no desire to ever see this woman again. She abandoned me with this monster just to save herself.

I know exactly what you are thinking now; that I'm just filled with teen angst and really don't hate my own mother. That's because you do not know what I know, at least not yet. I can no longer keep this life a secret. I need to get help soon, before it's too late.

*   *   *

There's been this voice inside my head ever since I was a little girl. Sometimes it's my friend and other times it's my own worst enemy. The voice has the power to turn me from sympathetic to irate in as little as two seconds. Over the past few years, I've been able to gain control of this voice. I'm not perfect though. Every once in a while it manages to escape the cage I've locked it in.

The voice first started talking to me not long after my mother left us. My dad spent those first few weeks drinking all day. I didn't know this at first; I had no idea why my father was acting so strangely. When my mother lived with us, my dad never hit me; I don't remember him even ever raising his voice at me. Everything all changed when she left. With nobody else in the house, I became his personal punching bag. Some days I could not get up to get ready for school because he hurt me so bad. Nobody ever said a word to me at school. They all believed me when I told them I had a cold. It was all Daddy, and he made me promise not to tell anybody or I would never get to see him again. Losing both of my parents was not something I was ready for, so I just kept my mouth shut.

The lunches my mom used to pack for me were what I missed the most. Daddy spent his morning sleeping off his hangovers, so I had nobody to help me get ready for school. Most days I didn't bring a lunch to school because there was nothing to bring. Daddy spent more money on booze than food.

*   *   *

I walk into the kitchen and notice a newspaper lying open on the table. Normally, nobody reads the newspaper, and it just gets tossed into a pile on the counter. I had cleaned up the kitchen the night before after dinner, but somebody had been in here since then. The painting on the far wall was now crooked, and there were dirty dishes all over the counter. Somebody had already made the coffee and spilled milk around the drying rack. I heard footsteps behind me, and as I turned around, I bumped into him.

"Woah, be careful. You need to watch where you're walking."

It took a couple seconds for me to process what was going on. Daddy was never up before I left for school, especially times like now when he was in between jobs. The whole scene just baffled me.

I finally managed to ask him, "What are you doing up so early?"

"I'm going to find a job," he answered.

With that, our conversation ended. I could tell he had already helped himself to his happy juice. That was not a good sign at all; nobody would hire Daddy if he showed up intoxicated. He had done it before a million times. Daddy always told me he acted sober better when he was buzzed. Even if he did get the job, he wouldn't have it for long; his bosses would catch on and fire him.

The only thing that was running through my mind is what would happen next. This situation could go two ways. Daddy could somehow find a job and come home and celebrate with drinking, or come home without a job and try to drown his feelings with alcohol. Neither of these options looked too appealing, but trust me, I would much rather have the first one than the second.

$$* \quad * \quad *$$

I came home from school not knowing what to expect. I noticed his beat up truck in the driveway; at least he made it home okay. When the bus stopped down the street, I couldn't bring myself to go into that house. So instead, I turned around and walked in the opposite direction. I didn't have any idea of where I was going; I just knew any place would be better than going home.

I walked towards downtown, figuring I'd stop to get some coffee and then go to the library. I needed to go somewhere where I knew he wouldn't find me. The library was the perfect place; all I had to do was say I had to meet with some kids from school for a group project. My plan was perfect. It was believable and got me out of having to go home.

The only issue was that the library closed at six. When six o'clock came, I had nowhere else to go but back to that house. It was getting dark, and I didn't want to get stuck walking the streets alone at night.

*   *   *

No matter how many times I walk into my house not knowing what to expect, I will never get over that sick feeling. As the little shack we call a house comes into sight, I get nauseous. My hands shake, and I try to focus on my breathing. It's a trick one of the nurses taught me after I had a panic attack in the middle of gym class. She also told me to try counting down, but that never helped; it just made me feel like I was counting down to my own demise.

I took a deep breath before slowly turning the doorknob. The last thing I wanted to do was wake Daddy up. He had to have come home several hours ago, so by now he had probably drunken himself to sleep.

Today must have been my lucky day. When I walked in, I found him with a six pack on his lap and his face hanging over the edge of his stained, olive green recliner. I went to my room to put my stuff down. About an hour, later I figured it would be safe to leave my room to go get some food. Skipping breakfast and lunch had left me famished. I probably shouldn't have had that coffee either; it only made me more susceptible to my anxiety. As I began to tiptoe across the hall, I could feel Daddy's loud, deep snores bounce off the walls.

When I got to the kitchen, I realized we had no food. I mean we had food, but nothing that looked appetizing. I made a mental note to go grocery shopping this weekend. I finally found some peanut butter and jelly and began to make a sandwich. When I went to get a knife, the world turned against me. The drawer got jammed, and in the process of pulling it out, all of the silverware came crashing to the ground. The sound the forks and spoons made was the worst noise I had ever heard. I knew I had woken Daddy up.

The crashing of the silverware woke up more than just Daddy; it caused the voice inside my head to come back. It started calling me names like stupid and incompetent. The voice told me to run before he came into the kitchen, but I couldn't move an inch. All I could do was stand there, petrified with fear of now knowing what my father was going to do next.

He burst through the door, screaming something which made no sense. Once he grabbed onto a chair for support, I was able to make sense of his slurred words.

"What the hellllll is going on here? Where you been all day? Didn't you think to call your faaaather and let him know where you were? You braaaat. You spoiled, worthless braaaat."

The rest of what he said was incomprehensible. He came charging at me with his hand clenched in a fist. I must've had luck on my side because he stumbled and fell to the ground face first. I used this as my chance to get out. I jumped over him and ran outside of the house, not bothering to grab shoes or a jacket.

*   *   *

I swear I ran for an eternity. Not once did I look back or even slow down. Adrenaline filled my body and gave me the ability to run faster than I ever had before. I eventually stopped at a park and climbed to the top of the jungle gym and just sat there. The voice began to speak to me, this time more softly. For the first time in years, I didn't try to stop it. I let the voice stay out of the cage, it had been right in the kitchen, and I should have listened to it before.

The voice was successful at calming me down. It told me it wasn't my fault and that I deserved better. I needed to stick up for myself and get revenge. Nobody had the right to say those things to me or try to hurt me. Eventually, the voice convinced me to take action.

I slowly walked back home, letting the voice tell me this was the right thing to do. It took a while; I hadn't realized how far I had run. I guess it was a good thing because the closer I got to the house, the more confidence I had in the voice's plan.

When I got to the property, the first thing I did was make my way to the shed. In there, I found exactly what I had been looking for on the middle of the work table. It was an ax. I didn't even know why we had one; we had no trees in our yard. After exiting the shed, I made my way to the windows. Daddy had somehow made his way back to the recliner, which was exactly what I had hoped for.

I walked back to the front door and slowly turned the knob so that I would not wake him. My lack of shoes had covered my feet in cuts and left deep red stains on the beige carpet. As I walked up to the recliner, I got another adrenaline rush. I could finally get my payback for all the times he had hurt me. I no longer needed the voice as my motivator.

As I stood over him, he opened his eyes. He turned pale and opened his mouth to say something, but no words came out. I just looked at him and gave him a crooked smile, enjoying the site.

When he finally was able to say something, all that came out was, "Why?"

This made me and the voice inside my head cackle.

"You know why," I said through my chuckles.

And with that, I killed the monster I called Daddy.

A Race Against Time

By Juliana Cole

―――༺⚬❀⚬༻―――

The clock struck midnight, as she hurried to grab her belongings before time ran out. Unlike the story of Cinderella, however, Prince Charming was not waiting for her with a glass slipper, and there was certainly no Fairy Godmother in sight. As Aarya rushed out the door of her small, tattered apartment, fairytales were the last thing on her mind. No matter what was about to happen, she knew her life was going to change forever. Aarya was ready to leave her life in Yemen behind; she knew it wasn't good for her and she needed to get out. But then again, she really didn't have a choice.

The Yemeni government had told Aarya just three short days ago that she was being exiled from her native country. She was given seventy-two hours to gather everything she owned, find a completely new place to live, and say goodbye to almost everyone she had ever known. Although she felt betrayed and helpless, she knew that even if she was given another chance, she couldn't have stayed in Yemen knowing that she would never receive the rights she deserved. Being a petite, twenty-one-year-old girl, Aarya stood no chance of changing the stubborn, impractical ways of the Yemini government. No matter how beautiful she was, she was a woman, and in Yemen, that meant she was completely powerless.

Aarya was being forced to leave for speaking out against the government one too many times. She had hoped that the woman's activist group she created with her friends would make a difference, but she realized now that it never stood a chance. They had organized a small protest in favor of women's rights outside of the national Yemini government building just last week and refused to leave for two days. When a group of guards tried to physically remove Aarya and her friends from the property, Aarya refused to budge and created a huge scene, kicking and screaming as they attempted to carry her away. But the guards took her into custody anyway and informed a Yemeni official what had happened within minutes. Without being given a trial or even a chance to tell her side of the story, Aarya was told that since this was not the first time something like this had happened, she was out of chances and had exactly three days to get out of Yemen.

It was now seventy-two hours later. Aarya had finally finished packing everything and knew that she had no other option but to leave. As she began to run down the cement steps of her apartment with all of her bags at exactly midnight, Aarya realized that she had forgotten the one trace she had left of her mother back inside. The golden locket her mother had given her right before she died nineteen years ago was sitting on the kitchen counter of her now former apartment. She knew that the police would be there any second to make sure she was gone, but she couldn't bear leaving the one connection she still had to her mother behind. Aarya turned around to quickly run back inside, and then noticed the red and white lights coming down the rain-covered street. As she stood there, frozen, with her hand on the doorknob to the apartment, the terrifying words that the Yemini official told her just seventy-two hours ago raced through her mind. "If you are not gone by midnight three days from now, you will not just be exiled from Yemen, but from life itself."

Knowing she didn't have any time to mess around, Aarya turned the doorknob to open the front door, trying not to lose grasp with her now sweaty palms. She sprinted inside to the kitchen and discovered that she couldn't see a thing without any lights on, but knew if she turned one on, the police would know she was still in there. She put one hand out in front of her to search the slate countertop for the necklace, while the other one grasped on to her heavy bags, and hoped the locket wouldn't be far from her reach. Time was running out; it seemed as if the police cars were already parked in front of the apartment, and they would be walking up the steps any second.

If she had any chance of safely getting out without them seeing her, she would have to run out the back basement door.

Finally, after searching for what seemed hours, her shaking fingers came into contact with the locket. She grabbed it and quickly zipped it in her jacket pocket. As she split towards the basement door, she heard footsteps and a key turning inside the front doorknob. She opened the basement door slowly, praying that it would not squeak. As she opened it just enough for her thin body to fit through, Aarya heard the front door open and the voices of what sounded like three men. She made her way onto the first step of the basement stairwell and began to close the door behind her, trying to be as quiet as possible. Once it had closed completely, she began tiptoeing down the set of carpeted stairs and let out a sigh of relief. It seemed like she was going to make it out just in time.

Once she reached the bottom of the staircase, she began walking towards the backdoor with her bags in hand and necklace in pocket. She was so relieved to finally be getting out of there. She couldn't wait to meet up with her boyfriend, who was waiting for Aarya in his car down the street, ready to drive them to the train station just ten miles away.

But just as she thought she was safe, Aarya heard the basement door open and the loud footsteps of the three police officers running down the stairs. Shocked and terrified, she knew that her only option was to dash to the door and get out of there as fast as she possibly could. She didn't have the luxury of time to come up with a better plan. As she rushed to the door and they ran down the flight of stairs, she could hear the three men yelling to her.

"We know you're down here!" one of them said. "Freeze right where you are Aarya! You don't wanna cause any more problems for yourself," shouted another.

But Aarya had made up her mind. She wasn't giving into them. She turned the doorknob, threw the door open, slammed it, and ran out into the backyard as fast as she could. As she hopped the fence, she could hear them coming out of the house and running after her. She didn't want to look back, but knew they weren't too far behind. She made her way onto the street and hoped that it wouldn't be long before she stumbled upon her boyfriend's car. As she sprinted down the street in the pouring rain with her bags hanging off of her shoulders, all she could do was pray that the cops wouldn't catch up to her.

Aarya noticed a ray of light coming from the dirt road she was headed towards. She began to get nervous, grasping that it could possibly be a cop car, waiting to take her into custody. As she continued to run, however, she realized that the lights weren't coming from a police car. Instead, they were the headlights of her boyfriend's run down car, which sat on the corner of the dirt road. She rushed to it as fast as possible, hoping that she would make it into the car before the policemen caught up. She could still hear them chanting after her, but wasn't sure how close or far away they were. She threw the passenger door open and tossed her bags in the backseat. Gasping for air and beginning to cry from anxiety, Aarya yelled at her boyfriend to step on the gas and to drive as fast as he could.

"Aarya, calm down! What's going on?!" Khalid asked his frantic girlfriend. His nose crinkled like it did whenever he got nervous. He was wearing a ripped leather jacket and jeans, with his hair was slicked back like it always was. His dark brown eyes glistened as he stared at his beautiful girlfriend, waiting for her to answer.

"The police . . . they're coming after me . . . right there . . . they can't catch me . . . they just can't . . . ." Aarya was able to spit out.

As Khalid began to speed down the road, Aarya went on a rant, trying to explain what had just happened. She could hardly catch her breath as she frantically told him that the police had chased her out of her house and that she didn't know what to do. She finally took a deep breath and turned her head to see if the three policemen were still running after Khalid's car or if they were now chasing them in their own car. She knew she wasn't let off the hook yet.

But, to her surprise, not one policeman seemed to appear in the back window of the car. In fact, no one was anywhere in sight. Only darkness and forest trees surrounded their car and the empty road as they headed toward the train station.

"Wait," Aarya said, confused, "Where did they go?!"

"The policemen? I'm pretty sure you outran them, Aarya," Khalid said as he looked over at his girlfriend with a smile. Her fearlessness made him love her even more.

"That's not possible. They were just behind me. I could still hear them when I got in the car!" Aarya thought this was way too good to be true.

"Aarya, there's no one behind us," Khalid reassured her. "And even if there was, I would protect you."

Khalid and Aarya had been together for over two years. He loved her more than anything in the world, and realized at this moment that there was no one else he would ever want to be with. He was planning on asking her to marry him once they found someplace to live wherever they ended up, and he could hardly wait to spend the rest of his life with her.

"I can't believe that just happened," Aarya said, beginning to feel relieved and accomplished. It had sunk in. She was safe. "I'm being exiled from my country and was just chased by three cops, yet right now, I feel invincible."

They both smiled as Aarya looked at her boyfriend and realized how much he and all of this meant to her. She had dreamed of getting out of Yemen for so long, and now it was finally about to happen.

They turned into the train station parking lot. Khalid parked the car in a spot to be left there since they weren't planning on coming back.

"You know what?" Aarya said, "It doesn't matter where we end up in the morning. Anything's better than the life we've been living in this country. All that matters is that we're out of there and that I'm with you."

"I love you," Khalid responded, as he ran his fingers through her long, brown hair, still wet from the rain, and admired how her olive skin almost sparkled, just like her eyes.

"I love you too," Aarya said, as she leaned over to give her boyfriend a kiss. She began to gather her bags from the backseat and opened the car door. As they walked towards the railroad tracks,

Aarya reached into her pocket with her free hand and grasped her mother's locket.

This is the way it should be, Aarya thought to herself. *And I wouldn't change any of it.* They walked up to the station to await the arrival of the train that would mark the beginning of the rest of their lives.

I'm Not in Texas Anymore

By Kimberly LeDuc

As the engine of the 747 aircraft began to accelerate, I knew take off was about to begin. The cargo area suddenly seemed like the wrong place for me to be. I warily peeped through the holes of my pink crate and looked at my surroundings. Suitcases piled on top of one another shook as the plane struggled to reach its cruising altitude. Cries and barks echoed throughout the dark bowels of the plane. I was relieved to hear that I was not alone on this terrible endeavor. To keep myself from going crazy from the loud roar of the engine and lack of light, I fantasized of where this big bird was taking me. Would it be warm? Will they think I'm cute? Will I even make it there or will I die from fear first? If where I am going is anything like where I am now, I don't want to go! How come I'm the only one of my family that had to leave? Will they be going where I am too? I can't be without them! All of these questions raced through my mind and thankfully distracted me from the turbulence.

I could feel the plane lowering from the air and descending to its destination, which to me was unknown. After a couple of bumps here and there, I heard the wheels release to prepare for landing. Anxiousness and fright filled my body. We hit the pavement and glided until coming to a stop. I had arrived at this unfamiliar place, and it was time to explore.

I patiently awaited my turn to be carried off of this loud machine. I wondered where I would be taken to next. My soft fur began to sweat as my nervousness increased. I heard footsteps stomp closer and closer, and then I was lifted into the air and brought onto a truck. Beside me were other dogs, most of them older than me. The truck came to a short stop, and I anxiously waited to be picked up again. I was carried into a room crowded with humans talking. When they heard the door open, they immediately turned around and stared in awe at me and my fellow travel partners. A teenage girl came running up to my crate and looked inside at me.

"Mom, Dad, she is so tiny!" she screamed.

She unlocked the latch to my crate and reached her arm inside. Gently, she picked up my two pound body and held me close to her face.

"Be careful, Emily," the mom said, "She's just a baby!"

I couldn't help but wag my tail and show signs of happiness and excitement. As she held me up to her face, I stuck my tongue out and began kissing her as a greeting to break the ice. Emily and her parents began to walk out of the room and we went outside. This place did not look like Texas, and I began to get worried. The grass was something I was familiar with, but was missing my siblings and parents. Emily put me down and stood back up.

"Go potty, Riley," she said to me.

"Potty?" I thought to myself, "What's that mean?"

I sat down in the grass and stared up at her. Her parents began to giggle, and she picked me back up. On the walk to the car, I overheard her talking to her mother and father.

"Do you think Bella will like her? She's smaller than we thought!" Emily's mom said.

Who is Bella? Why wouldn't she like me? I began to feel nervous all over again. We got in the car, and I laid down on Emily's lap. I began to feel tired from this trip and fell asleep in her arms.

*   *   *

The bang from Emily's seatbelt hitting the side of the door startled me, and I jumped up, fully awake. We pulled into the driveway of a big yellow house with green shutters and a huge backyard. I looked out the window and realized none of my siblings were outside playing. I felt a sense of sadness as Emily carried me out of the car, but I was anxious to see if they were inside waiting for me. As Emily opened the door to the house, I heard barks. My tail wagged and my body squirmed with excitement.

"They're here!" I thought to myself, "I can't believe they came here too!"

Emily put me down, and I ran to where I heard the bark coming from. I reached the room with couches much like the ones back in Texas, and saw another daschund, but this wasn't my sibling. Instead, I was faced with an overweight, long, barking hot-dog. I had never encountered a problem with another dog, especially one of the same ethnicity as me. I backed up as she continued to bark and inch towards me.

"Bella! That's enough!" Emily's father yelled.

Bella listened to her master and immediately came to a hush. She waddled her way towards me and began to sniff my fur. I ran away and sat on Emily's feet. I only felt safe around her. Bella did not seem too friendly, and I did not want to take any chances.

"Mom, look at her! She is scared! I told you Bella would be mean."

Emily picked me up and cradled me in her arms. My fear of the mean dog disappeared, and I gave Emily a kiss to tell her thank you. We sat down on the floor, and she showed me my toys. I had never seen so many toys, and to think that they were all mine was mindboggling. I wanted to go explore, but I could see Bella sitting on the other side of the rug watching my every move. I had entered her territory, and she was not very happy about it.

Emily kept removing me from her lap and placing me on the rug, but I would immediately hop back in between her legs. For some reason, I did not feel safe without her; almost like how I did not feel safe in Texas without my siblings, even for the slightest moment. It became evident to Emily that I did not want to go anywhere around the house on my own, so she moved us to the couch. I laid on her lap and curled up into a little ball. It was finally nap time.

* * *

"Emily! Dinner's ready!" her mother shouted from the kitchen.

Emily stood up and sat me on the floor. She walked away into the kitchen and expected me to follow. I knew Bella was right around the corner, and I was too scared to walk by her. The only thing I could do was sit right where she left me and cry for her to come back and pick me up. Within seconds, Emily's feet were in front of me, and she bent down to lift me from the soft rug. She lightly kissed my head and brought me to the kitchen table. On the way, we passed by Bella, and when she saw me, she began to bark again. This dog was not very friendly, and I could already tell that she didn't me stealing Emily from her.

"Emily, put her down. She can't sit on your lap at the *kitchen table*. I think she can survive ten minutes without being in your lap," her dad ordered.

Emily placed me on the ground next to her seat, and I saw Bella staring at me again from across the floor. I felt nervous again and needed to be in Emily's arms. My attachment to her grew by the second, and I was not sure why I needed to be in her arms at all times.

While I sat there crying and staring up at her, I thought about my family back in Texas. I wondered if my brothers and sisters missed me, or if they didn't even notice I was gone. I was so used to always having them around to protect me, but now I was in the real world with other dogs that didn't even like me. My dependence on my family left me lost in the world of being on my own, and I realized I needed to toughen up. I stopped crying and walked over to Bella. I sniffed her fur for a change and licked her cheek. I just wanted to become friends, since we would be living with each other, and this was the only way to do it. Surprisingly, Bella reacted well and licked me back.

A sense of relief ran through my long body, and I ran over to my toy basket. Even though Emily was still eating dinner, I was ready to explore more . . . on my own.

Brotherhood

By Laura Vallejo

———⁓⌒⌒⌒⌒⌒⌒⁓———

Maybe if I just plug my ears and close my eyes it will all go away. It never worked the other times, but maybe this time will be different.

There I sat in the only room we had in the house. It was my mom's bedroom. Looking back on it, it was not much of a bedroom at all. It was more a mattress in the middle of a blue carpet. Blue was my favorite color, and the carpet made me feel special as if my mom picked the color just because she knew how much I loved it. It was the only thing that made me think that my mom had ever noticed me, let alone loved me. It was stained with dried up beer and liquor that had been spilled and never cleaned up. There were so many cigarette burns in the carpet you would think it was part of the design.

They were at it again. My mothers' screams were so loud that it hurt my ears and her boyfriend's voice so deep and full of rage it sent a chill down my back. The worst sound came right before my mom's scream when you could hear his hand hit her body.

I felt a teardrop down my face, then another. I tried to hold it in and stop the tears; it only made it worse. I was scared. Helpless. My breath quickening. I was starting to hear myself cry. The breaths got even shorter and with each gasp of air came a sound of weeping from my mouth.

I felt a hand moving along my back side to side. Opening my eyes, I saw my brother sitting next to me. He was only three years older than I was. It was not hard to figure out we are brothers. The light skin, piercing blue eyes complimented by the pale, almost white hair is what we had in common. Besides him always being a little chunkier than I am, you would think we were twins. We used to get stopped by the most random people to have them ask if we were. It brought me such a sense of pride that people thought I resembled him, since he was the one person I looked up to the most.

Through the tears fogging my vision, I could see him sitting there. I took my hands off my ears and started wiping my tears. The sound of the commotion going on in the next room intensified only to make me start to cry harder.

"Billy," my brother Joey said, "It's alright, you just need to breathe, okay?"

I squeezed my eyes shut as tight as I could and nodded my head "yes" in between my breaths.

"Billy look at me," he continued, "Just take a really deep breath in like this." He sucked in as much air as his lungs could hold and held it, but did not exhale. "And count to three Mississippi." Then he exhaled.

It was my turn. I took a deep breath, filling my lungs to what I thought was the maximum capacity. One Mississippi, two Mississippi, three Mississippi. I exhaled. For those three seconds, nothing else was happening in my world. Everything stopped, and those seconds felt like their sole purpose was to piece me back together.

"Whenever you get upset like that, just do this. It will work every time, I promise. I would never steer you wrong. I love you," he said while embracing me with a hug.

"I love you too Joey," I replied.

That was one of the best lessons I have ever gotten out of life. My mom ended up getting arrested for drug possession. I was bounced around a lot of foster homes, but the advice my brother gave me that day got me through some of the hardest times of my life. He was my best friend, and when he was gone it was like a whole piece of me had gone missing. We had been put in the same foster homes for a while, but he started heading down the wrong path by age twelve. By fifteen he was so far off on the wrong path, leading the life we both vowed we never wanted. He was locked up for a while when he was sixteen, and I haven't seen him since. I remember that day they said Joey would not be returning home, and it was that day that I promised I would make something of myself.

I did just that. I somehow made my way through college, and I recently graduated. I wanted nothing more than to have my mom and big brother see me in that cap and gown. I wanted to make them proud. God only knows where they were though, and I decided not to bother wasting the time or money walking down and getting my diploma. I would be the only kid without anyone there.

I was starting my career at a marketing company. The hours were long and unusual. I was being way underpaid for the amount of work I was doing, but it was what I had to do. Start at the bottom and eventually make my way to the top. It paid the bills, but I decided to take a bus boy job a couple days a week to get some extra money. I took that job to save up. Truth is, the biggest dream I have is to have a house one day. Joey and I talked about that a lot when we were younger. I wanted somewhere I can call my home, something that I never had. I want it to be decent size, yet cozy and blue. Anyways, all the money, every single cent I made as a bus boy, I put in a box in my closet. It was safe there; hidden in a shoebox among thousands of other clothing items and shoes in my closet.

I had just arrived home from a long day spent at the marketing company. I stopped home for a second to get my bus boy uniform and grab a quick bite to eat. When I took off my jacket, I heard something hit the floor. I looked down to see my phone lying there. I picked it up and flipped it open. I had a missed call and a voicemail. Looking at the number, I had no idea who it could be so I decided to listen to the voicemail.

The voicemail started with a clearing out of the throat.

"Uhh . . . hey, Billy," the strange, yet all too familiar voice said.

That is all I had to hear for my heart sink to the top of my stomach. Not even noticing it, in that same split second, my body, guided by the wall, sank along with my heart. By the time my bottom hit the floor, I realized I had missed the rest of the voicemail.

I took a second to regroup a thousand thoughts running through my head. Billy. I repeated the name in my head. That was the first time in years I had been called that. Only one person ever called me that.

Now anxiety was setting in. That knot you get in your stomach, the sudden nauseating feeling when you cannot figure it out, but you know that something is not right. There was that feeling swelling up in me. Overwhelming me, I could feel it slowly making its way through my body.

"Just take really deep breathes like this," I said in my head as I flashed back to when I was six years old again. I inhaled as hard as I could. One Mississippi, two Mississippi, three Mississippi. Exhale.

Twenty years later, and it still works. Did I really want to listen to the rest of the voicemail? I could just hit delete, forget about it, and go on with life as if nothing had ever happened. Nevertheless, how could I just ignore this feeling? How could I live with the "what ifs?"

I redialed my voicemail slowly and entered my password. Taking a deep breath in, I pressed pound.

"Uh . . . hey, Billy. It's me," the voice started.

I knew exactly who "me" was. Only one person ever called me Billy. If that didn't give it away, the Bronx accent sure did.

"I heard your living in Rochester now, and I'm in town. So yeah give me a ring back will ya?"

I wrote down the number he gave me. I punched it in my phone and stared at the screen for a good three minutes before pressing send. Each ring seemed to be ten times longer than usual.

Please don't pick up. Please, please don't pick up, I thought in my head as my heartbeat quickened.

The ringing ceased. My heart dropped again.

"Hello, Joe speaking."

"Joe? It's Bill"

"Billy! God it sounds so good to hear your voice again kid."

I went numb. There was a lump in my throat.

"Billy?"

"Yeah, yeah, I'm here. It's good to hear you too, Joey."

"Listen I have to go, but can we meet up?"

"Yeah, I work until eleven tonight, but let's meet at the diner in Broad River at 11:30"

"Great, see ya then."

The line went dead before I could even say goodbye.

After a seemingly endless shift, I made my way to the diner. I parked and sat there debating whether I should go in or not. My fingertips tapped on the leather steering wheel, and my knee shook up and down nervously. I looked in the rear view mirror and pushed my hair to the side trying to tidy it up. I stepped out of the car, pulled my pants up, straightened my collar on my busboy short, and made my best attempt to brush off lint that was on my clothes. I took my time walking into the diner. I kept my head down staring at the ground blankly. All I wanted to do was turn around, but for some reason my body kept moving toward the diner door. I looked up, and through one of the windows, I saw him staring back. We made that quick awkward eye contact before I put my eyes back at the ground. There's no turning back now, I thought.

I walked through the doors and turned toward the booth he was seated in. There was my big brother who always had my back, the one who always had the best advice, the one that had been missing for the majority of my life. The only difference was we no longer looked alike. He was no longer the chunkier one; now he was thin, sickly thin. In fact, everything about him looked sickly. His hair was now turning a light gray. He still had those piercing blue eyes, except they were diluted and bloodshot with heavy gray bags under them. His skin was still pale, only now it was tinted with a sickly gray color.

We greeted each other with a hug before I sat down. I learned that he ended up getting out of jail at 18 only to be put back in and out a few more times. We reminisced on the bad times, the good times, and the embarrassing times. We laughed at the funny memories we had. I couldn't remember the last time I had laughed so hard. Joey always had the ability to make me laugh until my insides hurt. At one point in the conversation, I could remember not even listening to him anymore and thinking how great it was to be with him again. It brought me a sense of warmth and comfort, as if someone had put that missing piece back in me. He said he was doing well now, but trying to find somewhere to live so he could finish getting his life back on track. Right away, I offered for him to stay with me. It was somewhat a selfish decision; on one hand I couldn't let him leave my life again. On the other, he was my brother, and it would be nice to have someone to come home to at night instead of just a lonely, cheaply decorated apartment.

He moved in and things worked out great. It was nice to have someone around, but it was even better that it was my big brother. I told him all about how I was saving up for that dream house we always talked about.

"When I find a job, Billy, all my extra money is going right there with yours," he told me.

I was not home much because of all my work, but the time we did have together was well spent. I noticed that Joe was a little different than I remember; a lot more private. Sometimes, I would come home, and he would be on the phone. As soon as he saw me, he would tell whoever was on the other line that he had to go. Other times, he would say he had to go out for a couple minutes, but never say where he was going and would end up getting back so late I was already in bed. This did not bother me all that much though.

I had just arrived home from one of my bus boy shifts.

"Hello? Joe you home?" I said walking through the door.

When I got no response, I figured he had just run out for a little while and decided to take a shower. I had just gotten paid today. Plus, tonight was busy, and I made off with some tips too. I went to go put in my shoebox, but I could not find it. I looked around a little more, and when I still could not find it, I started to panic. I tore my closet apart throwing every shoe, opening every shoe box, taking all my clothes, ripping them from the hangers, and throwing them outside the closet. It was when I stood there with my closet completely empty that I realized Joey did not run out for a little while.

There was that feeling swelling up inside me again. I felt a tear drop down my face, then another. My lungs felt like a balloon deflating, until there was finally no more air left in them. Gasping for air, I closed my eyes. Inhale. One Mississippi, two Mississippi, three Mississippi. Exhale.

Second Chances

By Nora Blake

—⁓⁓◦◦⊙◦◦⁓⁓—

Ahhhmaaaazzziinngg Grraacce! How sweet the sound? That saved a wretch like me! I once was lost, but now . . . .

Sam groaned at the sound of absolute garbage coming out of his car radio, grabbed the volume knob, and turned the music down until it was muted. He laid against the cool leather cover on his car seat and took a deep breath. Despite the air conditioning being on high, beads of sweat still managed to slide down his forehead. He felt the faded scar there too, the one his confused and drunken father gave him back when he was about seven. It was only 8:37 in the morning, but the temperature was at least 80 degrees. *Why am I even bothering to do this?* he thought to himself as he watched the time on the car clock slip away. Many thoughts were going through his mind. *Should I go through with it? Maybe give myself one more chance? But who would really notice if I died?* Sam reached over to the glove compartment and took out a brand new, loaded .22 caliber pistol. He toggled with the barrel in one hand and the trigger in the other. Debating on whether to pull the trigger now and end it or not, he finally threw the gun in his passenger seat and put the car in drive. *Guess I'll give myself just one more chance.*

The sun glowed as it rose over the horizon. Sam drove slowly down the narrow trail leading to the Green Willow Gospel Church. Patches of beaming sunlight hit the car windows, nearly blinding him. Despite his annoyance, he noticed something different. He opened up the driver's side window and gazed at the scenery as he drove by. The trees seemed more green than usual, the dirt path was homely, and the blooming flowers on the side of the road gave off a light but pure scent. Although he never really valued nature, he found himself in disbelief of everything outside, from the now light blue sky to the faint humming of cicadas in the distance. Usually just the sight of the area alone kept Sam on edge. *This is how I want to remember my hometown,* he whispered under his breath. By just viewing the natural beauty around him, Sam began to feel less uncomfortable with his surroundings and also remembered a time in his childhood where this old path made him glad. With that, he continued to inch his way towards the entrance of the church.

One specific memory stood out in Sam's mind that morning that entailed a past fishing trip he had with his father in the same area he just drove through. After fishing all morning, Sam's father sat on a log and pulled out a bottle of liquor. Sam, the seven year old clean-cut altar boy, sat down next to him. He began to sing Bible tunes, and stared in awe at all of the pretty birds flying in the sky and the compilation of multi-colored leaves that covered the bottom of the woods and adjacent pond.

But before Sam could even get through the second verse of *Amazing Grace*, a favorite song, his father grabbed him by the collar of his shirt and barked, "Boy, now I don't wanna hear you singing bout Jesus and all that crap, ya hear? He don't love you, never will. Your momma's lyin to you! He aint listenin, and singing one of His old songs isn't gonna do anything!"

Sam attempted to take away the now almost empty bottle of liquor. But before he could dispose of the poison making his father cruel, he felt a large hand reach out and scratch his forehead. Bleeding and in pain, Sam shouted loudly and whimpered until his father signaled for them to trek back to town. He remembered fighting back tears of anger as the drunken father and upset son made their way back to town, where they went their separate ways. Sam went home to his mother, while his father drove off into the distance, only to come back a few weeks later for some more "quality time" with his son. The only lasting remembrance that came out of that fishing trip was a physical scar and an even deeper emotional mark created by alcohol and a broken relationship.

The sunlight beamed directly into his eyes as the car neared the sign that read "Green Willow Gospel Church, Parking to the Left." Sam turned into the vacant lot and eyed a bottle of hard liquor in his back seat.

Green Willow was a *Christian community known for its outstanding faith and punctuality—Church is first!* That's what really turned Sam off to the idea of church. He did not like being forced to do things, particularly being dragged to church *every* Sunday by his mother, especially right after a hard night of drinking. Even as he sat in the surprisingly empty parking area, he slurped a half-empty bottle of Jack Daniels. The car clock's time was 8:57. Puzzled, but willing, he got up from his car, breathed in the fresh air, and exhaled the crude stench of alcohol. As Sam walked towards Green Willow, the sound of silence completely overwhelmed him, and he was very anxious as to what might happen next.

"Hey, anyone here?" he bellowed in his low Southern drawl. The inside of the church seemed so much bigger compared to the humble outside. Wooden pews were piled high with prayer books but completely empty in regards to people. Each wall decorated with large, expressive stained glass windows and the white tile floors only brought Sam back to his childhood, when his life appeared easier. What really caught his eye was the altar. The gleaming chalice almost blinded Sam and the snow-white tablecloth was soft and appropriate.

Sam came to go to one last mass, to prove to himself that he could do it before taking his life. And naturally, not one parishioner came in sight. He hunched over in a pew and looked down at his reflection on the floor. *What has my life become of? Am I really this screwed up? What am I even doing here?* The church clock read 9:04. As he stood up to go, a weak voice came from the entrance.

"Howdy! How are you doing today?"

Sam turned his head completely around to look at an old woman with a worn, wrinkly face and a wide, toothy grin. She began to shuffle her feet until she reached the empty space in the pew Sam was sitting in.

"Hey," Sam sighed. The woman came closer and closer and took a seat next to him. She opened a prayer book and began reciting verses.

"Love is patient. Love is kind. It does not envy, it does not boast . . ."

"Why are you reading those verses? No one's even here for church," Sam interrupted.

"Well," the woman replied, "Even though church is cancelled today on a count of the priest being away, I still need to have my place with the Lord, whether it be through real church or just some quality time with em'".

Those words hit Sam like a ton of bricks.

"Why'd you come all the way here to just sit and read from the Bible? Can't you do that at home?"

The woman simply said, "It's one thing to just read out of the Bible and call it a Sunday mass. But, if you wanna really get something out of your time with the Lord, you gotta work at it, even take a 20 minute car ride just to be in His house."

Sam looked down at the floor again and then gazed at the dazzling altar. The chalice holding the Eucharist definitely got brighter since the last time he looked at it.

"You see," he mumbled, "my relationship with the big man upstairs hasn't really been all that good since my Momma died and Dad left. I guess He reminded me too much of them. As a matter of fact, my favorite memories of being a kid started in this room and at the path and creek up the road. Man, all those good times."

The kind, old woman just gave him a quick smile and looked at the chalice with him. They both could not get over how shiny it was over the thousand other times they both looked at it.

Sam opened his mouth to speak, but could not get words out. Before he could even mutter a thought, the woman said:

"Are you Sam Roberts? That one kid who everyone knew was going to be someone, definitely a huge step above his hard drinking daddy?"

"Yeah, that's me alright. And look at me now. I'm a lowlife with nobody anymore. The only thing that keeps me going is where my next drink is gonna be. At this point I must be the Devil himself compared to my old daddy! I went from head altar boy to a full-blown alkie loser with nothing to live for!"

Sam put his fingers against his temples and took another deep breath. Although he was not sweating anymore, the same questions filled his head. *Would anybody notice or even care if I were to go? Do I matter to anyone?* He looked down at the floor and found the woman viewing herself in the reflective tile floor as well.

"I bet you already know that nobody's perfect, and everyone makes mistakes. But even though I only know your name, I know you're more than your last bottle of booze. I think that chalice is so shiny today because the Lord is looking down on you right now and trying to give you signs to tell you what an amazing man you are, just by being yourself. Heck, even I know that you're better than your daddy, uncle, and grandpa just because you made it to church today!"

She grabbed his shoulder and gave it a good squeeze. The church clock read 9:27.

"I gotta get out of here," she said hurriedly. "The Senior Bingo Tournament starts in a half hour, and I don't wanna miss it! I'll see you around Sam, maybe in church next Sunday?"

She used his knee to prop herself up and rubbed her silky smooth hands across his face.

"God bless you, Sam, and remember, you always have love in the Lord."

As she scuffed towards the exit, Sam dropped to his knees and began to pray, for at least an hour after the woman left . . . The more he talked with God, the more of a burden seemed to be lifted off of his shoulders. All he could hear as he kneeled with complete reverence was, *You always have love in the Lord. You always have love in the Lord. You always have love in the Lord. You always have love in the Lord . . . .*

He finally stood up and looked around the church in complete shock. Just like the old path leading up to Green Willow, Sam never realized the simple beauty of a place where he could find pure happiness.

Sam really did not know why he felt the sudden urge to go to Green Willow that day. Why that nice woman just happened to be there, or maybe even if she was right about the chalice. For now, he simply looked up at the ceiling, stared at the stained glass dove right above the altar and whispered:

"Thank You."

The day just began, and Sam burst out of Green Willow Gospel Church, beaming with pride. He almost forgot that his car was still parked in the lot.

He looked at the car, the interior, the leather seats, and the empty bottle of Jack Daniels and loaded .22 pistol. Shrugging, he hopped into the driver's side and began humming an old Sunday school song. He drove his car to the same pond and woods he loved as a young boy and crouched down to watch the water flow. He took out the gun and let it submerge to the murky bottom. Along with the gun, he threw his last empty bottle of Jack Daniels somewhere into the woods. *Man, am I lucky for my second chance today,* Sam said to himself. He looked up at the blue sky, listened to the water trickle, and found that the same accents that made these woods so important to Sam still lingered. The trees shook with vigor and brought him closer to his repressed memories.

Sam's forehead scar became all but a small mark on his head, and as if talking to no one, Sam shouted, "I told you Daddy! God is always listening! You just gotta believe that he's there! Just believe!"

And with everything in him, Sam began to not only proclaim Prayer hymns, but also read his favorite verse.

Search me, O God, and know my heart: try me, and know my thoughts, and see if there be any wicked way in me, and lead me in the way everlasting.

Untitled

By Devin Long

———∿⌇⌇∿———

The gravel crunched under the tires of an old pickup truck on the narrow drive. The absence of streetlights only made visibility a greater challenge in the heavy downpour. As though conditions could not be any more trivial, leaves coated the ground and were sure to stick to the worn rubber Chevy's wheels. Rawnie was hardly ever careless this way, but she had ignored the beckon of her destination for far too long now. For the past ten months, she had been returning there every night in her dreams.

Dawn loomed near by the time she reached the clearing in the trees she had been searching for. Rawnie pulled over and turned on her flashers, though it was apparent that the odds of another person traveling down the lane were slim. She sat watching the raindrops trickle down her window, catching other droplets along the way. She listened to the sounds of the drumming above her head, her favorite lullaby, half wishing she could lay back and close her eyes.

You don't have to be here, she told herself. But once she let that thought surface, she knew it was a lie. She knew that if she turned back now, her sacrifices would have been worthless and she would be overwhelmed with regret.

Rawnie cursed herself for not packing an umbrella. She scanned the trees for a place to take cover, but realized the trees were nearly bare by this point in the season. She would have to just suck it up. After all, she had never been the kind of girl to worry about her hair getting messed up by unfavorable weather conditions.

When she finally stepped out of the truck, the rain hit her harder than she had expected. It soaked through her clothes before she made it across the street. The woods were dark, as the sun had barely broken the horizon. Aside from the rain, it was unnaturally quiet, creating the sense that the rest of the world was gone. Rawnie's thoughts were sharper than when she was lost in the bustling of everyone else around her. The more steps she took in the soggy earth, the clearer her memories shone. The elated mood Rawnie associated with this walk was tainted by the weather. She remembered the time when she would walk here every Sunday with her best friend, her small hand wrapped around his finger. They never talked much, but they never needed to. His gentle demeanor paired well with her innocence, as if he was born to be a father. She was always eager to get to the end of the path, but he had taught her to enjoy the walk. His favorite season was autumn, he told her once, because he loved the way the leaves painted the scene just before they left the trees bare.

Rawnie was so deep in thought that the bridge was before her in what seemed like a few mere minutes. It was more weathered than she remembered it and some sort of plant had weaved into the bars that supported the railing. In the eerie light from the rainy dawn, the creek below played with her eyes, appearing much deeper than she knew it to be.

Rawnie picked up a pinecone and walked out onto the bridge. She dropped it in the water to watch it come out the other side. She and her father used to play this game, seeing whose stick or acorn or other scrap from the woods made it out first. The pinecones had always been her favorite choice. But this time it sunk. Rawnie could hear the echo of her father's laugh. It had a genuine ring, even when he laughed at triggers of Rawnie's frustration, like a sinking pinecone. Being at The Secret Place made her feel his presence for the first time in ages. But she knew that was impossible.

Why did he want me to come here? This is pointless. In a wave, she remembered all the reasons they had drifted apart as she grew older. It wasn't that she didn't love him—he was always the person she liked most—but she grew tired of his unlikely promises and of disappointment. But she had always believed in remembering people well, kicking herself for allowing her negative emotions to seep through.

Just when Rawnie was about to turn back to go to the old truck, something on a plank under the bridge caught her eye. The white silver glistened in the rain. Its delicate chain hung it from the plank, twisting the hanging trinket the way Rawnie used to spin when she twisted the ropes of her backyard swing.

It was her mother's locket that her father promised to pass down once he was ready to let go. The Celtic designs were ancient and took Rawnie's breath away every time she sneaked a peek at it in her childhood. Her father must have stowed it here before he fled. Rawnie thought the Nazis had taken it when they searched their home.

Hardly conceiving that the locket was before her, Rawnie would not have been surprised if its image slipped through her fingers when she tried to retrieve it. But when she knelt down and reached for it, she could feel the cold metal between her fingers. Rawnie could have sworn there was a sort of charge of energy radiating from it that made her feel safe and whole at last.

A Wall of Branches and Dying Leaves

By Victoria Price

The dry, February air made her winter coat feel paper thin as the occasional gusts of wind drove straight through it, creating pins and needles down her spine and neck. Yet, she still found herself in the empty park, leaning against the old tree she used to climb when she was younger, waiting for him to arrive. In earlier years, a battered wooden bench was completely visible below the tree, but as the time flew by, the growing trunk began to hunch, as though from old age and the branches began to extend downward like arms, engulfing the seat. For years, the nature-made hiding place had been her secret, but on that afternoon, she would share it with the boy she loved.

Through the wall of branches and the collection of dying leaves that never quite made it to the ground, she saw him approaching from the distance. Her vision was obstructed, but there was no mistaking the way he walked with his hands in pockets, eyes lowered, and the way his old North Face jacket hung loosely on his thin body. He was an image of perfection, from the black hair that gently brushed across his forehead, ending just above his eyebrows, to his icy blue eyes that gave her chills she couldn't experience on even the coldest of days, including that day in the park. She found herself getting lost in his every detail, but her trance was broken when she realized he had walked right past her and the tree.

She emerged from her hiding place and called out to him. The arctic air caught in her throat and she felt her chest begin to tighten as she struggled to breathe, yet his name still slipped from her lips, just loud enough for him to hear.

"Ben."

The sound of his name, whispered in the background, made him jump, but he smiled when he realized who it was. It had been two years since they had last seen each other, but she was just as beautiful as ever. The wind blew through her hair in the way it had when they were teenagers, creating swirls of black and brown about her pale face, accenting her hazel eyes and ever-rosy cheeks. In that moment, he stood silently, admiring what she had become.

Before he could comment on her sneaky entrance, she motioned for him to follow her into the trees. Although confused, he obliged and was pleasantly surprised when they arrived at the hidden bench. How could he have missed it earlier? The hole seemed too small for more than one person to sit comfortably, but he entered anyway, the close corners providing a sense of security between the two.

"What is this?" he finally let out, breaking the stillness.

More silence followed and, after what seemed like an eternity, her gentle whisper filled the quiet space.

"Our secret."

His entire body went numb with guilt at her the sound of her words and he began to feel that familiar burning sensation creep up behind his eyelids.

She hadn't heard his voice in so long. Its smooth, honey-sweet tone sent a warming sensation through her cold limbs, but when she tried to speak, the frigid air again trapped her words in her chest. She was barely able to choke out her short response, but it seemed to suffice as he smiled at her once more.

"Well how have you been?" he whispered as he leaned forward for a hug.

He had thin arms and a lanky body, but his embrace was warmer and stronger than seemed possible. It was something she had missed. She tried to cherish the moment for as long as she could, but it ended almost as quickly as it began. His touch managed to somehow soothe her vocal chords and she was able to speak.

"Uh I've been okay, I guess . . ." She murmured in a barely audible tone. "Work is work. I have an apartment downtown. It's small, but I mean, I like it, I guess . . . But how have you been? It's been a while . . ."

All he wanted to do was sit and stare at her, admiring her old conversational habits, like the way her eyes always seemed to make their way up to his and the way she always diverted them just before their connection could set off a spark. He lost himself in the way her leg was always lightly pressed against his when they spoke and the way she always crossed and tucked her ankles neatly beneath the seat. The way she constantly spun her silver ring around her finger was enough to drive him crazy. He could sit for hours listening to the melodic rises and falls of her gentle voice, admiring every detail of her existence. She was beautiful and, for the moment, she was his.

But he knew it wasn't right. He couldn't quiet the voice in his head that told him to just tell her what he had done. It was an honest mistake and he planned to fix it, but he didn't know how to start. Again, his eyes began to burn and his knees felt weak to the point that he knew he would have collapsed on the spot had there not been the bench underneath him.

Hours could have passed and she wouldn't have noticed. They spoke about everything the other had missed. She told him about her new home and the puppy she had rescued from the pound. He told her about his new sports marketing job with ESPN and showed her pictures from his UPenn graduation. Time blew by like the wind in her hair as they swam through oceans of deep conversation. She nearly forgot where she was, lost in his tales, but was brought back to reality by the sudden shriek of a cell phone's ring. He politely excused himself from their conversation, and she didn't mind, still lost in the smooth sound of his voice, until something he said caught her attention.

"Okay . . . I love you too . . . I'll be home soon . . . Gimme 10 minutes . . ."

The warmth drained from her body and she could feel her face turning white, not sure whether she would be able to speak. Again, she could feel the winter in her throat.

"Who was that?" she managed.

"My girlfriend. Sophia. I'm sorry. This has been great, but she needs me at home. I'll call you sometime this week and we can get, like, a coffee or something. I'm really sorry."

He hadn't even needed to look at the phone's battered screen to know who it was. Her beautiful pink face turned to a ghostly white. She seemed to have frozen in her seat, like the most perfect statue ever constructed. He couldn't wait there to see what he had done to her. He needed to leave. The bench, the branches, and the girl of his dreams were spinning in circles around him as he stumbled out of the hiding place. He could feel his stomach in his throat and the air escaping from his lungs as he struggled to keep his composure just long enough to make his way away from the tree. Once he felt safe, the tears began to flow like lava against his cold skin. He knew he couldn't call. He knew there would be no coffee. He knew he had ruined everything.

And with that, he was gone and she was again alone under the tree. She felt dazed, lifeless, as though she had just run a marathon and tripped and fell before reaching the finish. Every word of his goodbye sent needles through her skin, burning holes through her heart. Her body went numb and it was only when she felt the warm, wet drops fall from her face onto her exposed wrist that she realized she had begun to cry.

Match Made in Heaven

By Ricky Bretherton

I found myself on the footsteps of heaven. The golden gates stood before me, gleaming with an overwhelming awe. I thought its awe would blind me, the power of our great creator's realm ahead of me. I proceeded to take my first steps up the long stairs leading to the enormous archway. Once at the top, I stood there, awaiting entry into the great house of God Himself. Peering to the left—back to the right—nothing was in sight except for me, the stairs, and the gate extending far into the distance, farther than the eye could see. I continued to stand at the top of the magnificent stairs waiting for anyone, anything, to let me in. For nearly an hour I stood there, motionless. *It must be a test*, I thought to myself. Eventually, I grew tired and decided to leave. *It must not be my time, yet I was sent here for a reason.* This statement puzzled me, and before I could turn to leave, a great voice bellowed down from the sky above me.

"Who are you?" The voice resounded through my body and all around me. It was such a prominent and strong voice, I knew the owner must be God Himself.

"My name is Michael," I said with confidence. The initial question baffled me. *Wasn't He the one who brought me here in the first place?*

"You obviously do not understand the question. Who are you?"

His voice brought chills up my spine. I had no clue what He was talking about. I quickly searched my mind for an alternative answer.

"I am Michael, son of Raphael." I'd seen it in all those movies; it has to work this time.

Once again, He asked the same question. "Who are you?"

Infuriated with the question because there seemed to be no right answer, I shouted back, "I don't know!"

There was silence. Not a sound could be heard, but the beat of my heart reverberating through my chest.

"This is why I have sent for you here into my great domain. You once had the purest of hearts, but time has changed you, my son. You should know why you are here."

The moment these words left his mouth, I immediately began to remember the events leading up to my encounter with God.

There I was: the most successful individual the world had ever seen. I created a life of fame and fortune at an early age. Being the brightest one of my class and alumni of an Ivy League school, I was on top of the world. I was only 20 and had all the materialistic things I could ever dream of, yet I missed out on most important part of life: family. I lost all connection with my family and woke up one day to find both my grandparents had passed away. All the joys of life vanished before my eyes, and I didn't know how to react. I continued to work harder and harder, trying to escape reality, pain, and demise, yet my life inevitably came to a snapping halt. Driving my car eighty mph in a twenty-five, I crashed. My vision was blurred, and when I finally recovered some consciousness, I was being rushed to the emergency room. Lying on the Operating Room table, I just knew it was my end. Life had caught up to me all too quickly.

A tear rolled down my face when I regained consciousness and I quickly wiped it away. I could not show weakness in from of the creator of the world. I began to feel faint. Dropping to my knees, I began to weep. I could not stop it even if I wanted to. It was the first time I cried since learning of the death of my grandparents. I didn't care about my car, house, or anything. I just wanted my family.

"Am I dead?"

"My dear son, arise and wipe the tears from your face. You are not dead."

Regaining my composure and strength, I rose to my feet to find the entrances to heaven open. Within the golden gates was pure white. I assumed it was a portal to heaven.

"I have saved your life, yet you can't tell me why your life is worth saving. Thus I have created a great challenge for you. You shall play me in a great match of golf for the ultimate gift: your life. If you win, your life will be spared."

"This is not a game, this is my life we're talking about!" The white sky above turned gray. Lightning shot out of the sky, hitting the ground in the distance. Thunder crackled and a downpour started. God did not respond. I was left alone.

"So be it," I said, walking through the portal. I disappeared into the abyss, accepting the great challenge bestowed upon me.

I appeared on a golf course, lightning still lit up the sky as the downpour increased with ferociously. I was dressed in my golf attire head to toe. My lucky Cobra cap, in which I once scored a hole in one, sat upon my head. I also wore my favorite shirt and pants. The shirt, made of sweat repellent material, was a sapphire blue with white and black lines running horizontally. My shorts also fit snugly on my slender body. But what impressed me most was the new golf shoes God must have given me for good luck. They were so comfortable; it was as if I was standing on two clouds. I had to get a pair if I was to ever to step on Earth again. I looked at the company name, and to my surprise they read: *GodofGolf & Co.*

Should have seen that coming, I thought to myself. Little did I know that I was standing on my home golf course I used to play on for my high school team. *Ahhh, Shorehaven . . . my favorite course.* It was just how I left it five years ago. The smell of clean cut grass filled my nostrils as I trotted toward the club house. As I got nearer, a familiar face smiled at me from to porch.

"Hey Buddy! How ya been?"

"Carmine! You haven't changed one bit!" I was happy to see him again. He wore his usual collared shirt and khakis and held a hotdog in his left hand. He was always known to have an enormous appetite, as well as an upbeat personality.

"So how's the course playing?" I said, trying to strike up a conversation.

"It's playin' a little slow today, 'cause of the rain. Business is kinda slow too, I have to say myself." I looked around us. A once crowded golf course had no one in sight. Carmine interrupted my train of thought, saying, "Ah, you have a tee time reservation I see. Head up to the tee; He's waiting for you."

With that, Carmine pushed me along the path, grabbing my golf clubs and a scorecard.

"Good Luck!"

I looked back to see him waving and stuffing his face with the hotdog. *I guess God's the walking type; otherwise my clubs would have been on a cart.* The path leading to the first tee was quite the hike, so I had time to collect my thoughts. *Game time, Mike! No messing around, your life's on the line!* The more I thought, the more I started to become nervous. *How am I supposed to beat the Almighty One Himself? He'll probably get hole-in-ones every time! I'm only a regular guy, nothing more!* I became depressed with the thought that I would never be able to save my life, so I distracted myself by looking at the scenery as I walked along the winding path. The wind had picked up substantially and leaves began to whip by my face. Being near the ocean, Shorehaven is known to have powerful winds and violent weather, but a calm gentle breeze on a fair day. The rain pelted my face with every step as the trees shook fiercely, bending in the path of the strong wind. Yet I headed down the path, still with my doubts of ever winning this insurmountable challenge.

After several minutes, I reached the final summit to climb before reaching the tee. My mind raced as I climbed the hill. My palms turned sweaty, my heart was pulsating throughout my entire body. With each step, I neared my fate. *This is the end,* I thought. But it was just the beginning . . .

He stood on the tee, awaiting my arrival. The flash of brightness around him caused me to shield my eyes, but no more than a second. I looked on to see Him facing the sea, hands raised towards the heavens. His robe was thrown loosely upon His body, having perfect detail. The creases of the robe seemed to be delicately painted on a man no other than God. He threw His left hand down violently, then his right. As He did this, lighting shot out of the sky with His every command. He then proceeded to bring his hands up as if carrying profound weight. Waves began to rise in the distance, none like I had ever seen before. Rising hundreds of feet in the air, He continued to raise them higher and higher. With a quick, fluent motion, He threw his hands down, sending the waves crashing down before us. I was sure the waves would reach us any moment, quickly climbing the steep slope of the golf course from the sea. All of a sudden, the water approached Him, and I was sure it would overpower Him, for no one could stand that much force. I couldn't bare to watch because after Him, I would be next! Before I could turn to run, His hands once again shot up, fists clenched. The water engulfed God, surrounding every possible escape. He threw his hands open and the sea turned into a mist of rain passing over Him, leaving no trace of the destructive force that was there moments ago. He turned to me, His eyes piercing my soul, and without a word my feet began to walk towards Him. I had no control over it. In the distance I could hear him whisper, "Come here, my son." Soon enough, I stood face to face with God himself.

His eyes once again pierced through my stare, into my every thought and emotion. By His mere appearance, you could tell He was no mere human. For one, His eyes shone with an untainted color like none other. They could illuminate darkness itself, unlock truth in lies, and every other mystery untold. His face had many characteristics of any man, a full beard, long hair, and a distinctive scar on his right cheek bone. I peered at the rest of His body, and yet again it was a humanly as any other body.

"Michael, you have accepted your challenge. Prepare for the almighty power of all the heavens."

I thought we were friends! It occurred to me I would receive no slack from God. "It's your turn." That was my cue. I prepared for battle.

I took the weight off my shoulders, laid the golf bag on the ground, and selected a driver and other tools I would need. I approached the tee-box, dug the tee into the ground, and set my ball upon it. I searched the horizon for a safe place in which to drive my ball. The rain clouded my vision, but I could see far enough to find a safe haven for my ball. I took a deep breath, closed my eyes, and prepared myself. Looking back down, I wound up in my stance, and swung my hips forward in sync with my arms, driving the golf ball straight and true. With a clash, it disappeared into the clouds. *Guess I still got it.* Golf had always been my favorite sport and I was privileged enough to have played it many times over the course of my life. I now stood proud and tall after proving that I could, in fact, have a chance of beating God at His own challenge. I stepped off the tee and motioned toward God.

"The tee is yours."

Without a word, He set His ball down on top of His tee. He pulled out a golden driver and with a flawless swing, sent the ball flying toward the flag. My jaw dropped as He smirked, walking off the tee.

"I guess I've still got it." He walked off the tee and headed down the path, disappearing into the distance.

I was still amazed by His perfect form. *I can't believe Him! There's got to be an easier way to win my life back!* Still aggravated, I headed down the path after God.

He stood by my ball, motioning for me to come toward Him. The course was soaked with excess water. As I stepped onto the moist terrain, the muddy water narrated my every step with *squish-squash* until I finally reached my ball. God stood back, letting me have a look. My ball was submerged in a pool of water. I recalled back to my handy-dandy official rules book. *If my ball is in water or if my feet are in water, I can move my ball! Finally, some good luck!*

"You might want to move that." God motioned for me to place my ball somewhere dry, if I could find anything dry.

"That's just what I was about to do." I proceeded to pick up the ball and searched for a clear area. Finding a decently dry area, I placed the ball down. I took out an iron, turned my body toward the target, and unloaded a crushing shot, headed straight as an arrow toward the pin. Yet again, I proved myself worthy to fight on.

"Your turn," I said.

God turned and began to search the landscape for his ball. Forty yards ahead lay His ball. We approached it together. As we got closer, I could not believe my eyes. *Completely dry! But how? It's still raining?!?* But there it was, a dry patch of grass just large enough for God to step on to hit the ball. He approached the ball, sung and stroked the ball with great force, taking a divot with it. We then walked to the green, planning our next and every shot.

We walked together in complete silence, yet I felt like we spoke the whole time. We never met before, yet I felt His presence in me my entire life. The fairway soon turned to a clean cut green in which both our balls lay no more than 3 feet of each other. It was my putt. I took out my putter and approached the ball. I inspected the slope of the green. I had always been good at it. I have always analyzed everything before I've done something. I set up and began to practice my putting stroke. *Perfect, just like that.* I realigned myself with the pin. God took the initiative to tend the flag for me, a kind gesture. I peered down at the ball; back at the pin. In a moment's flash, the ball rolled into the hole for a well-earned birdie.

"Well done. Now, let me give it a try," God said, grabbing His golden putter and immediately knocking His own ball in for a three as well. *A tie after the first hole . . . let the match begin.* We headed towards the next hole in silence, but connected as one.

The next holes passed over me in a blur of the fierce battle for my dear life. From great shots to pitiful luck, God and I played through it all. I played for myself, my family, and God Himself. These holes did consist of all the same emotions that passed me in the life I once lived, the one I am living. God did not let up on me, nor did I let Him. It was my life to fight for, and I was going to make it worth fighting for. In these grueling and painful hours God and I spent together, we became no longer strangers. We shared a connection like no other, something only we could experience. The demanding game took a toll on me, and I found myself a stroke down with the final hole to play. My fate would soon be sealed.

The sun had finally broken through the cloud-ridden sky and appeared just in time for the sunset. *This is it. I leave it all here, and take nothing back.*

"I believe it's your turn, God," I chimed in.

He looked down at His score card, smiled, and approached the tee-box. Once again, He was able to hit the ball straight down the fairway.

"Not a bad way to cap off the day."

"Not at all," he replied.

I stepped up to the tee, nervous as could be. Trying to ease my worried mind, I took a couple practice swings and proceeded to swing my driver with perfect form, sending the ball flying towards the left side of the fairway. We picked up our bags and moved on.

What bugged me the whole match was how it had been raining and wet, yet God's robe stayed perfectly dry when my pat legs seemed to be pained in mud.

"How is it that your robe is still clean?" I questioned Him.

"It's pure . . . like the heart."

And with that, not a word was spoken until we reached our balls. I found mine in the rough, but playable. Only one problem: a huge oak tree was in the way. The tree loomed over me with a presence of massive force. It was at least a hundred feet tall, and blocked my way to saving myself. My heart sank, but it wasn't over yet. I had made it this far, I could think of something to get me there.

I saw God out of the corner of my eye looking around for His ball in the distance.

"Go ahead and look for your ball; I'll meet you at the green."

He replied, "Thank you," and hurried off to find His ball.

I stood contemplating my every option. I came up with the only one that could very work. *If I'm to ever get past this tree, I'm going to have to curve the ball.* With that thought in mind, I tried to remember how to hide a fade shot. With an idea in mind, I went for it. The ball took off like a bullet, traveling fast. Appearing as though it would hit the tree instantly, my heart sank. At the last moment, it curved around, reaching great heights and landing softly on the green. I sighed with relief. *One step at a time, Mike. One step at a time.*

God managed to chip His ball onto the green. He had been so good with His short game today, rarely missing a putt. For me to have any chance, he was going to have to miss the putt.

"Good luck," he whispered.

"And the same with you." Sweat flowed down my face now. It was now or never. God proceeded to look at His putt from every angle before attempting anything. He knew what was on the line and wasn't giving in. Determination showing on His face, He concentrated on the task ahead. The putt rolled slowly, but looked promising. After what felt like an eternity, it reached the cup. *It stopped! Why did it stop?* All of a sudden, the ball stopped rolling. The slope looked downhill yet it stopped. I still had a chance. God walked over and tapped His ball in for a par. It was up to me.

I marked my ball and examined every angle of the green. This *was* my life on the line. I took a couple practice putts, and placed my putter behind my ball and stopped. I looked up from where I stood. My brow was drenched with sweat, so I wiped it with my arm with a gentle touch. It was quite hot, but the shade of the enormous oak tree covered part of the green, cooling my face. I looked into the distance—into the horizon, for it could be my last sunset. The sun's rays penetrated through the clouds illuminating the waves lapping the beach. Crystals appeared in the sea, shining brightly back at me. The golden sand of the shoreline glistened as well. Sweat continued to pour down my face, stinging my eyes. I wiped my face for a second time and looked down at my ball. I proceeded step behind my ball and prepared for my fate. My heartbeat slowed, but it was the only thing I could hear. The birds' chirping ceased, the breeze vanished. It was me, the ball, and the cup. I slowly started my backswing and brought it forward, striking the ball and sending it on its way. As if in slow motion, it traveled on the path I planned it would travel. Nearing the hole, it was the moment of truth. Holding my breath, the ball approached the hole, pausing there. I let out my breath out, numbed by the results. I looked around, dazed. It had not hit me yet that I had missed the putt. My head turned heavy, my knees started to wobble.

I blanked out. My end was there.

"I tried, I tried!" I was barely able to open my eyes. I saw silhouettes of people rushing back and forth. I lay naked on an operating table.

"He needs oxygen, now! . . . What's his status? . . . He has a pulse!"

My thoughts were blurred, but I was alive. I didn't get it. Hadn't I missed the putt?

"Yes, you did miss the putt." Once again, it was my friend God. I searched my thoughts for Him, but it was just His voice.

"B-b-but why?" I questioned Him.

"Why did I save you? I thought you should know the answer to that. You gave me a reason to save your life. You tried."

"So you could call this a mulligan," I said, trying to laugh, but every inch I moved sent shocks of pain throughout my body.

"Stay still. I understand how much pain you are in, but remember, pain hurts, yet it is a constant reminder to you that you have survived your ordeal and are alive. I know you must have a bunch of questions for me, so I intend to answer them all."

"Why did you save me?" I asked Him this rhetorical question yet again because I wanted the true answer.

"You said it best, Michael, you tried. Do I save everyone? No. I haven't saved everyone because they didn't try. They gave up when the road ahead was tough, but not you. Everyone has great potential but it takes a true character to realize that potential."

"Why a golf match?"

"Different strokes for different folks, I always say. And speaking of you, Michael, golf was the perfect test. It is, in fact, one of my very favorite ways of challenging people. It brings so much, and it reveals—and this is what I love about the game—the mystery and the paradox of life itself. It giveth, and it taketh away. It contrasts humility and glory, urgency and patience, reason and instinct, conflict and understanding, penalty and reward, misfortune and joy." These were all the things I had learned in my encounter with God throughout every hole, stroke, thought.

"Last but not least, I'd like to revisit why I actually gave you your life back. Yes, it certainly is because you tried. But beyond that, was there a more profound reason? If you cannot answer this by now, I'm afraid you'll have to figure it out by yourself." Before the Almighty left, He deposited a small object on my chest, over my heart, then it disappeared into thin air. I then began to rest, knowing the battle was over and I had the rest of my life to live.

I knew God had saved my life because it was *my* life! With its ability to absorb, and learn from failure. With its capacity to improve. With its passion and its perseverance and its heart. God gave me the greatest gift of all: the best Michael I can possibly be!

Epilogue: Who are we? Michael struggles to find out the answer to this simple question taking him on a long journey he did not expect. He encounters no one other than God Himself, and is challenged to a round golf for his life. Stricken with fear, for he could never beat God at his own game, Michael finds courage to fight on, against the insurmountable odds. From great shots to pitiful luck, God and Michael played through it all. He played for himself, his family, and God Himself. These holes did consist of all the same emotions that passed him in the life he once lived, the one he is living now. God did not let up on him, nor did he let Him. It was his life to fight for, and he was going to make it worth fighting for. In these grueling and painful hours God and Michael spent together, they became no longer strangers. They shared a connection like no other, something only they could experience. It came down to the final putt whether he lives, whether he finds a reason to live for. This is something I'm lucky to say I have never experienced. Knowing my grandmother, you'd know how sweet of a person she is. Being able to spend your whole life with her, you would know what she does for everyone around her. She has touched my life in so many ways; I could have never lived fully without her. She has shaped the person I am and the person I want to be. I will never forget her loving personality and I am proud to say she has given me the greatest gift I could ask for: the chance to experience exactly who I am.

To my Loving Grandmother:
When you meet Him,
Tell Him who you are.

Untitled

By Michele Casalino

He sits there in silence and continues to listen to the sound of squeaky tires and people speaking around him. He thinks of his grandmother and how the sickness is taking over her entire body. The doctors said they tried everything, and that there is no way she is going to last another two weeks. But he has faith, a lot of it. He sits there and begins to quiver and weep silently to himself. He tries so hard to remain strong, but this feeling came over him that he felt he had to let all his emotions release out of his system. He begins to get sleepy with all the crying he's been doing.

As he weeps quietly to himself, a young woman in front of him turns her head and looks to see where the sound of crying is coming from. As she turns her head very slowly, she peeks through the crack between the chair she is sitting in and the one next to her and takes a quick glance. As she stares, she sees a mid 20 year old man with his eyes shut tight with his delicate hands covering his eyes. She continues to examine him, tilting her head slightly to the left with this confused look, as he removes his hands from his face. Suddenly appear three teardrops that fall down along the wrinkles and curves of his face; one teardrop following the other.

She turns her head quickly as her eyes widen as if she is in shock. Thoughts rush through her mind as she rests her head against the vibrating window of the bus. As confusion remains in her thoughts, she begins to frantically shake her right leg; she does not know what to do. She turns her head and looks at him once more and catches him looking right back at her as he quickly turns his head and wipes the tears off his face. She immediately shoots her head back and hits her head against her chair as she mumbles, "Oh boy, it is him." She feels like she has to talk to him now that he caught her looking at him. She slowly gets up from her seat and goes up to the lonesome man. She approaches him and her body casts a shadow upon his. He feels the darkness and knows she is standing right there, but he refuses to open his eyes and pretends no one is there. She stands there for a couple of seconds and just stares at him.

Eventually she says, "Johnny? Is it really you?"

He opens his eyes and stares back at her with his water-filled hazel eyes and says, "What a way to greet each other after 5 years."

She giggles under her breath.

"Did you miss me?"

He replies, "Lizzie, of course I missed you; I haven't seen you in a good amount of years. I cannot believe you recognized me."

Lizzie replies, "Of course I remember you; how could I not?"

John says, "Well, it has been five years since we have seen one another."

There is a long pause as Lizzie's eyes lose focus into the distance. John finally breaks the silence.

"But might I add, you look absolutely stunning. You haven't changed, not one bit."

Lizzie blushes making her cheeks even rosier than they already are.

"And those pink cheeks of yours were always my favorite; I could never forget those cheeks."

Lizzie giggles and looks up at Johnny as he forces a smile with tearful eyes looking back at her. At this point, Lizzie is still standing and asks Johnny if it is okay for her to sit down next to him.

Johnny replies, "Well no one's stopping you."

Lizzie sits right beside Johnny so that their legs are touching one another. Lizzie looks up at Johnny and wants to ask him if they can catch up on things ever since high school, but is hesitant in asking him. Lizzie and Johnny were high school sweethearts from the beginning of freshman year until the end of senior year. They even won cutest couple and most likely to succeed in their senior class yearbook of 1998. It all started when they met for the first time coming from different junior high schools. It was love at first sight. Johnny turns his head so that he is looking directly at her and says,

"So, it's been awhile since we have talked."

Lizzie replies, "I know, words cannot describe how ironic it is that I bumped into you after losing touch for at least three years now. How have you been?"

"I've been doing well. I am currently getting my bachelors in healthcare at Yale."

Lizzie replies, "Wow, that is such an accomplishment. I am so proud of you! Is it difficult for you?"

"It is pretty difficult for me. Everything basically comes down to competition. I do struggle sometimes, but I am dedicated enough to get the rest of my two years of college over with before I move on to getting my doctrine."

Lizzie says, "I always knew you were going to be successful."

A big smile comes across Johnny's face.

"And the family; how is everything with them?"

Johnny turns his head and faces the window with his eyes shut and his eyebrows slightly lifted. Lizzie knows Johnny inside out and can read him like a book; she knew something was wrong.

Lizzie's stomach begins to turn and she feels guilty for asking, "Maybe I shouldn't have asked, I am sorry."

Lizzie looks down to the floor and attempts to stand up and leave Johnny to cool down, but Johnny immediately grasps her right arm with his strong masculine hands and says,

"No, do not apologize. Don't just walk away to get out of a situation; it doesn't work like that anymore Lizzie. We're adults now."

Lizzie says, "Johnny lets not bring up the past. The past is the past for a reason".

Johnny clears his throat and sighs. He looks out the window for two minutes looking at the paved road in silence. He cannot stop thinking about his grandmother. Johnny shakes his head and clears his throat.

"Grammie Rossane is in the hospital."

Lizzie's eyes grow big in shock. Lizzie was Johnny's grandmother's favorite girl. Grammie would always say to Johnny, "You know Johnny, Lizzie is the brightest and most genuine peach I know." Grandma Rossane treated Lizzie like she was her own granddaughter. Johnny and Lizzie were practically inseparable. Everyday after school, she would go over Johnny's house and find Grammie baking her classic 'vanilla chilla' cookies, just because they were Lizzie's all time favorites.

Lizzie, in shock, stays quiet as all these thoughts rush through her mind at once.

Finally she blurts out, "Well is she okay? Is everything going to be okay? We need to visit her and see if she needs our company!"

Johnny just sits there in silence picking at a scab under his right wrist.

"Johnny stop fidgeting, you always do that when you are upset. Talk to me; is everything going to be okay with Grammie? Is that why you were crying?"

Lizzie has this concerned look on her face as she is staring back at Johnny. Johnny tries to stay strong, but the emotions begin to take over him. He begins to weep silently. Lizzie wraps her delicate arms around Johnny's fragile body. She then kisses him on the cheek and says, "Everything is going to be okay, Grandma's a strong woman."

Johnny looks up at Lizzie and gently takes her arms and places them on her lap.

"Lizzie, she has cancer all throughout her body. It is eating her alive. I do not know what to do or even what to say."

Johnny stops himself and does not tell Lizzie that Grandma is only going to last another two weeks; he still has faith.

Lizzie replies, "Johnny, I am truly deeply sorry to hear about Grandma, but I am sure everything is going to be okay. You just need to be strong and get through the whole process in one piece. As Grandma would always say to us, 'If you have faith, you can conquer any obstacle you are faced with.'"

That was Grandma's favorite quote and she wanted Johnny to live by it for the rest of his life; so he does. Every single day before Johnny left the house for school, she would always say, "Remember, if you have faith, you can conquer any obstacle you are faced with." She felt that if she repeated it to Johnny he would eventually listen to the words and be inspired. Johnny never really paid attention to the saying until Grandma starting getting sick; that is when he started reciting her quote to her every time he would leave her hospital room.

"I know, I still and always will have faith. I take that moral with me everywhere I go. If I have enough faith, maybe, just maybe, Grandma will be okay," says Johnny.

Lizzie replies, "That is the Johnny Peterson I know. You really have not changed one bit, Johnny."

Johnny changes the subject and blurts out, "Lizzie, what ever happened to us? How could you do that to me after all the years we'd been together? Why leave me when you were the one who made the mistake? Were you trying to get out of the situation by running away? You hurt me and left my heart broken."

Johnny had promised himself he would not bring up the past, but he just could not stop thinking about it.

Lizzie looks up at him and slaps Johnny in the face.

Johnny wakes up and finds himself on the bus with Lizzie nowhere to be seen, like she has disappeared. Johnny frantically looks around for Lizzie, but she has vanished. It was all just a dream. Johnny slaps his head and mumbles to himself, "Another dream about her? When am I just going to let her go?"

Johnny sits in his seat remembering his Grandma's famous quote, "Remember, if you have faith, you can conquer any obstacle you are faced with." As Johnny opens his eyes, he sees Lizzie standing above him with the man, Rob, she cheated on Johnny with their senior year in high school.

"Johnny, is that really you? Do you remember me, it is Lizzie. Rob and I are just taking the bus to his parents' house up in New Jersey to give the big news!"

Johnny wishes this is all another dream but it all seems so real. He slaps his face to wake himself up but he realizes that this is not a dream, it is all reality.

Johnny clears his throat and says, "This is all a shock to me, what big news?"

Lizzie exclaims, "Me and Robbie are getting married!"

This rush fills throughout Johnny's entire body and he exclaims, "What? After everything you have put me through, you greet me by telling me you are getting married to the guy you cheated on me with?"

Lizzie and Rob look at each other and laugh. Lizzie says, "Johnny can you take a joke! Rob and I are partners in this new project we are doing for a college assessment; we are just going to New Jersey to take interviews."

This is too much for Johnny all in one day. He doesn't know what to believe.

Rob says, "Well, I am just going to go back to our seats. Nice seeing you, Johnny."

Johnny rolls his eyes and says, "Yeah, sure," as Robbie walks back to his seat.

Johnny looks up at Lizzie and tells her about the entire dream he had about her, in detail, and how ironic it is that she ended up being on the bus the entire time. Lizzie is in shock, and they start talking and laughing about the past.

Lizzie looks at Johnny and says, "Remember Grandma's old saying 'If you have faith, you can conquer any obstacle you are faced with?' Well, I have faith in us. I missed you, Johnny. I just want to apologize for what I did in the past. I wanted to tell you this a long time ago, but I just did not know how to say it, with you being in college and all."

A big smile comes across Johnny's face, so that every single pearly white tooth is visible.

Johnny says, "I have faith too, and always will."

Johnny and Lizzie end up getting off the bus together to go see Grandma in the hospital, and Lizzie ends up leaving Rob all by himself for the assessment. Johnny and Lizzie are thinking about starting a life together. They both look at Grandma as she is lying in the hospital bed peacefully. She is so happy to see Johnny and Lizzie together again.

Grandma forces out the words, "Having faith is what brought you two together."

Johnny replies, "And us having faith is what is going to keep you alive and staying strong, Grammie. We love you."

Unanswered Goodbyes

By Maria Baldi

An American Airlines plane flew over the top of her beat up 1992 Honda Civic through the cotton-like cloud as she drove home from work. She looked up at the plane as the sunset reflected off her eyes, creating a honey-like texture that any bee would confuse with its favorite meal. An unusual amount of tears collected in her eyes and instantly dripped from their crease to the top of her heart-shaped lips, caused by the memories she knew would play back and forth until they finally met again. Picturing their precious moments together, as if they only occurred yesterday, from the tenderness of his lips to the soft tone of his voice when he first confessed his love towards her. But she knew that her only option consisted of reminiscing about the past if destiny never decided to reunite them in the future.

Suddenly, her thoughts came back to reality as she reached the George Washington Bridge Toll, and she began searching for the only cash remaining in her navy blue Dooney&Bourke purse she had received three years ago for Christmas. Once she drove off, the Honda Civic's engine roared, crying for an oil change, but the memories, disregarding the noise, unconsciously processed their way up to her mind for the second time. She knew his departure created a form of closure to a relationship she thought would be never-ending. But she couldn't help to think of the last hand gesture he made while walking into the gates towards the plane at the JFK airport, as he disappeared from her vision. She recalled the last words he said to her: "Just trust me baby. Believe in me, it's for the better," while at the same time she pictured the plane bringing the love of her life back to his homeland, taking her beloved away from her until what seemed like forever.

She recollected her thoughts and dried her tears on her white button-up, forgetting she wore her Colossal Maybelline Mascara. She then got herself together and reached her destination. She parked her busted piece of metal on wheels, which she preferably enjoyed referring to as her vehicle.

Jennifer walked up the stairs towards the second floor to the entrance of her condominium, her door reading *37B*. As she opened the burgundy-colored door, she observed her mother standing on a tiny black chair, attempting to regain signal on her textbook-sized television that was placed on the top of the refrigerator, in order to continue watching her favorite *novela*.

"Mami, get down from that chair before you fall back and hurt yourself!"

"Well 'Hello' to you, too! I'm fine, thanks for asking," replied the 61-year-old woman as she stepped off the chair.

"Listen Ma', it isn't exactly the best day for me, so I'd appreciate it if you stopped naggin' at me, at least just for today. Please."

"What is it now, mi nena?"

She stopped and stared directly into her daughter's eyes. The dark marks created by Jennifer's running mascara made Dona Carmenza realize her only baby had been crying. Not only that, but the odd black smudge on the top Jenny's shirt also gave her away.

Her mother tried consoling her as she put her overworked hand on her left cheek.

"Honey, tell me, what is it? Did somebody hurt you? Did someone disrespect you at work?"

"No, Ma," answered Jennifer coldly.

Then it hit Dona Carmenza. It was that depressing time of the year again. The calendar had hit March, and although the climate became warmer, her daughter only grew colder.

Exactly three years ago, at the beginning of March, Jennifer's boyfriend of four years left for Venezuela to visit his family for what he said would only be three months, but he never returned. He left without giving her a reason, but the only words of hope she remembered were: "Just trust me baby. Believe in me." Those words replayed in her mind day after day, especially in March when she thought of him the most. Whether it was a year, two years, or four years later, she knew they would play in her head repeatedly like her old scratched up Backstreet Boys CD.

"Jenny, you know I've been here from the start and I plan on being around an' trying my hardest to help you get through this," continued her mother with her distinct Hispanic tone. "It may be stormy now, but it cannot rain forever. Just like your Abuela Ana used to always tell me. Remember everything happens for a reason. It's time to try and let go, mi reina."

"You don't think these past three years I've tried? Do you honestly believe I wish this constant pain upon myself? I may only show it occasionally, but it crosses my mind everyday Mom, every damn day! Being left without a reason isn't something you just forget about after a four year relationship!"

"I never said you have to forget, did I? It isn't always a negative thing to go through hardships, Baby. That is what makes you stronger."

Jenny looked up at her mother, shocked at her words. And although Dona Carmenza was right next to her, she felt misunderstood, alone, isolated, and ignored.

"You'll never understand. And I do not want you trying to!"

She walked up to her room ignoring her mother's yelling, demanding her to come back. When Jenny entered her room she headed directly to her queen-sized bed wrapped in the dark green bamboo pattern bed covers that she had been sleeping on every night for the last couple of months. The sun beamed through her chestnut-colored curtains, giving the room a lively feel, but that meant absolutely nothing to Jenny. Her room did not reflect what she felt like momentarily. She sat for hours, staring blankly at the bone-colored walls that caged her in, thinking of a reason why Jonathan had left her without saying goodbye, with thousands of unanswered questions. For an endless amount of time, Jennifer remained motionless on the bed, until she fell asleep, the only time she felt at peace . . . except tonight.

As her brain drifted into a dream and entered the sleep stages, Jenny saw herself at an unfamiliar yet beautiful place, alone. She stood up in her fuchsia bikini and headed straight to the amazing palm trees located at the end of the beach. She suddenly heard a voice that immediately grabbed her attention. The voice repeatedly called out for help, causing hysteria in her actions as she looked around everywhere, only to find nothing. Jenny recognized his voice as soon as she heard the passion behind it when he yelled her name. It was Jonathan, but she couldn't see him. He continued to yell for her help, followed by loud coughs in between the screams and short gasps for air. That was the last she heard of him in her dreams before waking up to her alarm clock going off at the first snooze alarm. When she opened her eyes, she was back in her bedroom. As she looked at her alarm clock, it read 5:35 a.m., two minutes later than the time of her usual awakening.

Her clothes from the previous day remained placed on her body as she wiped her eyes from the overwhelming tears she was unaware of, attempting to adjust to the sun's rays that were flashing through the window cracks.

That morning was just like any other. She followed the usual routine, doing the same actions that slowly transformed into tradition to Jenny's everyday life. She took her twenty-eight minute shower, brushed her pearly white teeth, got dressed for work, brushed her short layered brunette hair, said "Good Morning" and "Goodbye" to her mother as she received the coffee Dona Carmenza would make for her every morning, and headed out to work.

This routine was followed for the next two months and thirteen days, until something caught Jenny's eyes as she collected the mail from her mailbox. On June 21st, 2010, there was an envelope that read her name and address.

Jenny Garcia Santos
37B Brookstone St.
White Plains, NY 10603

It was a yellow envelope from Jonathan Mendoza, all the way from Caracas, Venezuela.

Her heart raced feeling as though it would stop any second if she continued to read his name at the top left corner of the envelope. She felt relieved, excited, anxious, and delusional all at once. She couldn't believe what was happening. Had he finally remembered her? Could he have possibly not forgotten about what they once shared? Could they still have a chance to continue?

Jenny dropped the rest of the useless envelopes and magazines, and finally opened the folded yellow paper that carried what she had awaited for the past three years. She read the four pages Jonathan had written over and over again, until, after the fourth time, the words in the letter automatically sunk in her brain.

She dropped to the floor, still holding onto the four white pages that had just changed her life and made her feel dysfunctional, unmotivated, and destroyed. Tears streamed down her cheeks like the rain falls from the sky during Spring. Jenny yelled, cried, hit the floor, cried again and yelled some more, not being able to find any other actions that would fit what she was feeling. All she wanted to do was close her eyes and never see light again.

She got up and walked up the stairs once again to reach her apartment, entering the room with the letter still close to her heart, her eyes fire red, containing tears of despair, that seemed as though she had been crying for the last five weeks. The veins in her forehead popped out more and more as every tear fell from her eye.

Dona Carmenza ran to her and hugged her as soon as she realized her daughter's horrible conditions, not knowing what was happening.

"Mija, what is wrong? Talk to me, please!"

"You were right mom," said Jenny through her short-taken breaths that sounded as if she was close to losing her life.

"I was right about what Honey? Speak to me. Porfavor!"

"There was a reason. There's a reason for everything Ma'."

"A reason for what Jenny, let it out!"

"He did love me, he loved me more than anything in the world."

"Jonathan? When did you hear from him, Jenny? How?"

"He had to leave. For the better. He believed leaving caused me less pain."

Her mother became frustrated and confused as she took in the situation with complete obliviousness. Not knowing anything that was going on, she still found herself crying with her daughter after witnessing her go through the worst pain she ever expected Jenny to experience.

"He had cancer, throat cancer. Now he's gone forever. Forever Mom, forever!" yelled Jennifer as she felt her life changing, her heart breaking, and her tears falling.

Finding Jimmy Murdaw

By Lydia Krenicki

—⁓∘◦◟◉◟◉◦∘⁓—

I got there early, before the sun even rose. I set up my blanket and sat on the side of the road, patiently waiting for what was to come. The grass pushed through the stitches in my makeshift seat and tickled my legs. Sitting in the grass, I watched the sun rise higher in the sky as people started to arrive. They lined the streets with beach chairs and noise from the small crowds started to fill the street with a buzz.

The excitement in the air came through my lungs and filled me with impatience. I lurched up with my sudden enthusiasm and started pacing the street, abandoning my blanket by the roadside. Crowds of people were storming up the hill and I could barely see the tops of their heads as they as they reached higher and higher. The heat from the sun seeped into my shirt and warmed my back and the top of my head. I returned to my original seat, which was then occupied by a family, my blanket stuffed in a ball in between the grass and the curb. I shoved myself into the small space between groups of people, not bothering with my blanket.

The drums thumped and shook the street, the music blaring as the marching band rounded the corner of the avenue. The instruments' golden surfaces gleamed with the light of the burning sun. The shadows of the players darkened the street, making the band extend to twice its size. The flags twirled; swirling colors into exotic shades of red and blue. My jaw dropped as they passed, and I pressed my hands together, trying to stop time and keep the moment with me. I looked across the street and saw that a little blonde boy was doing just the same thing. Normally, I would have looked away, but the way his smile brightened his face reminded me of my brother, who passed away a few years before.

The rest of the Memorial Day parade passed by in a blur of wonder and awe. People packed up their belongings as quickly as they had come, disappearing over the hill. The sun started to fade and the shadows covered the street with an eerie aura. As I stepped away to leave my place of amazement, I stopped to look and remember my perfect day, one last time. In my mind, the band danced down the street and balloons filled the air. My vision was disturbed by a muffled scream, as I whipped my head up, pushing my long blonde hair out of my eyes to see what the commotion was about. The small boy I had seen before, about the age of seven, was being forced into a white truck. I was paralyzed with fear. Ice shot up my spine that even the warm memories of my day could not melt.

I ran. My feet beat the pavement in fury, trying with all my might to reach the little boy. The realization that I was not going to make it pushed me even further. The car sped off before I was even close enough to read the letters on the license plate. My heart thumped, pumping blood through my body, but I could not feel it. My hands and legs were numb with fear and the air had a sudden chill to it. I picked up my phone and dialed 9-1-1.

I tried to keep my voice steady. "I just saw a little boy," I said, "He was taken in a big white van. I tried to stop it." My voice sounded strangled even to my own ears.

"Take a deep breath and tell me where you are," a calm voice replied from the other end of the line. My stomach sank with the realization that nothing was going to happen fast, and I had a feeling it was going to be up to me.

That was the day my life changed forever. At twenty years old, I enrolled in the police academy and ever since then, I have been searching for some hidden clue, a little hint that will help me find the boy that has now taken the place of my brother. This has engulfed my life in a way that nothing else has. My meaning in life is to find the piercing blue eyes that stared at my running figure through the window, begging me to help him.

His name is Jimmy Murdaw, and he is the son of a rich investment banker and his young bride. He was four feet tall at the time and had hair that was so blonde it was almost white. His eyes are what I remember most. They were the most beautiful color blue I had ever seen. I would not stop searching until I found them again.

"Eva," Bob's deep voice rang through my daydreams, "you stayin' late again?"

Bob is my boss and he is one of the only people who understand why I have to find Jimmy. He is a big man, standing at six foot four with a middle that is almost as wide. His handlebar mustache gives him the perfect cop look.

"Yeah, I just have to finish some things," I said, fighting back a yawn.

"Don't you stay to late, ya'hear." He gave me a reproachful look over the top of my cubicle.

"Yeah, yeah, I'm almost done."

I was nowhere close to done. I shook the mouse until my computer screen came to life. I searched for hours through the scans of family pictures and belongings that might give me a clue as to who took Jimmy. The clock on the wall ticked endlessly as if telling me I was running out of time. It reminded me I was no closer to finding him, a fact that I could not face. I had to find my brother.

My head jerked up to a tapping sound on the glass door at the entrance to the office building. I rubbed my eyes, staring at the clock.

"Five a.m." I gasped, my energy suddenly finding me. I ran to the door and saw an old woman standing there. I undid the lock and pushed open the door.

"Hello, can I help you?"

Her voice was soft and scratchy as she said, "I found a video in my mailbox . . . I . . ." Her face drained of color and I brought her inside, bringing with her what may be the key to finding Jimmy Murdaw.

The moving figures flashed across the television screen in a way that made it impossible to distinguish the shapes as the camera turned. It steadied, and in the corner of the screen was a flash of blonde hair.

Advantages

By Kyle Capone

—⁓∾⌇⌇⌇∾⁓—

I don't understand what happened that night on the trip to Chicago. I just went to see my kids and now I'm stuck in this adventure. It all started when I went on a train from Connecticut. I went to see my divorced wife and two kids, Jake and Jess. I didn't get to see them lately, due to the fact of my job. I had to travel all over Connecticut in source of new business partners. I worked in an advertising business. Really, I hated the hell out of my job, but whatever paid the bills.

I started to look around the train at a few people. There was a man in a top hat who was smoking a cigar. He made a perfect circle with each blow. Then, while studying this other woman, the Conductor came to me and said, "Ticket please." He had some sort of coldness in his voice. I just handed him the ticket. He took the hole puncher and slammed it hard and gave me back the ticket and walked away. I felt pretty threatened by that man for some reason, but I decided to pay no attention, and fell asleep for the five hour ride.

"Here we are, destination at the Chicago Train Station; we hope you enjoy your stay!" I was startled by the announcement and jumped up and screamed. Everyone just started laughing at me. One old man made a nasty comment to me, so when he turned around I just flipped him off. I grabbed my bag off the seat next to me and I was on my way.

I took one step off the train and the first reaction I had was what a dump. It was dirty, windy, and disgusting. I could feel the wind as it brought in the smoke from the factories. Cold, harsh, alone, the wind was brutal. I just put on my hat and kept walking to find the nearest taxi. I kept looking at all the posters on the wall of "Support our troops in Korea!" and "Stop the COMMUNISM!" I couldn't help thinking what a joke it was. Telling people to sacrifice their lives for a country that doesn't have a democracy. It's a free world. I just stood for a minute to look at myself and then I saw a taxi. I jumped at it and raised my hand. He didn't notice me and just splashed me from yesterday's rain. I started to curse at the taxi and looked like a fool to the people around me.

I had to wait a half an hour to wait for a frigging bus, then. Finally, the bus came at a quarter to five. It was the late winter and already February, and it was ten degrees! I jumped onto the bus without hesitation. I looked at all the faces around me. I coldly put in the nickel for a ride to 34th Simonsen Street. I saw an attractive young lady and sat next down to her. She smiled at me and I smiled back. Then she stared out the window and I tried to see her finger. While doing that, I fell. She reacted quickly and helped pick me up. She started to giggle and asked me if I was alright. I snickered back and said I was alright.

"What's your name?" I asked.

"Violet," she responded.

"Like the color?" I said.

She started to laugh and I joined in too. I guess she liked my corny sense of humor. She looked at me and asked where I was headed.

"I'm going to see my little cousins. Great kids!" I couldn't believe I lied about my own children for a date maybe. She was so fascinated with me that she kept asking more questions and I just kept lying like an idiot. Finally the bus came to my stop and I told her I had to go.

"Wait!" she called.

I turned around, and right there in front of me was a piece of paper with her number on it. I smiled and jumped straight out of the bus. Then the bus drove away and I waved to her only if she could see me. Then I looked at the piece of paper and it said on it, "Watch yourself, call me: 1-203-911-3279." I looked curiously at the note, but didn't care and ran down the street to find my favorite ex!

I finally reached the street and was thrilled I was there to see the little buggers. Honestly, I loved my daughter the most; she was the oldest out of the two. While I was thinking of my beloved Jess, I just happened to reach the door and I knocked on it in a catchy jingle. Hopefully my ex wouldn't get angry at me for that. I waited two minutes, and no one still came to the door. I checked my little piece of paper my lawyer sent to me with where her new address was. I knocked harder in anger and then the door opened automatically, which was kind of creepy. I opened the door all the way and walked right in.

"Hello! Jess? Anyone?"

Next, I turned the corner into the kitchen and I found three dead bodies. I jumped in fear and went closer to look at the bodies. One was stabbed deeply by a kitchen knife and the other was penetrated by a fork in the back. There was blood all over the floor and I looked at the bodies closer to find that all were males. I realized the kids were not there and ran to look for them. I ran into every room and finally upstairs. I looked inside the kids' bedroom and I heard some breathing. I looked to the corner and heard it from the closet. I grabbed my son's baseball bat in waiting to open the door for danger. I could feel the sweat going down my back I as I held the knob of the closet. Then I threw it open, to only find my daughter, Jess, in absolute fear with a pistol in her hand. She fired at me, but lucky she missed me by an inch of my left shoulder. I grabbed it and hugged her while she cried.

"What happened?" I said.

"They took Mom and Jake!" Jess said.

I looked in desire to hope that was not the truth. Instead, after searching all the bodies, all I found was a business card.

"We have your son and wife here; we will give them up for a tiny profit, and don't try to get the police involved! Look into this man's pocket and you will find a treat."

I looked into the pocket and found a ticket for at eight to hop onto the next train and go to New York City. I took the tickets and grabbed my daughter's hand before she could say a word, and we ran out the door. When I tried to open the door, it was locked. It was jammed!

"Dad look out!"

A flying chair was right headed for me and I ducked before I could even hit me. There was a man with a ski mask and switchblade that had gone through the window. I ran up to him and hit him in the stomach. Boom! Then he hit me twice with his fists. Bam! Then kicked me in the shins and I was on the floor in tears. Right before he could take out his blade, I heard a chuckle from him and then said, "You can't do anything." He started laughing until I heard a shot go off. I looked behind me to see that my fourteen-year-old daughter had pulled the trigger. Then, I turned around to see a hole through the man's chest. He fell to the floor without a word. She looked at me and said, "Let's go." She ran out that door after grabbing her ticket. I didn't stutter and just followed her.

We just ran up to the train station and had to use the two tickets to get on the next train. On the train, this young man kept stalking me, and finally I turned around asked what he wanted.

"Nothing sir I'm just trying to find my seat," said the man.

Of course his seat happened to be next to me. He took his seat and I didn't even bother to look at him, and really, I did not care.

"So, sir, what are you going to New York for?" said the man.

"I got some business to take care of," I said.

"Yeah? So do I. I gotta tough job."

I didn't listen to his bull, so I just fell asleep right against the cold window, trying to cover my face from seeing his. Then I dozed off.

"We are here in New York City, Dad!"

I woke up and panicked. Then I realized it was just my daughter that woke me up.

"Alright, let's go to this address and find these jerks."

We called a taxi. One, out of nowhere, immediately skidded right up next to my daughter and me.

"Jesus Christ! What's your problem bucko!?"

"Get in the damn car!"

We heard gun hire from behind us and ran in the car. Then the driver turned her head around to pull out. It was Violet. I couldn't believe it!

"Duck!" yelled Violet.

Jess did; I didn't. I wanted to see who it was. There was a blue Mustang car and one Cadillac behind us. Since when did those hooligans get better cars then me!?

A bullet came through the window right beside my arm, so then I decided it would be a good time to duck. Violet was an angry driver. She steered the car through at least five alleys and couldn't get rid of them. She went back into the lanes, but there was so much frigging traffic. We tried to dodge all cars that came our way. Then a bus came out of nowhere and Violet then steered to the sidewalk with pressure and screaming. The Mustang had good reaction time, although the Cadillac did not make it. The bus hit it and kept going in the same direction without stopping. It looked as though the whole thing was planned. We were now on a strip of streets stretching for a while. Violet kept dodging all the damage it would do to the taxi.

Finally, she pulled into a dead end ally and slammed into the wall.

I woke up a second later looking for my daughter and found her unconscious next to me, so I hugged her to keep her safe. Then I threw all the scrap metal from the car off me and walked out. As I crawled out of the car with Jess, I saw Violet casually walk out of the front seat. Then the thugs' car pulled up. They shook hands! Then I heard Violet say, "He's over here!"

A very old, grey man came over to me and I looked up at him. It was the one from the train.

"Nice to see you again." He said, and then he pulled out a pistol and shot me.

I woke up to the smell of a bunch of crabs, and looked around for clues I may see while still trying to gain consciousness. I realized I was in some sort of abandoned deck storage room. I looked at where I was shot and saw it was a needle type of bullet that injected me with something? I looked around and I found that there was no one around, but I looked out to the deck and saw that there was a boat coming. There seemed to be over about four people on the boat, then it pulled up and I saw my ex-wife with a gun in her hand. She came out and walked right to me.

"Hello you bastard," she said, then hit me across the face with the butt of the pistol. I fell back in my chair. Either way, I couldn't get up because I was tied to the chair with rope.

"What do you think? I'm the head of a nationwide gang," she said.

"I knew you had drug problems, but I never thought you'd gone this far!"

"You're really stupid; I owned a drug lab ever since were married. You know I only used you for money, right?"

"Sadly, I knew it ever since we were married. I hoped that you would love me for who I was and you would have had changed, but you didn't. I hoped for love and now I can't believe it."

"That's too bad; you know, I looked for the same in you, but you are a real piece of crap."

She then pulled out her pistol again and called over a girl from the corner with a hood over her head. Then my ex-wife pulled off the hood off the girls head and it was Violet.

"Violet teach him a lesson, would you," my ex-wife said.

Violet then pulled out her magnum and pointed it at my head. "I'm sorry."

I looked down the barrel of the gun and then closed my eyes hoping to not feel the pain.

Bam! Bam! Boom!

Then I fell down hard I thought my life flashed in front of my eyes. Then I fell and opened my eyes and saw Jake breaking open the door with ten other police officers. Then I saw Violet turn around and shoot my ex-wife and the two other men, including the old one and the other one I saw on the train who I didn't notice before. Then I saw Jess pick me up and yell something, but I couldn't hear because of the bullets. Then she pulled me out while tied to the chair. Then I turned around and looked at Violet. She was about to close the doors to create some protection for her. Then she closed the door and took cover. Then I saw a recon boat coming from the boat. Then entered the storage deck and then shot all the gangsters inside. Then they went through the open doors and shot all remaining people inside. They had shot three police officers and then, of course, Violet, and I fell down. I slowly saw her fall and around her neck came flying off into my hand a necklace with a "Detective of New York City" badge. Then I saw the man that shot Violet run up to her. He had an officer cap on. He was crying. I dropped it and then I saw Jess came and pulled me away. I saw too much blood from the fallen and I couldn't help but faint.

I woke up in a hospital in Queens. I looked around and all I saw was Jake and Jess. When I opened my eyes and saw them, they were overjoyed and jumped in the air.

"Dad! Are you okay?" said Jess.

I couldn't even speak, as though my lips had been stitched, but they weren't, and I just said, "Fine". All I asked was what happened out there. Then Jake and Jess looked at each other.

"Listen, you know mom was a drug addict for a while. After you divorced her, when we were little, she started to do some crazy things because she needed to be loved," said Jake.

"You didn't realize it, but when you left her, she actually loved you, but you looked at her faults and at your job instead of a person that needed help . . . and now she's in the infirmary fighting for her life," said Jess.

I just sighed with grief thinking how come all these years I have been so selfish and did not think of the person I loved the most. The things she said back there must have been lies, and she must of have been so hurt that she took on more medication and addictions. I knew what I had to do then.

I stood up, and Jake and Jess both feared for me that I would fall, but I was alright. I had some stupid hospital clothes on and I grabbed the cane next to me. I started to walk down the hallway. Then, all of a sudden, I fell and had a flashback the day I wanted a divorce:

"Roger, come on, Sweetie, you're going to be late for dinner!" Jane, my wife at the time, said pleasantly to me.

I remember I came down drunk and hit the table, furious at my boss for having to move again.

"I don't care! Leave me alone." But I was already at the table.

"Come on, do we need to move again, Honey?" said Jane.

"Screw you, bitch, we need the damn money."

"Honey, please don't talk to me like that, especially in front of the children."

I remember I stared in her eyes and said I need the money or we'd starve.

"Aren't there more important things than money?"

"No, not at all."

"Not even the children or me?"

"No, now shut up!"

She started to tear up and I remember that sad look in her eyes and I slapped her. She was on the floor crying. I just stomped out and didn't even look back at the kids or her. My last look before I opened the door was seeing her grabbing some aspirin.

All of a sudden, I stood up from the hospital floor and knew what I had to do. I ran down to her room and waited outside the emergency room until the doc's were down operating. I waited outside for two hours to think of what I had really done and realized what she actually wanted from me in the docks. Love. When I looked up, I saw that the emergency room lights had turned off and saw them pushing my ex off into her room. I followed right behind them. I sat in a chair for two hours waiting for the medication to drag off. Then she woke up. I ran to her bedside and hugged her, to find that she was okay.

"Honey, I'm so sorry for what I've done to you all those years ago! I'm a terrible husband, can we please be married again?"

I started to cry and she didn't know what to say. All that came out was a yes and that was all I heard. Then, before we could kiss, her pulse just stopped. All the doctors came running into the room and tried to recover her, but sadly, it was too late for her and me. She was gone at that moment when I had just loved her again. I could of have done a lot years ago to prevent this from happening to her and me. You just have to take advantage of the good things that life gives you, like your lover, and not care about the non-important things that do not make a person, like money. After all these years, that money cannot bring her back, nor my mistakes I had done to her in the past. I know now I have to make the most of my life and not what I have been doing before. I need to give back instead of taking things from people, like their emotions.

I walked out of the hospital that night went to the bank and took out all my money and ran to a shelter, charity, and church, and got rid of all my money. Finally, for once in my life, I was proud of myself and felt happy. All I could hope for is Jane would feel the same way about me right now.

Just What Was Needed

By Katie Baritz

——⟨⟨⟨⟨⟨⟨⟩⟩⟩⟩⟩⟩——

Get a 3.5 GPA or higher, get into college, be state champion in both diving and gymnastics, manage a job, clean the house, do community service. Did I forget anything? Probably. I can only remember so much. For a sixteen year old, though, I think I'm doing pretty well. Ask my mother on the other hand, and she will tell you that I'm not so successful.

Monday through Friday, my alarm goes off at six—my alarm being the sound of my mother's voice screaming at me to get my lazy self out of bed.

"Wake up! I'm leaving. Make your own breakfast."

"I'm awake."

"What time does the meet start?"

"Four."

"See you then. Empty the dishwasher before you leave."

Just so she shuts up, I get out bed of relatively quickly and hop in the shower. The hot water causes me to want to crawl back to my cozy queen bed and pull the covers right over my head. I have a diving competition today; I should have shaved my legs last night. I get the razor and the shaving cream, and begin putting the foam on my hands and then spreading it across my tanned, toned legs. I knew it was a bad idea to shave in the morning; barely awake and of course I cut myself about three times. I wash the shaving cream and blood off, get the knots out of my hair, and get out of the shower. It seems like I was in the forever, but I gaze at the clock that says only ten minutes have gone by.

Staring at myself in the mirror, I want to smile back and think of the many things I've accomplished. I have offers from several

Division I schools, I have received employee of the month more than once at Hallmark, I currently have a 3.8 GPA, and I manage to give back to my community of Lima, Ohio, at least twice a week. Realizing all of this, I give myself the slightest smirk. Not enough where you can see my semi straight white teeth, but enough where you know that I'm somewhat satisfied. Standing there with my dark green towel wrapped around my body, I begin running a brush though my long, light brown hair. It's straight, so it usually does not take me too long. Gosh, how I wish I had curly or wavy hair. Straight hair is so boring. I look like my mom, with the exception of my eyes and the amount of wrinkles on my face. I have my father's eyes; almond-shaped dark green eyes. I think my eyes are the reason my mother avoids eye contact with me. Every time, she is reminded of my father, a man who is no longer with us. When my father passed away, the compassion in my mother passed away too.

"Hey, you've reached Evan. I can't get to the phone right now. Leave a message, but I probably won't listen to it if you do."

Evan always ignores my calls in the morning. He's my best friend and basically my ride everywhere. If I don't call him at least three times every morning, we would always be late to school. I call three more times, and then on the fourth call, he picks up.

"I'm awake. Be there in fifteen."

Before I can even respond, he hangs up. I start rummaging through my pile of clean clothes. I end up throwing on a pair of faded blue jeans, a gray tank top, a black zip up sweatshirt, and a pair of black flats. I find myself standing in front of the mirror again, just staring at myself. I'm looking into my own eyes now. I miss my dad so much. He would be making me breakfast if he were still here. He always used to on the days of competition.

Before tears start running down my cheeks, my thoughts are interrupted by the honking of Evan's car. I lost track of time, didn't eat breakfast, didn't put the dishes away, and didn't even make myself lunch yet. I grab my school bag, run down the stairs, grab a blueberry pop tart, and dash out the door. Evan is not a morning person, so when I get in the car, I don't even say "hello". He just begins pulling out of the driveway, and we speed off to school.

We get to my least favorite place in the world (school), and it's still early enough that everyone is just in the parking lot talking to one another. Both Evan and I just sit in the car though, staring blankly out the window.

"Are you hungry?" he asks.

"I'm starving."

"Good. So I didn't stop and Dunkin Donuts for nothing."

"Why didn't you tell me this when I first got in the car?"

"I was tired."

"You're selfish."

"If I'm so selfish, why did I stop and get you food?"

"Good point. Thank you."

Evan reaches into his backseat, grabs the bag of food, and tosses me a bagel with cream cheese. Food has never looked this good before. I begin biting into it and before I even realize it, the whole bagel is gone.

"What time does the meet start?" he asks.

"Four. Are you coming?"

"I'm your ride there, aren't I?"

"Good point, once again."

"Are you okay? It seems like something is bothering you," Evan says to me.

"I'm tired and nervous. And I cut myself shaving this morning. And I didn't put the dishes away," I snapped.

"Oh."

"That's it? 'Oh'? That's all you have to say?"

"No."

"I'm waiting for you to be a best friend and comfort me."

Evan says nothing. He just looks at me, shrugs his shoulders, and then smiles. Next thing I know, we're pulling out of the parking lot.

"Where are we going?" I shout.

"Don't worry about it. I'm being a best friend and comforting you."

I just let out groan and close my eyes. I'm too nervous and tired to even care about not going to school. I have only missed three days of school this year, and it's May.

"Wake me up when we get to wherever it is you're taking me," I say to him.

I fall asleep for what seems to be hours, but after the slam of the car door, I realize that my eyes were only shut for twenty minutes. I stare outside the window of the suburban and see Evan standing near the edge of a lake. The breeze causes ripples across the glossy dark water. Surrounding the whole lake are tall evergreens. Evan turns around and signals me to get out of the car. I just stare at him, though. He towers over me when we're next to each other; he is six foot three. His dark jeans and blue sweatshirt fit his muscular body so nicely. The wind ruffles his brown hair.

I get out of the car and stand next to him, just staring at the blue sky's reflection on the lake. All of a sudden, I feel Evan's hand holding mine. I do not pull away though, I just move closer to him. Staring at the lake, I realize how much good I have in my life. Life at home may not be ideal, but outside of that environment, I am lucky. Evan puts his arm around me, and the gesture feels right.

"Feel better?" Evan asks me.

"Much better."

"I'm glad. Now what do you want to do?"

"Go to school."

"You're joking, right?"

"Yes."

He nudges me away gently, laughing at my response. We both begin picking up rocks and skimming them across the water. My dad was the one who taught me how to skip rocks, but instead of crying over the memory, I smile at the smooth rock I hold in my hand and say to myself, "This one is for you, Dad." I look at Evan who smiles at me and then looks away. He never looked so attractive before. He has always been my best friend and I never thought of him as anything more than that . . . up until now, that is. I walk up to him and put my arms around his neck. For a second, I forget what I am doing, but then I go up on my toes and bring my lips towards his. His lips touch mine and we stay this way for what seems like a lifetime. Our lips break and I'm left staring into his dark blue eyes.

"I'm sorry," I say to him.

"For what, Michelle?"

"I don't know what just took over me."

"It doesn't matter. I liked it."

"I love you."

The words slipped out of my mouth. I stared at him with big eyes wondering if he would even say anything back. He stared back at me, looking confused. I was positive that within the next thirty seconds, I was going to throw up.

"I love you too."

After those words leave his mouth, I just smile at him and hug him. We walk back to his car and sit there holding hands. The radio comes on and it is just advertising, so he turns it off. Evan looks at me and kisses me on the cheek. His move takes me surprise, but in return I kiss him back. Never did I picture something like happening between us.

"Want to go see a movie?" he says.

I nod my head in approval and then we begin driving towards town. The car ride is silent with the exception of the car's engine. Was this how my parents fell in love? I never got the chance to ask either of them. Evan is just gazing out through the window, with his eyes focused on the road, but it looks like he's going into deeper thoughts. I wonder what is going through his mind. Is he thinking about what just happened? Or he is regretting it already?

"Why are you crying?"

I bring my fingers to my cheeks and realize that they are wet. My cheeks begin to burn from embarrassment.

"I don't know. I'm sorry," I reply.

He flashes his perfect white teeth at me and focuses on driving again. Now I'm trying so hard not to think of what happened at the lake. It happened and that's all that matters, right? I close my eyes and try to fall asleep, but too many thoughts have taken over my mind. My eyes remain shut and I begin thinking of my dad. His face comes perfectly in my mind. The image of his tan skin and dark green eyes appear so perfectly. His grey facial hair always tickled my skin every time he kissed me on the cheek or forehead.

I open my eyes and then, all of a sudden, the car begins spinning out of control. Evan grabs my hand and tells me to hold on. The car continues to spin off the road and the sound of the tires on the dirt takes over. I look out of my window and see a large rock in the path of the car. I brace for the impact and then the car is up in the air and back on the ground in a matter of two seconds. I slam my head on the roof of the car and my mind slowly slips into unconsciousness.

My eyes start to flicker and all I hear is beeping. I turn my head, but a sharp pain shoots down my spine. All of a sudden, my mom and brother are standing over me. I look down at my body and I'm covered in blankets. I lift my arms a little bit and see IV's coming from my wrists and hands. I try to speak, but nothing comes out. Both my mom and brother Chris take a seat and move close to me. My mother grabs my hand, a gesture that she has not done since I was a child. Christopher begins speaking to me.

"You suffered a serious concussion. You were in a car accident, remember? You didn't break any bones thankfully, but don't be surprised when you see your face and it's a different color." He laughs. "They want to keep you here one more night, but they think you will be okay."

I stare at him and just blink my eyes slowly. I understand what he's saying to me, but don't know how to respond. Then it crosses my mind.

"Evan. Where is he? I need to see him."

Chris and my mom look at each other and I see tears form in my mother's eyes. Before either of them says anything, tears fill up my eyes as well to the point where I can't see out of them. Evan is dead. There are some things someone can sense without anything being said, and this is one of them. My brother grabs my other hand and I begin to sob uncontrollably. My best friend is gone, all because he wanted me to be happy. I asked him to be a good friend and that's what he did. It was what he always did.

The rest of the day was spent crying. I didn't eat or talk. I just stared out of the window of my hospital room. As night time came around, I asked my brother and mom to leave. The crying didn't stop after they left. It only continued. I cried myself to sleep for the first time in years. When I woke up in the morning, both of them were back. The whole day was a blur to me. I ate my food, but ended up throwing it up from crying. I was discharged and the ride home was silent. When I arrived home, I went straight to my room, locked the door, and laid in bed. My life felt like it had fallen apart; first my father and now my best friend. I close my eyes and now I see Evan's face, his perfect face. He smiles at me and he says, "Get up and look in the mirror." A thought had never felt so real before.

I walk over to my mirror and looked at myself. My forehead still had stitches and my chin is still scraped horribly. I stare at myself, directly into my own eyes. In the reflection of the mirror, I no longer see just myself, but Evan also. He was as real as could be, his body untouched by any damage from the accident. He opens his mouth and I hear his words so clearly.

"I'm always with you. Don't forget that. Me and your dad, we're always with you. Don't let anything hold you back from doing what you know you can do. We both love you."

I shut my eyes and open them and he's gone. I blink again, hoping maybe he will come back, but then I think back to the words I heard. He is always with me. He does not need to physically be with me. I then remember that my dad is still with me too. I know that I'm never alone.

*   *   *

It's been fifteen years since Evan died. I went to college on a gymnastics scholarship. I work as secretary now. My mom and I fixed our relationship; I know she loves me now, and I know that she never stopped. Evan's death changed me. Losing my father was never needed. Losing my best friend was never needed. But with both devastating events, I became stronger. It may seem crazy, but they both guide me every day. I am grateful for having told Evan that I love him. I would never be able to live knowing that he never got to know. He and my dad will never let me be alone, and my love for them will never go away. Losing such important people is not what I needed; it was the lessons that came from them.

Random Days with Kilgore

By Nic Tejada

Dedicated to Kurt Vonnegut

He had a horribly misshapen mustache. He was going bald, a condition which, with the last strands of wiry hair, he attempted to conceal. He was scrawny and had a bad limp. *He was my idol.* He stumbled onto the faded white porch in a hurry. I asked him where he was going, sure he had something important or philanthropic in mind.

"The bushes," he gestured toward the brush behind me. It looked like anything but bushes, obviously long dead.

"Oh. Why?"

"To take a piss," he said in a what-the-hell-do-you-want-to-know-for tone. He had the ability to communicate extra sentences with his tone. *I loved him for it.* He burped with his crooked back facing me; he was taking his piss. Swaying back and forth, he was obviously drunk. I looked anywhere, at everything but him: the dilapidated shack he called "home", the outhouse turned tool shed in the back, the hairs that had just burst through my skin, hairs of which my pride was evident. The steps creaked and my eyes instinctively focused on him blundering up the stairs. His fly was wide open. When I pointed it out, he thanked me and flashed a smile. Put mildly, it was the ugliest smile I've ever seen. He was missing his front teeth, making his straggly mustache stand out even more. He had a cut on his cheek that opened every time he flexed a specific muscle. You could watch his food slowly break down through it while he ate. "A little x-ray of sorts", some called it. He sprang onto the table in front of me. It let out a moan and he hopped off. Pouting, he sat in the chair he had avoided before, the reason being he was a foot shorter than I when sitting in a chair of the same height. It wasn't only because he almost had the privilege of being referred to as a midget; it was also because, for a fourteen year-old, I was abnormal, standing at six foot two and a half. Whenever I was in his "esteemed" presence, I was made to either sit down or crouch. I preferred the first.

"Well, Angela, what brings you here?"

He enjoyed calling me girl names and called me a different one each time we saw each other. I was touched at how much effort he put into this abusive hobby of his, never a repeat.

"Well sir, I kinda wanted to know more about you," I said in a I-have-no-hope-you-will-actually-take-me-up-on-this-suggestion-but-I-might-as-well-try tone. Maybe it was the booze or maybe it was the well-done execution of his unique ability, but he responded,

"Well, of course!" Running his stubby fingers over the craters in his face, craters that he tracked and named, he said, "My exciting life began on a cold winter night . . ."

*   *   *

Her right earlobe was missing. It was shaped like a horseshoe and she kept it in a vial, hoping one day she could afford to pay for the surgery to sew it back on. For now, she had a habit of doing a hair flip too often and too violently in order to hide her unique deformity. She had varicose veins which everyone, excluding herself, seemed to notice, yet were too embarrassed to point out to her, and mercury fillings in nearly all her teeth. She was obese in the abdominal region compared to the rest of her rag-doll body, so her pregnancy went mainly unnoticed. It would've proceeded as such until her unexpected outburst at work: a bizarre-sounding vomiting. If it hadn't been for the circumstances, half of the room would've applauded her and inquire how she made those inhuman noises, while the other half would envy or begin retching themselves. Crandy Culler, the one-armed, one-eyed Evangelical and owner of the sweat-shop flinched so wildly that the phone he had perched in between his shoulder and lopsided head slipped out. He had been on the phone with his wife, who was having a "secret" affair with the Turkish pool boy. It was only secret to Crandy, but everyone was so disappointed with the unoriginality on the wife's part that no one bothered to tell him. Presently he was on his way to ruin someone's already dismal life by firing the person who caused him to lose the line with his wife. He surveyed the musty shop that had brought him his fortune with a look of pride over what he had created. The only person left in the room was that girl with the freakish ear. Somehow he recognized her, even though she was covered in sweat and what looked to be vomit. When she saw him she started laughing. Her ability to laugh in these situations was the only unique quality this otherwise dull girl possessed. She continued to laugh as she was thrown out of the shop. It took two of his best men to do it, as she was pretty far into the pregnancy but Crandy wanted her to be thrown out and he always got what he wanted. She continued to laugh as she burst through the door to her 4'x4' apartment. Only when she settled down in her bed did she start to cry. Nothing really changed except for the tears running down her unremarkable face. The first tears with the adventurous ones, cutting the path that the later tears would soon follow. She went to sleep curled in a ball. Two hours later her water broke. The shoes she had since she was eight pattered briskly against the pavement in a rhythm that was roughly that of her favorite song, the Star Spangled Banner. It was also the only song she knew. When she arrived at the hospital, she passed out. She awoke to the face of a deformed baby staring at her, and her heart stopped trying. Angelina Pelco died two hours after childbirth, due to unknown complications.

*   *   *

"Then I crawled to this shack and lived here the rest of my 83 years in peace."

"Really?"

"No, actually everything I just told you was complete bullshit from my stinking drunk mind".

"Oh."

I sat, thinking about what I was just told and finally came to a conclusion. "So you're trying to teach me a lesson? That one should always be skeptical?" I asked. My hands were clasped in hope.

"No. Not at all."

But he was. I was sure of it. *He was so wise.* His breath floated in my face, making it hard for me to see. It was toxic, a mixture of alcohol and burnt rubber permeated through my pores. As I pondered this odor escaping his chapped lips, this story I had just been told, and this profound lesson he had entrusted me with, he stood and entered the shack without saying a word.

*   *   *

Two weeks passed until I was on that faded white porch again. I'd had much time to think about his life story and all the lessons that were hidden behind the words, all the themes and messages he had imbued them with. What was the significance of the missing earlobe? Was it symbolic of Angelina's lack of listening skills? Why was the Star Spangled Banner the only song she knew? Was it an attempt at irony because of the lack of rights women had in the U.S? I had so many questions for him. I had decided to ask him to mentor me. To impart to me all the wisdom he had acquired over his years on this earth. He was such a Buddha, albeit one with a few hairs and a taste for illegal substances.

A noise like that of a footstep, but subtler, broke my concentration. He was crawling up the stairs again. I helped him up and, noticing a black matter on his lips, wiped his mouth with the back of my hand. *I would do that and much more for him.*

"Thank you Kayla." His voice was raspier than normal.

"No problem, anything for you, sir. Is everything okay?"

"Yes, everything is okay. Why are you here?" His tone only communicated one word now, and the word was tired, tired, and of course, drunk.

"Well," I cleared my throat, "Sir I was wondering if you could maybe give me some lessons on life, some more like that story you told me the other day. That left me thinking for quite long—powerful stuff."

"What story?"

"Well, the one that wasn't true."

"All of mine aren't true except for the ones that are."

"The one you told *me* that wasn't true."

"I can't remember. I was probably in an altered state of mind and, to tell you the truth, you aren't very important to me."

"It's okay sir. So will you teach me?"

"What do you want to know?"

I didn't know what I had expected. "I don't know tell me about what's important in life".

"Well, Michele, obviously money is the only important thing in life. I mean, look at my house, my clothes, my face." I had always thought that money was not important at all but since he said it, it must be true.

"I learned this lesson many years ago on a cold winter night . . ."

*   *   *

Her thin hair grew unevenly, leaving several holes through which one could see her pale scalp. Her eyebrows were nonexistent but she did have a considerable mustache. Her teeth were brown and her nose broken. She was wanted for several crimes in several states. She was perfect. Everywhere she went, that "weird kid with the missing front teeth" followed. When she robbed the liquor/toy store, *he* was standing outside. The owner and entrepreneur Andre Ford, who ingeniously sold toys and liquor in the same store so alcoholic parents could get themselves and their kids forms of entertainment in one stop, asked the kid to help him. He did not, instead choosing to follow his love wherever she went. Finally one day, she confronted him. "Why are you following me?" Her tongue seemed to be too big for her mouth.

"I love you," he said.

"Kid, don't you know that love doesn't matter? The only thing that matters is money. Now let me go get some and leave me alone"

He stood, frozen to that spot. Perhaps it was the cold, perhaps it was the tearing of his heart in two. Probably a mixture of these factors. Steam rose from the two streams of salt water on his cheeks.

Finally, after she had been long gone, he stirred. He walked to the police station. The face of his love was on wanted posters throughout the building, and under it, although he could not read, he noticed a long line of numbers. He told the nice officer everything he knew about her and in exchange he was rewarded the only thing that matters. Angelina Pelco was arrested days later.

*   *   *

"She taught me that and I thank her for it everyday."

I thought about what he had just told me and responded, "You used the same name for the last story."

"Oh, I used the first name that came to my head." He coughed into his shirt. When he lifted his head, it was stained red.

"So you just made that up again? You are so deep sir." I paused, shifting my attention to the stain. "Is that blood?"

"Yeah. Yeah." He seemed completely unworried. "I'm sick, Katie." Another name, he was so thoughtful. But he had called me this before. Something was definitely wrong. When I lifted my head to point this out, the only thing I saw was the glint of the sun bouncing off his beautiful bald head as he entered the shack.

*   *   *

He had left me with so much to think about. I loved hearing his stories, learning from his mistakes, embracing his philosophy. Why aren't more people taking advantage of this great thinker: this Friedrich Nietzche, this Søren Kierkegaard?

I had to see him again. I stumbled onto his faded white porch in a hurry and this time he was there already and, from what it looked like, sober. He did look worse however. His cheeks were gaunt, his "x-ray" not as noticeable. His mustache was stragglier and his head balder. I knew how much he loved his beer, so I brought him a six-pack of Pabst.

"I brought you this sir. I know how much you love it," I said, handing him the pack.

"I can't even drink anymore, Riley," he said with tears in his eyes. I cried with him. He told me to stop, that it was girly. I did as I was told. *He was always right.*

"This will probably be my last day. Write a book about my death, make some of that important green stuff. Try to glorify me and dramatize the events." I would do as I was told. I was just needing one more lesson, one more story. I asked him for one.

"Listen son, being sober and all, I can actually tell you a true lesson for once. This is the only one you should actually take heed of: don't ask others for the answer to life. Develop your own philosophy, your own ethics. Make your own stories. Live your own life, don't live it through others'. Screw those self-help books. I learned from my mistakes and I don't regret a single one," he said this all in one breath. He didn't take another.

I left him on that chair that day.

What a downer. I was expecting a better lesson. I wanted him to tell me what to do. I won't include that in the book. Time to find another old guy. So it goes.

Leaflicker and the Beetle

By Yatish Parmar

———∿∾◦⊙⌦⊙◦∾∿———

The radiant sunlight pierced the dense canopy to entice me into waking up. At that point, I noticed my peers watching me. Why were they staring at me? Had I done something wrong? Was I not like the others? Like the other newly germinated plants, I was healthy, but I felt different for some reason. The older plants viewed me with awe and fear. The eldest plant in our field asked me, "Where are your parents?" but I could not answer, for I had just been born. I decided to play with the other seedlings while the adults talked.

I, like the others, had the privilege of naming myself and asked the others what they were going to call themselves. I soon picked my name and exclaimed it: "I am Leaflicker." One of the seedlings had already marked his territory in the soft, moist patch of earth, and named himself Feeder. Soon all of the seedlings had announced their names to each other while I simply looked around, amazed at this new world I had entered.

For months, I had been stuck in the uncomfortable trappings of a pod and when I felt the sun beating on my seed shell, I started growing and soon broke free to stand tall. I noticed the world: saw the adults reaching for the sky and stealing the comfortable beams of heat. I could feel my roots absorbing the trickling water underneath and hear the annoying parrots, with their arrogant, multicolored feathers, just waiting to forage the seeds we noble plants shot out. I could smell the refreshing odors of the ground and finally saw the lush blooms of the mighty pineapple trees that loomed above us all.

The leader of the little clan of ficuses stretched down to confer with us and with his ruffling leaf blades under control, he told me bluntly, "Little one, you are not like the rest of us. We fear you may harm some of us when you mature. So we are going to tell everyone to stay away from you for everyone's benefit."

What? How was I going to hurt the oldest plants with my soft leaves and bendy stem? What was he talking about? With that, I turned away and my would-be friends left me on the edge of our growing patch. If only I could move, then I would be able to leave behind these beings that had shunned me. My leaves fell, as did my hopes.

But the biggest question I had was, "Why was I different enough to deserve to be alone?" I looked at my brothers and sisters and examined them closely. They were not different from each other. They all had pairs of leaves alternating on a central stem. How could they all unilaterally disown me when we were all born equal? I examined the elders and they dared not look at me, so I looked away and saw the birds flying and the monkeys bellowing. I felt a sudden pang of emptiness and concluded that I needed to eat. So, I shuffled as best as I could to enter the light with a shock.

As a pregnant cloud released its light, I indeed felt warmth and some comfort, but did not feel that hollowness subside. I could sense the empty feeling get worse, not better, and panicked. Was I doing something wrong? Was this why I was isolated? Was there a special method to eat the light as the other ficuses were doing? I saw them, stomaching the greatest possible amount of light as their leaves unruffled fully, basking in the bright nourishment.

I could not believe the elders. Did they shun me because I was flawed? I wasn't worthy of rights because I could not eat properly? An insect flew over our heads. As I was mentally screaming, I experienced a strange, scary encounter. It was like the top of my form was splitting in half and I was exposing my insides. Was I dying? Was this a cruel joke? Was I going to die with my dignity lost? But still I only felt that hollow and hungry feeling. The insect, a fly, landed on top of one of my exposed halves and I felt this excited feeling come over me. My exposed halves closed once again and liquids caused the fly to slip into my insides. This whole encounter ended with me nearly having a coronary.

What abomination am I? First I'm cut open, and then I eat something other than sunlight? I gazed at the other ficuses but they took no note of the incident since they still isolated me. I felt a shaking feeling and became even more scared when I realized that this fly was attempting to escape my body. And now a new feeling was overcoming me. I couldn't put a leaf on it until the shaking stopped: swooping glee. My leaves unfurled with swollen pride at this monstrous deed. I liked the fact that I had just eaten a fly.

But what was I? How could a plant eat meat? Plants never could possibly eat the flesh of an animal. I felt and now acted like a freak. So this was why they had shunned me. This was why they felt the need to throw me out of their lives and toss me aside like I wasn't worthy enough. I looked at Feeder's leaf blades swaying in the breeze and realized that they were all afraid that I would eat them too.

I felt like a monster. My eating of that fly felt delicious, but I had just killed something and ended its life. I was a plant, not a measly bird or monkey. I supplied life; I didn't take it. What sort of plant physically eats another creature? Was I cursed in some way to be like this? I tried to ignore the harsh sounds of the monkeys chattering as I looked down, defeated, at my leaves and they were shiny enough to see the beak-like structure that allowed me to consume the defenseless fly. I looked up to ask the elder plants what I could do but they would simply look at me, horrified. I turned away and stared at the crumbly earth for good measure.

*   *   *

It was torture. I needed absolution. My family was literally two feet away and I could confide nothing in them. I was a freak.

"Hey Feeder!" I called out, hoping to possibly earn some attention and make friends. He looked at me then quickly turned away, immersing himself in rapid conversation with the other seedlings pretending to not hear me.

As the ball of light above dipped out of sight, I immediately became heavy. My leaves drooped and my entire form sunk slightly. I winked out of consciousness.

*　　*　　*

BAM! A hard nut hit me over my little feelers. I groaned and remembered what had happened and tried to go back to sleep to leave this hateful world behind.

BOOM! Another nut nearly knocked me over and I sighted my attacker, one of the most feared predators of plant life. I had heard voices in seedhood about this beast and the way it could physically rip apart a plant and cause it to die a horrible, and even worse, a dry, death. With a squeal of deathly terror, it approached and I saw him: the deadly lemur.

He was terrifying: his fierce black eyes, intimidating striped tail, and jaws able to tear apart bark. I had heard stories; they would many a time bring down a whole banyan and use its bark to color their fur and to coat their black skin that reminded everyone of their true nature. He stealthily advanced, instilling fear in every plant, insect, and probably even the nuts in the vicinity.

I quickly folded my leaves in and hoped he wouldn't see me. He approached and dug his little claws into the earth, searching for seeds. The others simply cowered and tried to make themselves as small as possible. He sniffed me, smelled the meat from the fly, and moved on to the others. I nearly wanted to stop living. Again. The ferocious lemur ripped out my peers, my fellow seedlings. Leaves and stems went flying as the crazed animal searched for seeds.

I witnessed the massacre of our little colony as the lemur swiftly transformed the entire community into shambles. I saw Feeder's little roots disperse in the air and saw the older plants get thrown aside like common ferns or weeds. The monkeys' shrill cries still pierced the air and I sadly looked around at the desecration that this lemur was causing, yet I was powerless.

And as quickly as he had come, he left.

I stared at the spot where he had liberated his bowels and could not let myself believe that my freakiness had saved me. Was I that horrendous that even a lemur could not face me? I stared down and immediately stared up at the sky because on the ground there was a leaf from good old Feeder. Poor guy. I kept staring at the sky, wishing for all of this to go away because surely, no one could suffer this much.

*   *   *

I stared at the light ball, watching it move until my leaves got tired, and mustered the strength to look down. Aghast, I noticed a Hercules beetle on the ground, munching into a leaf with lobster-like behemoths of pincers.

"Hey, bud, what are you lookin' at? Can't a guy eat his brunch in some peace?"

"What's wrong with you? That's my friend you're mutilating!"

"He didn't seem like a good one," he said as he took another painful bite. "What do you say? I stick around for a bit to make up for this mess and you tell me about your former friend."

"Fine." I had nothing better to do.

"So what's wrong?" he asked as he continued to devour the leftovers of my other friends.

"Well, I'm not like the other plants. I eat bugs."

At this, the beetle fell over. I didn't know if it was from eating a tough part of the leaf or from what I said.

"Well, to each his own, right?"

"What? You're not going to run away and hope I don't eat you?"

"You, sonny? Of course not. If I stay down here, then you can't hurt me. And a slight breeze could knock you over; you're too soft."

"I am not! Wait 'til you see! When another fly comes around, I'll show you!"

"Get rid of the flies. They keep me up at night."

This beetle had long since finished the leaf. Was he trying to eat me too? When would this stop?

"Why are you here?"

"I don't know, it's interesting talking to a Venus Flytrap. Not too many of those around."

"A what?"

"Venus Flytrap. You are a carnivorous plant. You eat bugs. That's why I'm not going to climb you, or else you'll kill me. Imagine how angry my wife would be then."

"So what do I do? Do I keep living like no one cares about me?"

"What are you talking about, kid? You're different, so accept it. You're not crazy. I'm a talking beetle. You don't see too many of those around. Listen to me; you are not like other plants. You like flesh, but the most important act is not what you have, but how you can better things around you. I bring home bundles of leaves and dried fly wings to sleep on for my family. That's what my father told me and now I'm talking to one of the most dangerous creatures on earth for bugs, and I'm not even hurt. Am I crazy?"

I watched him and he gave me a backwards glance as he approached a root. With a munch, he continued.

"Don' think that I'm no' scared of you kid. Sure you got the mouth for eating my folk, but something tells me you won't."

"How do you know? I just ate a fly."

"So what? You don't think parrots don't eat small bugs or seeds? Well, who cares about them? They're evil. My point is that each of us has a role in society and this ecosystem. That golden tamarind up there, Barusha, he yells all day hoping for someone to listen. Yet he eats fruit. Should he be punished because he ate what you people produce? It's his need. He has a right to life, don't you agree?"

The bold tamarind happened to catch my eye and threw a rotten fruit at the vicious lemur, which sped back into the depths of the forest. I laughed and the beetle rolled over in pure shock.

"What was that for? I'm telling you that you have a purpose and you think this is funny? Trust me, boy, I'd rather be hunting for better leaves, but I'm stuck here mentoring a plant."

I stared up again, noticing all of the shrill cries of the tamarinds and howlers. I felt my double-flapped lips open and they relaxed because now it seemed real that I could be a part of this world and change it positively.

Elated, I asked the beetle his name and annoyed, he replied, "Names aren't important. Actions are. Go do something." And with that, he left, searching for more of my friends to exhume.

Jumper

By Alex Libre

—⁓∘⦿⟋⟍∘⟋⟍∘⁓—

Staring over the ledge into the water, I feel alive. With my toes hanging over the rock and nothing but shorts on, I raise both my hands as if to ask a question. How far will I fall this time? No one replies. From this view of northern California, it isn't so bad. The warm air tickles my underarms, so I propel them downward and lunge.

I hit the water with a surprisingly bold feeling of accomplishment. All my life I was told I was inadequate, that I wouldn't be able to compete with other boys my age. But, hell, I was tall, strong, and coordinated. Today, I proved myself. Today, I jumped.

"That was a nice flight, Blake. I'll videotape it for you next time," shouts someone on shore. I hear the rest of them snicker. I'm not an idiot. I feel stronger than any one of them, yet their words penetrate me like the water I split moments ago. The waves guide me to the shore, where I find my towel and dark sunglasses. They protect me from more than the sun. They protect me from people who don't understand and people who don't feel. These people jump from cliffs every week. But, I'm glad they jump with their eyes open, planning each run-up step before they leap. To them, cliff jumping is a sport; it is a competition in which they know exactly how high the ledge is before they free-fall.

To me, it is an escape. When gravity and I are alone, nothing else matters. The world I leave behind disappears. And still, I jump with my eyes closed. Inching towards the edge until I find where rock meets air, I have an entirely different challenge. All I can do is lean forward and hold my breath. Opening my eyes wouldn't help much anyways.

No. For a blind kid, cliff jumping is definitely not a sport.

*   *   *

"Hey."

"Hey, Blake. How was school?"

"I didn't go."

"Jesus, you know you won't graduate—"

"I jumped off Hoyt's Ledge."

"Hoyt's Ledge? That's eighty feet! You could have killed yourself trying to fit in."

"It's more than fitting in, Mom. I proved myself."

"To who? The kids that made fun of you since we moved here? There are some things you just don't realize, Blake."

"No, you don't realize something. I don't need to be a part of their group or a part of any group. I just need to be remembered. Adults like you grow up and forget that, but if people don't remember you when you die, your life meant nothing."

Shaking her head, she clicks her tongue as she walks upstairs.

I knew she wouldn't understand. She never understands. But I still tell her about my first real jump because it is the best news I have to tell in months. I sit in my room and look out the window. I try to imagine what it looks like to everyone else, because I see something, too. Some people think that blind people can't see. Wrong, I see. I see with my mind, conjuring images from what I've heard and smelled and felt and believed. Sometimes, I think that what I see is what's actually out there. Maybe everyone else is blind.

But this thought is too revolutionary, and most people never give it a chance. They overlook me, saying I'm just an idiot, a blind outcast who fails his classes, stays inside, and only goes out to jump. But now that some of the kids at school respect me, I plan on telling them about my idea. Maybe, someday, they will see like me.

At school the next day, I hear some kids talking about another cliff they plan to hit that day. I listen from a distance, only long enough to know how to get there. At 2:15, I walk to the trailhead, using my embarrassing, white cane. I climb to the top and realize

I'm not alone. Luckily, none of them have jumped yet. I can hear them moving back and forth, as if knowing the exact height of the drop would make it safer.

"Looks like ninety to me."

"No way. Has to be over a hundred."

Instead of fearing the height and peering over the edge like the others, I take the chance to beat them. I tied them at Hoyt's Ledge, because everyone's jumped there. But today I will be the only one to jump. I throw off my shirt, but leave the shoes. I will break my feet if I don't. This time, they walk me to the edge out of respect. I take three steps back, then three steps forward, and I fly. It feels like I fall forever, but the thrill is worth anything. By the time I swim back to the surface and take a breath, I'm greeted with ubiquitous applause. I just jumped one hundred feet. And best of all, I'm respected for it.

The next day in school, one of the kids that led me to the edge pulls me over in the hallway to talk. He tells me that what I did "impressed" him, and that he wants to see more. His name is Derek, and I know this already, but he does not yet know me.

"Blake. The blind kid that you used to call an idiot."

He apologizes. He tells me that he didn't know that someone like me could jump. For once, I understand someone else, and as it releases something within me, I feel good. I have a friend now, and his name is Derek.

Later that night, he calls me. He says that he and some of his buddies are thinking about jumping off a bridge near Sacramento. He says he can drive if I read him the directions. We both laugh, but I take him up on the offer. That weekend, we head over to the spot. It is a breezy day and the metal of the bridge feels cold, contrasting the rock I usually stand on. They chant my name as I step up onto the ledge and hold onto a pole nearby for balance. Derek brings almost twenty people to watch me this time, and I feel proud. No one else has hit this ledge before, but it doesn't matter to me. I let go of the cold metal bar and lunge forward, feeling a rush of life fill my body. This time, when I return to the earth after my short stay underwater, I'm greeted with cheers.

"Blake, Blake, Blake!" they shout. I dry off to find that Derek drove home without me. Someone else tells me that he was angry that I jumped something higher than he has. I forget about it, still absorbed in the glory of my accomplishment, but Derek doesn't talk to me for weeks.

When he finally does, I have jumped off more cliffs than anyone else at my high school, including him. I am, in all honesty, a celebrity. "The blind cliff diver," as they refer to me. But, still, I pick up the phone for my friend.

"Hello?"

"Hey, Blake, I wanted to let you in on a trip I plan to take soon. You've heard of The Ridge?"

"Yeah."

"It's 180 feet down, and there's a guy who just did it without any injuries. What do you say you and I take a look at it?"

I think for a minute about the pros and cons of the jump. If I reject this offer, I throw away my reputation as the daring kid I am. But what's the worst that could happen? I break a wrist, an ankle? Hell, even if I died on impact, I'd be remembered. I once read that it's important in life, not necessarily to be strong, but to feel strong, and to measure yourself at least once. Jumping The Ridge, regardless of the outcome, would be a true measure of my strength. As The Blind Cliff Diver, I accept.

"Count me in."

*　　*　　*

It is a perfect evening. No wind, but warm enough to feel comfortable. The drive takes well over an hour, so I sleep on the way here. Feeling fully rested, I open the door and step out at our destination. Something feels weird.

I touch the ground beneath me, and it's soft dirt as I expected. I feel two thick pine trees on either side of me; perfectly normal for the sylvan district we are in. My shoes are tied tightly, my favorite shorts hang from my waist, and I am brave. Still, something is wrong. Suddenly, I hear the sound of a truck's horn. I hear no cars or movement of any kind around me. The ground I stand on is not fit for traffic. This is not The Ridge I know, The Ridge I've heard so many stories about, The Ridge over water. The truck's horn must have come from below, and I know cars do not drive on water. I realize that the ledge Derek takes me to is over solid land.

Suddenly, I get the urge to punch him in the face. I am stronger now than I ever was before and am stronger than this liar for sure. I step down off the ledge and pretend to whisper something to him, then grab him by the hair and connect my knee to his temple. Something releases within me and it feels good. Derek tried to kill me over something as mundane as jealousy. Some people just don't see like I do.

With no sounds from Derek for five minutes, I release my grip on his chest. He is unconscious, but still breathing, so I leave him and walk along the trail. The grooves of the handrail are soothing. With each indentation equally as deep as the next, they hum monotonously as I slide my hand along the surface. The soft noise relaxes me and I think as I walk: I may not be able to see what happens in the present. I may not be able to see memories of the past. But I'm able to see the truth in every situation; in this way, everyone else is blind.

I come to the conclusion that there's a reason that Derek brought me here. After all, I have never backed out of a jump. This is the ultimate test. A jumper shouldn't always know how far he will fall. If I always thought before I leaped, I would have backed out of half the cliffs I hit before. I am blind, and that itself attests to my bravery. But some people don't understand. Some people don't see the way I see.

At least they will remember me. They will remember this.

What I do in the next sixty seconds will go down in the newspapers as a suicide and in my family as a tragedy. It is neither. I am a jumper, and I always will be. This is just another cliff, just another obstacle. If I die in sixty years, people will forget that. People will forget what I see. People will forget Hoyt's Ledge. People will forget me. But if I die in sixty seconds, I will die as the bravest blind cliff jumper that ever lived. People will remember what the blind boy saw.

I step up onto the railing, built to prevent this very act, and feel for the evergreen next to me. When I get my balance, I raise both hands in the air, as if to say goodbye. No one replies. I open my eyes and look around. I see a world of people who misunderstand, people who ignored me until I was something special. Before I was a jumper, I was nothing.

I stand one hundred and eighty feet above the ground, preparing for the plunge of my life, and my mind is caught up on a thought most blind people never have: it's a damn nice view from up here.

No, this is not suicide. This is the measure of my inner strength. I lean forward, and let go. In the calmest voice I can muster, I leave my last words to echo between the cliffs of northern California for eternity.

"I'm not an idiot."

Nothing but a Bet

By Hayley Gola

"That's it, the last box," she says as she puts down the packing tape. She had just finished packing up the remains of her dorm room. It had been a week since she graduated, and she had finally snagged down a place to live after senior year. She would be moving in with her boyfriend, Zach, whom she had know since before she was born. Their mothers met in the hospital. They were roommates after they had Sophie and Zach. They had been dating for a little over a year, something that everyone knew was going to happen.

"Finally! Now, lets put it in the car and bring you over to the apartment." He smiled and grabbed the last box, shaking out his shaggy brown hair as he walked to the door. Sophie sighed and looked around the room, the memories filling her brain. Memories of late-night study sessions and all day movie marathons with the roommates were all fun. Now, reality was sinking in. She needed a job.

*   *   *

"Nothing. Absolutely nothing," she says and she shuts off the laptop. There were no jobs out there. Not for a fashion designer. Yes, the economy was in the tank right now, but there needed to be something out there. People needed clothes!

"As much as I would love to help you, I must get to work," Zach says. Zach was in a new up-and-coming band called "Winning".

"Fine, go. Go be a big rock star; and leave your best friend here with no hope and no job," she says, knowing the guilt would get to him.

He walks over and puts his head on hers and his arms around her from behind. "Soph, stop it. You are an amazing designer and you are going to find a job." She sighs and reopens her laptop.

"I know, I know. You should get going. I'll pick up dinner," she says. He gives her shoulders a rub and heads out.

Three hours later, Zach returns with a big smile on his face.

"What's up with you? Get an implant of ego?" she says, shutting her computer off. Six applications, and one Frappucino later, she was exhausted.

"Nope, even better. I got you a job," he said, sitting down across from her. She looks up at him, confused. Did he just say what she thought he said?

"You got me job? Are you serious?" she says, standing up and walking over to him.

"Yes, I got you a job. An old friend of mine needed a designer and I knew you would be perfect for the job."

Sophie's smile drops. An old friend? That could never be good. Zach didn't have the prettiest of pasts. In college, he got in with the wrong crowd and started up a lovely gambling habit. It took two therapists and lots of tears before he was able to break the addiction. But why was he in touch with an old friend? She thought he hadn't talked to any of his gambling friends in months.

"Old friend? Why are you talking to an old friend? Are you gambling again?" she spits, paranoia slowly taking over.

Zach stands and holds her arms. "I'm not gambling anymore, Soph. I would never think of doing that again. He contacted me because he knew what you did and needed someone. I swear".

Soph cocks her head and stares at him. "You better not be lying to me, Zach." He kisses her forehead, trying to reassure her. She shrugs off his arms and turns back to go to the kitchen.

"Fine. Dinner is in the living room," she says, grabbing plates and forks. She joins him as he sits down on the couch, Chinese food carton in hand. They eat and watch TV, eventually falling asleep on each other on the couch.

*   *   *

It had been a few months since Sophie started the job with Zach's old friend Brian Atwood. She was hired to design clothes for one of his many magazines.

It was late and Sophie was up working on a new outfit for a photo shoot that Brian was having. It would be a royal blue evening gown for the fashion section of that month's issue.

A ring in the distance snaps her out of her trance and she looks around for the source of the noise. She drops her colored pencil and looks around, eventually finding the source of the noise. It was a phone she had never seen before. It wasn't Zach's, he would've told her if he had gotten a new phone, and she could clearly see his Blackberry sitting on the table next to his sleeping body.

The phone stops ringing and then beeps once more. "One new voicemail!" the screen reads. Sophie takes the phone and sneaks into the bathroom, shutting the door and immediately calling the voice mail.

"Zach, it's Brian. Really like your girl. She is definitely the right choice for this company. We must have bets more often. Ta ta!" the voice on the other line says, then nothing.

Sophie stares at the phone, her mind blank. So her paranoia was right, he was gambling again. He even brought her into it this time! She couldn't believe he had lied to her, her of all people. Her heart beat fast as her mind raced. Why? How? When? All of these questions ran around in her mind like tiny mice, nipping at her brain.

*   *   *

The sun rises slowly and so does Zach, he doesn't get out of bed until 10 am. She, on the other hand, didn't sleep at all. Her determination to finish her design and to bust Zach had her going all night.

"Morning. Looks like you were up all night," he says, rubbing his eye and giving a kiss on the head. She has no time for his flirtations. She means business.

"Morning. Looks like you had a good sleep. You even missed a phone call," she said, and she took out the secret phone from her pocket. All he could do was stare at it, as if he had laser vision and was trying to blow the phone up.

"Where did you get that?" he asked, his voice slightly stammering.

"Heard it ring this morning. Thought I would never find out? Too bad," she said, standing up, but keeping a distance between them.

"I don't know what you're talking about," he said, standing perfectly still. He thought he was going to get off so easily. He needed to think again.

"My job was nothing more than a bet to you. I can't believe you would do that. I can't believe you would lie to me about it! I thought you were over this! I thought that we had worked this out. I thought—" she stopped herself from rambling. Angry tears stung the corners of her eyes, making her eyes red and joining the dark circles that appeared from last night.

Zach grabs her shoulders, brown eyes meeting brown eyes. He has his puppy dog look on, something he had perfected over the years. She wasn't going to take it, wasn't going to let it wash over her and push out the anger she held.

"Stop it, they aren't going to help you this time. What the hell possessed you into thinking that this was a good idea? Are you insane?" she said.

"You were upset. I wanted you to be happy again, to have a job. I knew he owned a magazine. We played a little and then talked," he said, trying to meet her eyes again,

"So, I guess that means you think I can't get a job on my own then, right?" she says, snatching her arms away from his hands and starting to walk away.

Zach takes her hand before she can make it too far. He pulls her back to him and his nostrils huff. "I never thought that. Sophie you are the greatest designer I have ever seen. You look at a color and can create an outfit from that. You were going nowhere and I needed to help you. I couldn't leave you helpless, just staring at the computer," he says.

She sighs, not knowing what to say. Her eyes stared right back at his, her hands lying limply at her sides.

"Just . . . . don't do it again. I want to get this job fair and square. The bet is off," she says, her finger poking him in his chest. He smirks and lets her go.

"Perfectly fine. I will call Brian right away," he says. She doesn't move, only stares at him, making him more nervous.

"You got lucky this time," she says. "This happens again, and I'm out of here." He only swallows and looks at her.

"Never," he says. She actually wanted to believe him, wanted to believe that this was just a slip up, a lapse in judgment. Problem was.

And he didn't. She was proved wrong.

By Gina Groseclose

Tuesday has always been my favorite day. It really has no significance, but in my town, it only seems to rain on that day.

"Stop staring out that window and do your work, Luke. It's only rain," my teacher called.

"Sorry, Ms. Bray," I replied.

English was always my worst subject. Having to share my feelings, or put myself into a story for all to see, has troubled me since I was around eleven. Teachers always give me a hard time about it.

Ms. Bray was the worst when it came to teachers. Not that she was a bad teacher, but she was the kind that wanted to know her students and personally connect with them. She always told me I could tell her my secrets, like I had something to hide, or she had an obligation to me. I didn't want her to know those secrets, and I couldn't stand that Ms. Bray thought she knew everything about me. Worst of all, the things she didn't know, she filled in herself, kind of like a mad lib titled: *Luke's Life.*

"Luke, come here," said Ms. Bray.

I peeked up from my paper, hoping I had only imagined her voice, but as I looked up, she smiled and nodded at me. Lowering my head, I walked to the front of the room.

"Luke, I wanted to talk to you about your writing. You're great in class when it comes to discussion, but I just wish you could put those ideas down on paper."

"I just don't really like the idea of writing, Ms Bray. It makes me nervous when people read what I have to say. It's . . . it's different."

"Hmm . . . well, I think you have so much potential to be truly good, so I am giving you a head-start on this assignment. I'd like you to write about someone you would like to spend a day with, if you had the chance. Be sure to include details about why you chose this person and what you would do. Alright, Luke?"

"I guess so. I'll try."

I walked back to my desk, gathered my things, and moved to a desk right next to the window. Until the bell rang I stared at my reflection on the glass as the rain passed through it. Who would I write about, I thought, and why was Ms Bray being so nice to me?

For some reason, this Tuesday seemed to drag on forever. Sitting in class, I could almost hear every tick of every second as the clock teased me. This paper was such a simple assignment, yet I couldn't figure out why it was still in my mind. Finally, the last bell rang.

As I waited for my sister, I decided to sit in my car in the school parking lot so I could listen to the rain pound on the roof. It reminded me of spilling candies, like skittles, all over the floor, but I found it to be relaxing. My eyes closed naturally and I tried to fill my mind with different thoughts, like the car I was sitting in: a dark green, 1999 Jeep Cherokee with a dark gray interior. It was my mom's. Everything had stayed the same. From the air fresheners my mom left, tucked between the cushions because she thought they were ugly, to a hairbrush in the glove compartment, I wanted everything to stay the same.

Dut Dut. Carrie was knocking on the window.

"Open the door, Luke. What are you doing?" she screamed through the window.

"Sorry."

I shifted my car into reverse and left my sport without glancing over my shoulder. The rain had completely distracted me. My sister began babbling about the day's gossip more than usual, but my mind was clear.

"Luke . . . Luke . . . Hello! What's wrong with you?" she said as she cut her stories short.

"What are you talking about? Nothing's wrong."

"Yes, there is. Literally every Tuesday you change and I don't get it. If you don't want to hear me talk, you can just tell me, but this silence thing really sucks."

"It's," I took a deep breath, "It's nothing."

"Tell me."

"Carrie, you wouldn't understand. When are you going to grow up and just let things go?"

She spun her head quickly toward the window and struggled to swallow, her body shifting with the car from not wearing her seatbelt. I knew I upset her. At the next light, I took a left turn and took the long way home.

"It's the rain, Carrie."

"You're such a liar, there's no way it's that. I don't even want to know anymore."

"Fine. But when you change your mind, you know where to find me."

Carrie had the door open, ready to jump out, before I put the car in park. I sat in the driveway, turning off my music and lights, and listened to the candies click on the roof. I knew who I wanted to spend a day with.

*   *   *

For the next two Tuesdays until the paper was due, I wrote only as it rained. It brought back the most memories for me, and made it easy for me to share my thoughts with the paper. By this third Tuesday, I was stuck, back to where I was when Ms. Bray first told me about the assignment. As the cursor tauntingly blinked at me, I found it harder and harder to focus while the rain slowed to barely a drizzle.

Carrie and I hadn't talked since the previous Tuesday when the same conversation came up. Only this time, she chose to throw in a few choice words. I wanted her to know I was serious. I wanted her to know what happened. And I wanted her to understand why the rain was so significant to me.

Our dad had changed, although he said he never would after the accident, and it changed my sister for the better. Before she was daddy's little girl who depended on him and my mom for everything, but now she's independent. Watching her grow and take advantage of everything has become my inspiration and helped me get through the years. Seeing her mad and confused because of me tore me up inside. The pain was almost as bad as the day our family was torn apart, and I couldn't handle the feeling.

I got up from my computer, put on a shirt and hat, and walked down the hall to her room. I tapped on her door lightly with the tips of my fingers so she would know I wasn't in an up-tight mood.

"Carrie, please open the door . . ."

She was strong, never let her emotions get in the way of each day. But I think that's what troubled her. Our dad could never comfort her or me and now she had a thick shell keeping us out. Carrie had spent a lot of time figuring things out on her own and so she kept to herself. I didn't want to accept that this was the way our relationship was going to be.

I hesitated to knock again. By the stuttered breathing, I could tell she had been crying. So, without waiting for an answer or knocking again, I opened the door.

"It's me. Don't cry, Carrie. I'm sorry. I don't want to fight with you. You're my baby sister, and I want to be able to be here for you."

"Luke, I just don't understand why everything is this way. I want to understand."

I sat next to her on her bed and hugged her. We sat for what felt like hours and talked about everything that had happened in the years passed, and when we were done, I kissed her on the forehead and said good night.

I walked to where my father sat up watching re-runs of the night's game on ESPN. His eyes were opened so wide and glassy he looked frozen there.

"Dad, you need to talk to Carrie. She misses you. We miss you and we want to be here for you, just as much as we want you here for us."

He didn't respond, just turned the volume up and went back to memories of before he had a family. I went back to my room, printed out my essay due the next day, and got under the covers.

The next morning, I was awake before my alarm clock, but pressed snooze anyway, just to keep up with my usual pattern. I put on my favorite baseball shirt from the *Mariners*, pulled on my corduroys, and grabbed my keys, almost leaving without Carrie. For the past few weeks she had refused to accept my rides, but now she was finally ready to forgive me.

I especially wanted to be on time today to share my essay on who I would like to spend my day with. I was actually happy to be able to share my thoughts with everyone.

"Good morning, Ms. Bray. How're you?"

"Morning, Luke. Are you ready for today? I'd like you to present first."

I smiled and sat down, not wanting to seem too eager. My leg shook in nervousness and excitement. I hoped everyone would take my presentation seriously.

"Alright, students. I hope everyone is prepared with their papers and ready to present," Ms. Bray addressed the class.

A hand in the middle of the room shot up before she could finish her sentence, "Ms. Bray, Ms. Bray! Can I go first?" The over achiever, Ingrid Hernson, insisted on sharing everything and always volunteering.

"Relax, Ingrid. Luke is going first today." Ms. Bray smiled at me, bigger than usual. "Luke, the floor is yours."

My body felt heavier than usual and my stomach seemed to twitch more and more as I got close to the front of the room, but I had made it.

"Okay. So I decided to choose my mom to spend a day with."

As soon as I finished my sentence Ingrid called out, "why would you pick your mom? I can't stand being around my mom."

She continued her rant about her mom, but I tuned out until she was done.

"My mother is dead." I replied.

Ingrid's face went pale. As she slinked down in her desk, everyone in the class glared at her and let out a sigh of relief that they hadn't asked, because I knew most of them wanted to.

"Luke, I'm sorry you have suffered such a huge loss," Ms. Bray said sweetly, "but we would love to hear all about her if you are still willing to share."

"Thank you, Ms. Bray. I chose to spend a day with my mother because I haven't seen her in six years."

I paused to breathe for a second because I had never shared anything about her before, and skipped around on my paper to find what I really wanted to share.

"I'd want to be with her on a Tuesday because she's the one who made me fall in love with that day. She gave me my love for the rain, and if anyone every noticed, it only rains on Tuesday in this stupid town. When I was young, she would tell me that the rain gave her peace, and calmed the earth itself. It washed away all the impurities man brought to it, and gave the earth a new start. Even though people would keep committing horrible acts or hurting the planet they lived on, the rain would always come and wash it all away, forgiving them. I think of her every day, but thoughts of her fill my mind every Tuesday. I stare out the window at the rain every time and see a little piece of her, falling to the ground, soaking into the earth, and blessing it."

I looked up at the ceiling and then quickly to the floor.

"That was very deep, Luke." Ms. Bray cut me off.

I got nervous and I thought she had stopped me because it wasn't what she wanted to hear, but I could see her fighting to keep in a tear. Besides, I didn't even care if anyone liked it or not. I loved it.

"Is there anything else you'd like to add, Luke?" Ms. Bray asked.

"Her name was Sunny, and she was as beautiful as the rain."

Sunny's Smile

By Susan Hatchman

—⁓⦿⦿⦿⁓—

Abelino

She looks so adorable, dressed in her Cinderella dress, twirling and dancing to the music that's blaring through the speakers on the streets. Even for seven years old, she looks like a real princess. And she is my princess. *Yeah, Princess Kristen is now leaving the Carnival.*

She looks like her mother had before she passed: a heart-shaped face with big eyes and a button nose. I can take credit for the onyx ringlets hanging past her shoulders and the way her face is so expressive. That's why I call her Sunny, always lighting the world with her smile. Even if she's upset, she smiles. She can't help it. I watch her graceful spins trying not to be the over-baring father always holding his kid's hand. Her mom warned me about that with her last words, but I can't help the fact that my heart lurches every time she balances on the curb and does her spins there.

"Daddy, look! A pink bear!" she calls out as she rushes to a nearby stall that the Carnival had set up, selling stuffed animals. There is a giant pink bear with red hearts all over it. I walk up behind Sunny, now jumping with excitement, and ask the vendor how much the bear is.

"This bear? Oh, yes, it's seven," he spoke with a heavy accent that I couldn't place. Maybe Italian? He was dressed in a dark velour sweat suit, and his dark hair was thinning. He took my ten and made the change.

"Thank you," I said, as he handed the bear over. I turned to Sunny, smiling from ear to ear.

"THANK YOU, THANK YOU, THANK YOU, THANK YOU! I love you *so* much! Thank you, Daddy!" She hugs the bear as if it's her best friend and claims to never let go of it, but she will in about ten minutes when she is too tired to continue to walk, and we go home.

It's late as we walk down the streets, but everywhere I look, there is pulsing life and laughter from the festivities. I look around to see cafes full of people along with the souvenir stores filled with tourists. A man working for the Carnival is handing out flyers and Sunny takes one because of its pretty colors. There was a guy standing in front of an ATM. He had a dark brown mustache and a duster coat on, looking up and back at the machine.

There are lights of all colors hanging from the street posts, and signs hanging everywhere. The roads are covered in confetti, streamers and trash. I see a lady with many bags carefully navigating around the mess so she won't slip.

That was how I met Sunny's mother, Jenna. We were both young and lost in the crowds of happy people. She had bought many gifts for her family and was struggling under the weight of them all. She slipped and fell, landing on all of the bags. I remember the embarrassed and hurt look she had on her face and I rushed over to help her.

"Are you okay?" She was startled by my voice and tried to wipe away the tears as she turned to me.

"Thanks, I'm fine. It's just that I think I broke some of the glass in my bags." And with that statement, I feel in love. I didn't know how she felt about a stranger, but I offered her a helping hand and, over time, she loved me. It was the happiest time of my life.

Two years later, we were man and wife. We moved here and were planning for a baby. Three months later, we got the news that she was pregnant. Everything was going great. She was healthy and I had a steady job that allowed me to miss work to go with her to the doctor appointments or stay home with her. It was not until the beginning of the third trimester that Jenna started to get sick. She lost weight, became weaker, and couldn't stay asleep for long. It wasn't a major concern until she started spotting. The doctors were worried about her and put her on bed-rest until she came to term.

Jenna was strong enough when she was in labor, she just didn't make it to see her baby girl.

I shake my head, reminding myself that that it was all seven years ago. There isn't a need for tears when there is Sunny around. I look down to tell her it's time to leave.

"Sunny, it-" my breath freezes in my throat. Where is she? She was just right next to me. I start to walk around, trying to keep calm and not cause a panic, all the while, the empty feeling in my heart festers. "Sunny," I call out, waiting for the answer that didn't come. "Sunny? Where are you?" Still no answer. I start to jog, pushing people out of my way, looking for the face I've seen for the past seven years.

"Sunny!" I shout, not caring anymore about the people around me. They were in the way. I needed to find her. "Kristen!" I felt the sting of tears as they threatened to fall down my face. I scan the faces of everyone—

There!

Spotting a flash of blue down the street, I sprint towards it, relief filling me. I was going to have to tell her not to wander off as I got closer.

"Sunny, what were you thinking?" I grab her shoulder so she sees me, "You can't go doing that—"

It wasn't her. Instead of light blue eyes staring up at me, they were hazel. I now realize that her hair is too light.

"Sorry," I mumble as the familiar feeling of loss seeps through my veins. I see colors all around me, but I can't make out a shape.

She's lost. My princess is gone.

Vincent

"Mommy, please can I have it?" a little boy dressed as Zorro asked with the puppy-dog-look. Oh, please buy the blue bulldog for him. It's only eight dollars.

"No, Johnny. It's time to go. Your father is getting the car warmed up." She pulls the boy away by the arm, his clear look of longing on his face as he stairs back.

Damn, I thought. That was probably going to be my last customer of the night. All of the parents drag their kid's home for their "bedtime". What they should be doing is buying their brats more toys. They should be paying me more for the temporary happiness of the kid.

I go to the back of my stall starting to pack up the rest of the junk. Bags and boxes filled with the cheap toys, half of which are already broken or ripped. It doesn't really matter, as long as they sell. I try to keep an eye on the front, in case there is that one kid who wants to steal from me.

I pick up the last pink bear and remember the guy who bought it for his daughter. Full head of black hair, black leather shoes, Oxford shirt and a Rolex on his wrist screamed money. He was the kind of guy I like, rich and willing to buy anything for his kid. I was hoping for another sale after theirs, but thanks to that mom, I won't.

Tomorrow, I will probably raise the price on the smaller stuff and lower it on the big ones. I don't need to keep huge, candy colored animals in my apartment. Maybe I can find some old candy to add to the stall. Yeah, get rid of candy and toys, saying it's for a non-profit cause. Not a bad idea.

"Excuse me, sir." A young voice calls from behind me. He has a natural flow of voice that says he's not a tourist. Time for my act.

I turn around to see a couple, neither one of them past twenty years old; the girl was smiling up sweetly to her boy. He probably got suckered into buying a cheap toy for her. I smile slightly while thinking that this will be a sale.

"How can I help you?" I lay my best Spanish accent I had. People don't usually try to talk to you too much if there is a language barrier.

"How much for the purple dolphin?" He points up to make sure I understand. *Hook, line, and sinker.*

"Eight-fifty."

He hands me a ten. I hand him a dolphin that will fall apart in a day.

"Keep the change."

"Thank you, thank you." I nod my head to show my gratitude.

He hands the toy to his girl and they walk away arm and arm. They look happy, but they won't last any longer than that toy in her hands.

It reminds me of my girl that I used to be with. She always wanted money. Money needed for clothes, shoes and jewelry. I just walked away. She has clothes and the shoes on her feet are fine. Then, she asked me for money for groceries. I said that she doesn't need more food. She needs to lose weight. She wanted to go out for a nice dinner. She must have thought she was funny. A nice dinner costs money. I earned that money. I am not going to go spend it on someone else who only complains for the whole world. She left, and since then, my little money wallet has grown significantly. Of course I still have a fling here and there, but they don't cost much.

I check my watch and see that it's past 10:00 PM, time for me to go. I have to get up early in the morning to work at a construction site and then come back here to sell more rubbish. I look out to see all of the adults partying harder now that the youngsters are home. The drinks come out and so do the cigarettes.

I was half way done with packing up when a man came up. He was wearing this year's yellow Carnival T-shirt; his hat covered his eyes and most of his nose. I've never seen him here before, but then again, I just stay in this one spot.

"Hey, can I get one of those dogs?" he asks, avoiding eye contact. He was probably one of those high teenagers that works here. I decided not to do an accent this time.

"Sure, that's eight dollars." While I reach for the dog he holds out the exact change. He takes the dog with no further comment and disappears into the hoards of people.

"Druggie." He probably screwed up with his girlfriend and is trying to make amends. Not going to happen.

I went back to my packing, thinking of ways to get more money, maybe by getting some smaller key-chains and pens. Adding bright

Christmas lights and a miniature disco ball would attract more kids.

As I turn off the overhead lights in the stall, I hear a man shout in the distance. Great, a fight is just what I need to block my way out of here.

The shouts continue to get louder as I load everything onto a cart and head to my car. It was like this guy was calling for help from this person who obviously wasn't going to do anything. When are the police coming to break this up?

It's times like these that I am glad I don't waste my money on liquor. You get drunk and then do stupid things, like fight and shout for help that will never come. Since I stay sober, I am able to know that the only person who can truly help you is yourself. No one else can help you and no one will.

I edge my way around a crowd to see a man running around like he is being chased by death. Poor guy, he needs something to pull him back to this world. That something just won't be me.

Robert

I love my job.

I travel around the world to take pictures for multiple companies; they pay for everything from the travel expenses to the meals at the hotel. I go around taking tours of places and take pictures. My passport is filled with different stamps from different countries.

I adjust my duster, covering all of my cameras and equipment. I know I look suspicious in this, but I like the way I feel, like I stepped into a Western novel and I am ready for the draw. I am so unlike the scenery around me now, but I'm good with that.

Coming from a small town high in the mountains may make me wish to see the desert and experience the west as it was written in so many stories. But, I'm here in this rural town during an amazing Carnival.

Lights outline every store and tree. Earlier, there were floats passing through the streets, going around and around. I have many

SD cards filled with pictures, and I think I might keep some of them as keepsakes. I might even give a gallery show with my memories of all of the places I've been.

What I truly do love is that all of the costumes are just better here. The princess costumes aren't synthetic material, but satin or silk. The masks aren't some cheap plastic, only hand-painted plaster with ribbons and jewels. Once I saw one painted like the desert; I had to buy it, but I ran out of money.

"Can you hold it for just a minute?" I pleaded, as I ran to scour the nearby streets for an ATM. I was about to give up hope when I saw a bank two blocks away. I did a quick walk to get there before anyone else.

"Sorry," I muttered, as I bumped into a Carnival worker handing out flyers. His stack was very thin, so he was able to keep a hold of all of the bright papers. I didn't stay to hear his remark.

I reached the machine and tried to punch in the right codes, changing the language to one that I know.

Why do these machines take so long? I asked myself silently, *Hurry, come on. I know this computer can go faster.* I looked up to see if there was a line behind me, surely it's been that long for one to form. Thankfully there was none. I did see a little girl in a Cinderella dress, though. This one stood out from the rest, more expensive and skillfully made.

I turned back to machine to complete the transaction. Waiting . . . and done! I turned and rushed back to the vendor before he closes up. I pass by crowds of teenagers, some carrying stuffed animals that they might have won or bought for each other.

As I get back to the stand, I find that the vendor did hold the mask for me, but he's now charging me for just saving it. Luckily, I did get enough money to cover all of the costs.

"Thank you very much." I didn't care about how much it cost, I felt that it was worth it.

Now, back to work.

I got my camera out and started to take pictures of the Carnival scene that changed with the rise of the moon. A couple walked hand and hand, stealing kisses when they thought no one was looking, and a woman carefully walking around the trash on the streets, avoiding getting her red heels dirty.

It's amazing that, even at this time when many are slumbering, there is life right under their noses, I think, staring at the covered windows of apartments. There is music blaring from the square where the main party is.

I walked back to the bank, hoping to see that little girl again. She had such an innocent look about her, like she could really be a princess. I walked around the corner to see that she was still there. It looked like she was with her older brother. He was the worker I bumped into earlier. He now looked like a giant compared to her tiny build.

He was giving her a blue dog, but she was holding tightly to a pink bear that required both of her arms to hold. He was bent down to stare into her eyes, and all I could think of was that this would make a wonderful picture. Her smile was bright enough to light up the surrounding area.

So, I start to press the button multiple times, just to make sure I get the picture. Though, the guy was wearing a baseball cap, blocking out the view of his eyes. It was a heartbreaking picture. Still, I had to get at an angle to see his eyes.

After 25 pictures I finally got a picture with his eyes in it and started to put the camera away. I juggled the thought of apologizing to the boy, but when I turned, they were already walking away, still holding the blue dog and her arms still filled with the pink bear. I decided against it. They were happy and going home. The little girl tired from a long day at the Carnival.

I continue down the street, just enjoying the sight and feel of everything. I truly believe that I will miss this place, nevertheless, I must move on to the oceans to try to get pictures of aquatic creatures and the beaches of southern Italy.

I might even come back.

Kristen (Sunny)

"Where are Beary and Spot's friends?" I ask. "I can't wait to show Daddy all the friends we've found."

"They're just around here," John says. He's one of the workers here at Carni-Val's party. He said that Beary had friends that he will miss if I don't take them with me. He said that we could surprise Daddy with them all.

Daddy has been sad lately, so it will be great to see his happy face when he sees more friends! Just like my friend John.

"You must be getting cold. Here, put this on." John takes off his jacket and holds Beary while I push my arms through the very long sleeves.

"Can I have Beary back?" I reached up for him.

"Here you go Sunny."

We continued walking for a long time. My feet started to hurt, and I just wanted to lie down and sleep. Daddy might get mad that I am staying up so late. I pulled on John's sleeve.

"John? Daddy is going to be mad that we've been gone for so long. Can't we get Beary and Spot's friends tomorrow?"

John stops and turns to me. "We're almost there, Sunny. Can you hold on a little bit more? I can call your Daddy while you meet all of their friends." Instead of waiting for my answer, he grabs my arm and pulls me through a dark brown door. He lost the nice look, and a look of pure hatred covered his eyes as he stared at me.

"Where are we? Why are the lights off? John? JOHN?" I call out into the pitch black. Fear crawls up my back as my voice echoes around the room. I turn around to try to find the door again, but I'm lost in darkness.

"JOHN?" this time I hear laughter. "WHAT'S GOING ON? I WANT TO GO BACK TO DADDY! DADDY?" I scream at the top of my lungs. My throat hurts, but I still scream, hoping for an answer. "DADDY!"

I feel a pinch in my arm as I inhale for another scream, "Shhhhh, this will only hurt a little." The chuckling voice says.

My arms lost their strength and Beary falls to the ground. I follow soon and land on top of him. I hear foots steps coming as I my eyes shut.

*   *   *

A scream fills the square, over the loud music.

People turn to see what the outburst is about and then scream themselves, backing away from the sight.

Leaning against the center fountain is a little girl, covered in blood. Her once beautiful princess dress is torn and stained with her blood. Her shoes were left near her feet, which were now burned and more blood trickled from many gashes. Her face is swollen and there is more blood coming from her broken nose and mouth. Her hair is flattened and some sections seem to be pulled out, leaving bald spots. Her chest slow rises.

A man rushes through the crowd, pushing and shoving as he calls out, "Sunny? Sunny!" He runs to her forgetting about the blood or anyone else. He holds her in his embrace, tears from his eyes fall on to her face.

"Someone call for help!" he shouts, barely able to get any sound behind the plea. He rocks back and forth, whisper prays and telling her everything will be all right.

Many bystanders pull out their cell phones, dialing 9-1-1 to get an ambulance. Many of the vendors called for help from the medical tent, and are now standing by, watching the tragedy unfold before them.

Her father is trying to find the source of the blood and gasps as he stares at her arm.

Her arm from the shoulder to the wrist is bruised and twisted at a terrible angle, but worst of all, her hand was cut to the point that it is only being held on by a few bits of skin and tendons. Her father tears off his coat and tries to stop the blood flow. He quickly glances at he legs and sees more warped positions.

"Sunny, who did this to you?" He whispers through his tears. He brushes hair away from her face like he's done so many times before. Only this time, he smears blood.

The girl tries to answer but only coughs up more blood and other liquids. Her mouth hangs open, trying to suck in air. Everyone sees that tongue as been cut in half and most of her teeth were pulled out.

Her blood has diffused over the ground, nearing the frozen bystanders' feet, mixing with the trash from a party not so long ago. None of them are able to move, to care about anything anymore.

The paramedics finally arrive and race to the little girl, bleeding in her despairing father's arms.

Diablo

By Michael O'Callaghan

—∾∾∽◌◠◯◠◯◠◌∽∿∾—

"Behind you!" Tim looked in his rearview mirror and swerved left. He shook his head, trying to bring himself back to reality.

"Right!" He heard the voice again and again and Tim obeyed. The Mercedes C300 behind him braked hard and spun onto the sidewalk.

"One down." Tim always seemed to speak out loud to himself. He heard the hum of the engine as he pressed his foot down. His Lamborghini Diablo roared ahead of the competition. The stoplights seemed to turn green for him perfectly as he drove through each intersection. Truthfully, they were probably all red, but who cared? The infractions on these streets were given for *not* speeding. Mistakes on these streets didn't land you a ticket, they just killed you.

"He's *gaining* on you!" Tim looked around the car frantically. He knew there was no one there but the voice. An omnipresent voice that called to him from the empty passenger seat and outside the car.

He recognized the voice—Sammy. Sammy was someone from Tim's past; he remembered playing pretend with her. He always liked to be king and queen of the castle. He was King Timmy Karl and she, his Lady Samantha Donohue.

Sammy screamed at him from the passenger seat, "Tim!" She was very real to him now. His eyes were back on the road; even though mere seconds had passed since he was racing towards a wall. He glanced to Sammy for help, but she was gone. He made a sharp turn and he was back on his course but the distraction cost him the lead. A chrome Audi A8 sped into first position.

"Idiot. The bridge, the bridge!" Sammy was angry now. He shook his head in fear. Wasn't the bridge out?

"I could swear they're doing construction on the bridge . . ." he mumbled like it should have been a thought.

"No, they aren't! Not a right, Timmy. Take a left, take a left!"

"Leave me alone!" Tim screamed aloud. He never understood why Sammy could be so mean. She always got angry at him and he hated it.

"Turn!"

"Please, Sammy. No," Tim begged.

"The bridge, Tim."

"What?"

"Yes, Tim, the bridge, the bridge!"

"We'll die, though!" he shouted back. "The money . . ." he began.

"Why are you always concerned with the money? Don't you want to be with me again?"

"I've gotta win . . . I need that envelope," Tim licked his lips.

"Not the money, Tim! Why not me, Tim?"

"Cash . . . cash. Yes, money," he muttered. "Why turn?" the phrase was awkward.

"So we can be together! Turn, Tim! Left, Tim! Turn-*turn*!" And he did. Tim Karl closed his eyes and turned right.

When Tim opened his eyes he was alive, quickly accelerating to 100, 110, 130, 145 miles per hour! He looked at his rearview mirror, expecting his doom, and instead of the edge of a bridge, Tim saw the Audi A8 with the driver slamming his fists on the wheel. Tim slammed his foot on the brake and even threw the E-brake for good measure. He stepped out of the car, woozy from the sudden lack of speed, and saw everything around him spinning.

"Damn, Timmy! Great work, man!"

"Yeah, you had 'em there, Tim!"

He saw an envelope put in his hand, but couldn't feel it. Squeezing it felt good, but it was as if it wasn't there. Tim licked his lips, lusting for the cash in his hand. But, the world started to fade—he had seen cars and . . . a wall? Maybe. He wasn't sure. All he knew was these Benjamin Franklins in his palm. But there was Sammy in the car, crying. Everything around him looked upside down or discolored, and then Tim saw nothing.

*   *   *

Tim awoke early the next morning. He stood up and saw the clock read 7:30. He had strange dreams of gunfire and other odd things last night. He looked out his small apartment window over beautiful New York City. He just looked for a while. Someone watching the scene would have assumed he was waiting for coffee or something. Literally, no thoughts could have been running through his head.

That morning, Tim Karl was the same man with a different consciousness. He remembered nothing of being a street racer and didn't hear omnipresent voices. The Tim that was present now was raised by honest, loving parents, grew up in a beautiful suburban home, and would never hurt a fly.

In his apartment that morning, Tim Karl did not hear voices, was not suicidal, and did not hallucinate. For him, Sammy was the girl who grew up across the street from Tim. She died in a car accident when she was seventeen years old as a brand new driver. The years following her death were the most difficult of Tim's life. But now, he felt relieved. He had come to terms with his best friend's death.

Tim looked back at the clock and saw 10:36. Tim was glad he had slept late that morning. A thick envelope lay on his bedside table. He opened it and found it full of $100 bills. Shrugging, he assumed he had gone to the bank yesterday and forgotten.

Tim was a money-maker just like his parents; he knew they were proud. His father, James Karl, was a lawyer; his mother, Marylou Karl, a doctor. If they had taught him anything, it was to make money. And now, here he was, an NYU chemistry major, ready to make big money. His parents raised him to live honestly and earn a respectable living. His science experiments had earned him huge prizes across the country and he nearly foamed at the mouth thinking of the stockpile under his mattress.

*   *   *

His hands gripped the wheel tightly. Tim was always ready to race. He knew his Diablo would dash, no, *glide* into another win. Revving the engine, he looked around and sized up the other drivers. They were lined up across the street, a Porsche Carrera GT and himself looking most prominent. It dawned on him that all the drivers had their windows rolled up, but he knew they spoke to him.

"Come to me Tim."

"I see your wrists!"

"I know you want to kill yourself, Tim."

"You're nothing—we're something."

But the other drivers looked forward, pressing their foot on the gas, eager to speed off into the race. He knew more than anything that they were screaming at him, but they weren't. The voices came from all around him, but then he saw her, Lady Samantha Donohue in the passenger seat. She was begging him to come to her. When Sammy had passed, he split his mind. This was the part of Tim that could never grip the pain.

His foot bounced on the accelerator, as if playing a kick drum. Engines roared in fury as drivers were ready to go.

Just then, a beautiful woman walked in front of the cars, dressed in a mini skirt and tube top that made the drivers' eyes wide. Tim licked his lips in lust.

"I like her. I like her a lot." It should've been a thought but Tim *had* to say it out loud. He didn't know why. Sammy began to cry next to him.

The girl counted on her hands:

One. She stuck a solitary finger in her mouth sexily.

"Sammy, it's okay . . ."

Two. She aimed a peace sign at the drivers.

"Hit the wall? Come to me?"

Three. She threw her arms in the air.

The drivers sped past her, the Porsche taking the lead.

"Let's go!" Tim screamed to no one in particular. Then, the other two cars moved forward to drift neck and neck with the Carrera. Tim rubbed a $100 bill between his fingers.

"You're nothing, Tim."

"Please, you can't win!"

Her voice came from everywhere, but Tim knew there was only Sammy.

"Screw you!" Tim wailed as he soared past the other drivers. Naturally, Tim won. He closed his door after stepping out of the car before a single other car completed the circuit. He felt another envelope of cash pressed into his hands and he relished it. He liked that girl . . . she smiled at him. He decided to talk to her, but Sammy pleaded.

"Screw me? No, Tim. Why Timmy?" she cried and cried.

"No, Sammy, please. I didn't mean to—"

But, the world went black.

*   *   *

Tim Karl woke again, a new man, in the comfort of his apartment. He smacked his alarm clock silent. It was 7:30, just on time. He rolled on his back and stared at the ceiling. When he finally rolled out of bed, the clock read 8:15, but Tim had not fallen back asleep. He shrugged, grabbed his keys, and headed to class.

Tim found himself always dozing off in class. He knew he was smarter than half of his professors; Tim was on his way to being a millionaire! He didn't have time to listen to old guys talk. Often, he was asked his opinions and had no idea how to answer since his thoughts were floating so high, away from everyone else. Many times it wasn't because he had been sleeping either—he had just zoned out.

Tim checked his phone. He found a text from Amanda.

"Amanda?" he said aloud. "*Can't wait to see you Tim. Mwah!*" it read. Assuming he had accidentally slept with someone last night he texted her back, "*When will I see you?*"

Suddenly, Tim realized it was the girl who started the race last night, which seemed to cause an intense migraine. Tim didn't remember anything about a race, but it seemed so real . . .

"Mr. Karl? Tim?"

"I, uh—" Tim shook his head. "What the hell just happened?" He slapped his forehead. "Shoulda kept that one in my mind," he said out loud again.

"Tim? Tim, are you alright?"

"Yeah, I just . . ." he paused. "Professor, I honestly have no idea how the hell I got here."

"You want to go home? Maybe you're just feeling sick."

"No sir I—I'm alright." His professor was not convinced.

"I don't feel sick sir, this is quite normal for me."

"Do me a favor and take the rest of the day off, alright? Sleep."

"Yeah—alright. Thanks?" he wasn't sure if this was the right response. "Jeez, man. What's my deal?" he asked himself as he left the room.

The professor shook his head, "This is becoming more and more frequent." The class agreed.

Tim got home and decided to call his parents, but when he picked up the phone, he blanked on the number. Tim stood there, phone in hand, for about 15 minutes, but he didn't even notice the time go. He blanked on what he was doing entirely and just decided to go to bed.

Once he laid in bed, he spoke to himself, "Maybe I'll call mom . . . she's a doctor, she'll know what to do." And after unnaturally narrating his thought process to himself, Tim got up to call his mother.

Upon standing, Tim felt extremely woozy. The migraine intensified and the world seemed to spin around him. He stumbled a bit and passed out halfway to the phone.

*   *   *

Tim woke up in serious pain. He checked the clock and realized he had been out for about an hour. He rubbed the top of his head, feeling warm wetness. He looked at his hand and saw that it was covered in blood. Rubbing his temples to bring focus back to the world, he saw he had hit his head on his bedpost.

"Oh," he moaned. His phone buzzed.

"*Soon* ;)!" the text message read.

"The girl from the race?" he asked himself.

"Timmy!" Sammy's voice wailed in his head. There she was, standing by his bedside. He shook his head and Tim was a student again.

"Jesus Christ!" he looked around for the originator of the voice, but realized he had scared himself. "Crap, I need to call mom. This isn't good—I shoulda' thought to call her before."

Suddenly, he broke out shrieking. "Help me!"

"I'm here! I'm here! What do you need?" His hands flew to his chest. Tim was having a conversation with himself. The street racer was screaming for the help of the Chemistry Major.

"What the hell?!" He bit down hard into his arm, trying to wake himself up from this nightmare.

"What's going on?!" He began to sob before he bit himself again. He pulled his head away hard and left a gash in his arm.

"Help me . . . Jesus Christ, help." But this voice wasn't his—Sammy was calling for him.

Nothing was going through his mind but his money. His brain was conflicted on how he had acquired it, but he knew he needed it. Both Tim's were drawn to the green paper.

"Just jump out the window, Tim. Be with me," Sammy begged.

Tim had blurred memories left. His life was replaying in his mind. He felt as if days passed when a few minutes went by. Sammy's screams made Tim walk out of his apartment, only to stumble into the girl he liked from the race.

She said, "Hello," coyly and he pushed her aside. He had to get his car. She gave him the finger and stormed off. Tim didn't care.

"Timmy Karl, you get back here!" Lady Sammy Donohue acted like the queen of the world again.

He opened the door and started shivering. He sat down and felt the world spinning. He smashed his head against the wheel. Then he did it again. Elbow by the window, he put his head into his hand like a frustrated cab driver. He had no idea where he was or whose car he was in. He reached into the console and found two envelopes of money. Tim took a huge whiff of the envelopes. He licked his lips, almost sexually aroused by the smell of the bills.

KNOCK. KNOCK. KNOCK.

"Crap!" he screamed, like a knife had been thrust in his leg.

The girl jumped back from the window. He shook his head and opened the door.

"Sammy? What?"

"What did you call me?"

"I—sorry," it wasn't Sammy. It was the girl from the race, but Tim couldn't tell.

"Tell her to go away!" Sammy shouted from somewhere. Tim looked around for her.

"What was that all about?" the girl at the window asked.

"Who are you?"

She smacked him across the face. "Don't touch me ever again. Will I see you at the race tonight?"

Tim felt like this was all a bad acid trip. He had no idea who this woman was, even though he had just bumped into her. He just looked out the windshield without answering.

"I hope not," she stared him right in the eyes. "You're insane."

It was coming to him. Memories of his parents' home in Ohio, childhood memories of winning the spelling bee and another of beating the winner unconscious, getting his Diablo from his parents for graduation but winning it in a race . . . there were two lives in Tim's mind. He began to realize it.

"Hello? Are you there? Jesus, what's wrong with you?"

Growing up in a happy, loving family and growing working for drug dealers and shoplifting. Pleasing his parents with his great grades and being beaten for failing to do what he was told. Racing cars and going to college . . . something wasn't right.

"Jerk."

As she walked away, the world melted away and he only saw her. She walked out into fuzzy world of shapes and shadows barely distinguishable from each other. Sammy smacked him across the face.

"Why don't you care about me?" And then even Sammy was gone.

He laid his head back in exhaustion. He realized that something had been hurting him like hell, but the shrieking voices blocked the pain.

"The money, the money . . ." he stammered. Sammy was a figment of Tim's imagination. The racing and chemistry were unreal to him. But the money . . . for Tim, the money was real. Tim's realization that he had lived two lives was driving him insane. But it did another thing to him. He ignored everything else.

*   *   *

As he pulled Tim Karl out of his car, the EMT noticed a head wound had seeped onto the back of his shirt. The other paramedics helped him get Tim onto a stretcher. An envelope of money fell onto the asphalt, full of $100 bills. Both Tim's had been clutching to it.

"Poor guy."

Winds of Vengeance

By Domenick Gasparro

It came, and it came fast. People fled for their lives as it approached, running from their homes and filling the street with chaos. They ran from it, speeding across the cobblestone streets with whatever valuables they could carry. People were knocked over in all directions as others crashed into them, spilling their items in the process. A few made it to the city gates, but the panic in the city and the darkness of the night slowed everyone else down. Then, all of a sudden, it struck. Destruction filled the air as objects and dust flew everywhere, barring even the most sharp-eyed from sight. It smashed houses to pieces, for their wooden structures did not have the strength to best it. Screams and the splatter of blood rose sharp in the atmosphere, only to end up blotted out by the sound of sheer power. Peasants and noblemen alike died in large numbers. And then it went away. Piles of debris littered the ground, making the town unrecognizable.

A few days later at the castle, the King of Zephyrus, a tall man with black hair, sat upon the roof in his marble and gold throne, wondering if he had made the right move. The people and the nobles recently questioned his rule, and he would not tolerate it. Why could they not understand that they deserved punishment for what they did on that day long ago? He, as their king, could rule them as he wished. He therefore justified himself in having sent the tornado over the city.

"My king! My king!" shouted a servant as he ran into the outdoor throne room.

"What do you want?" said the king in his usual cold voice.

"One of our spies says that there is a resistance forming. Men of every rank are forging weapons and armor."

"A resistance?!" yelled the suddenly angered king. "When will these people ever learn? I cannot tolerate this. Have they not felt the sting of my wind magic enough to know that I won't back down?"

"My king, that is the reason they are angered," said the servant. "They are mad that you cast a tornado upon them. *They* seem intolerant of *you*." When the king heard this, he put his hands forward and sent a blast of wind at one of the decorative marble pillars surrounding his throne. The gust knocked it to the ground, crushing the servant to his death.

"*That* is what will happen to their resistance." The king rose from his throne and went to his speech post at the front of the castle's roof. "ENFORCERS OF THE ZEPHYRAN ARMY, GO TO THE ARMORIES IMMEDIATELY! PREPARE FOR WAR!" As soon as the king issued his order, the Enforcers marched to the armories and grabbed swords, shields, axes and maces. They soon began to train upon the grassy fields surrounding the castle. The sound of metal clashing filled the air as the practice battles commenced.

Meanwhile, in the Forest of Terra (some three kilometers away from the castle), many survivors of the tornado gathered. They, like the king's army, came armed with weapons. The group had no less than five hundred men and women, and had gathered in a large clearing surrounded by trees of golden wood. This was the resistance. A short brown-haired man named Frank stood on top of a branch, making a speech to the group.

"My fellow Resistors," he said. "Our king has been corrupted. Do you not remember the time that he was good? The time where he treated us well?"

"AYE!" the crowd screamed.

"My friends, he was an excellent king. That is until he began to control the wind. His powers have corrupted him. Now, we are treated like slaves!"

"AYE!" the crowd again screamed.

"He now refuses to give us even the slightest of freedoms. We cannot hunt, we cannot petition, and we are even forbidden to interact with those other than our families. We have sent messengers to ask him why this is, and he kills them before they can speak. Regrettably, my friends, we have no choice. We must destroy our king."

"DESTROY THE KING! DESTROY THE KING!" the crowd began to chant. Meanwhile, Frank stepped down from the branch. He had satisfied the Resistors.

He then took a walk away from the clearing. The forest became quiet as he walked away from the crowd. He began to think of his sister, Maria. He then remembered the tornado. He remembered how the black, swirling air mass came straight at his house. He and his sister had hidden under the table.

"Frank, will we be alright?" asked the eleven-year old.

"Maria, we'll be fine. Don't worry." He remembered looking at her face, seeing her black hair and her brown eyes. And then the twister lifted them off the ground as it struck the house. Frank heard Maria scream as the tornado sucked her up. Then, the wind blinded and deafened him, and soon enough he entered free fall. He landed on a hay bale. For that moment, Frank felt lucky, only to see his sister's blood-drenched head impaled on a large splinter sticking up from the debris. It lacked a body. He got up from the hay bale, and became angry. Frank then came out of his horrid memory, not bearing to think about it any longer. However, the anger followed him, and he clenched his fist. "Maria, I shall avenge you."

"Send them forward," said the King to the General. "The enemy is near. I can sense that they are in the forest."

"FORWARD!" ordered the general. The army of Enforcers marched towards the gate of the castle grounds. They had a mission to kill every person that would rebel against the king. Nothing could hinder them. They would not fail their king.

The king whistled and his horse, a creature coated in a dark brown, came running. He mounted the animal and rode forward with the rest of the army. Those people would get punished one way or another. As he rode, he again remembered that fateful day, and the reason why the people should get punished. Ahead of him, the king saw the Great Greens, with the Sea of Skies and the Forest of Terra in the distance. They rode for hours over the grassy terrain; the combined footsteps of them and their horses shook the ground. They stayed in perfect ranks as they went over the hilly fields of the Great Greens, with their king and general in the back. Not one soldier truly became tired, for the Enforcers ignored all tiredness, as they valued their duty to the crown over their physical bodies. They drew near to the forest, yet continued to march until the king abruptly told his general to halt the army of Enforcers.

"HALT!" the general ordered. "What is it my king? Why are we stopped?"

"I smell the rebels getting closer. Let the foul scum march out of the forest and we shall surprise them right here. Order them to form a semicircle around the exit to the forest."

The resistors marched through the sea of trees, headed for the Castle of Zephyrus. Frank figured that they would camp at the edge of the forest, cross the Great Greens in the day, and invade the castle at the next nightfall. Frank wondered why it had to come to this. He had met the king a long time ago, and he seemed like a wise ruler. Why would he turn like this? How could he kill something as innocent as Maria? Then Frank thought of all the other people he saw. Arms and legs had littered the grey cobblestones, all stained with blood and without masters. The tornado literally ripped some people to pieces. He could not let this happen again. "I will avenge all of you," he muttered under his breath, still lost in his memory.

"Frank!" shouted a rebel.

"What is it Henry?"

"We are nearing the Great Greens. Do you wish to make camp here, at the edge of the forest?"

"Yes," replied Frank. "We will march across the Greens tomorrow. The troops need rest."

"Very good sir," said Henry. The rebel remained silent for a few seconds, and then spoke again. "Frank, I can tell something's bothering you. What is it?"

"What do you mean by asking that?" said Frank. "The king is oppressing our people! We have to do something."

"No, there's something else. Why are you leading the Resistors? Did something happen to you?" asked Henry. Frank remained silent as he thought of Maria. He wondered if he should tell Henry about his sister. He decided against it.

"Nothing happened," he said. "I just saw that these people needed a leader, and decided that I had nothing to lose. The king needs to be stopped, and if I hadn't stepped up, no one else would have."

"Come on, Frank," said Henry. "You don't have to hide anything from me. It's not like I'm a spy trying to probe your mind. I will be fighting at your side when we raid the castle." Frank thought about this. He had known Henry for a while, and he seemed like a nice person. How much harm could it do to tell him? Upon these thoughts, Frank spoke.

"My sister, Maria, has died in the tornado sent by the foul king. I must avenge her. Why do you ask?"

"I was just a bit worried about you," said Henry. Then the rebel marched away.

"Well?" asked the king. "Are they planning on coming out now?"

"No," replied the spy. "Their leader, Frank, is setting up camp just beyond those trees."

"Great!" said the general. "We can attack their leader during the night. If we kill him, we can show the fools some real punishment." The general seemed ready for battle, and he wanted to get on with this one.

"No," said the spy. "That would be a death trap. I have seen all that goes on in the camp, and his tent is well guarded. Plus, those fools will be enraged by a rude awakening, and, therefore, will be much more dangerous. They keep maces under their pillows for such occasions."

The king again spoke. "We need to lure this Frank out of the camp somehow. Do you have any more information on him?" he asked the spy.

"Yes. His sister was lost in the tornado. He wants to avenge her. That is all that I know."

"Very good," said the king. "I know just how to lure him now. You have served me well, Henry." The king rose and said, "General, tell the troops to stay in position. I will only be a moment." As the general issued the order, the king wandered into the forest.

Frank busied himself by setting up the camp with the rest of the troops. He nailed the thick wooden supports for the tents into the hard ground when he saw something out of the corner of his eye. A young girl with brown hair and brown eyes stood beside a tree. She then ran off into the woods. "No, how could it be?" he thought aloud.

"What is it Frank?" yelled one of the troops.

"I thought I saw something. There was a girl behind that tree there. She looked like . . ."

"What did she look like?" asked the troop.

"Never mind. I'll go investigate. Meanwhile, you keep setting up the camps," he ordered. When the soldier left, he went in the direction of the girl. "Maria! Maria!" he called. It just had to be her. But what made this possible? She died in the tornado. He had seen her bloody head in the debris.

Frank traveled deeper into the trees, calling out Maria's name. He saw the edge of the forest, and then he glimpsed her again. She stood by another tree, and disappeared. He had no doubt that it was her as he ran across the soft soil, past the golden-wooded trees, and out onto the Great Greens. "Maria?" he said weakly.

Then he felt a hand on his shoulder. A cold voice said, "Not Maria, but *me*." Frank turned and found himself face to face with the king. He had rows of armored troops behind him, his Enforcers, and they soon surrounded them. "So, you are the leader of the group that calls themselves the Resistors. They are a pitiful group to follow such a fool."

"Where is my sister? What did you do to her?" asked Frank.

"Perhaps I should ask you the same question. She's dead, of course. Do you not know that tornados can kill people?" replied the king.

"But, but how? How did you make her image? And what do you mean 'ask me the same question'?"

"Perhaps *this* should reveal things to you." The king took a step back. He drew his sword, a long curved scimitar, and raised it skyward. He started to glow with a purple light and his features began to change. His hair and beard grew long and white, and his robes changed to purple. The king had transformed into an old man. "My name is Darkengale, the Wizard of the Winds. I have killed your king and taken over Zephyrus."

Frank stared at the wizard in awe as the army of Enforcers also magically transformed. Their armor chanced shape and turned purple. "Darkengale?" Frank pondered the name for a moment. He went over the history of Zephyrus in his head. "Do you mean the famous Darkengale? The one who could change shape and was the Lady of the Mountain's brother?" Darkengale gave a crooked smile at Frank, acknowledging him. "So, you disguised your famous Gust Knights as royal Enforcers? And you changed shape to impersonate the king and my sister?"

"Very good, Frank," said Darkengale. "You have figured it all out."

"But how did you know what my sister looked like?"

"The wind lends me its eyes, Frank. Magic is quite powerful. And, now, let me ask you, do you know the fate of the Lady of the Mountain? *My* sister?"

"She was executed in the city for a crime she didn't commit," answered Frank.

"Yes," said Darkengale, "*your* people killed her. And ever since that fateful day I have wanted revenge." Darkengale began to get hyper. "Your people deserve to be punished for what they did!" he yelled, making Frank take a step back. "And for that, I will begin either killing or torturing those city people, starting with you. I can't wait until they see what has happened to their foolish leader." Darkengale took his scimitar and pointed it at Frank's throat.

However, just before Darkengale thrust it in, a battle cry arose from the forest. Before anyone could move, the Resistors charged out of the forest, weapons in hand. They went and collided with the Gust Knights, beginning the battle. Darkengale got knocked backwards by the collision, giving Frank time to draw his broadsword.

Clashes of metal filled the air, and blood stained the grass as the Resistors and Gust Knights killed each other. In the middle, Frank fought Darkengale one on one. Frank found out, as he fought, that Darkengale had a large amount of experience with his blade, having developed a swordsman's skill over the many years of his life. The scimitar flowed naturally in the evil wizard's hand, and after many clashes with the broadsword, cut Frank in the cheek. Frank tried to return the damage with a series of thrusts, but Darkengale parried them all. Then, he mysteriously backed off. Frank spared a slight moment to wonder why, but then he saw a purple ball charging in the wizard's hands: a spell.

Frank charged in, and with a three hundred and sixty degree spin, gashed Darkengale in the arm. Darkengale became angry as his spell failed, but then he backed off further and raised his sword. The spell succeeded this time and he transformed again. Frank now found himself face to face with . . . Frank. Darkengale turned into a doppelganger, an evil copy of Frank. Frank tried some horizontal slashes, but Dark Frank parried them all with pinpoint accuracy. The real Frank backed off a moment, but Dark Frank used his own move on him: a charge followed by a sword spin. He gashed Frank in the chest. Frank, now angry, wildly swung at Dark Frank, and the swords locked. Each of them pushed against the other with all their strength. The moment intensified as their muscles began to shake. Then, with the old wizard's skill and the young man's strength, Dark Frank managed to push Frank to the ground. Frank watched his life go before his eyes as his doppelganger raised his sword. As it came, everything seemed to slow down. Frank's senses began to act on a deeper level. He heard each individual clash of metal from the surrounding battle. He tasted the blood from his cheek in his mouth. Above all, he saw the shadowy figure of the doppelganger in front of him, lowering the sword. Then, before the blade had a chance to connect, Dark Frank's head exploded. Frank saw a spiked steel ball in its place as the individual pieces floated to the ground. One of the Gust Knights had mistaken him for the real Frank, and killed him with a mace. Frank quickly got up and began to shout commands to his army.

"Form ranks! Get into diamond formation! We'll surround them and close in! Get your spears out!" The Resistors followed every order and surrounded the opposing army. They formed a diamond around the Gust Knights, and slowly began marching towards the center with their spears extended. The enemy had nowhere to go as the Resistors closed in. Wave after wave of Gust Knights fell, until only a small group remained in the middle. At that moment, Frank yelled "Thrust!" and the Resistors thrust their spears towards the center to finish off the enemy. Not a single Gust Knight remained alive on the Great Greens. Frank had led them to a swift victory.

Thirty days later, the city fared well. The people had repaired all the damage from the tornado, and now lived cheerfully. Word could be heard all around about the wind wizard Darkengale, and Frank's astounding victory over him. Children ran through the streets with sticks, trying to replicate the duel. Meanwhile, at the Castle of Zephyrus, Frank stood upon the roof before the marble and gold throne. His broadsword hung at his side. Crowds of people gathered all over the castle grounds, waiting. A servant walked between Frank and the throne. He had a crown in his hands.

"My friends, this fair kingdom of Zephyrus has suffered one terror that goes beyond imagination. We have suffered the rule of an imposter named Darkengale, who has tormented our people with his wind magic," said the servant. The crowds remained silent. "He has sent a tornado at us, trying to kill every one of us, and has acted relentlessly when we asked him why. However, one man has helped to end this struggle. One man has lead our people to their salvation. One man has defeated the evil which plagued the kingdom." The servant then placed the crown upon Frank's head. "All hail King Frank, the Great, the man who led the resistance against the evil wizard and saved our kingdom." The crowds began to cheer.

"ALL HAIL THE KING! ALL HAIL THE KING!" they chanted. However, as they chanted, a single voice rose up loudly, hitting everyone's ears.

"I object!" it said.

"Who dares object to the King at his crowning?" asked the servant. "Show yourself."

An old man garbed in red appeared before the crowd and said "My name is Pyroclast, the Wizard of Flames. I object to the crowning of your Frank. He is a cruel man with many ills."

"Wizard, you should know your place!" shouted the servant. "Our king is-" but King Frank interrupted him before he could finish.

"Why, Pyroclast, do you object to me? What have I done against you?"

"You have killed my friend Darkengale," said Pyroclast. "I will not stand for a King who has murdered such a noble wizard. So, now, I shall kill you." The crowd became silent. They stared at the Wizard in disbelief.

"Pyroclast," said King Frank, "your friend killed my sister and many other people with that great tornado of his. He had to be slain or the entire kingdom would have perished under him. Also, you should know that I am not the one who killed Darkengale. One of his own Gust Knights killed him by mistake."

"It matters not to me," replied Pyroclast. "Your resistance caused a battle that resulted in his death. And, anyways, you should have thought about the consequences when you killed his sister, the Lady of the Mountain. I remember that fateful day."

"Pyroclast, we are not the ones who killed the Lady. That was one hundred years ago. Our ancestors committed that act. I was not even born yet," said King Frank. Pyroclast seemed taken aback. He had no words left to use on the king. "Let us keep the peace," continued King Frank. "The winds of vengeance have passed. We must not let them return. We must all learn to forgive."

Pyroclast thought about this for a moment, and then he spoke. "Then you may forgive me, King Frank. I, as a wizard, have seen hundreds of years, and did not take into account that the people in the kingdom now were not even around then. Your words are wise, and I have misjudged you and your people."

"You are forgiven, Pyroclast. Now go, and let this kingdom enter a new era of peace." At the King's words, Pyroclast left the castle and went into the distance. The crowds watched him until he disappeared deep into the Great Greens. Then, they let out a cheer that lasted for several minutes. As they cheered, the servant spoke to the king.

"You really did save us. You really did bring an era of peace. I can see a future of fortune with you on the throne."

The crowd's cheer broke into a chant. "ALL HAIL THE KING! ALL HAIL THE KING!" they screamed. Trumpets from musicians standing around the walls of the castle began to play, and the new king marched to his throne and sat in it. At that glorious moment, Frank completely overcame vengeance and forgave, perhaps even thanked, Darkengale in his thoughts. The evil old wizard had taught him how not to rule a kingdom. After these thoughts, Frank, for the first time in a long time, sat and enjoyed himself. He watched the crowds celebrating, and the musicians playing their trumpets. He looked out upon the Great Greens, the Sea of Skies, and the Forest of Terra—his new kingdom—and relaxed. The Kingdom of Zephyrus would remain in peace for a long time.

A Disastrous Night in Podunk

By Steven Curran

It was a cold, dark night in Vermont. On a hill sat a big house that fit in nicely with the woods around it. A dog was outside running around happily and alone when two men appeared from the shadows. Both were armed with shotguns. The dog noticed them and gave a low, angry growl. One man had the dog's attention, while the other snuck around the dog. The man came from behind and hit the dog over the head with the butt of the gun. The only noise made was one loud yelp that came from the dog.

*   *   *

After a day of skiing at Mount Snow, we went back to my Cousin Sam's house. It was deep into the Vermont mountains and isolated from other people. The nearest neighbor was probably close to a few miles away. The house sat on top of a hill surrounded by thick woods. It was a nice, quiet spot that makes you feel calm and relaxed.

Sam and I sat in the living room as Aunt Maryann made us Ellio's pizza in the kitchen, which was open to the living room. We were sitting on the couch, and I could see over the kitchen island to the stove, noticing the pizza was ready. Uncle Chip and she were not eating with us because they were going out to a friend's house for dinner.

As we ate our food quickly, Aunt Maryann said, "Let Henry outside in a little bit, but remember to let him back in." Henry was their big, friendly yellow lab. We let him out right after Sam's parents left. Forgetting to let Henry back in, we went upstairs to play Xbox.

After fifteen minutes of playing Nazi Zombies, the power suddenly went out. Neither one of us wanted to go to the basement to turn the power on.

"Steven, go down to the basement and turn the power back on," said Sam. Going downstairs into the mudroom and then into the basement to the fuse box was too much work.

"Hell no, it's your house and I'm lazy. You go down," I said. Sam couldn't really argue against that.

"Come on, both our phones have flashlights and I don't know what to do. Just come with me," said Sam. For some reason I ended up going with him even though I didn't want to.

We got to the mudroom, put on our sneakers, and were about to open the door to the basement when we heard just one loud yelp come from outside. Immediately, both of us froze in fear and just looked at each other. It had to be Henry. It sounded like him, and what else could make a noise like that? We stood there in complete silence, hoping to hear him bark, but all we could hear were our hearts pounding. Too afraid to find out what happened, we both ran back upstairs, pushing and shoving each other the whole way up. We hid in Sam's room and both of us were out of breath. Our hearts were racing and all we could think about was what was outside.

Scared out of my mind, I whisper to Sam, "What the hell just happened?"

"Dude, I have no idea," he whispers back. We were both too afraid to speak loudly. So many possibilities were going through my head that it scared me thinking about them.

"What if someone's out there?" I said. From the look on Sam's face I could tell he didn't like that idea. He looked more scared than I did. "Sam what if—?"

"—Shut up," said Sam, "you're probably right, but what do we do if you are?" I knew Sam wasn't going to like what I was about to say, but someone had to say it.

"Sam, we have to go downstairs." I thought I was scared, but when I looked at Sam I could see he was shitting his pants.

"No way," said Sam.

"We have to. What if they try to get into the house and get us?" Sam eventually agreed that we had to go downstairs.

"Okay, but what are we going to do when we get down there?" said Sam. I had to think about it, but really, it was simple.

"I'll go down and lock the doors, while you go get your dad's shotgun," I explained, "The shotgun is still in his room, right?"

Sam said, "Yeah, it's still there. You get the front door while I get the slider door on my way to my parent's room." Even though the plan was so simple, it seemed so difficult. We walked out of Sam's room and got to the top of the stairs. We were walking down quietly because all I could think about was if they were already inside. I really hoped they weren't because then anything could happen. We got to the bottom of the stairs with no problem. Sam was about to go his parent's room and I was headed for the mudroom when we heard someone speak.

We could hear the voice say, "Hey, don't forget after we check this room we'll check the master bedroom and then grab anything valuable." We could tell the voice came from the office, which was right next to the mudroom door. Neither of us moved an inch, too afraid to make a noise.

Then we hear a second voice say, "Alright, but what if there's someone still upstairs? We don't know if everyone left." I looked over to Sam relieved that they had no idea we were here. I wave over to him to sneak closer to me, so I can whisper to him. Right as he gets closer to me we hear the first voice again.

"I don't think anyone is here, but if there is just blow them away," said the first voice. When I heard that my jaw dropped. They had a gun and were going to kill us on sight. I look at Sam and can see the sweat dripping down his face and I wipe my own away.

I whisper to Sam as quietly as I can, "We need to get the hell out of here." All he did was nod in agreement. We were going to have to bolt for the mudroom door and get to the woods. Forget the gun, we needed to get help. Making things worse, we were in the middle of nowhere and had no cell phone service.

The second voice spoke again, saying, "No don't do that. We don't want murder on our hands too. Just threaten them, so they'll do what we say. That way we can tie them up and get out of here."

"Yeah, alright," responded the first voice.

Either way, I didn't want to stick around to find out what they would do. Using my hands and other body expressions I explained to Sam what we would do. We would go through the mudroom and run for the woods. We would keep going until we reached the road again and then get help. It was the only thing we could do because there was no way we would stop them when they had two guns and we had none.

I put my hand on the doorknob, ready to open it and run with Sam just a few steps behind me. Just before I open the door I hear a loud sneeze from behind me.

The voices both yell, "Someone's here!"

All I said was, "Shit Sam! Let's get out of here!" I threw the door open and ran for the next door leading outside. I didn't look back once. All I heard was yelling coming from Sam, the two men, and probably mine too. Most of the yelling was just everyone cursing at each other.

I made it out the front door and headed towards the woods. On my way out I saw their ax next to the firewood and decided to grab it on my way by. I kept running up the hill, through the snow, and into the woods until I was far enough away and out of breath. Finally, I looked back to see if they followed us all the way out here. They weren't coming, and from what I could tell when I moved closer, they must be in the house still because the lights were back on. I thought it was odd that they didn't follow us out of the house. Then it hit me. Where was Sam? He wasn't with me, so those guys must have grabbed him as we ran outside!

What the hell could I do? I was in the middle of the woods with an ax and my cousin was being held hostage by two guys with guns. I sat there on the edge of the woods unable to think of any way to help Sam. At that moment I saw headlights coming towards the house and turn into the driveway. I was so relieved. Sam's parents were back and Uncle Chip would be able to help me or get help. The car was getting closer to the house and that's when I noticed something. It wasn't their car; it was someone else. I watched four more armed men get out of the car, and sat all alone in the cold Vermont woods, helpless.

Not Your Ordinary Short Story …

By Patrick Odierno

Today started out like any other regular day, sleep deprived, awaking to the harsh sound of my alarm clock reading 5:00 A.M. After I slammed the snooze button, I laid back for a few minutes trying to remember last night's dream. After a few minutes of thinking, I remembered my dream was a dream that has been occurring for a few nights now. I'm watching myself getting arrested at work, but wasn't the person being arrested.

I tried to figure out if there was any relevance, but I couldn't since I haven't done anything noticeably bad while in the United States. As I stumbled out of bed, I opened up the curtains to see the array of lights that filled the early morning Manhattan sky and all of the yellow taxis and normal cars on the street from people commuting to work.

At 5:10 A.M. I proceeded down my narrow hallway into the bathroom to take a shower. I turned the squeaky handle to the left and heard the sharp, hissing sound of the water hitting the tile floor of the shower and the plastic on the shower curtain, and jumped in. After I finished resting my head against the shower wall, I daydreamed for a few minutes, still trying to think of any hidden meaning coming from my dreams, but found nothing.

I tried to keep my mind off of it to keep from going crazy, and then I went to my room to get ready for work, threw on my black coat, dress shirt, dress shoes, and dress pants, and headed downstairs for breakfast. As I ate my Frosted Flakes, I realized that I had some extra time, so I looked up some of my old photos from my past.

For about ten minutes I looked over photos from early childhood up to my teen years when I came across a picture that I hadn't seen in a while. It read, Dmitry Markov, 6'1", 185 pounds, Age 22, hair: black, eyes: black, scar above left eyebrow, affiliation: Russian Mafia, and Correctional Facility: Moscow State Prison.

You may be wondering what that is all about, but yes, I am a member of the Russian Mafia and went to jail for seven accounts of murder, and yes, I have the distinct Russian accent when I speak. The only reason that a person like me is on the streets today is because the Russian Government made a promise to me that if I became a spy for Russia to find out government information on the United States, they would set me free. Coming from the very prestigious Moscow State University, the Russian government gave me this chance because they knew how smart I was. I agreed to take the job and was soon off on a plane to New York. This was about five years ago, and now I'm 27 and work for the Secret Service of America. You also may be asking why the US government would hire a killer, a mobster, a demonic creature. Well that is quite simple. I changed my name to Andrei Draganov so the US Government would have no clue who the real me was. I have supplied the Russian government with many secrets about the U.S. Government. My new objective for them is to find out where the President will be at 12:00 P.M. tomorrow—where he will be assassinated by the Russian Mafia.

At 5:30 A.M, I made my way to work. As I closed the door behind me and headed for my black Mercedes, the usual New York City stench overwhelmed me. I sped off to work and got the usual annoyances on the road such as beeping horns and hand gestures.

I pulled into work and entered the building, greeting my fellow employees, but today nothing felt normal. Everyone was looking at me like I had five heads. I thought to myself *just play it cool and act normal, maybe I'm just imagining something*. In the back of my mind I knew that something was up.

Sitting down in my cozy work chair, I tried to get my mind off the thoughts of getting potentially found out for being a Russian spy. About two hours had passed, it was almost time for lunch, and all had been going well, but I was still felt very uncomfortable. The clock finally struck 12, and I sent an email to the Russian Government that I was coming back to Russia with the information

I obtained. I bought my plane ticket and as I walked out the door I heard someone say, "Hey! Get back here!" but I figured that it was just my imagination. I felt as if I had made a clean escape from what might have happened. I returned to my car and retrieved all of my valuable belongings from my house.

I rid the house of anything to do with the Russian Mafia, especially the picture I was looking at this morning, get all of my money and passwords from the US government, and then head off to LaGuardia. I felt sort of like a real gangster again, leaving the U.S. and not getting caught with doing one of the worst things you can ever do to a government. As I raced down 95 towards LaGuardia I saw in my rear view lights, blue and red.

It's a cop car! But I knew that if I just took off, that would only make things worse for my sake, so I pulled over. Two cops exited their vehicle, and as I pushed the electronic button I heard the squeaking sound of my windows go down. I asked the officers, "What is the problem, officers?" with my Russian accent. The officers asked for my driver's registration and license and walked back to their car. I acted cool, but inside I was sitting on a bed of nails. I was frozen in my seat with my mind racing. What could they have found out about me?

About two minutes passed and I see the cops have exited their vehicles. It turns out that it was a routine traffic stop and that they are just giving me a warning because they found out that I am a member of the U.S. Secret Service. I was reluctant to go as I drove off, but I knew I had to get on the plane before anything else happened that could lead to me getting caught. As I pulled up to the airport, I felt a sense of gratitude. I felt as if I was just that much closer to escaping, but I had a thought still stuck in my mind that I was still as close to leaving as to getting caught.

When I arrived at the airport, I smelled the vibrant fumes of the gasoline and I saw the gigantic 747 planes rushing out of the airport. As I entered the airport it sounded like the roaring of 100 lions because of how loud the people were talking, and I made my way through the maze of people awaiting their flight. I then stepped up to the TSA baggage claim to get rid of my bags. The bag weighs

66.5 pounds on the scale, which means that I have to pay an extra twenty-five dollars. I try to argue with the TSA attendant, but she won't budge and I have to pay the extra twenty-five dollars. I sighed and had a little bit of anger building up inside of me, but there should be nothing to worry about because this is the least bad thing that could have happened right now. As I walked down to the plane, I started realizing the couple of military officers that were in the airport and remembered that I will have to go through a security checkpoint. I swiftly checked my pockets to make sure that I had nothing that can get me arrested. I reached into my pocket and found out that I had my old switchblade in there when I felt it pierce my skin. I discovered that my hand started to draw blood and rushed to the bathroom before my shirt received a blood stain. As I entered the disgusting bathroom, I tried to clean myself quickly before anyone in the bathroom recognized my strange behavior. When I finished, I saw a dark red stain on my white T-shirt. I then went into one of those disgusting stalls and got my jacket out of my carry-on bag and threw it on over my ruined my shirt. As I reached the security checkpoint and I went through security, nothing beeped and I thanked God. I tried to keep a smile on my face so I could enter the plane as quickly as possible. I grabbed some food from the nearest Starbuck's and then showed my ticket to the flight attendant and was finally on the plane. As I reached seat B-23 I let out a huge sigh of relief and knew that I finally made it. I would finally make it back home and show my fellow comrades what I have obtained from the foolish U.S. government. After I was finally done scrambling for my iPhone, I called one of the associates from the Russian Government. We then speak in Russian, "I have all of the information we need to take down the President."

He says, "Good, good Dmitry. When are you getting back to Russia?"

I went on saying, "I will be back in Russia tomorrow, and pick me up at the airport around 12:00 P.M."

He then said, "Ok, we will see you there, Dmitry. Mr. Putin will be very pleased with you," then I heard the click of the phone call ending.

I then retrieved my headphones from my bag and plugged them into my iPhone and started listening to some of my Russian music. I thought about sending the information about where the President will be tomorrow on email, but I hadn't gotten much of sleep lately so I just figured I'd wait until I get to Russia. I fell into a light sleep, and in about 20 minutes I was awakened from the overhead speaker and realized that we were on our way to proceed onto the runway. I heard the roar of the jet-engine start and tried to go back to sleep. A couple of moments later the jet-engine shut off and there was a quiet whisper inside the plane; I wondered what was going on. I took off my headphones and tried to eavesdrop onto what was happening from the distant voices inside the plane, but picked up nothing. A couple of minutes have passed and nothing is happening. Suddenly, I heard distant voices coming from outside the plane door saying, "Move! Move! Move!"

The doors burst open with a loud noise, like a metal door slamming, and I saw the faces of police officers storm the inside of the plane like wildfire. The police sprinted right toward me with their guns drawn saying the words, "Get on the ground!" Before I could even argue, I was already on the ground with the ice cold, steel handcuffs on my wrist.

One of the policemen said, "You have the right to remain silent. Anything you say can and will be used against you in a court of law. You have the right to an attorney. If you cannot afford an attorney, one will be appointed to you by the state." It happened so quickly that I really couldn't believe it until I was in the backseat of the police car.

Now I heard the sound of the siren and saw the flashing blue lights through the reflection of the wet roads as the cops rushed me to the nearest precinct. The cops started to ask me questions. The driver of the police car, who was a strong looking white man in his late thirties, asked me, "Do you know why we have arrested you?"

I replied "No, I have no idea officer, sir."

The cop then went on to say, "Well Mr. Markov you are under the arrest for treason of the United States government." My face then turned as red as a habañero pepper and the air was vacuumed out of my lungs. I did not reply because I knew that I had no chance of escaping now. As the cops drove me down to the nearest precinct, it felt like it took three hours. We finally arrived to the Midtown Precinct on 54ᵗʰ street in Manhattan. As I exited the car, I was hit with the pouring rain and only heard the roaring of the rain drops crashing down on the busy New York streets. The cops sent me to a holding cell inside the precinct and the last words they told me were, "You have one phone call, you're held without bail, and you will head to Rikers Island by 12:00 A.M." As they leave and I hear the click of the locking door, I think to myself, *was it all worth it? Is this the way that you could have started a new life I America?* The last thing I thought to myself was *do I have any regrets . . .*

Aftermath—After Dmitry's trial, he is found guilty for treason of the United States government and is put on death row. Dmitry receives death by lethal injection about a month after the trial is over so he could not feed anymore secret information to the Russian government through letters or phone calls. The United states President, however, was not assassinated because the information did not reach the Russian Government in time. However, many other secrets were revealed to the Russian Government because of Dmitry. More importantly, Dmitry's actions intensify the hatred between the two governments. It turns out that the only proof they have on Dmitry was that last day on the Secret Service job when the boss needed the proof to know that he was actually committing treason against the US. When he caught Dmitry sending the final email before he left, the boss was the voice saying, "Hey! Get back here!" and he sent the police to the airport after him. Before his execution, the last thing Dmitry says as he turns to the government officials is, "Thanks for making my job as easy as possible!"

They Say Nobody is Perfect

By Eleni Petridis

—~~~◦~◦⌓⌓~◦~~—

Growing up, my brother Adrian was my hero. I wanted to be just like him and I tried to imitate everything he did. He was the quarterback of the football team, so when I was old enough, I tried out for quarterback of the football team. He listened to rap music, so I listened to rap music. He got his hair buzzed cut, so I got my hair buzzed cut. It never seemed to bother him that I copied everything he did. If anything he embraced it and enjoyed doing things with me even though I'm 8 years younger than him. Of course we fought like all siblings do, but after a couple of hours we both forgot about it. In my opinion, we had the best relationship two brothers can have, and it stayed that way up until he graduated from high school.

You see, my family is not poor, but we don't have money to throw around, either. All of Adrian's friends went away to big universities, but my parents couldn't afford to send him to school for $30,000 a year. Especially since my dad lost his job. In the end, he ended up enrolling in community college about thirty minutes from where we live. So while all his friends were out starting new lives in their college towns, he was stuck living at home.

My parents and he started fighting a lot more, but I thought that's what all kids do when they get older. At least when I watch television I always hear them talking about teenagers and their mood swings. I didn't really think anything about it until he started acting differently with me.

"Hey Adrian, wanna go down to the courts and play some basketball?"

"Tyler, don't you see I have more important things to do right now? Go ask one of your friends to play with you."

I know it doesn't seem like a big deal that a guy in college doesn't want to play basketball with his eleven year old brother, but to me it was a big deal. It wasn't the fact that he didn't have the time to play with me. That happened all the time. It was the fact that he just didn't seem to care anymore. Sometimes it hurts more to have a person ignore you than it does to have them angry with you. At least when they're angry with you, you have some of their attention. It got to the point where I didn't even bother asking him to do anything because I knew the answer would be no.

One night my dad and he came home really late. My dad came into the house yelling more than I ever heard him yell before. They thought I was sleeping, but I couldn't sleep with all of the commotion.

"I'm not going to keep coming to your rescue every time you get in trouble!"

"Dad, you don't even understand!"

"What I do understand is that you're throwing your life out the window, and if you keep acting the way that you are it's only going to get worse!"

"Oh yea, well since when do you care so much?"

"Your mother and I have done everything that we can for you. It's up to you to take some responsibility and get out of this mess that you're in!"

"Okay. Whatever."

I heard him walk upstairs and into his room. I got out of bed and went to talk to him. He has changed so much over the past few months that I got nervous starting conversations with him. It's sad to think that now I hesitate to talk to my own brother, who I used to tell everything to.

"Hey can I talk to you for a minute?"

"Ty, now is not really a good time."

"Why have you and dad been fighting so much lately? I wish it could be like old times when we all just got along."

"You're too young to understand. Now go to sleep. It's late for you to be up."

If there is one thing I hate most it's the phrase, 'You're too young to understand.' I bet you I'd be able to understand a lot of things if he would just talk to me. But even after all that has happened, I continued to make excuses for him, like maybe he's just having a hard time at school or maybe he got into a fight with his best friend. I even went as far as thinking maybe it was something that I did that made him act this way. I didn't want to believe that he changed. That's why it was so hard for me the day my mom told me the worst news I'd ever heard in my life.

"Your brother got arrested for something very bad, and we're not going to see him for a while."

At first I didn't know what to think, and I just sat still. My mom didn't tell me what happened, but said Adrian is in a lot of trouble. To this day, three years later, I still don't know what my brother did that landed him in jail until he turns 25. Adrian used to tell me that I'm too young to understand, and maybe he's right. Maybe I am too young to know what he was going through, but there is something that I do understand. I understand what it is like to idolize someone and place them on a pedestal above everyone else. I understand what it is like to grow apart from someone who you thought would be there for you forever. And what I understand most is that no matter how perfect you believe a person can be, they need to realize it for themselves.

Once Upon a Sign

Jack Kelly

—∿∿◦◦⁀◦⁀◦◦∿∿—

I didn't always want to rob banks. I didn't always feel the need to pump my tired veins with adrenaline, but at age 83, hell, I guess life really is full of surprises. If you tune into channel 9 WKTX, you'll hear about a senile old man who held up the First National American Bank over on Jamestown Boulevard last week. Well, that senile old bastard is me, Red Dawkins, except I'm not as senile as the local police of Goliad, Texas would like to hope. The fact of the matter is that I like to rob banks, plain and simple. I guess its rooted with the fact I need something to distract me from the fact that my wife of 48 years, Jill, died 3 years ago. She was my world and when she left, well I had to cope with my lifeless days.

Most folks my age are so hopped up on prescription pills that their whole life revolves around socks in sandals and Anderson Cooper with CNN. But not me, I don't know why I chose to rob banks as my extra curricular activity, but it just fit. The rush is a high that no other prescription pill or CNN anchor could ever meet. I love the facial expressions of the accountants whose pretty little faces seem to wrinkle like the dirty, unfolded clothes that undoubtedly reside in the best apartments that an accountant of a midsize local bank chain could afford. I love the way the manager's sweat from his nerves mixes with his Rite Aid-brand knock off cologne, which he bought to hoping to get the new 22 year old intern with dirty blonde hair between the sheets, it creates a musty smell that seems to engulf his short, stocky figure. Thirdly, I love the sound of police sirens, most people get scared shitless when they hear one, but I love them. I look at them as a chance to add some excitement into my dull life.

That's the problem with today's youth. No one does anything to piss people off anymore. When was the last time you heard about a rock-star throwing a TV out of a hotel window, or a group of kids rioting in the streets simply because they wanted to? Everyone complies with laws and doesn't push boundaries anymore; it's kind of ironic how I'm the one robbing banks, huh? I suppose robbing banks would have been more fun in my youth. When you're old, everyone just assumes you thought the money was free or that the bank was your house; everyone patronizes you, but I guess that's the glory in it all. You see, this is the third time I've robbed a bank. It's all the same God-damn procedure, the Goliad police catch up with me half way down I-35, ask me condescendingly how my day was, as if I wasn't aware of the federal crime I had committed, they take me to the station, take my picture, and leave me in the cell until judge Daniel Richard can see me. I tell Judge Dan I thought the money I was taking was from my account, he assumes I've learned my lesson, and I'm out in time to have my dinner. The perfect crime.

The strange thing is, just once, I wish I would be treated like the federal offender that I am. I want to feel the hard steel of the rusted, Texan jailhouse bars press against my old bones, and in the last years of my life, that's about as high as my aspirations can be. It's funny how I spent all the 60's revolting against the police and doing all I could to stay out of jail; yet 50 years later, the one dream I have left is to live out the remainder of my days in jail, because it's where I truly believe I belong. It's where I'll reach the end of my road, maybe not the one less traveled on, but then again, Robbie Frost is no Red Dawkins.

Only once in my life I felt like I belonged, and it was with Jill. We were High School Sweethearts and she was the light that broke my bedroom window every morning, and gently made its warm, sweet tenderness onto my face as she greeted me with a kiss. We lived our days in the quieter part of town, away from the already quiet city of Goliad, where the closest thing to the modern world was the one gas station on our side of town, with the bright red sign and the chipped paint that would peel off a little more each day and settled in a small red pile beneath the Diet Pepsi vending machine. That was it. That, in its simplicity, was all Jill and me needed. Just the paint chips and us, but, like the paint chips, she faded away. When the cancer hit her, hell, she was more accepting of it than I was. I cried for days on end, and in the end she was the one consoling me! I suppose it was better that way, because she died the way she wanted to, caring for me.

The funeral was too much for me to bear. After I received my condolences and apologies from people I didn't really know all that well, I wondered why the hell I had to have other people there. No one cared for Jill like I did, and I felt almost angry that it was me, her in the earth, and I realize how twisted that is, but the heart knows what the heart wants.

I got home from the funeral around 5 and walked outside to soak in the cloudy Wednesday evening, and I notice how all the paint chips have finally peeled off and left a bare sign, a sign with no past and no future. It was bare, like I was. I get drunk to cope with my loss and head into town to visit Sweet Rosie's, the best cathouse in all of Texas, and that's where I meet Vivian. She's a young 35 year old brunette with rough eyes from being in the dark all night, but she was beautiful. Maybe it was the Jack Daniels talking, maybe it was the loss of Jill, or maybe I was just in the mood for change, but I went to a party with Vivian later that night, and that's where I realized that old age is a bitter son of a gun. Everyone around me was dancing on each other, doing things I haven't done in 30 years, but the real blur came when the drugs were passed around. I had never done drugs before in my life, and here I am 83 years old going down the binge shoot in the back of the place. This is the moment that the rush of youth and danger come back into my life; this is the night that I commit my first robbery.

It wasn't a tough gig. I stagger into the 7-11 on oak street at about 3 in the morning and pretend to look around for a little bit, shuffle through the latest issue of Rolling Stone, but really I was looking for exit signs, noting how many people were in the store and the size of the cashier. I pick up some jerky and walk up to the cashier, he was a small Mexican boy named Rodrigo, we have our small conversation that every human has when interacting with another for the first time, how are you, some weather were having, it's all the same bull. I ask for a pack of cigarettes to get him to turn his back, the leading ingredient in whatever those kids gave me has now reached it's peak. It's scary yet exhilarating. I take the 0.38 caliber pistol from my pocket and point it at young Rodrigo, he looks at me as if I'm joking and asks what I want. I'm too excited to get the words out, but eventually, in my blinding state, I manage to squeeze out the word "Money."

He grows pale and arches his eyebrows; I could tell he had lost whatever touch Rodrigo had with reality 7 minutes ago. He hands me all $47 and I quickly leave the store. It was the greatest rush I could have ever gotten, and maybe I was spiraling out of control, but I loved it. I walk back to Vivian's house and fall asleep on her couch, the happiest that I had been in a while.

I wake up the next morning with a raging hangover and some kind of crusty substance moved in on my face, but the $47 form the night before that was still in my hand was all I needed to get me going again. By this time Vivian is gone and I'm alone in a strange house, in a strange part of town, but it doesn't matter because for the first time since Jill died, I was happy. I had to get the rush again. I put on my Levi's and the Dallas Cowboys t-shirt I had on the night before and head to local bank on Davidson Road. I had never walked with so much confidence before. Nothing could stop me, and I dared to try anything. This was the day that I robbed my first bank, my orientation to the truth.

But that was a long time ago, I'm older now, less wise I'd like to think. So when you sit down to eat your dinner tonight in front of the TV, in front of Channel 9 WKTX, I only ask for some lone youthful listener to look past the humor of an 83 year old man in handcuffs, and to think for a minute that maybe he's not a crazy old bastard, maybe he's grabbing life. So many people let life pass them by, so many people sit back and watch their dreams and their passions escape from them, but I'll tell you one God-damn thing, if an old bastard like me can find where he belongs, anyone can. I was sentenced to life in jail, and I couldn't be happier. I'm finally where I belong, my paint chips have finally faded from my sign, and I can gently float to the dirt floor below, waiting to be swept into the nurture of the wind.

Taken

By Alexis Noonan

Isabelle awoke to her mom's soft touch. "Time to get up, sweetie," she said. Isabelle groaned and rolled over, only to see that it was 6:00 and way too early to get up.

The sun streamed in through her window, blinding Isabelle as she sat up and yawned. She pulled off her pink polka dot sheets and stood up to stretch. She then walked into the kitchen to see her mom cooking breakfast and her dad sitting at the table, reading the newspaper, and drinking a cup of coffee. She sat down at the table and helped herself to a stack of blueberry pancakes, some bacon, and a glass of orange juice.

"How'd you sleep last night, honey?" asked her dad.

Isabelle responded with a simple, "Fine." She hated when her parents asked her questions like that. They always asked the same questions and she always used the same answers. What also bothered her was the fact that neither of her parents acted like they cared about what she said, they were just trying to start a conversation that always ended up going nowhere.

In the midst of thinking about this, Isabelle forgot that she had yet to get dressed for school. She glanced at the clock and realized that it was 6:45 already. She had to get to school early today to make up a test for AP Calculus, and she couldn't afford to be late.

"Oh my gosh! I have to get ready!" Isabelle gasped. She hurried to her room and began rummaging through her drawers, trying to find something to wear. She decided on something simple: jeans and a tank top with a cardigan over it. She walked into the bathroom and quickly put on some makeup. She didn't have time to do her hair so she just brushed through it and put it up into a messy bun.

She grabbed her black Northface backpack and rushed out of her room, only to forget her chemistry book that was sitting on her desk. She went back in, grabbed the book, and went back out to the kitchen where her parents were still sitting.

"Alright I'm gonna go now," said Isabelle. "I'll see you later. And mom, don't forget that tennis practice is over at 4:30."

"Don't worry, sweetheart. I'll be there, and maybe we can get something to eat after."

Isabelle loved when her mom treated her after practice. It really gave her something to look forward to, and she was actually excited to spend some time with her. She hadn't seen her very much since tennis season started and she started hanging out with her friends more.

She walked out the front door and began the ten minute walk to school, just like she had done every day since middle school. Even though it was almost May, it was still a little chilly out, and Isabelle wished that she had grabbed her jacket on the way out.

The walk to school was pleasant, but nothing special. She usually walked with some of the other neighborhood kids, but since she was so early today, she had to walk by herself. She used this time to think.

As she walked, she thought about the test she had to take in roughly twenty minutes, and thought about how much she could not wait for the week to be over so she could enjoy her weekend.

All of a sudden, a black Mercedes pulled over to the side of the road and a man got out. He was tall, dark, and handsome, wearing sunglasses and a sleek black suit. He looked upset about something, and Isabelle felt bad for him.

"Excuse me," the man said, "I'm sorry to bother you, but my dog seems to have run away and I can't find him anywhere. I figured I'd ask you since you've been walking. He's a little Yorkie puppy. Have you seen him?"

Isabelle hesitated to answer. She knew that you weren't supposed to talk to strangers, but she couldn't just ignore the guy and walk away. She thought about it for a second and decided that she was fifteen years old, not five. There was no harm in just talking to the guy. She would simply tell him that no, she hadn't seen his dog, and then she would continue her walk to school and he would drive away.

"No, I'm sorry, sir. I haven't seen him," Isabelle said. She turned around and began walking away.

All of sudden the man started talking to her again. "You know, if you're on your way to school, I can give you a ride," he said. "I know it's just down the street, but it is kind of cold out here and I'd hate for you to be late."

Isabelle also knew never to get in the car with a stranger. But she was freezing and she needed to get to school in time to take her test. She was already five minutes behind schedule and she couldn't afford to waste any more time. It was only a two minute ride down the road. Against her better judgment, she got into the car.

They drove down the street in an awkward silence, and the whole time Isabelle could feel her heart beating out of her chest. The drive felt like an eternity, and when they finally pulled up to the front of the school, she felt a sense of relief. She exited the car quickly and thanked the man for the ride, making sure to avoid eye contact.

After that, Isabelle's day went as planned. She took her calculus test, went to all her classes, ate lunch, and at the end of the day got changed for practice and headed out to the courts. She started to warm up with her friend Hannah, when she spotted the black Mercedes that she had rode to school in, and inside, was the man. "Why would he be here?" she thought to herself.

For the rest of practice, she found it really hard to focus. She just couldn't wait for her mom to come pick her up so she could put her mind at ease.

When it was finally over, the first thing she did was check her phone. She had a voicemail from her mother, saying that she was sorry that she couldn't pick her up, but something came up at work.

"Great," Isabelle mumbled to herself. How was she going to get home now? All of her teammates had rushed home and she was the only one left. The worst part was that the Mercedes was still there, and she was actually getting really scared.

The only thing left for her to do was walk home. Sure, it was a short walk, but something about the fact that that man was here made her uneasy. She thought about it and realized that there was no other choice. She grabbed her backpack and her racquet and began walking home, at a little faster pace than usual.

Her heart was beating at a thousand miles a minute and she could barely breathe. However, she realized that there was no one in sight, and that made her feel a little bit better. She slowed down a little and allowed herself to catch her breath.

All of a sudden, the strange man that had been stalking her all day appeared, and Isabelle's heart stopped.

He didn't say anything, but looked at her and smiled. Isabelle froze and hoped to God that she would be okay. She thought about running, but feared that he would outrun her. She also considered screaming, but there was no one in sight to hear her. All she could do was stand there, frozen with fear.

Before she could do anything, he grabbed her so she couldn't move, and covered her mouth to prevent her from screaming. All of her belongings were dropped and left on the sidewalk. He dragged her away from the road and behind some trees in the park down the street from school. He had parked his car there and Isabelle noticed that the trunk was open. She tried to scream but nothing came out. Before she knew it, he had thrown her into the trunk and slammed the door, leaving her in complete darkness.

She was laying in a fetal position and the space was so small that she could barely move. She tried to reach for her cell phone, but didn't have much luck. After about five minutes of crying, she attempted to grab her cell phone again. This time she was successful and she managed to unlock her iPhone and call her mom.

"Hello?" her mom answered. Just as Isabelle was about to answer, she heard a beep and saw that she had no service and her call was lost.

"This can't be happening!" Isabelle mumbled.

With that, the car stopped shortly and she heard the door open. "Oh no," she said.

The trunk door opened and the light hurt her eyes.

"Get out," the man said, "Now!" He grabbed her and pulled her out of the trunk.

Isabelle looked up to see a mansion overlooking the city. It was easily the most gorgeous house she had ever seen, but given the situation, she couldn't even enjoy the beauty of it.

The man grabbed her and pushed her towards the front door. Once inside, Isabelle marveled at how stunning the foyer was. The white, marble floors sparkled beneath her, and the large staircase was right out of a fairytale.

"Get in here," the man said. As Isabelle walked in to the gourmet kitchen she was amazed once again at how beautiful this house was, but at the same time, she wondered why he had taken her here. She had expected to be taken to some abandoned motel in the middle of nowhere, like in the stories on the news.

Isabelle feared what he was going to say but to her surprise, he was nice. "Do you want anything to eat?" he said.

Isabelle was extremely confused. The man who had just kidnapped her and thrown her in a trunk was actually being nice to her and offering her something to eat. Instead of just saying yes, she blurted out what she was thinking. "Why are you being so nice? I thought you were supposed to be a kidnapper."

"Whoa, whoa, whoa who said I was a kidnapper?" he said.

"Um, hello? You just kidnapped me!" Isabelle said with disgust. She couldn't believe that this guy was acting like such an idiot. Did he not remember the past few hours?

"What are you talking about? I didn't kidnap you. I just wanted to spend some time with you . . ." the man said.

"Wait, what?" Isabelle said.

"I mean I've been watching you for the past few weeks. I've watched you walk to school, go to practice, and home from school. I just needed to meet you and spend some time with you, but I knew you wouldn't come with me unless I just took you. I didn't mean to scare you."

Isabelle couldn't believe what she was hearing. Right when he said that, she realized that this guy probably had severe psychological issues. It seemed that he was obsessed with her, and she realized that she had to get out of there as soon as possible. But how? While the man's back was turned, she took a peek at her phone, only to see that it was dead.

"I made up a room for you upstairs. It's the second door on the left. I hope you like it."

Isabelle didn't really know what to say, but it was getting late and she was kind of tired. She would rather sit in a room by herself than down here with this guy.

"Okay, thank you. I'm gonna go to bed now."

She ran up the stairs and entered her new room. She stood there, pacing back and forth, trying to figure out what to do. She needed to plan an escape, but how? She figured that she would act normal for a few days and leave when he least expected it.

Before going to sleep, she looked around the room. The drawers were filled with clothes, all her size, and makeup covered the dresser. Had he really been watching her that closely? It occurred to her that he had been planning this for a while, and that really scared her. She had to get out of there, and fast.

In the midst of all this thinking, Isabelle fell asleep and woke up to the man staring intently at her. "I made you breakfast," he said with a smile.

She sat up as he placed a tray on her lap, filled with a plate of scrambled eggs, toast, bacon, and a glass of orange juice. Not even her mother served her breakfast in bed, so Isabelle found it rather strange that a perfect stranger was going through all this trouble for her.

"By the way," the man said, "I have to go to work for just a few hours today so I hope you don't mind having this house all to yourself. There's plenty to do. I have a big screen T.V, a computer, and video games downstairs." With that, he walked out and went downstairs. She heard the front door shut, so she raced downstairs. This was her opportunity to escape.

She couldn't just walk out though. She had to figure out a plan considering she didn't know where she was or how long it would take to get home. Her first thought was to try to find any mail that would say the address, but she couldn't find anything. Next, she went into the den and turned on the computer. While she waited for it to load, she tried to open some of the drawers, none of which opened. She clicked on the internet explorer icon, only to find that he had disconnected the internet. In fact, he had disabled all uses of the computer except for Microsoft Word and solitaire.

Next, she tried to find a phone. Thankfully, there was one in the kitchen, but when she had tried to dial her home phone number, it said that all outgoing calls were disabled. Isabelle started to cry because there was no way for her to reach anyone and she was hesitant about just walking out of the house. However, that seemed to be the only option.

She went to the front door and grabbed the handle, only to realize that it wouldn't open. She ran to the back door, which also wouldn't open. Her pulse was racing as she discovered that she was trapped inside this house with no way out. Her mind filled with thoughts of how else she could leave, but nothing came to mind.

It seemed like it had only been a few minutes, but two hours had already gone by and she heard the garage door open, meaning that the man was back. She ran upstairs and opened the door to the storage closet. She managed to squeeze in between two stacks of cardboard boxes and sat there, praying that he wouldn't come in. She could hear him calling her, and felt the footsteps as he searched every room. The door to the closet opened and her heart dropped.

It was silent, and she couldn't see the man, but she could sense that he was looking around for her. She held her breath, but luckily he left just as fast as he had came in.

Once he left, she waited a few minutes then stood up and cracked open the door. She heard him yelling and cursing downstairs and then heard his car speed out of the driveway. She crept downstairs, being very careful not to be seen, just in case. She walked into the kitchen and out of the corner of her eye she saw that the door from the garage into the mudroom was left open. She walked out of the garage, and because the man had left in such a hurry, the garage door was left open. This was her chance, and despite not really having a plan, she was going to leave.

She started walking down the long winding driveway. She decided it would be a better idea to jog until she got away from the house and into town. Once there, she got onto a main road she stopped and took a breath. She stopped and sat down on a bench on the side of the road, and right then, she saw the man driving down the street towards her. He pulled over and jumped out of the car.

"How could you leave like that after everything I had done for you? Can't you see I just want to be near you?" he said.

"But why?" Isabelle asked. "I had never seen you before yesterday."

"It doesn't matter. Come with me, we're going back to the house."

Now that they were in a public place, Isabelle screamed for help and shouted, "Call the police! Please! He's trying to kidnap me!" The people around her gasped and pulled out their cell phones, rapidly dialing 911. Isabelle struggled to keep the man off of her, and tried with all her might to keep her ground.

In what seemed like only a minute, a police car arrived and two officers jumped out of the car with their guns up. "Let the girl go, sir. Now!" they shouted.

"No!" he said. "I love her. She has to come home with me."

"Let her go or we'll shoot."

After a second of hesitation, he let Isabelle go and one of the officers raced towards him to handcuff him. The other walked over to Isabelle to comfort her. They called her parents and they hurried to the scene. They had not seen their daughter in 24 hours, but not knowing where she was made it seem like 24 years.

Isabelle sat there with her parents, crying and hugging. She was so happy this was all over and was so glad she was back with them, where she belonged. She lifted her head off of her dads shoulder and saw her kidnapper in the back of the squad car. That guy had serious issues, and her thoughts of what could have happened made her shiver. She was just glad to be out of there alive. Sure, she hadn't had the perfect life before, but who does? This whole experience made her thankful for the life that she had, and made her see that she wouldn't trade it for anything.

He Was Her Everything

Tiffany Arredondo

―――⌇〰⌇○⌇〰⌇―――

A boat floating on the dark blue water, swaying with each subtle wave that stroked its side. There was no sound. Only the water's movement along the boat was audible. It was complete serenity. Complete quietness. Peace in this beautiful evening.

A figure appeared. He waved from the boat. Happiness danced around him. Emma raised her hand to shield the sun. There was no face to this figure, but she felt her heart soar out to him. He was everything. He was her air, love, forever there.

The sky was painted with warm yellows, dewy purples, and bright pinks as the sun set over the horizon. It was as though the heavens themselves had painted this beautiful scene for the people on earth to admire. So many colors that were growing darker and darker as the sun dipped lower. Beyond the colors, where the sky grew darker, she could see the intricate patterns of the constellations begin to appear as nighttime crept upon them.

She looked above her. The clouds' edges absorbed these bright sunset colors the same way they would with just normal sunlight. Shifting colors. Moving. The white masses floated slowly across the sky. Watercolors blending on a white canvas.

The sky darkened all of a sudden. Fear settled inside of her. Panic. The bright sky changed further. Absolute darkness surrounded her. The waves became more violent. The boat was thrashed against the water. She watched in horror as the small boat was completely submerged beneath the colossal waves and swallowed from sight. Hungry waves taking what didn't belong to them.

She ran. Water splashed around her, and lightening streaked the sky. The boat was gone though. She couldn't see it. Couldn't see the sole figure anymore. Her heart fell. She stopped running. It was pointless.

The boat was gone.

He was gone.

And she was alone.

She woke, feeling her heart beat rapidly in her chest as the tears slowly slid from her eyes. Reid's arm was around her, and although it normally brought her comfort, nothing could settle the knot of nerves building inside of her. No matter how hard she tried, she couldn't shake the feeling. It was so much more than a dream. Her heart told her so.

Often, when Emma dreamed at night, she dreamed the sort of dreams that were only beautiful if they were never spoken aloud. They were lovely to say the least, and they kept her wanting to close her eyes and let sleep carry her away while she was awake. She dreamed of sitting on a white beach and as far as she could see in every direction, there was no dark form of an approaching figure, set aside the one next to her. Together they listened to the birds above them sway in the ocean air, sending their calls out. She felt happiness and love and peace.

Then there were the dreams that made her wish so desperately that she had never fallen asleep in the first place. They were the dreams that made her feel as though something was horribly wrong. Dreams filled with darkness and pain. She had been having the same reoccurring dream over and over for two months now. The same boat. The same beautiful sky. The same storm. Her heart always falling as she realized she was alone.

It never stopped. It was always around the time that Reid went out in his boat for a few hours, and even though she never saw the face of the figure in her dream, she knew it was him. He was always the one sitting beside her on that white beach smiling and laughing, and he was always the one that was swallowed by the violent waves of the ocean. It was always him.

He was her everything. He gave her everything. He gave her so much when she was close to having nothing. He gave her a home, happiness, and a reason to keep living life when everything around her just washed away into nonexistence. Losing him wasn't an option. She would die before that happened.

Each time she had the dream, she feared for Reid's life. She feared that the one person that meant the most to her would vanish like everything else. She just couldn't shake the feeling. She never could. The fear only grew when his departure drew near.

He left at noon. Sometimes later, sometimes earlier, but he always went. That one day where Emma prayed and wished that he would be okay. She would wait and wait and watch the horizon from the back window of their house for a sign of his return. She couldn't allow herself to move until she knew that he would be lying beside her at night again.

He breathed out over her neck and pulled her back closer into his chest. "You finally awake, Ems?" She didn't want to say anything. He would be able to tell she was upset with one word. Instead, she laced her fingers with his and gave his hand a squeeze. Her entire body felt numb.

The warning she felt was the strongest it had ever been. She tried to focus on the heat radiating from Reid's body, and the feel of his skin touching hers. Anything to make what she felt go away. None of it worked. She silently cried and wiped away tears all morning, and when the time for him to leave finally arrived yet again, it felt like she was going to collapse with all the emotions she was feeling. It was too much.

The water crept close to her toes as the blue waves fell against the sand of the small sliver of a beach. The sun shone down its rays and made the water reflect like a million distant stars in the night sky. Sea birds flew above her, their calls mixing with the rush of the ocean, bringing a calmness to the evening. With each push and pull of the ocean's waves reaching the shore, a new gift was given from the vast waters. A variety of shells dotted the sand—different shapes, sizes, colors, all unique in some way.

It was truly a place that anyone could feel at peace, and yet, Emma just felt fear. She pressed her toes into the wet sand and took in a deep breath, smelling the ocean air and trying to stop the tears that wouldn't stop.

The pain was unbearable. The fear was terrifying. With each soft touch of the warm wind grazing her face, the emotions she felt rose to higher altitudes. The wind was off. It felt strange.

The screen door behind her banged shut, and she wiped at her eyes quickly as Reid made his way down to the dock. She wanted him to stay, by God did she want him to just forget about the trip, but she didn't feel right to ask that of him. He went out on his boat once a week. It was something that he used to do with his father when he was still alive. Every week they would go out into the water and every week they would enjoy the quietness of the ocean. They didn't fish. They didn't swim. They just sat and listened. Reid had to continue the trip every week, even though his father was gone. He never missed it, and Emma wasn't going to stop him. She wouldn't be selfish.

She managed a small smile when he held his hand out for her to take, and walked with her to the end of the dock. Unlike her dream, they didn't live on a long and never-ending beach of white sand. They lived in a small house that was surrounded by trees in every direction, and only had a small expanse of pebbly sand beside the dock that Reid's boat was tied to. And it was perfect. She loved their home. She loved everything about it. Any place with him was perfect to her.

"You feeling alright?" he asked.

"Mhm," she kept her face hidden with her hair, "just be careful okay?"

"I'm always careful."

"I know, I know. Just . . . be careful."

He stopped and looked at her curiously then. The fear was plain on her face, even if he could barely see it. "You have a bad feeling, Ems?"

He knew that she sometimes felt like there was something very wrong. It had happened many times before. It wasn't just the dream that time though. The air didn't feel right, and she knew in the pit of her stomach that something wasn't right. Every single time in the past she was wrong. Nothing bad happened, and it made her believe that she was foolish to ever think otherwise. How could she possibly know when a perfect day, much like that one, was going to end terribly?

She smiled weakly at Reid and shook her head. "No, I'm fine."

"Emma," he began, looking out at the water, "if you don't feel right about me leaving today, I won't go." He shrugged and rested his hands on the sides of her face, moving a strand of light hair behind her ear. "I have no problem staying here with you. You're actually not that bad," he joked.

Reid would never do anything to upset her, she knew that. If she said to stay, he would stay, but it was just a feeling. It was just a dream. "I'm never right, Reid. Go. Okay?"

"You sure?"

She nodded and reached up to kiss his cheek softly. "Have fun."

He wrapped his arms around her waist and lifted her up the few inches from the dock. "I'm going to have to take you at some point. Eventually. I think you'd like it."

It would be a while before he was okay to do that. His father hadn't even been gone for a year. Emma wasn't entirely sure if she would want to go with him when he was ready. The nightmares were enough to keep her away. "Maybe," she replied.

"Maybe." He gave her two quick kisses before he set her down. "I'll be back in about an hour or so."

"Don't rush it, Reid."

"You're obviously upset. It's going to be a quick trip this time and I'll be right back here with you," he reassured her. "I promise."

She watched him step into the small boat and lift the thick rope off the dock post that kept it in place. "I love you."

He looked up at her and smiled, the gold of his eyes shining in the light. "I love you too, Ems."

As he turned the key and slowly drifted away from her, she rubbed her lips together and sat down. She didn't always sit out there and wait, but she had to be sure. She wanted to see him on his way back when he was only a speck on the horizon. That would be enough to calm her nerves.

Until then, she waited. She sat beneath the warm rays of the sun and stared out at the water like a statue. The time ticked away, and what felt like an hour was quickly behind her. There was no sign of him. She waited more. The fear started to settle in even deeper, and it felt like there was something lodged in her throat, making it hard to swallow. He'd be back. She knew it. He always came back. This time was no different.

As if to remind her how wrong she was to think that, the wind caressed her face. It felt so wrong to her.

The sun started to set, and she watched as the sky began to match that of the one in her dream. It had been more than an hour. She knew it, and she began to panic. When it started to rain, she had to fight back the tears. It was just a storm, she had to remind herself. It wasn't any different. The tears blended in with the rain splashing against her face. The large drops soaked through her clothes and created millions of ripples in the blue water. It was like the sky could feel her pain and it too was sad.

Where was he?

She kept her head down and stared at her hands, the small diamond ring reminding her of what he promised. He said forever. He would never leave her alone. He would always be there for her. The events of her past would never hurt her if he had anything to do with it. Reid had been her rock. He kept her from falling apart when she almost lost everything. He would never leave her alone.

Emma pulled her legs up to her chest and buried her face. The sun had long set and still she waited. The flashes of lightening couldn't move her. Neither the heavy rain nor the absolute darkness that consumed her surroundings before each violent flash of light could move her. Nothing could. He should've been back. He said it would only take an hour, and he was always careful. He said he would be. He should've been back.

The dream was almost taunting her in the back of her mind. She could've stopped him, but she didn't. It was her fault. How could she let him go? How could she ignore something that was so strong?

Her dream. That bad feeling she had since this morning. She didn't want it to be real, but she knew it was. Reid wasn't coming back. He wouldn't, and the pain it brought her was even worse than all the hurt she had felt in her life.

She couldn't bring herself to move no matter how hard she tried. The ocean had taken him, and she wanted him back, so she waited, and waited, and waited. The day would never come, she knew that, but nothing could make her move. What was the point? What did she have?

"Reid," she cried quietly. She lifted her head and looked out at the dark water being churned by the storm. Her hair was sticking to the sides of her face and she shook with a chill. She didn't care. She didn't want to feel anything ever again.

She had a bad feeling in the pit of her stomach but she ignored it, and now he was gone.

Her everything.

Entre Tus Heridas

Jazmin Sanchez

———◦◦◦◦◦◦———

Let me open your eyes to a world that, for so long, you have ignored. The one you see so far, yet it is so close; the one that you conceive as a fantasy, a tragedy, a story, that you will never be part of until it hits you, deep down, in a place where scars are easily made, and the memories are never forgotten. It is a story found in between pages, in different books, all written in the darkness, because that is where I found them. The events are not in order because there are truths that should never be told, but all you need to do is close your eyes, and then you will see clearly; through me, into him and his past.

I wake up and I look around, it is past midnight, and slowly I get down from bed and walk to the bathroom. I open the door slowly, but before I move I can see him close his eyes and let his body rest against the wall. Slowly, he pulls up his arm and closes the door. I know that soon he will be gone, what I didn't know is that he would leave behind his past, at least a part of it. It will do no harm to leave a note, to leave the past hidden in those pages of books not made for untold stories, an unexpected place to forget all that has been hunting him. Flashbacks, hallucinations, dreams, memories, people, his life, left written in the back of dictionaries as if it would give a new definition, in fiction tales, as if it would make it unreal.

A day has passed and he is gone, gone for good, and in his usual manner, he leaves a note. A note saying bye, a note that welcomes my journey into the story of a man I will always love. Just yesterday he told me to be like a butterfly, to expand my wings and fly, no matter what the distance was it would not tire me, but give me strength.

To be like a butterfly and show my colors, I had a whole life ahead to wear black, and he was still not dead. I grab the note and stick it inside the first book I pulled out from the shelf. Just yesterday he was sleeping in my room while I stayed at the guest room, just to make him comfortable, and now he is gone. As I place the note inside the book, I notice his hand writing and I tell myself that tonight I will read his last message. The day goes on and the room is dark. Everyone is in bed, and I'm wide awake. I get up, trying to find my place in the darkness of the room, and grab the first book I can reach. I close my eyes and I start to cry; I can remember last night as he too sat here and started to write. He is not a writer, you must know, but this is the way to liberate the pain he carries, to cover the scars, or to just let them bleed out.

As dark as it may be I can still read his last message. The light of the lamp outside is enough to outline the page and make every word legible.

"The best way out was to cover the harm, to not look back. For he stood up so tall and great, who was I to shame his name, who were they to believe the truth? You hear the laughter, you feel the joy, and I feel the pain and his hand in my skin. You see them around el abuelo, sitting, talking, and sharing their time with their loved ones. I see myself in the darkness; I share this space, as he makes love and produces pain, and leaves a mark. I'm only five and he is thirty, I'm just a boy, he is a man, I tell lies, he has learned to tell the truth; the truth in his eyes, as he hides what he should have never done. He was the author of my life, a sexual act that gave him pleasure and chose the direction of my path."

I close my eyes and I still feel the pain, a knot in my chest, as I could picture what he went through. It only makes me think of where that man could be and what is of his life. It makes me think of those who experience what he went through and how, until this day, his secret is safe. His story is still unpublished, his acts soon to be revealed, his memory still inerasable, his act still causing damage. If I could just be close to him, hug him and take the pain, but I'm too young and I cannot understand why it would have to be this way. I flip the pages and realize that there is no more, I look at other books and find the missing pieces to his puzzle.

"I have what you need, I need what you have, but in a time like this, I will take whatever you give. Depend on something and your life will not function properly. I need drugs, I need drinks, and I give whatever they will take. I walk to the train station, down the stairs, and into the tunnel. I see three people standing; they look at me and nod, two women, one man. One puts her arm around me, she is Colombian, I can tell, her great figure gives it away, her accent confirms my thought, and her beauty draws me close. The second women is Puerto Rican, not as pretty, but with a strong personality, her eyes say determination, and her movements show control. The man comes, and with a nod signals us to walk up the stairs, out of the tunnel and into the streets. They give me drugs if I pay, the money I have is limited, it's not even mine—if it belongs to anyone it would belong the little mouths waiting at the house. A house where I don't belong, a family that I don't deserve, a sister that I cannot love, and a niece that waits for the one she considers her father. But for now I cannot think I need what they have, and I'll pay with all I can. The Colombian girl comes and whispers that it will cost more than the money I have, but I can pay with my body. Drugs, it's all I have, it's all I need, at least for now.

I can still remember that night, but I cannot remember him coming with anyone else. He walked to the door and fell to the floor. His black hair hard and bushy, his golden brown skin lost its glow, his face lost its figure and he turned into a sunken skull. My mother looked at me, her face was tired, her body was low from the weight of her stomach which carried my sister, and her eyes were wet from all the tears. She told me to push my uncle as she would pull him up the stairs. Yet, as we walk you could already feel the smell, he had pushed his bowel into his pants. I could tell this would be another rough night, there was cleaning to do. The next morning, it only got worse. My mom walked out of the room as he came out of the shower, she saw him and hugged him,

With a voice as gentle as a mother, for she had been his mother all this time that my grandma was unable to be with us, she said, "Manito I want you to change."

"Things will change, I promise," he said. Those were his last words, and then he was lost in the big city. A city that we all knew so well, for we lived in it, but that hid those who got lost in the shadows.

I didn't see him, he never came back, and all that was left were his things in his room. His Enanitos Verdes CD, his Caifanes wall post and the smell of cigars. I remember praying each night for him to come back; we ended up moving and then my prayers were heard.

I'm sitting down where he sat yesterday, thinking of the day he finally came back. It took him three years, in which he lost his mind, his health, himself. I remember walking out and seeing him looking at the house. How had he found us? I did not know. All I knew was that he was back and that was all that mattered. Things were not the same, yet he was still the same with me. Three years had passed; I had grown my hair long and brown, my skin had his golden tone, my eyes were black, and my smile slowly fading. He did not talk, he could not talk, and he did not want to talk. He wrote everything down, this way no one would listen to his voice and find out where he was. 'His people' had placed a microphone in his throat and could easily find him. There were cameras everywhere for the people to spy on him. People wanted something from him, they wanted to keep him, to kill him, and so he would not eat. I never knew who 'his people' were; all I knew is that whatever happened while he stayed in New York had changed him. Every question I had he would answer it by writing, and in his writing I would find the answer. I got up and looked through more books.

"Sometimes I found myself starving with nothing to eat; I stayed under the tunnel at the train station. During these times, anything that would wet my mouth and touch my taste buds was good, even if it meant eating my own coagulated blood that came from my nose into my stomach."

The thought of seeing my uncle under the tunnel with nothing to eat but his coagulated blood-filled buggers produce such hate inside of me that I could only let out by crying. For the past three years I had enjoyed a good life. I ate whenever I pleased, and whatever I desired, I got; yet any misunderstanding shifted my world. A small problem, because the cause of desolation, while my uncle lived such a life in which it was impossible to think, took the last energy out of my body. I close the books, I have read enough. Two hours have passed and I'm still sitting here. Thoughts fill my mind as feelings penetrate my heart, and I cannot help it but to cry.

Where is he now? He is where he belongs, trying to make up for all the time that was wasted. He tries to make a new life, a new future, and forget the past. It has been easy to forget, not because memories are easily forgotten, but because the drugs affected his brain. What I cannot forget and will never forget are his last words,

"Voy a ser un guerrero de sangre para que nadie te haga daño, quiero verte como una mariposa volar alrededor, vencer el mundo y sus barreras, y nunca temerle al dolor."

"I could write a whole book if I wanted to, but I only want to open your eyes not live that world for you. I want to show you that in life we have to go beyond that wall that divides our lives into an illusion and reality, into your world and mine."

The Cycle

By Tiffany Volpe

───∽∾⌒⊙⌒∾∽───

"Don't talk to any of them. They'll tie you up—they'll get you. They're all whores."

I knew by the screaming and hollering of the inmates that there was a new patient being admitted. I rolled over on my cot and looked up at the cracks and chips in the ceiling, 1,837. That's how many dots are on the tiles; I know because I've counted them.

"Ms. Marshall," one of the staff members called me, "Ms. Marshall, you need to get up and dressed for the day."

I did not want to move from my rest. I sulked and sat up.

"Coming!" I said.

I shuffled my feet across the floor, making slight scuff marks on the linoleum tiles, as I sauntered to the cafeteria. I looked at the buffet options. Dark green peas that looked dried out, along with a soupy mix of chopped meat, and mashed potatoes to go with it. Repulsed, I walked to an empty table, foodless.

"Honey," I heard a tender voice call. It sounded just like how my mother used to call to me, "You need to eat something, its part of the protocol here."

A peppy, blonde lady was telling me to eat that disgusting food, "Are you kidding me?" I responded with a blank stare.

A second lady with dark hair approached me with a tray of slop. She dipped a spoon in it and said, "Open wide."

At that point I lost it. I pushed my seat back, the chair legs skidding across the cold, unforgiving floor, making a wretched screeching noise. I got up and kicked one of the women in the gut. As she tried to make her way up, I slapped her across the face. I was soon ambushed by three bulky security men. They escorted me back to my cell. I did not resist, however, because part of me wanted to go back anyways. Upon returning to my cell I went to sleep. While sleeping I dreamt of a memory from my childhood.

I was on my bathroom floor in a puddle of some sort. I soon came to realize it was my own blood. My mother was huddled over me, crying, and my father was grabbing towels off the cabinet shelves, trying to create a tourniquet to stop the bleeding from my wrists. That was the day I was committed here. That was the day that I was deemed a hazard to myself. What my parents didn't realize is that was also the day I found out Tony, my boyfriend for over a year, was cheating on me. I didn't know how to handle it, so I coped the best way I knew how. I put the razor's cold, smooth blade against my wrist and dragged it across. I had been "cleansing" myself this way ever since I was 13, after being abused by a family member. Now, at 18, it was different. This time though, this time I made a mistake. The blade went in too far and cut too deeply, and the loss of blood caused me to pass out. My parent heard the thud of my body hitting the floor and I became partially paralyzed, unable to move. Whether it was from shock or some sort of physical damage, I don't know. The next thing I remember was waking up in the emergency room, laying on a stiff cot, my wrist bandaged with gauze and medical tape. The clearest memory for me, though, was the smell of the hospital. It smelled like an old person. Not grandma's perfume or grandpa's pipe, but that crusty, general yellow smell, of an old person.

I was awoken from my sleep by the blinding light of the sun creeping in through the curtains. I tried to roll over and go back to sleep, but I was interrupted by a gruff, male voice. It sounded very manly, almost like the person was over-compensating for an area they lacked in.

"Ms. Marshall," the voice called, "you need to get ready for your therapy today."

Crap. No. This cannot be happening. I recalled last night's antics, when I assaulted the female staffers after they tried to force feed me. I told them no, but they didn't listen to me. Maybe I can just hide under the covers like I used to when I was younger and knew I was in trouble. I pulled the cold imitation cotton fabric sheets over my head. It smelled like the emergency room blankets.

A smell of sorrow engulfed my nostrils. I lay silent under the covers, not daring to move, keeping my breathing monitored. The next sound I heard made my heart stop. My door was kicked open, and I heard slow, heavy foot steps moving towards my bed. A large shadow began to fill all the cracks of light in my room.

"Amber you need to stop this," he spoke. How did he know my name? I never told anyone my name before. I didn't care what this clever stranger said, though, I did not budge. The next thing I felt were strong, masculine arms simultaneously ripping off my covers and picking me up. I punched and screamed, but not even the pounding of my frail fists could deter him from his mission. I was carried unwillingly to the electroshock therapy room. My eyes gazed eagerly at all the wires and machinery. I found some humor in the fact that this room was all white, symbolizing purity and morality, and yet this was one of the coldest, most unsympathetic places I knew. The male nurse spread petroleum jelly on my temples after strapping down my arms, legs, and head. I closed my eyes and took a deep breath. *Here we go again.* The next thing I felt was a shock traveling up and down my spine at the same time.

I awoke back in my room. I was tired and sore. I decided to go for a walk to the bathing quarters and freshen up. As I walked out of my room, my bare feet stung from the cold floor. I tried to ignore it and kept walking.

"No! Get away!"

I heard screams coming from down the hallway. "Another patient must be going in for therapy," I thought to myself. I kept walking forward. An older woman approached me. She had disappearing gray hair, and her eyes had a lost look to them.

"Pray for salvation, child!" she screamed at me, "They're coming. They're all coming to get us! No one is safe anymore, nothing shall be the same!"

I stood dumbstruck looking at her, and then I passed on by. I learned not to take anyone seriously here, because sooner or later everyone was driven crazy, but not me. I'd never let myself get like that. As I walked into the bathroom the piss stained floors let off a

God-awful stench. I wondered how this could be a humane place to live.

"Buh!" I heard a scream come from a stall.

I turned around and saw no one there. *Okay Amber, keep it together. You're just stressed out, no one's there.* I walked over to the sink and turned the water on. It gushed out in spurts for about thirteen seconds before a steady stream would flow. I looked in the mirror; my once perfect cheek bones looked grotesque and overtly apparent. My eyes were sunken in with dark circles underneath them. My blonde hair was now dirty and greasy and fell down in strands. *At least my nose is still perfect.* I splashed the cold water onto my face. As it dripped down I opened my eyes, half my face was melting off!

"What's going on?" I screamed. "No, stop! Ahhhh!" I furiously began clawing at my face and maniacally splashing water. This time, though, when I looked in the mirror my face was normal. Had I imagined it? It seemed so real.

"Aaaaaaamber . . . Aaaaamber . . ." I heard a singsong voice calling my name. I couldn't stand it. I hated hearing my real name. It reminded me of when life used to be a happy place for me. I cupped my hands over my ears and yelled.

"Stop it! Stop! Stop! Stop! Stop!" My screams became pleas. As I continued pleading with my mind, which was slowly driving me insane, my body collapsed to the floor. As my side smacked onto the hard cold bathroom tiles, I became physically paralyzed. As I lay on the floor, internally bleeding, unable to make a sound, I couldn't help but think how ironic it was that my life was ending in the institution the same way it began. On a cold, tile floor. Maybe this was all planned. Maybe this is all just a cycle.

Demon Slayer

By Carly Mammoliti

———〰〰≈≈≈〰〰———

Constant. Never ending. That is what these dreams are, and oh, don't forget annoying. I hate them with such a deep passion I'm beginning to see an unhealthy obsession forming from it.

These dreams don't just haunt me while I sleep, though. They have started to show up while I'm conscious. At first, I thought all of it was one big hallucination, but to dream about something and then see it happen makes me wonder.

Maybe I'm going crazy. What if the entire thing is just a dream like the movie *Inception* or something? Jeez, I need a life.

What if this is just my brain trying to entertain me because of the lack of friends I have? Whatever this is, it's driving me crazy. Pretty soon I'll be wrapped in a straightjacket and brought to one of those scary, padded rooms.

"Lucy, it's time for school," my mom said to me from down the stairs.

I couldn't help but to think about what lies ahead of me today. "Hmmmm," I thought out loud, "will it be one of the shadowy figures pretending to be a 'popular', or maybe I'll have to deal with one of the colored guys who are constantly watching my every move."

Talking to myself, a habit I recently picked up to help me feel like I was still sane after all of this began to happen. "Go figure, right."

Now the shadowy people falling in with other people's shadows was something I thought I was just imagining, but when I started to notice odd looking creatures staring at me through windows and discreetly watching as I walked to and from school, I honestly thought I was going mental. Though, for some reason today felt different. Who knows, maybe the insane images my brain has started to create will leave me alone for just a day.

I got up and got ready for school, running down the stairs and shouting a "bye" to my mom while heading out the door and starting my journey to the prison also known as high school. I hate it there; I have no friends because every one already thinks I'm a freak. "Oh, if they only knew," I said out loud, as if by chance some one could hear my plea for sanity.

While I was walking, I saw them. There were about three purple creatures in tan trench coats and bowler hats sitting in a 50s-styled car; not even trying to hide the fact they were staring at me, almost as if they where spies.

Though today, I just feel exhausted. "You have got to be kidding me! I'm so done brain, just done," I said again to no one and walked over to the car to give the odd looking creatures a hand gesture my mother would scold me for if she ever saw me doing to anyone.

I knocked on the window, taking in the look of shock and surprise on the purple creature's face. "Hey buddy, I don't know who you are, or why you guys keep following me. Frankly, I think this is all an illusion my brain made up, but do you think you could just lay off? I would much prefer my sanity," I said rather rudely but quietly, in case someone sane happened to walk by and saw me talking to a parked car, or worse, I could be talking to absolutely nothing.

"I'm sorry miss, but I cannot do that. I would not be doing my job, and that would cost me more than my job, miss," the creature said to me. Oh great job brain, it speaks! I have officially lost every marble up in that big empty scull of mine. Some one call the mental institution, time to have Lucy admitted.

I guess I have a look of shock and confusion on my face because the one in the driver's seat started to talk next.

"Miss, I'm afraid you have already seen and *heard* too much," he said looking at the *thing* next to him. "You will be coming with us, I'm afraid, miss."

I think by now the shock is completely gone, and confusion has taken over my facial expression. I just can't seem to comprehend what that creature just said to me. Did he just tell me I'll be coming with him? Coming where?

Before even having a chance to ask myself another question, I was pulled into the back of the old looking car and it sped off into a brick wall. A BRICK WALL?

I was about to scream when the front end of the car hit the wall, covering my face for an impact that never came.

"Okay, what is going on? I'm taking it my whole 'it's all in your head Lucy there's no such thing as purple beings' is all a lie. So then what, exactly, are you, then?"

"I'm afraid that is something we cannot tell you, miss," said the one in the driver's seat again. "That is something only the master can explain."

"Okay, well who's the master? And where exactly am I?" I had so many questions, and I just wanted them to explain some of them.

Now it was the one next to me to speak, "all in due time, miss. All in due time."

What was that supposed to mean? How did I even get in this screwed up situation? I thought I was on my way to school. School, I mentally sighed to myself, never in my life have I wanted to be there so badly.

As the car drove, I looked out the window, noticing a pink sky with black clouds and no sign of a sun in sight. Knowing that the creatures with me in the car wouldn't answer any of my questions, I just continued to observe my new surroundings.

I was so consumed in the odd sight of no trees and just black houses everywhere, I almost missed the creature next to me speaking. "It will be a long drive, miss. The master would prefer that you try to sleep now so you are not tired upon arrival of the estate," he said rather formally.

"Oh," I said, caught of guard, "okay." I took out my iPod and pretended to listen to it while I closed my eyes. There was no way I'm missing any of their conversation while they think I'm sleeping.

However, as the minutes ticked by, the car was in complete silence. But I still didn't trust these strange beings enough to let my guard down. Heck, I was being kidnapped if you wanted to get technical about the situation.

It felt like I was stuck in the car for hours before it finally stopped in front of a large-looking mansion. "We're here," said the creature next to me. "That's great," I thought to myself, but where exactly is *here*?

However, I was soon broken from my thoughts by one of the purple guys. "The master would like to see you now, miss," he said to me. We had walked into the building and all I could see were winding staircases and hallways full of doors.

"Okay," I said, "take me to your master." I had to stop myself from laughing at that last part. It feels like I'm in an alien movie. That thought made my mind begin to wander and wonder if the purple creatures before me were aliens. They don't look like aliens. Then again, I wouldn't personally know what an alien looks like.

As these thoughts raced through my mind, I was following the purple creatures up one of the staircases, down a hallway, and up to the third door on the left. The one in front knocked on the door, asking permission to enter.

A muffled "come in" was heard, and they opened the door, pushing me in and leaving me to fend for myself in front of the 'master.'

"Hello, Lucy," the man in front of me said. He looked normal, tall, with dark hair and matching eyes. The man couldn't have been more than twenty, and seemed friendly, but how did he know my name?

"How do you know my name?"

"Oh come on now, I know you have noticed my men keeping tabs on you for me," he said to me in a bored tone.

"Alright," I said to him, "let's pretend that this is all real and I'm not completely insane. Now, where exactly am I, and what do you want with me?"

These weren't all of the questions I had, but considering I think I'm dreaming and going to wake up any minute there's a time limit here.

"Oh that's right. Where are my manners? My name is Zachary Adams," he said, "and I'm afraid this isn't a dream Lucy. You are in my world now, Magia. Also, there are certain reasons why you are here, Lucy. Reasons that have to do with the dreams you've been having, and the things you can see that happen to people."

"How do you know about those?"

"I thought we went through this, Lucy. My men, or rather trolls, if you want to get technical, have been watching you for quite sometime now," he said to me in all seriousness.

His world? Magia? *TROLLS?* Wasn't it bad enough that I already thought I was an insane loser with no friends, but now I find out that this is all *real?*

"Okay, so pretending like I'm not about to freak out or feint," I said with the look of a panic attack coming on, "what exactly is it that you want from me, and what's in my dreams, or the weird shadow things?" I was beyond confused and heading into insane territory again.

"Precisely that," he said with a slight smile to his features, "you have dreams about these shadow people and my trolls because you can see things before they happen. You're psychic, Lucy."

"Alright, that explains the weird dreams. Now what about the shadow things? Are those your 'men' too?" In the few minutes I've been here I'm doing a good job of not showing how freaked out I am, but I guess I learned how to hide it about the same time the dreams and seeing things started.

"No, not at all. These shadow things, as you call them, are demons. Not very nice creatures, I'm afraid. They tend to be attracted to humans whose souls are un-pure. They feed off of sins and encourage the human 'host', if you will, to commit more acts of evil."

As he was explaining this, the pieces began to put themselves into place. Well, in an odd way. Still confused about why I was psychic and what that had to do with these demons, which I didn't even think really existed.

"What does any of that have to do with me being psychic? I didn't even think demons really existed," I said to Zachary.

"Well Lucy, you are one of the few 'chosen' who can see them and destroy them."

"So what you are trying to tell me is that I'm in some different world called Magia, I'm psychic, and I can kill demons?" I said, not believing a word of it, "and I thought I was crazy before! When am I going to wake up from this completely mental dream?"

"Well for starters, we are known as Demon Slayers, and I'm afraid I'm telling you the truth," said Zachary. "I apologize if it is a bit much to take in all at once, but we need you.

"A war is about to begin. Demon Slayers against demons. On our side we have the Nymphs, or Fairies, and Pixies, and also those trolls and other creatures that have turned to see a better life on the 'good side,' against all demons and every creature that inhibits the Underworld."

"Yeah, that is a lot to take in all at once," I said, "But what do *I* do about it? I'm just one person."

"You may be just once person, Lucy, but you are not the only Demon Slayer. We have teams all over your world, protecting humans from demons, and we need all of us to help in this war," he said looking remorseful about there even being a war.

"I see," I said trying to let him know I understood when I really didn't. I couldn't think straight, everything just hit me like bricks and I felt like I could fall down and be crushed by the weight of it all on my shoulders.

"So, I'm guessing you want to use my psychic abilities to help in this war, right?" I was going out on a limb with this suggestion, but I didn't think I was wrong.

"That is correct," he said, "I don't mean to ask to use you, but it may be the only way our side has a chance at winning this war and preventing many deaths.

"However, the choice is your. You can choose to help us, or you can choose to return back to your world."

I thought about what he was offering me. A life of fulfilling what I was born for, or one of constantly questioning my sanity.

"I'll do it," I said, looking the stranger directly in the eyes with as much emotion I could muster up for the time being.

"Well then," Zachary said, "we must begin your training immediately, and study your psychic abilities further."

"Training?"

"Oh yes. I wouldn't just throw you out into a war, vulnerable and not knowing how to destroy a demon," he said to me as he gestured for me to follow him out the door, down several hallways and staircases, until reaching a blue door that stood out from all the other brown ones. "We begin your training now."

And I did. I trained every day for what seemed like months, but was only a few weeks. I learned to control and use my abilities to benefit the war and before I could catch my breath, it seems, the war was beginning.

As I came face to face with the shadowy creatures, who were more slime than shadowy up close, I had to remind myself to focus on my training instead of them. Using my psychic abilities to predict their every action I was able to warn other members on my own side before fatal blows were delivered to them.

I was fighting the demons next to Zachary, helping each other when needed like he had taught me to do in the previous weeks. We had grown to be friends during the sleepless hours we had spent together on days end. The thought of possibly loosing the only friend it seems I have was the worst thing imaginable.

We fought for hours, casualties only seeming to accumulate on the demons' side; until finally they had surrendered with a quarter of their 'men' laying on the ground.

"Thank you," Zachary said to me after hearing news about the surrender, "we could not have one this war without you."

"Well I am a Demon Slayer after all, it's what I do."

It seems that life around Mangia could settle down and I could experience a calm life here compared to one of constant fear of the war.

As the Demon Slayers' side began to retreat in victory, an arrow suddenly flew by my face and headed directly towards Zachary's back. Before I even had time to blink, he was on the ground, motionless.

Falling to my knees a simple "no" escaped my lips. The entire battle field falling into an eerie silence, I closed my eyes, and the silence was broken by a strange beeping noise.

The noise got louder and louder, like I was getting closer to the source. When I was finally able to open my eyes, I was staring straight at the light blue ceiling in my bedroom.

"Lucy, time for school," my mom said from down the stairs.

I was back in my own world, and I knew what was going to happen today. I knew what I had to do.

Go through today just like I did in my dream, and at the end of the war, save Zachary.

Stuck In the Waves

By Kelly Mulvehill

—⚬⚬⚬⚬—

"How could he do this to me?" Sydney couldn't help but get mad at her dad for making them move again. With him constantly traveling for work, they never spent much time in any one place. And of course now they had to leave as soon as Sydney was finally making friends. She picked the picture of her mom off her bed to pack it away, and remembered all the good times with her. Sydney was only four when this picture was taken, and their smiling faces made her wish she could go back to that time. Her mom's warm smile always made her happy, and she thought of how proud she would be of her for making friends.

"Mom wouldn't have made me move again," she thought to herself.

The rumbling of the moving-truck's engine shook Sydney's room and her dad yelled up the stairs, "Come on, Sid, we've got to go!" She stroked the old wooden frame of the picture, pushed it into her suitcase, took one last look at her favorite home, and said goodbye, knowing she would never love another home the same way.

After eight hours in her dad's cramped 1994 Nissan Altima, they pulled up to their new house. It was much too big for two people, and had an old, colonial look to it. Sydney was looking at the paint color—an ugly mustard yellow, when she looked next door and saw an old lady gardening in her yard. Sydney had been through this before—moved into a neighborhood of old people—and it only made it harder to make friends. "Great," she thought, "No kids."

The next day Sydney had to go to school, and although she new she would make friends, she was terrified. "Are you sure I have to go, dad?" she pleaded.

"Yes, Sid," he said, handing her lunch for the day, "Go ahead, it won't be bad, everyone'll want to be friends with you." Sydney grabbed her lunch and shoved it into her backpack, groaning at her dad's optimism. She swung the front door open, and took a step into the bright sun and a brand new school day.

On the way to school she thought about all her other first days of school and how they were all the same, and finally gained some confidence. That was until she got her schedule and found out she had swimming first period. She tried with all her might to explain to the guidance lady why she couldn't take that class—she couldn't even swim! Ever since that day at the beach—no she wouldn't let herself thing about that, not here, not now. "Just please, ma'am, I need a schedule change." The guidance lady just stared at her with cold, beady eyes, with no sympathy for her. The decision was final.

Defeated, Sydney left the guidance office and heard the secretaries laughing together, "Oh please, who doesn't know how to swim? What a pathetic excuse to get out of class, everyone knows how to swim!" they mocked her.

Giving up with convincing these women, Sydney headed to class to change, and prayed the teacher would be more reasonable. "Excuse me? Mr . . . ." she peeped, looking down at her schedule, ". . . Rich?"

"What?"

"You see, there's been a mistake. I can't be in this class, I don't now how to swim."

"Ha! Nice try, kid. Next time try something more believable, like 'The dog ate my homework!' Ha!" he jeered, fat, jiggling jaw sending spit flying into Sydney's face, "Get in the pool!" he suddenly shouted, angry now, and blew his sharp, ear-splitting whistle, sending kids scrambling into the pool

It all happened so quickly, one boy ran past Sydney and gave her a little shove to get her moving, sending her off-balance. She immediately tumbled over and felt herself falling through the air. She wanted to scream but was too terrified to even produce a sound. She felt a rush of air whiz past her and the cool water engulf her body. Terrified, she looked up at the blue world surrounding her and thought this was the end. The surface was getting farther away, and the water getting darker, and before she new it the world around her faded to black.

*　　*　　*

"Ha! Wee! Catch me! Ha! Stop it!" Laughing and smiling kids filled the beach on this sunny summer day. Parents lay in the sun and built sandcastles with their kids, and the waves crashed loudly on the shore. The salty breeze cooled the air on this record high day of 105°F. It was the perfect day at the beach, and the water was beautiful blue and welcoming. Sydney ran up to her mom and snatched her hand. Looking up at her with the beautiful blue eyes of an innocent five-year-old, she smiled at her mom, "Can we go swimming, Mommy?" she asked, "Will you take me?"

"Sure, honey, just hold my hand, the waves are big," she told her.

"Bigger than you mommy?" she asked, amazed.

"No not bigger than me, Sid," she laughed, "But bigger than you! Just stay with me and we'll be fine."

Excited to get in the refreshingly cool water, Sydney pulled her mom faster towards the water and they waded in together. They started splashing and jumping over waves, having a great time. Sydney's mom always had a way of making her laugh. Sydney thought they were invincible; nothing could hurt her with her mom there. The chilly waves splashed Sydney's face and made her giggle, forgetting about the other people on the beach. Suddenly, Sydney felt a huge wave come crashing over her head, and her mom's hands get ripped away. Panicked, she looked around for her mom, but couldn't see her. "Mommy! Mommy where are you! Mom!"

*　　*　　*

Sydney jumped and shot her eyes open, trying to figure out where she was. She was lying on wet concrete surrounded by twenty some-odd kids staring and laughing at her. Her teacher leaned over her and got angry once he saw her come back into consciousness, "Why didn't you tell us you couldn't swim?"

Humiliated and annoyed, Sydney went to the nurse's office, hoping to go home. Nurse Betsy, however, sent her back to her second period class with a clean bill of health. She soon found out how fast gossip spreads in a small school, for the rest of the school day she had to endure stares and taunts from her fellow classmates for being the freaky new girl who didn't know how to swim.

"There she is!" a boy named Roy mocked her, making faces and acting like he was drowning. Once satisfied with making his friends laugh, he approached Sydney at her desk, "Nice job today, new kid. What's your name?"

"Sydney."

"Well, Sydney, I don't know where you're from, but around here everyone knows how to swim. Welcome to the wonderful world of living in a small costal town with nothing better to do." She just gave him a cold stare. "Well if you're looking for friends, you're not going to make them at the bottom of a pool. I can help you there," he said with a mischievous look in his eye.

Sydney looked at his small brown eyes and thin crew-cut brown hair. He was a skinny little kid and not very tall. She suddenly recognized him as the boy who pushed her into the pool, and she looked down to see him leaning on her desk with his hand on top of her open history book. She looked up at him then slammed the book shut with all her might, crushing his hand. "Ouch!" he shouted, making the teacher look up, "Hey! You—"

"Roy! Take a seat, and leave Miss Reynolds alone!" the teacher reprimanded him. He gave Sydney a dirty look and stormed away to his seat, clutching his hand.

"Okay class, today we'll be learning about . . ." the teacher's words faded away as Sydney drifted off in thought, annoyed at her terrible first day.

"So what if I can't swim? What kind of a town cares about that anyway?" she wondered. "Now I really don't fit in and no one will want to be friends with the weirdo who embarrassed herself in front of everyone. And what happened in that pool? That dream, it felt so real. Like it really happened. But I couldn't have—"

The bell rang, bringing Sydney back into reality and as she picked up her books she was thankful the day was over and wouldn't get any worse.

She got on the bus and looked for a seat, only to be greeted by cold stares and whispers—no doubt about her incident this morning. She sat by herself in the front of the bus and waited to arrive at her stop. The bus drove through the center of town and Sydney noticed the town was so small they only had one traffic light. Once they left the hustle and bustle of the town center, the bus drove past the beach that was ever so important to this town. Only one side of the beach looked suitable for tanning or swimming while the rest of the land consisted of rocks and large boulders creating sheer cliffs and choppy water. There were hardly any tress and Sydney thought it was a terrible beach and certainly not one to be proud of. The dark blue-gray water disappeared from view as the bus continued down the road and Sydney was glad to leave it—she hated beaches.

The bus screeched to a stop and Sydney stood up to get off. She set off down her street and was about to reach her house when she heard footsteps behind her.

She jumped around and saw none other than Roy and his group of trouble-making friends walking behind her. "What do you want?" she asked.

"We just felt bad about earlier today," he said, "maybe we can all try again, you could be our friend."

"Trust me, you're the last person I would want to be friends with," she said, although she wasn't sure she meant that herself—at this point she was sure no one else would be her friends.

Suddenly, Sydney's old lady neighbor came out of her house and into her yard noticing Sydney. "Oh my, hello Sydney, dear," she said, "why don't you come in with your friends?"

"Yea Sydney, bring in your friends," Roy said.

"Yea bring in your friends," his friends echoed.

"No, no, Grace, they're not—"

"—Come in!"

Sydney groaned and the kids all filed into the house. She sat down in the living room and Roy and his posse did the same.

"I just wanted to get to know you a bit better, and it looks like you're so sweet you already have tons of friends," Grace said.

Sydney didn't bother telling her they weren't her friends. It seemed like no one listened to her anymore. She looked around the house and noticed how untidy it looked. Papers were everywhere and everything was covered in dust.

"I'm sorry my dad and I haven't visited yet," Sydney said.

"Oh it's okay, pumpkin. Honestly I've been too busy lost in all this paperwork," she said, suddenly looking like she may cry, "I'm piled up in debt, and the bank may take this house away from me, and I—"

Sydney saw she was getting too flustered so she tried to change the subject, "That's a beautiful necklace you have on," she said.

Grace stopped short and forgot about worrying. She grabbed the extremely large green-blue gem around her neck and said, "Oh this? Thank you. I love it too, it's been in my family for years," she said, smile fading again, "although I think I may have to sell it to pay off my debt. Oh . . . . excuse me, I . . . I have to go." She pulled the necklace off and put it down, running out of the room covering her face. Sydney felt like she said everything wrong and should go check on her, when Roy stood up.

"Man, this old lady is lame, let's go," he said, motioning for everyone to go.

"What? She's sweet. We need to check on her, she was so upset," Sydney said.

"Man, you're lame too, new kid," he said.

"No I'm not."

"No? Then prove it. You want any friends, then . . . take that," he said pointing the old necklace.

"What?"

"Take it," he said as everyone stared at her and waited for her move.

Conflicted, Sydney didn't know what to do. She knew it was the wrong thing, but she needed friends. And if they didn't like her, no one would.

She reached out and snatched the necklace, "Let's go," she said and the kids ran out of the house.

"Nice job Sydney," Roy said, suddenly much nicer to her. "Now give me that," he said.

Sydney opened her mouth to argue, but closed it again, not wanting to get on Roy's bad side again. She handed him the necklace, instantly feeling guilty, but trying to ignore it.

"Okay, later," he said, "we're out." The kids all turned around and followed Roy away, leaving Sydney alone.

She walked over to her house and went inside and up to her room. She started working on her homework and before she new it the clock read 12:30$_{AM}$. Exhausted, she got in her pajamas and climbed into bed. As soon as her head hit the pillow she drifted off to sleep.

* * *

The water crashed over Sydney's head and she couldn't feel the bottom. "Mommy! Mommy!" she yelled over and over again, voice muffled each time she swallowed water. The cold, salty water crushed Sydney and made her eyes sting, and she could feel herself getting tired.

Just as her head went under she felt hands grab her and pull her back out. "There you are Mommy, what happened?" she asked as a pair of arms carried her back to the beach. Mommy didn't respond, though, and she felt herself being laid down on the sand. She opened her eyes to see why her mom didn't respond, but when she did all she saw was her dad walking away from her. People suddenly crowded around her, and she couldn't see her dad anymore. She tried to look around the people, but they wouldn't let her. "Move, I want my mom," she yelled, starting to cry, "Where is she? Daddy! Daddy, where's mom? I want my mom!" She suddenly heard someone tell her to rest and felt a hand on her shoulder push her back down.

*   *   *

The alarm clock buzzed and Sydney woke up to turn it off. "What's with these dreams?" she wondered and got up to take a shower. She got ready for school, not looking forward to seeing Roy or anyone else, but the day wasn't too bad. Some other people talked to her that day, and Roy didn't mention the necklace, so she didn't have to worry about that. "Maybe taking that necklace wasn't such a bad thing after all. People are actually treating me normally," she thought to herself. On her way home, however, she passed Grace in her yard and saw the strange looks she gave her. She hurried past feeling immensely guilty and went inside her house. The rest of her week went about the same way only her nightmares kept getting worse. Always the same one, a day at the beach that goes terribly wrong, and they only reminded her of her fear of the water.

One day next week Sydney came home to find her dad home early. "What's going on, dad? What're you doing home so soon?" she asked.

"Have a seat. We need to talk," he said and motioned to the chair across from him, "Grace Brown notified me that you were over at her house the other day with a group of friends after school. She said she showed you a necklace of hers that then went missing as soon as you left."

Sydney couldn't believe this was happening, "How could he have found out so soon?" she thought. "I don't have it, dad," she said.

"Come on Sydney, let's not make this harder than this has to be. She said she's not going to press charges, but she needs that necklace. She's just an old lady, she needs the money."

"I don't have it."

He stared at her and said, "You're grounded."

"But dad—"

"No arguments! I didn't think I raised a daughter who would lie to me, or take advantage of an innocent old lady. I didn't know this move would change you," he said.

Sydney heard his car turn on and screech out of the driveway. "I'm not a bad person," she thought, "why did I take that necklace? I have to get it back." She grabbed her backpack and ran out the door as soon as she knew her dad was gone. "I've got to find Roy," she thought to herself, "and fix this."

She jumped on her bike and peddled off in search of Roy. She rode for ten minutes when she went past the beach and had to stop short when she saw Roy and his posse messing around on the rocks. Anxious, Sydney parked her bike and took a hesitant step onto the beach. "Hey! Roy!" she said, walking up to him and keeping as far away from the edge of the cliff as possible, "I've got to talk to you."

"Oh hey, Sydney! You come to hang out?" he asked.

"No. I need that necklace back."

"What?" he said sitting up off the ground and getting up, "I knew you were too lame, new kid."

"Look, I don't care anymore. I should have never taken that necklace. Now I just need you to give it back to me."

"I don't have it."

"Yes you do, Roy. Now give it to me!"

"Oh you mean this necklace?" he said pulling it out of his pocket and holding it above his head so Sydney couldn't reach.

"Yes, come on and drop it. Just give it to me."

"Oh sure, I'll drop it," he said, "You're right, sorry." He took a step closer to the ledge and held the necklace over it.

"No Roy, don't!" she shouted, but it was too late.

He let go of the necklace, and Sydney saw it plummet through the air and land in the dark water. "Go get it, new kid," he said laughing at her, "Come on, guys, let's go." Everyone left leaving Sydney there panicked. She could barely breathe as she looked over the ledge at the choppy water below. The rocks created a huge drop-off and the water below crashed as the wind blew through Sydney's hair. "What do I do?" she thought, "What do I do? I can't just leave, I have to do something. I have to get that necklace; otherwise no one will believe me."

She couldn't believe she was about to do this, but she threw off her backpack, said a prayer, and dove. She hit the water and the cold shot through her like a thousand knives, making her gasp and swallow the water. "What am I doing?" she asked herself, "I'm so stupid!" She surfaced and gasped for breath, barley able to hold herself up over the huge waves. Memories came flooding back to her of those terrifying nightmares, of the water crushing her and her not being able to touch the bottom. The water pushed her over and she tumbled under the water, not sure which way was up and which was down. She could barely see through the dark water, and could feel herself drifting out of consciousness. She couldn't hold her breath any longer, and just when she was about to give up she saw it.

Not ten feet below her, the green-blue necklace glittered in the sunlight through the water and caught her eye. "I can reach that," she thought. She held on to her breath and tried to swim for the necklace. She just reached the necklace and stuck her hand out to grab the gem but couldn't hold her breath any longer. She felt the smooth gem touch her hand and as the world faded to black she made an aimless grab for it.

*   *   *

"Sweetie lay down," a woman said, but Sydney wouldn't listen. She tore away from the woman and ran through the crowd, stopping short at the waters' edge. "Mommy?" she whispered in shock. One hundred feet out in the water, a small dot Sydney could recognize as her mother was having trouble staying above water. A rip tide had pulled her out to sea and she was not a strong swimmer. Sydney's dad had fallen to the ground in the shallow water, weeping, knowing the lifeguards would

never reach her in time. The entire crowded beach had turned silent and everyone was on the shore, watching.

"Mommy!" Sydney shouted, starting to cry. This time no one came over to stop her and she just lay down and sobbed. "My Mommy!" she cried, "Mommy . . ."

Her Mommy never made it back to the beach, and the lifeguards did not reach her in time. "How did this happen?" Sydney asked herself, "It's all my fault; I made her go swimming with me." She couldn't stop crying and afterwards her dad barely talked to her.

Their family became distant and for the longest time Sydney's dad acted like nothing happened. They were never the same. There was always something missing in the house, and although the community was supportive, soon they had to move, and Sydney never went near the water again.

*   *   *

Sydney woke up on the cold sand, soaking wet and drowsy. It was dark and windy and she couldn't believe she was awake. "I'm alive?" she asked herself, sitting up and coughing. "Those nightmares, they weren't dreams at all, they . . . were memories," she thought.

"Oh thank goodness," said a voice behind her, "what were you thinking, kid? I'd thought I lost you." She turned around and saw a soaking wet man sitting behind her.

"How . . . how did you find me?" she asked.

"I come by here every day, and I was walking along the rocks when I saw you in the water. You went under and didn't come back up so I went in after you."

"Thank . . . thank you," she said.

"What were you doing anyway?"

"The necklace!" she thought to herself. She grabbed her pocket and felt inside it—no gem. After all that work and she hadn't even gotten it. "Nothing," she said. Now no one would ever believe her.

"Well are you feeling okay?" he asked, "You ought to head home, it's getting late."

"Right, okay. Thank you again."

"No problem, kid. Glad I was here."

She got home when it was pitch black, and she saw her dad's car in the drive way. She quietly walked into the house and snuck up to bed, remembering she was grounded and hoping her dad didn't know she was gone.

She went to sleep and for the first night in weeks she slept soundly. In the morning she went downstairs for breakfast, got ready for school, and left for the day.

She got to class to find Roy talking to a bunch of kids. "Yea, a real rotten egg," he said, "Can you believe it? She actually stole from an old lady!"

Sydney couldn't believe it—he was actually telling everyone *she* stole the necklace and making her seem like the bad guy. "You and I both know that's not true, Roy," she said.

"Come on Sydney. Don't accuse other people of what you know you did," a classmate said.

"But I didn't!" she said.

"Not cool, Sydney," another kid said.

"Kids sit down! It's time for class!" the teacher said.

Sydney was devastated. Everyone in the entire town thought she was a thief, even her own father.

She sat by herself again on the bus home and when she got to her house, she walked in to find her dad packing boxes.

"What's going on?" she asked.

"Where were you last night? I explicitly grounded you, and I come home to find you out, who knows where," he said.

Sydney didn't know what to say, no one would ever believe her. "What's with the boxes?" she asked.

"We're moving," he said, "I asked for a transfer, you need a new environment. One where you aren't influenced to be a bad kid. Starting next week you'll be taking classes at an all girl's reformatory boarding school, and I'll be working in Detroit. Go pack your bags."

Sydney ran upstairs, unable to say a word. She had tried to fix everything, but failed miserably. Now her father didn't even trust her, and Grace and the entire town thought she was a thief. "I'm sorry, Mom," she said looking at the picture of them and packing it into her trunk. "Why did this happen to me?" she asked and lay down on her bed and started to cry.

Heist

By Elle O'Hara

I remember the day. It is forever tattooed to my brain. I keep playing that day over and over in my head. What was I thinking? My name is Allen. Allen Edwards. And this is my story.

I was always a drifter. I never really fit in anywhere, and that was a problem. During a time of prohibition and depression, the loneliness was unbearable. But that's just something I had to deal with. Like everyone else, I had no job, no money, and nowhere to go. The only places where I felt like I belonged were speakeasies. They satisfied the need for an adrenaline rush that I had always had. Butch McGuire's down on the South Side of the windy city was my regular spot. And that's where I met Foster, Foster Dillinger that is. Foster was a dreamer, that's for sure. He was very similar to me. We shared the same height of 5 feet 11 inches. Our hair was casually pushed back, and our faces perfectly shaven. My eyes were a golden brown, but always had a dead look to them. But Foster's eyes, yes Foster's eyes had a spark that you could not forget. When he stared at you, you couldn't help but stare back. He put you under a trance. You could tell he was a dark, twisted man, and he had big plans for his future.

We ran into each other a few more times over the next couple weeks. But I always kept my guard up. Besides, I overheard a bull session between a couple of guys, and they all said he was bad news. He had some beef with the other gangsters in the South Side and owed them a lot of dough. That's when I began seeing the wanted posters.

WANTED:

Foster Dillinger.
5 feet 11 inches.
160 lbs. Brown hair.
Hazel eyes.
Wanted for bank robbery and murder.
Reward: $1,000

Foster was dangerous. But as I walked down the alleys of Chi Town, alone, with no money or family, all I could think about was what he was wanted for: bank robbery.

He had something going there. What was I to lose? I had nothing anyways. I needed some dough now and fast. I needed to find him.

I found out that he was hiding in some abandoned warehouse, so I met him there.

"Foster, I've heard you been scoring some real dough lately," I said.

"Talk is cheap. They don't know what I've been doing," Foster said.

"I'm not here to rat you out. I want in."

"How am I supposed to know you aren't messing with me?"

"I need the money bad. And money ain't something I mess around with."

"If you ain't messing with me, then meet me at McGuire's tomorrow at sundown. Now scram, and you never saw me."

I did what he told me to. I got to the underground bar just as the sun finally faded away. He was there too, and he had his gang with him.

"So, you weren't kidding were ya?" Foster asked me.

"Nope. So what's the plan?" I asked.

"Slow down there kiddo, we are about to set out the plan. Now this is what we got to do." Foster points to two guys standing in the corner with gray fedora hats and tailored suits that cost more than any money I ever had.

"Buzz and Red, you guys will go stake out the First National Bank here on the South Side. That's our target," Foster said.

The two patsies nodded and headed out with their submachine guns to go scope out the bank. Then Foster turned to me.

"You're gonna have the hardest job. I need you to get a job as the bank's teller. I've—"

"I have to what? How the hell am I supposed to get a job when I don't have any experience?"

"Kid, pipe down. I have connections with some guys on the police force, and they have some references for you to make sure you get the job."

"Okay, so I just walk in and get the job."

"Yes, that's your job for now. I'll let you know the rest of the plan, as we get closer to the date. We can't do this without you. You need to be our inside man. Now beat it, and do what I told you to do."

*   *   *

"Dinner Time!" the prison guard yelled.

I was sitting in my cold, dark cell that only contained a metal bunk bed, a sink, and toilet. My roommate was not a threat to me, which is not what I can say for most of the guys in here. I was staring at the rotting white ceiling, and then, at that moment, I realized where I had went wrong. Foster said he knew some guys on the force. I should've realized that he was no good. Foster just could not be trusted.

I turned my head to look at the "so-called" meat and vegetables that were on the plate in front of me. I took one small bite, and then pushed it away from me. This place is hell.

*   *   *

The next morning I woke up at 5. My apartment doesn't have water, so I had to find a place to shower. Foster made it clear that I needed to look like I meant business. I was able to find an old, run-down shower in an abandoned building. The water was cold, but it worked. I got in real quick, and then started getting ready. I slowly and carefully shaved the hair off my chin. I grabbed the suit that Foster gave me, slicked back my hair, and headed out to the bank.

"Hello, sir, how can I help you?" asked one of the bank clerks.

"I am here for the bank teller position. Do you know where I am supposed to be?" I asked.

"Oh yes sir, we have been waiting for you. Follow me this way."

He walked me back to an extravagantly decorated room in the back that was covered in marble. When we walked in, another man greeted me, and started my interview. It was only about 2 minutes into the interview when he told me I got the job. I felt a smirk appear on my face.

That night I went back to the joint where Foster and I had first made the plan.

"You did good, kid. Your next step is to get the keys to the vaults, and find out all of the security codes. You're gonna have to be the one that gets us in."

"I can do that," I said.

The next day, I arrived at the bank at 9 am. The bank clerk I had the day before told me everything I needed to know. He told me where the vaults were, he gave me the keys, and of course the security codes. It was like taking candy from a baby. This plan was going to be easy.

Foster had contacted me and told me that Wednesday at noon would be the date of the heist. He told me to meet him behind McGuire's that morning before I went to the bank.

The days went by fast and all of sudden it was Wednesday. I woke up early. The bank robbery finally hit me. Today was the day I had been waiting for. As always, I made my way to the joint where I met Foster, Buzz, an d Red. We all knew the plan, and we were about to score big.

I left the gang and went to the bank as instructed. It started out just like any other day. The people came in and out one by one. I watched the clock as it slowly made its way to each hour.

The clock rang at noon.

I went to the back door, punched in the code, and let Foster and the guys in.

"C'mon scram, bring us to the damn vault already!" Foster said.

"Easy, it's right this way." I said.

They followed me back to the vault in that same extravagant back room where I was first interviewed. I used my recently made key to open up the vault. Foster started to grab the wads of cash, armfuls at a time. That's when we heard the siren go off.

"What the hell did you do?" Foster said.

"I didn't do anything, I swear!" I said.

Foster grabbed the last bit of rubes and was off. When I saw the cops coming in, I ran outside to the meeting place we had decided on. But when I got there, Foster was already closing the car door and then he sped off.

This was all a set up. Foster had double-crossed me. I was the fall guy.

I felt a sudden burst of pain and fell to the floor. I looked up and the cops were on top of me, handcuffing my hands behind my back.

I faintly heard one of them say, "Stupid kid, you can't trust Foster."

This must have been the guy he knew from the inside. Foster had set up this whole thing, so that I would get him in the bank. He was planning on ditching me this whole time, so he could keep the money all to himself. I couldn't believe that damn bastard.

"Allen Edwards, you are hereby under arrest for being a co-conspirator in a robbery. You have the right to remain silent . . ." the cop continued with his speech.

My trial date was set for three weeks from that day.

Those three weeks flew by and it was time for my trial. The judge welcomed me, "Please take your seat son," he said.

The district attorney pleaded his case, and my lawyer made his rebuttal. Unfortunately, the jury was not sympathetic of me and sent my ass right off to jail for a minimum of ten years for co-conspiracy in a robbery.

There was no way I was going to let Foster get away with this. These next ten years will be filled with plot-making for my revenge.

So that's how I got here. Living poor as dirt doesn't seem so bad anymore. The slammer is hell. I don't know whom I could ever trust again in this town. But I do know one thing. When I get out, Foster Dillinger is going down.

Never Forget

By Taylor Kennerly

—·—

"Promise me."

Cold eyes, the color of blue ice stared back at me, but I felt no fear. This was my best friend, my protector from playground bullies.

"But you're moving away," I said, tears beginning to swell in my eyes. He took my hand and squeezed it.

"I'll be back," he said, "but only if you promise." I looked at Victor. At first view, anyone would have thought he was a normal third grader with his pale blond hair and olive skin. But anyone who took the time to look into his eyes would see only darkness, a quiet storm beneath them. It's what kept kids away from him and what drew us together from the start. Two lonely kids; two weird pairs of eyes. The recess bell rang and I came back to reality. He licked his chapped pink lips and squeezed my hand harder.

"Promise me?" he whispered. I nodded my head as my chocolate brown hair fell into my face.

"Okay, I promise. I won't forget you. I promise we'll be best friends . . . forever."

8 Years Later

My name is Katherine Epps, Kat for short. A nickname endowed to me for my slanted eyes. One blue, one green.

I adjusted the straps on my laced tank top. It was supposed to be hot today, never the less, my curly hair hung down well past my shoulders, finally tamed after years of being what my Dad used to call "borderline bird nest". A car outside honked its horn signaling its arrival to pick me up and I booked it out the door.

"Come on, I have a paper that I have to turn in before school starts," she said.

I laughed at my best friend Candice. "What kind of extra credit are you doing now?"

She stuck her tongue out at me as we pulled off down the street in her candy red convertible. We drove quickly, but even at a normal pace our school was no more than 10 minutes away. Riverside was a small community made up of green lawns and cul-de-sacs. In the short ride to our school, you were given a tour of our whole town. The small white city hall, family owned stores, and the old movie theatre, all bordering a river, made up the center of all our activities. We pulled up to a stop light and Candice pushed back the loose strands of blonde hair that had escaped her french braid.

She pushed up her glasses and smiled, "So, did Andy ask you to the bonfire yet?"

I laughed at the question she'd been asking me every day this week. "No, but there's only a few days left. He'll ask me soon . . . maybe even today." I smiled to myself at the thought.

"I don't know why you're so intrigued by my love life when yours is so interesting."

Candice rolled her eyes as she pulled into the school parking lot. "Oh please, you know I don't have time for guys."

Easily one of the prettiest girls in school, Candice was also the smartest. Between college prep courses and academic clubs she viewed boys as, "not part of her game plan", and ended up breaking hearts all over town.

We stepped out of the car and walked into school. Candice hurried off on her quest for academic excellence.

"See you third period!" She winked at me.

"Good luck!" I shook my head and went to turn around, accidently bumping into someone.

"Kat?"

I looked up into familiar blue eyes. Elementary school memories flashed in my head as a strong hand helped me to my feet. I stared back at my old childhood friend. He'd grown several feet taller and gained a few pounds of lean muscle. His black V-neck t-shirt accentuated his pale skin, making him look like he hadn't been outside for months. He smiled crookedly as he took my hand and squeezed it.

"I told you I'd be back."

I was speechless, still in shock at the sight of my old best friend. He frowned down at me, the storm beneath his eyes raging.

"Don't tell me you've forgotten me."

I quickly pulled back from him plastering a smile on my face.

"Of course not," I stuttered, "how could I forget my best friend?"

He smiled brightly and leaned in to give me a hug.

"Hey Kat!" I turned around and Andy embraced me in a tight hug.

"Ready for math?"

He looked over at Victor still behind me and smiled draping his arm over me protectively, "I'm sorry, are you new here?"

Victor stared back coldly and put out his hand for Andy to shake.

"I'm Victor, Katherine's best friend."

My eyes widened at Victor's self-given title.

"Weird, I thought Candice was your best friend," said Andy.

I tried to quickly back pedal out the situation. "She is," I explained quickly, "Victor and I used to be best friends, in elementary school."

It wasn't hard to see the hurt in Victor's eyes. The warning bell rang for the start of first period.

"I really have to go Victor, or I'm gonna be late. I guess I'll see you around?" Andy turned me around and steered me to class before Victor got a chance to reply. I turned back to see Victor standing in the same spot I'd left him. I tried my best to smile back at him, "I'll see you later okay?" and I hurried off to Pre-Calculus.

Andy and I walked into Pre-Calculus and took a seat at our desks.

"That Victor kid is kinda weird. How did you two even become friends?" he asked.

I took out my books and flipped through the pages, trying to look focused on yesterday's homework.

"I was kind of a loser when I was little. So was he. I guess we just kind of got drawn to each other," I shrugged. "Anyway, he ended up moving away in like third grade. Eventually I grew up, got some new friends, and that was it."

"Well, I don't know. He still seems kind of weird to me, but I guess if you guys were cool, he's okay." He paused for a moment and then smiled at me. "That reminds me of something I've been meaning to ask you . . ."

All day I thought about Victor and the look in his eyes. I couldn't believe how he thought that we were still best friends, let alone that he had reappeared in Riverdale at all. Even when Andy asked me to the bonfire that afternoon my mind was elsewhere.

"What's up?" said Candice on our drive home from school, "you look distracted."

I shook my head, unwilling to give up any information until I had figured it out for myself.

"It's nothing."

She shrugged her shoulders and turned the corner on to my street.

"Well I have interesting news. During my study hall today I was helping Mrs. Pricely, you know the school nurse, file some stuff. While she was out helping a student, I found this huge file on a kid that had everything you could think of when it comes to the mental department. Schizophrenia, multiple personalities, anger management, everything I swear," she shook her head. "I can't believe they'd even let someone like that into the school."

I shivered and erased the thought from my mind. "Well, even if they did I think they'd have enough sense to put him in those kinds of separate classes."

I got out the car and shut the door. "Later," I said.

As she drove away, I walked up to my front door, reaching into my pockets in search for my keys.

"Kat"

I turned around and there was Victor, standing on the side walk.

"What are you doing here?" I asked surprised.

He looked up and down the street and shrugged his shoulders, "I just remember where your house is, that's all. I forgot to ask you if you were going to the bonfire this Saturday."

I stared at Victor for a moment, contemplating whether to lie or not, and finally decided to just tell him the truth.

"Yeah, I am actually. Am I gonna see you there?"

"Yeah," he said, his smile brightening as he brushed his hand through his hair.

"Hey do you mind if I come in . . ."

"No," I said abruptly, "I mean, I actually have a lot of homework to do and my parents are weird about having people over while they're out," I lied, rummaging through my back pocket and finally finding my keys.

"But I'll see you Saturday!" I quickly put them in the knob and turned, pushing through my door.

"Bye!" he yelled, my door slamming in his face. I leaned against the door trying to slow my racing heart. It made no sense for me to feel this way; Victor and I had once been inseparable. But it seemed like the eyes that once used to comfort me gave me chills like everyone else. I walked into my kitchen and looked out the window at the spot where Victor had stood a few minutes ago. The same spot I had met Candice in 6th grade, on the first day I moved into my new house . . .

(Ring! Ring!) I jumped at the sound of my kitchen phone. I took a deep breath, telling myself to calm down. I was sure I was jumping to conclusions. Besides, what was the worst that could happen?

Bonfire
Victor

I sat in the car looking at the pill bottle in my hand. It was just one of many that I had given up on. Taking medicine never worked, the voices always came back. I looked in my rearview mirror at the gathering of teens behind me, laughing and standing around the golden bonfire. It scared the crap out me. I hated the music. I hated

321

the glow of the fire. But Katherine was there. I had to go in. I knew she was expecting me to show, and I was her best friend, why else would she come? I threw the bottle onto my passenger seat and stepped out my car, making my way across the parking lot. I walked through the different groups of people, accidently bumping into a short, stocky guy I recognized from the local high school.

"Woah, freaky eyes man," he laughed and shoved a beer can in my hand, "welcome to the party!"

I sneered at the can in my hand and continued on. I just had to find Kat and then she and I could leave and go some place quieter.

I scanned the crowd again, distractedly sipping the warm beer. It was against the rules of my release, but I didn't care. I needed to calm down and this was the best solution to the problem right now.

I ended up drinking a few more beers, just standing around scanning the throngs of excited students. Finally I found Kat sitting on a rock near the edge of the river. I breathed a sigh of relief as I made my way towards her. I was so close, finally. I just needed to talk to her. To know we were still best friends, like she promised. I stopped when I saw three kids I didn't recognize run up to her.

A pretty girl with blonde hair went up to Kat and gave her a huge hug, introducing her to a shy boy with glasses and model features. I looked closer and recognized the other boy with them as that jerk, Andy, from earlier this week. Kat's face glowed as she stood up to greet him. And that's when it happened. He kissed her.

The shock of the kiss was like a punch in the stomach. I could feel myself slipping out of control, the alcohol taking over. Each voice in my head egged me on, until soon, I was there.

My fist in his face. Blood everywhere. I couldn't stop. The screaming was nothing to me, it was the hands that dragged me away. I struggled against them. "Kat!" I called, "tell them to let me go! It was an accident! Tell them, you know me!"

Katherine stared back at me in horror, cradling Andy's bloody face in her arms. Her look of horror then turned to disgust, and then to one of hatred.

"Get him out of here!" she yelled, "I hate you!"

I stopped struggling against the arms that pulled me back. Her look was so familiar. So many people hated me, gave me looks before they even knew me, but not my best friend; she promised.

I shook my head, tears running down my face, but then I stopped, and began to laugh. The arms that once caged me let me go, backing up cautiously. The voices inside me began to whisper, growing louder with each strangled chuckle. I laughed and laughed, backing up, taking in all the faces. Their judgment filled me with wonder as they began to change. Faces of brain dead ward patients and psychologist stared back at me, ready to drag me back to the hell I had just escaped. I stood up on one of the stones surrounding the flame of the fire, heat swelling against my back.

"This is my home!" I shouted, "I'll never leave again, and anyone who has a problem can kiss my . . ." My sentence was cut short by a hard slap to my face. Kat stood in front of me, her face tear and dirt stained face filled with anger. I stared back at her and the voices in me swirled in anger. They began to yell, pounding my skull from the inside. As she raised her hand, poised to hit me again, I reached out my hand and grabbed her wrist.

"If I can't have her, nobody can."

I yanked her towards me and we fell into the blazing circle.

That was two months ago, and as I sit in this jail cell, rocking back and forth, the voices still whisper to me. The drugs keep me quiet and confused, but that night rings clear in my memory, echoing the burns that mark my skin. So I sit and wait for my chance to escape this place. I have to go see Kat, to let her know I forgive her, to tell her we'll always be best friends. I will see her again. I won't forget her. I promise . . .

Effects of Teenage Bullying

By Katie Tolla

———⁓⁓∽◦ᑫᡕᲐᲑᲒᲓᲔᲕ◦∿⁓———

Days like these are always so difficult.

As I trudge half-asleep into the kitchen, my mother asks me, "Is everything okay? You know, if something is bothering you, you can always talk to me about it."

There is no way I would talk to my mother about this; just another day of school with inevitable teasing.

It's Monday, first period of the day, which today, happens to be Health. I walk into the room and instantly freeze as I look at the board: "Today's topic: obesity."

Oh no, they will all be thinking about me, I know it. They'll find some way to relate everything she says back to me.

A sophomore aggressively pushes past me, "Sorry freshman."

With a sore arm, I walk to my second-row desk with celerity. The bell rings, and the majority of the class is present and seated in desks surrounding mine. I can faintly hear two girls behind me whispering and giggling, probably about some rumor.

"Today we're going to talk about obesity," the teacher said, "you probably hear about it on commercials, or maybe you hear adults say it when they warn you about fast food. So, can someone give me a definition we can work with?"

"Fat," someone a few rows behind me called out.

"Yes . . . but I was looking for something more specific," the teacher responded.

"Unhealthy?" said a girl who appeared to be my age.

"Closer. Obesity describes an individual that is 20% over the normal body weight; 18% of children your age are affected by it."

"Aw Laura, you're not alone!" said Kelly, the girl in the seat behind me, as the people around her started to laugh.

The sound of my name almost made me jump. Of course that would come as a surprise to them. In a rich town like this, if you weren't naturally a size zero, you either starve yourself or have Daddy buy you all the latest diet plans and pills. It's just an unwritten rule of teenage society.

Kelly's friend raises her hand, "What's wrong with them? Are they poor or do they just hate themselves?" Emily says in an innocent-sounding voice.

The teacher answers, "There are all sorts of reasons. Sometimes it's genetic, other times it's from lack of exercise. There are many possibilities."

I hate it when teachers do that. Obviously, those comments were directed toward me, but she treated it like a legitimate question. Sometimes I truly believe that even teachers think I'm worthless.

A few more classes pass and then it's time for lunch. After getting my usual three slices of pizza, which drip grease every time you pick it up, I step into the cafeteria and pause. Choosing a table was always such a difficult task. At the first table I see, there is a group of girls each dressed in denim jeans and the same brand-name boots. The next table is crowded with people in their different sports jerseys, talking about their victorious game from the night before. After them, I see a table with four kids I recognize from various classes. This is probably the best option for me, so I sit down, and shyly say, "Hey."

Hayley, from my Civics class, responds, "Hi."

I try to make small talk with all four about our classes, but they seem hesitant to talk to me, and they keep going back to their previous conversation about whether or not two of their friends would make a good couple. I feel unwanted in this conversation, so I grab my things and leave. As I walk away I hear Matt half-whisper, "Why did you let her sit with us?"

"I don't know, why not?" Hayley replies.

"Because, she's weird."

Two more periods pass without any problems; no one even notices me. Then, there was last period, Geometry, which was going well, until Mrs. Mills gets a call from her husband and decides that talking to her husband is more important than teaching math for the last twelve minutes of class.

Matt is in my math class, and so is Kelly, the one from Health. They talk to each other obnoxiously for a little while, and then Kelly taps me on the shoulder.

"Do you get any of this? We don't," she says in her sweet, manipulative voice, pointing to the board with a jumble of letters and numbers.

"Umm . . . yeah . . ." and I proceed to explain to her everything she missed when she was too busy texting to pay attention to Mrs. Mills. She asks me many stupefying questions, until I am completely frustrated with her. After everything she's said about me and to me since school started, helping her was more than I could take.

"Thank you! Oh, and I love your shoes," she finally says at the end.

"No you don't. Why are you even talking to me? I know you hate me," I blurt out, mainly by accident.

Kelly seems too surprised to answer, so Matt does it for her.

"At least you know by now," he says cooly.

The bell rings and I leave not knowing what to think. Maybe I should blame myself for being unlikeable, or perhaps I should be angry at them for not giving me a chance. Either way, I get home bitter and exasperated.

I sign on to my Facebook, and look at my newsfeed. I scroll down a little and see Kelly's status: "Some losers need to be nicer. This is why they don't have friends." Twelve people have liked it, including Matt. Someone had said in response, "Don't let Fatass bother you. She isn't worth it."

The next says, "Why does she even go here? It's not like anyone likes her."

I cannot get that name out of my head all night. I can't even concentrate on homework. I've never understood why they feel like they have to pick on me. Yes, I was rude today, but I never used to be. They made me bitter.

I don't come back to school the next week. Hayley told me they all figured I had just switched schools, but they didn't say much else. Perhaps they feel guilty, or just didn't care much. Either way, I am better off here. I've been spending some time at home as my parents make phone calls all day with various teachers and secretaries from my old school. We have not made any real plans yet, but I will probably just transfer to another school outside town, not that I expect much to change. It never does.

Broken

By Ashley Ramirez

———~w───e~o~c~re~o~o─~w───

"Sophie! Sophie!" A woman calls in the lush green meadow, filled with flowers. The smell of roses, lilies, violets, and daisies fill the air. A young girl plays in the green grass, picking flowers and watching the clouds as the sky passes overhead. As she lies there, the older woman with brown-blonde hair and those sea-green eyes that drag you deep into their owner's soul, sits next to the young girl.

"Sophie?" the women asked as a confused look passed over her kind features. "Yes?" Sophie answered while looking to the clouds as the sky starts to turn dark with the coming night, and stars begin to appear.

"What are you looking at sweet girl?" the women asked with a soft, sweet voice.

"Nothing Auntie Laurel; I'm just thinking," Sophie says, getting closer to her aunt.

"Thinking 'bout what?"

"Well, I'm thinking about all the stories mommy and daddy used to tell me." Laurel watches as a few stray tears start to slip from the little girl's clear blue eyes and down her cheeks. She uses her soft hand to wipe away the stray tears.

*   *   *

Laurel remembers a night a year ago; her sister had asked if she could watch her niece for the day. Laurel had agreed, and arrived at the house soon after. Laurel and Sophie had spent the day at the zoo. They spent most of their time looking at the zebras and the giraffes. Sophie seemed to like the giraffes the most, so Laurel stopped and bought her a stuffed giraffe on the way home. Sophie clutched it in her arms while laughing with a bright smile, and named her new giraffe Sheldon. Every time she saw him, she would pick Sheldon up, and he would make her laugh and smile.

Laurel made spaghetti for dinner that night. Everything was great until the doorbell rang. Laurel knew something was wrong. She wasn't expecting her sister and brother-in-law home until midnight, and it was only nine. She walked from the kitchen after making sure the stove was off, and paused on her way to the front door to check on Sophie. She was fast asleep on the couch with Sheldon in her hands. Laurel walked in, turned off the TV, and put a blanket on her nine-year-old niece. She paused once more to look in and see how cute her little niece looked with her strawberry-blonde hair all tangled, and her small hands holding Sheldon tight to her chest with the patched up colorful blanket on her. Laurel could no longer ignore the ringing of the bell since it had gone off twice already, and started for the door. As she walked, everything slowed down, and she saw the silhouette of a single person through the glass frame of the door. It was a relief until she opened the door and saw that it was a police officer. She thought something must be horribly wrong. The officer looked up with a sad expression as the door opened.

"Laurel Levy?" he asked.

"Yes," She replied.

"Maybe you should sit down. I have something to tell you," the officer said.

"It's okay," Laurel said, "just tell me what's wrong." Laurel knew it had to be something horrible, otherwise the officer wouldn't be here.

"Well, Miss Levy," the officer paused and sighed, "your sister and your brother-in-law were in a car accident."

Laurel looked devistated.

"Are they okay?" she asked.

"I'm sorry, but they both passed away."

With that said, the officer again said he was sorry for her loss, and turned and left. Laurel closed the door, turned around, put her back against it, and slid down to the floor and cried.

Sophie had woken up and heard everything. She saw her aunt, the strongest person she knew, breaking down and crying. She couldn't believe it.

Sophie tried to comfort her auntie, but Laurel was trying to regain her confidence to tell her young niece what had happened to her parents. Before Laurel could tell her, Sophie's face contorted to one of unbelievable pain, and tears started to run down her face. She fell to her knees with her giraffe by her side. She slid into her auntie's arms and Laurel held her tight. She couldn't believe how much her niece understood.

Sophie cried herself to sleep in her aunt's arms that night. Laurel was so tired; she fell asleep next to her niece on the couch.

*   *   *

Laurel was taken back from the memory, and pulled the little girl into a tight hug.

"Baby girl, don't cry, they're in a better place now," she said.

"But what if . . ." Sophie starts to say.

"Shh, it's okay. Don't worry little girl, they are always looking after you, they're your guardian angels," she said whispering into Sophie's ear while still watching the stars.

"Hey do you want to hear a story?" she says to the small girl once she had calmed down. Sophie, with a loss of breath, brought Sheldon up to her chest and nodded to her auntie.

With her acknowledgment, Laurel started her story.

"Alright sweet girl, this story starts with a little girl almost like you, but this little girl would wander her back yard after it got dark, chasing fireflies. One night, she wandered into the woods just beyond her backyard chasing a small, dazzling firefly. The little girl had never been this far in the woods and now she was lost. The girl ran from place to place trying to find her way. When she couldn't, the little girl got frustrated and started to cry. All her thoughts turned to how she would be lost forever. A kind deer pranced past the clearing where the crying little girl was sitting. He heard the crying and wanted to know why she was in the woods when it was so dark out.

"Sweet girl," the deer said, "why are you in the woods when it is so dark out, and may I ask why you're crying too?"

The girl thought to herself how polite the deer was. Through her sobs and hiccups for air, the girl said, "I'm lost. I was chasing a firefly and I lost my way. Can you help me get home?"

The deer didn't want to see the sweet girl cry anymore so he said, "Yes," and walked her back through the forest to her backyard, and led her home.

Laurel finished the story and turned to find her sweet ten-year-old niece clutching her giraffe close to her. Laurel thought of that giraffe. It had been through the death of Sophie's parents, the day she broke her leg soon after when she fell on the playground, and he had some scrapes and thorns from Sophie running through the forest near the house. She picked up her sleeping niece in her arms and walked carefully to the car. She placed the young girl in the car, and wrapped a blanket around her and Sheldon. With that, Laurel drove them back home through the starry night.

The Deceivers

By Julien Monick

———〰️〰️〰️———

Jeremy Bethol rose from his bed at 5:00 A.M. with a sense of effortless ease. He bounced around the sunlit room searching for his best set of clothing. Today was an extremely important day for him, but also a day for a very difficult choice. However, as though ignoring the internal conflict rising inside him, the 29 year old man grabbed his black and navy blue suit. He threw it on the silky bed and moved to the shower.

After allowing the warm and calming water to wash away the pains of his mind, Jeremy reached for his towel with a hand that seemed to be etched with a strange marking. The strange marking gave his hand a mysterious vibe, as if there for a reason. He looked at himself in the mirror and saw a well postured young man with long, straight black hair, blue eyes, and skin as tan as gold. His welcoming face had deceived many people, but the scar over his right eye could never lie, and it only echoed sadness.

It was time to head out. Jeremy put on his suit and left his penthouse suite, one he seemed suited for, but perhaps that, too, was a lie. Jeremy closed his eyes on the elevator ride home and drifted off into a daydream. He gathered his anxious feelings and calmed his nerves as he had trained himself to do over the years. The doors opened with a chime and he walked out onto the street.

"Good morning Ben. It sounds like there will be lovely weather today," Jeremy said to the doorkeeper as he left the hotel.

"Yes, it does appear to be so Mr. Bethol. Do you need a chauffeur for the day?" replied the doorkeeper, seeming thrilled to mince words to someone of such stature.

"I was born with legs, might as well use them," Jeremy stated with a philosophical sense and a half smile.

The truth of the matter is that he simply could not be under the watch of any prying eyes. Where Jeremy was heading, he did not need a car. As he exited the hotel, he took a right, moving towards the job interview he had been rehearsing in his mind for over 3 weeks. It was his chance to turn his miserable life around for the better.

The bustle of the New York City traffic filled the air, even at such a ghastly hour in the day. Seems as if Jeremy was right about the chauffeur, it would only slow him down and he needed to move fast. Moving past alleyways and dark corners of the city of life, Jeremy pulled himself towards a door with the same marking on it as his hand had. He knocked on the door, and a small slit opened, revealing a set of cruel eyes.

"He who enters never leaves unless with a bearing to the right direction," they said.

Jeremy picked up his right hand and showed the marking. A circle surrounding a triangle with a small "z" cut in the middle. As the cold eyes saw this, they moved away closing the slit. Four small clicks came from the door and it opened, revealing a bald-headed man with a similar marking on his hand, except instead of a "z" there was a "g".

"Mr. Z is here sir, I'll buzz him up," he said.

Jeremy nodded to the man and continued up the building. On the outside, the building appeared to be a broken down mess, but the inside was exquisite. It appeared as if everything was touched by the hand of Midas.

As he was walking down the stairs he thought about what he was about to do. These people were extremely dangerous; he knew this because he has been one of them since the day he was born. They were known as the Deceivers. A group of silver-tongued, killers that dedicated themselves to ridding the world of those people who only bring suffering to it; the Deceivers were an organization that spread across the world. Yet they remained undetected for centuries. This is because those who enter never leave.

They were hired to eliminate those who "deserved" to die and carried out what they believed was necessary work for the good of the world, and perhaps it was. Each member was given two scars. One etched on their hands as a constant reminder of who they belonged to. The second isn't so much a scar as it is an attitude. Each member had been taught to master the art of observing others and knowing how to lie accordingly. Henceforth, those who mastered these skills were known as master Deceivers.

Jeremy, being a master Deceiver for nearly ten years now, has done many gruesome things for them before, and all in the name of making the world a better place. He has been scarred both mentally and physically, but it has made him the virtuous man he is today, and that man has finally found love and a future. It was his time to leave the Deceivers, but this wasn't a decision to be made lightly.

He reached the bottom of the stairs and was greeted by a woman dressed in white. She brought him to a large oval room with a man dressed in black sitting behind a wooden replica of the desk in the white house. The man looked as plain as day, but his face screamed of power. The grit in his smile revealed a few golden teeth, and his buzzed-cut, black hair seemed to rustle at his unexpected visitor.

"Welcome Mr. Z, it's good to see you today. Have you completed your quota for the year so soon?" said the man.

Jeremy looked him in the eye and grinned, "All done, and I have a favor to ask of you."

"And what might that be?"

Jeremy knew this was the moment. He wanted freedom to start his own life without having the Deceivers controlling him. He wanted to stop the lies, but as they have always said, "all those who enter will never leave." They were never really specific with this meaning, but with the Deceivers, it could never be good.

His hands shaking, Jeremy said, "Sir, I have been part of this group for my entire life. I have served faithfully for years and I have taken care of over forty-four dastardly souls who have deserved what they got. But I am asking now from this service, may I be relieved from my duties from the Deceivers? I have fallen in love and found a job that I can do to help those that deserve it. Sir, I'm asking for my freedom."

The mysterious man looked at Jeremy for a fleeting moment and said with a reserved tone, "Then Mr. Z, or shall I say Jeremy Bethol, you are free to leave. Enjoy the rest of your life, no matter how long or short it may be."

The woman dressed in white reached for his shoulder as the man in black turned around. Jeremy let out a big sigh and turned his back on the Deceivers.

As he left the office, the man in black hushed something on the phone, but Jeremy was too happy to care. This was it, the moment he has been wanting for years now.

As Jeremy walked up the winding staircase, he thought to himself of the future he would soon have. He thought of how his job as a clinical psychologist was a good way to take what the Deceivers had taught him and use it for good. His fiancé would sure be happy to see him again, and this time he wouldn't have to worry about the demons of his past interfering. No looking over his shoulder for spies loyal to those he had killed, no being nervous just to make a decision, and best of all, no more lying. He would be able to live his life with his fiancé in peace. His dream was finally coming true.

He reached the top of the staircase and waved to Mr. G one last time. Mr. G seemed tense though, as if he had been told bad news. He pulled his weapon in what felt like slow motion as he focused in on his target. He fired two rounds into Jeremy's chest. The sound of the gun startled him as he fell back and hit the wall behind him. He could feel the bones in his spine crumble as the shell of a dying man sank slowly to the floor. The world seemed blurry to Jeremy as his dream faded away. The man in black rose from the staircase and walked to Jeremy.

"Leave us," he directed to Mr. G.

"Why?" Jeremy said with a fading voice, "why did you do this?"

"Jeremy, you should have known better. We hide behind a wall of lies my friend, we deceive the world and I deceived you. We do not get to be free; all those who enter will never leave."

Jeremy's eyes slowly shut and his life came to an end.

Stolen Moments

By Kaitlin Oliver

—⚬⚭⚬⚭⚬⚭⚬—

*   *   *

Why do I have to go to college? I'm not ready; I haven't gotten a chance to be a kid. I've lived in a shadow full of despair and loneliness. My life is flashing before my eyes. I don't know what I'll do with my life. My mom says it's the right time and that I'm ready, but I think otherwise.

Julia was an 18 year old girl getting ready to go to college. She wasn't one of the star students, but she tried her best. She struggled in school because she was always so sick, due to the fact that she was diagnosed with Graves' Disease at the age of 10, an autoimmune disease that affects the thyroid, causing it to enlarge to twice its size or more. This causes someone to have a low immune system, along with a low white blood cell count, and hyperthyroid symptoms such as increased heartbeat, muscle weakness, disturbed sleep, and irritability. She also suffered with low self esteem, since she had very thin, stringy, black hair from her hair loss, and her big brown eyes stuck out like a frog. People teased her constantly, so she tried to keep to herself as much as possible.

Julia thought she was not ready to go away to school because she wasn't able to have a normal childhood after being diagnosed with this illness at such a young age. She didn't have many friends because people saw her as strange and not the smart, outgoing girl she was. It's too late now, Julia is dying and she is here to tell us the most affecting memories and moments in her life and how they changed her.

336

*   *   *

My mom and I leave the doctor's office and she takes me out for ice cream to get my favorite flavor, cotton candy on a sugar cone. We sit on the bench closest to the ocean, watching the seagulls fly and the sun setting. I can tell she is crying and I ask her, "Mommy what's wrong?"

She turns to me, and what came out changes my life forever.

"Julia, the doctor said you are very sick."

I really didn't understand what was wrong with me, but I knew I wasn't well.

Now Julia lays here in this white hospital room, staring at the ceiling, thinking why this had to happen to her. She wished she never thought about making her life different, because as soon as she wished for it, her life was changed for the worst, not the better. She wanted to have friends that she could talk to about anything, be known in her school as someone important, and not have to worry about any problems that went on around her. Now she had many different tasks that had to be done and worried about, like take gross medicine every morning, and have several trips to a new doctor, where only old people went to get her blood drawn. This was the task that Julia hated the most because she couldn't stand needles. Whenever she went to the doctors she had to have the same nurse, Nurse Gigi, because she knew how to control Julia, and stop her from crying and fidgeting at the process of getting her blood drawn. Julia had to stop being a kid and handle these responsibilities like an adult to better her health, and she didn't like it.

*   *   *

"Frog face, frog face!" I can hear the middle school kids calling me as I walk down the hall to my class. I hate school; I wasn't one of the popular kids, the sport athlete, or a scholar, so no one really knew who I was.

"I wish my life was different," I would think constantly, "I wish I wasn't sick."

As school continued to progress for Julia, the teasing continued and she began to believe some of the things the kids were saying. They would call her frog face because of the way her eyes bugged out, ugly, old lady because of how pale she was, and her hair was falling out. It was getting so bad that they began to follow her home from school and throw things at her. The teasing bothered her so much that she stopped taking her medicine so these features and side effects would go away. If her mom found out, she would kill her, so she didn't let her know.

Every morning, Julia would just take the pill in her hand and throw it out whenever her mom wasn't looking. She knew this was a bad decision because it created a bigger chance of her disease to get worse, but she felt like this was the only way to go back to her normal, care free life. One day, as Julia was walking home from school, she heard the group of kids that followed her everyday get closer. She had thought this day would have been different, since she left school early, but it wasn't; so she began to run home so they wouldn't catch her. Because she hadn't taken her medicine she knew she wasn't suppose to do extreme athletic activity, so as she ran, she felt herself having shorter and shorter breaths, but she continued to run as the hot sun was beaming down on her. She didn't want them to catch her today; and they weren't.

Her body gave in and collapsed right on the hot, hard pavement. The group of kids saw her fall and just ran in the other direction because they didn't want to get blamed for this. She doesn't remember anything after that; all she does remember is waking up in the bed she is laying in now.

She regrets wishing that her life was different, and that she could wait to go away to college; because now, she would not be able to experience it. Now she is dying and has so much to offer the world that she won't be able to share.

*   *   *

When asked what I want to be when I grow up I say, "I want to be a lawyer!"

I've aspired to be a lawyer since I was 8, and plan on accomplishing it. I love to argue points with friends, family, and even teachers; it just gives me some type of power that I never had in real life. Everyone would actually listen to what I had to say and not worry about what I looked like or judge me by how intelligent or unintelligent I was for once.

Her life forever changed because of this terrible disease and now she will never know who she could have become in life. She could have become a lawyer and actually liked college, only if she wasn't so scared of the changes occurring in her life. Being diagnosed with Graves' Disease caused her to achieve poorly in school, get bullied a lot, and not have a true childhood of carefree fun. Now that her life is ending, she wants to leave all of us with this: In life you may come across many challenges that you are afraid to cross, whether it be going to college like Julia; or even performing in school, don't be afraid to work through them because something worse could come around that can change your life forever, like it did for her.

Destination

By Kerry McCabe

Eight months, six days, and three hours.

That's how long I've been trapped here in this lonely room, and each day I have starred at the plain white wall, watching the cheap paint peel. My room is about the size of my old closet, which used to be filled with more than enough clothes that I would never get the chance to wear. I was stuck in the same grey outfit every day. The grey cargo pants with a beige pin stripe down each side, and the plain white tee-shirt with the all girls Six Points Correctional Facility logo in the top left corner. I was forced to wear the ugly white nurse shoes that you only see your grandmother wear because they have "good support" and "are safe". When the days get cold in the small town of Burke, New York, we are allowed to pull on a hoodless, grey sweatshirt, accompanied by the logo once again.

It was always there, reminding me of where I was, and how I went from living the life of a privileged teen to being trapped in a small room with nothing but a single, lumpy bed, and a nightstand where I keep the photos of my past life locked up. When I look in the mirror, I don't see anyone I know. My perfectly tanned skin has turned into a pale and pasty white, and the split ends on my once perfect head of glossy, brown hair have become unmanageable. Dark circles from a lack of sleep have become permanent around both of my eyes, and the scar on my forehead from falling off of the swings when I was four seems to be more noticeable than ever. The muscles I gained from being the star of the tennis team at both my high school and country club have all but disappeared, and all I am left with are limp arms and soft legs. I hate that person I see in the mirror, maybe even more than I hate the person I was before I got here.

My name is Kendall, and despite the popularity I had at home, not one of my friends has written to me. I'm only allowed family visitors, but I haven't seen any of them in three months. My dad was the last one to visit, and it was only to explain that he wouldn't be able to see me as much anymore because he was putting in more hours at the office. I'm guessing it was his excuse for not dealing with me, or my mother, perhaps both.

My mother hasn't looked at me the same ever since my doctor diagnosed me with anorexia about a year ago. Not a day goes by that I don't think about how much better my life would be if I hadn't gotten my annual physical. Everything was normal at the doctors until they weighed me and saw that I had dropped twelve pounds since the last time I had been there two months ago for the flu. After that, my life became chaotic and filled with different doctor's appointments. My mother took me to each one, and every time she would have a greater look of disappointment on her face.

It was her idea to send me here. She didn't want to have to deal with my problems when she had herself to worry about. So without any warning, she pulled me out of school and sent me here. I didn't even have the chance to talk to her about it, and I doubt she cares if I make any progress either.

So today, like every other day, I go back to my room after breakfast with no mail being sled through my mail slot, unlike every other girl here. Instead of listening to them giggling over stories they're now sharing with one another, I decide to go to group therapy early.

When I get to the group room, it's completely silent and still. The cushioned chairs are still in a circle from yesterday's session, and I pick my usual chair which looks out into one of the few windows so I have something to stare at while the others share their feelings. I usually never pay any attention to what any of them say, and hardly even hear when a question is directed towards me.

"Well someone's here early," Kyle said as she walked into the room, startling me.

Kyle was the only person here I had become friends with. I don't intend on remembering this place, so why become friends with the people in it? I tried explaining this to Kyle, but she basically told me I didn't have a choice, and it was necessary to be friends with her.

"What did I say about sneaking up on me?" I said bitterly.

"Whoa there Kendall, no one's trying to kill you. Relax," Kyle replied coolly.

Surprisingly, Kyle's here because she cuts herself. If you couldn't see the scars, you would never know that she's a cutter. Kyle's always so open and outgoing, but that just shows you that you can never really tell what someone's feeling, and the people that look happy are usually the most miserable.

I made myself comfortable as the rest of the girls filed in with their range of problems. There were the depressed fat girls, the depressed underweight girls, bipolars, bulimics, cutters like Kyle, and then the anorexics. Finally, Vivian, our counselor, came in and sat in her spot diagonal from me. She was always late, and way too happy for one person to handle.

"Good morning girls," Vivian said in her chipper voice.

A few of the girls muttered their hellos, and then the great discussion began. We always start off the session on how we feel, and surprisingly, most of these girls feel something different every day.

"Maya, you were a little under the weather yesterday," Vivian said, "are you feeling any better today?" she continued to Maya, one of the bipolar girls.

Maya replied with a smile on her face, "Actually, I'm feeling a lot better. I think it's because the sun's out today. The sun always makes me feel better."

Maya was one of the more "unique" girls here. Everyone knows she's bipolar, but she takes abnormal to a whole new level, and I hate hearing her constantly talking about how the weather determines her mood in her annoying high-pitched voice.

"I'm glad to hear that," Vivian said, "how about you Kendall?"

I was caught a little off guard since she usually either kept me for last or didn't even bother since my answer was the same every day.

"I'm fine," I said.

The last thing I remember is that look on Vivian's face when she disapproves of something. She knits her brows and purses her lips like I actually care what she thinks.

I woke up to Kyle shaking me.

"Kendall, wake up! We have to go to lunch," Kyle said.

I groaned as I stood up.

"Wow, third time this week you've fallen asleep during group," Kyle said, "nice work," she continued.

"Thanks," I replied sarcastically.

It was a quiet walk to the cafeteria. I really wasn't good at keeping up a conversation, but Kyle never seemed to mind.

When we got there, our trays filled up with turkey and swiss sandwiches and a side of soup.

I hated meal times. People watched you as you ate to make sure you were eating what you were supposed to, and they wouldn't let you leave until you finished. I've learned that the hard way. I mostly stare at my food, occasionally pushing it around as Kyle scarfs down hers across from me.

"C'mon Kendall, you know they won't let you leave until you finish. Might as well get it over with now," Kyle said.

I just starred at her. She didn't understand, and she got the hint because she quickly finished and stood up, ready to leave.

"I'll meet you in the rec. room when you decide to finally eat your lunch like a normal person," Kyle taunted.

As much as I hated it when she said that, it always seemed to get me to eat faster.

When I first got here, I was in the cafeteria for four hours because I refused to eat my breakfast. Now it takes me a little less than an hour.

I'm the last one to leave the cafeteria, as usual, and I head over to the rec. room where I sit next to Kyle on the blue-stripped couch and we watch her favorite show, *Modern Family*.

"What do you think one-on-one's going to be about today?" Kyle asked. One-on-one was our personal therapy session, and each day had a different topic.

"Hopefully nothing," I replied.

"Kendall, if you don't start opening up to these people, they're never going to let you leave," she said.

I knew what she said was true, but I don't like opening up to people. Especially not shrinks.

"Just talk to them like you talk to me," Kyle continued, "it'll get easier, I promise."

"I know. I just don't know where to start," I said.

"How about you start by actually answering one of their questions," Kyle said.

"Very funny," I replied.

"I guess I should get going," I continued.

"Go get 'em superstar," Kyle laughed.

I gave her my attempt at a smile as I walked into the empty hallway to my therapy session. My one-on-one therapist's name was Julie, and I liked her a lot better than Vivian. She was waiting for me with a smile when I came in and sat down.

"So, Kendall, I've been hearing you don't participate in group, and doze off during most sessions. Why?" Julie asked.

"I don't know. I never have anything to share," I answered.

"You know Kendall; it's good to let your feelings out. It's a natural stress reliever for the body and mind," Julie said.

"I know," I replied.

She hated when I gave one word answers. She said they lacked substance, and would get me nowhere.

"Kendall, I'm starting to worry that you're becoming depressed. You're lacking energy, you don't concentrate during group or in here, and you're persistently sad. If you don't open up, we can't help you," she said.

"I'm not depressed," I said quickly.

"Alright Kendall, this is what I'm going to do. I'm excusing you from all night activities, and you are going to do what you need to do to figure out what you want here. You need to want to get better in order to do it, and I hope your attitude will change soon," Julie finished.

All I could come up with was, "Okay."

I silently stood up and walked out only to go into my silent, cramped room. I'd rather be alone than in the rec. room with everyone else. It gives me time to think about everything.

I pulled opened my nightstand drawer and took out my old photos and immediately started to cry.

The girl in the pictures was so happy and alive, and I just wasn't that girl anymore. I would never be that girl again, so I ripped up my pictures and threw them across the room in fury.

Why did this have to happen to me? I used to have such a great life with great friends, and now I don't even consider myself a friend. And weren't my friends supposed to catch on that I was barely eating anything and was at the gym during all of my free time, even after two hours of tennis practice? Didn't anyone care enough to see what was going on, and to stop me before I got here?

These thoughts raced through my mind as they did every night until the pain from them became unbearable and I decided to sleep it off once again. Sleep was the only thing that seemed to calm me, and it was one of the few things I was good at, so I curled up under my covers and my dreams came in no time.

Eight months, six days, and fourteen hours.

His Final Piece

By Andrea Rosales

—ᴡᴍᵒᵒᵅᵊᵅᵔᵒᵔᵉᵒᵒᴡᴍ—

Finished. His latest piece stood before him as the young artist sighed in exhaustion. Light tinted the dim room through the dust-covered windows, old and broken, abandoned and neglected. The artist threw his head back and allowed himself to collapse down to the floor, his thin and worn body unable to hold him up. With the last bit of his strength all ready used up, he could do nothing more than to listen to the sound of his steady breath as he stared at a crumbling ceiling with lifeless eyes . . . eyes filled with nothing but fatigue.

A palette of colors covered his bruised and worn hands, hiding the scars and cuts gained in exchange for the beautiful works that filled the small studio. He possessed steady, yet delicate and slender, fingers, trained over years of practice and hands that used to move with such ease and confidence now lay still at his side, unable to move, too tired to try. The young man felt weak.

He closed his green eyes slowly, unable to look at the old ceiling any longer, disgusted by another pathetic reminder of the sorry life he led.

One more finished. Today, that makes 382, 382 art pieces in five long years; and still, not one is good . . .

His eyes opened weakly as the young man began to chew his bottom lip. The proof of the nervous habit could be seen in the various marks left on his chapped and mistreated lips. The artist stood up slowly as he looked around the studio he had become accustomed to. His eyes carefully searched each of his works, immediately finding their flaws, like a magnet looking for metal

The pieces were beautiful. There was no doubt that the young man possessed unimaginable talent. Yet, something was missing. No one knew better than the artist himself.

"Life," he said simply.

That's what it lacks. My artwork is . . . dead.

His tired hands began to shake as all expression left his pale face. The artist was exhausted. His body begged for rest, but he refused to give in. He was ready to collapse, yet was restless for change, for peace of mind. When had it all begun to spiral down for him? When had he realized he was falling and it was impossible to get back up?

Five years, 60 long months, 1825 painful days, 48 lost jobs . . .

Five years ago I was happy. Five years ago everything was simple. Five years ago they were . . . alive. It all ended with their lives.

His was the old cliché story. The young artist laughed bitterly, not a hint of humor in his voice. He had been a boy of seventeen, the only child in a warm and loving family with parents that encouraged even the smallest things he did, creating the artist he had become. The boy had grown blessed, never alone, for they had always been there to help him through his troubles and needs. However, life is fragile and theirs was proof of that. They had failed to last past their precious son's 18th birthday . . .

Boom, crash . . . Is that the sound their cars made as they met?

The young artist shook his head violently, unable to rid himself of the thought. They died, leaving him all alone. No one could encourage him anymore; no one could support him. The young boy of seventeen had nobody. Five years passed and the young boy of seventeen grew into a young and bitter artist with a loss of will. Five years had passed, as did the jobs, the people, and the strength.

He had learned to support himself, forcing his feet to move forward through stressful jobs, expensive bills, and crushing responsibilities. Left foot, right foot, the young boy had moved through the years in autopilot, not allowing himself to give in to the pain of loss, but somewhere along the line, he had given up. Life was painful. When they were alive, the boy had never realized how strong his parent's shield had been against the cruelty of the world. He had been such a fool.

Art, though, could be another shield, another escape. It was what kept him sane. It kept their memory alive. They had taught him to love it, and he would engrave their memory into his heart with each stroke of the brush.

Yet, the young artist lost control. The art had become an obsession for him, taking him away from reality, but he was grateful for it. The passion he felt he had maintained out of love had turned into nothing but a drug that could numb the pain. He had been desperate for anything to take him away from the sadness in which he dwelled. The artist was a fool.

382 pieces . . . and somewhere along the line, before I could even realize it, they lost life as I slowly lost the will to live.

He hated it though, hated the unfeeling machine he had become and the lifeless pieces this robot created. His life had become a factory, spitting out artwork manufactured without passion. He needed to change. They deserved a better son than this.

The artist refused to give up and settle for what he had stooped to create. He would do it. He would honor his parent's memory with the creation of a masterpiece. A beautiful work that radiated all the life he had forgotten how to express: how to pursue, how to enjoy.

One more time. Let's make 382 turn into 383, just one more . . .

He smiled weakly as his frail and tired hand picked up the brush and pressed thick paint onto a white and empty canvas.

383, I have a feeling you will be different. Will you save me?

The young artist began his work. The pain and exhaustion he had felt a minute ago was now long forgotten. He had a responsibility. Pain would not be allowed to come between him and his one true desire.

Minutes slowly melted into hours as the sun outside set and made room for the moon to roam at night, yet the artist continued to work.

"Almost finished," he muttered softly as his weary eyes began to close. "Tomorrow, it will be complete." The young man smiled hopefully as he put his supplies away, finally retreating to small corner of the room he had reserved for sleep.

The sound of cars awoke him as people rushed off to their jobs. Life went on, stopping for no one. It hadn't stopped for him when his world had ended, and it wouldn't stop now when he was desperately trying to win some peace back.

Remembering his latest creation the boy rushed up to the easel, eager to see the way it would look in the morning light, eager to finish it and at last find tranquility.

What he saw shocked him. The young artist's bright green eyes widened in disbelief. His painting . . . How could this be possible?

The young man knew his own work. He remembered each detail. He could still feel the way he had lovingly painted each feature in his mother's gentle smile, and his father's excited green eyes that had resembled his own before they had allowed life to leave him. The artist remembered it all. Then why did he not remember painting this face in the middle? Just who did it belong to?

"It's faded, as if it's having trouble showing itself," the young artist said in astonishment. "My father's green eyes, my mother's dark hair, pale complexion," he continued as his fingers lightly traced the canvas trying to find a sign that it wasn't real. "Is that face mine?"

Unable to understand why, the young artist found himself ready with a paintbrush at hand. His skilled hands did his work for him as he mindlessly continued the work he could not remember creating. He needed to complete the painting. He needed to be saved. The artist smiled weakly as he worked.

382 pieces, and their simple faces on canvas are what manage to bring back the life into my creations.

However, the young artist knew something in the painting was missing. It was not complete. He refused to acknowledge the piece as finished until his currently blurry smile looked as alive as theirs.

Up, down, up. He was unaware of what his hands were painting, letting each stroke of the brush surprise him as he mindlessly continued.

Up, down, up. With each stroke, his hand trembled slightly. The artist could feel himself getting weaker. Yet, at the same time he could see the way his portrait's eyes seemed to shine a little more than a moment ago, or the way his skin had begun to look so real he could feel the warmth radiating from it.

"It's coming to life." His voice was barely a whisper.

The young artist continued to paint. As the color left his face, it appeared in his painting's expression instead. His breathing became slower and more painful, but he refused to stop his progress. The young man's knees began to shake. He was not sure how much longer he would be able to stand.

Up, down, up. His brush strokes continued. His body felt cold and he knew he had lost all color. His painting's complexion had never looked so healthy.

Up, down, up. The artist stumbled slightly as his left leg gave out. Unable to understand his desire to continue through the pain, but unable to stop, the young man chose to kneel as he continued with his work.

Five years, 60 long months, 1825 painful days, 48 lost jobs, 382 paintings, 382 failures . . . This one will be different. This one can change it all. My life was not meaningless. Theirs was not in vain.

Up, down, up. He could barely control the brush now, too weak to even hold it up, too weary to even hold himself up. However, the artist refused to give up. He laughed weakly.

"Leave a piece uncompleted? As artists, I guess it's impossible for us." His words trembled just as much as his once steady hands did, but he continued painting.

It's almost finished.

Up, down, up. His body was trembling.

Up, down, up. The painting was radiating all the life that he lacked.

Up, down, up. The light in his green eyes was fading, leaving only an empty and unfocused stare.

Up, down, up. The young artist's shoulders shook violently as he coughed, leaving the bitter taste of copper in his mouth as trickles of blood managed to escape his lips.

Up, down, up, down, up.

The corners of his dry and bloody lips turned upwards in a weak but triumphant smile. It was complete. The artist's tired eyes shut themselves slowly as his paintbrush left his weakening hold. His head slumped back as his neck gave up the fight to hold him up. His worn body followed as it crumbled to the dirty floor. With the last bit of his strength the young artist forced his eyes open to catch one last glimpse at his last creation.

His gaze was met by a beautiful sight for sore eyes. Three pairs of eyes on the canvas met his own, three gentle smiles reassured him that all would be all right now. He had done it. He had brought life back into his art. The memory of his parents would now be alive for an eternity, along with his own.

The young artist shut his weary eyes, satisfied with what he had seen. Five years, 60 long months, 1825 painful days; his smile had never looked as happy, his expression as peaceful as it did in the painting, together with the family that he had yearned for.

Five years, 60 long months, 1825 painful days, and it had all finally come to an end. Now the young artist would never be alone again. The young man had been tired, desperate for rest, yearning for piece. He had found it. Now, he would be able to rest forever with the family he had always missed.

Together in his painting, they would all live for an eternity.

Too Far From Home

By Melissa Rojo

—⁓⦿⦿⦿⁓—

"Daddy come on! Liz's parents are letting her go! Its only one week, and I'll only be two hours away. Plus, what could possibly happen in the Caribbean?" complained Leslie.

"You know I heard there are actually some pirates in that Caribbean," slyly replied her dad.

"Just for the record, you're not funny." Leslie flipped her long chestnut hair and looked down at her white blouse. She concentrated on one of the buttons, contemplating whether she should use the power of her eyes to make her father succumb to her wishes. When she tilted her head just the right way so that the light glistened off her deep blue eyes, and she opened her eyes and pouted her lips just enough, her father was unable to say no. Usually this was a last resort technique, and rare was the occasion when she had to use such force, but her father was being so difficult, and she couldn't understand why. *Well, maybe just this once.*

"You know Leslie, hun, that eye trick stopped working when you were about . . . well when you were potty trained," said her dad with a certain smugness.

"You know Bob," started Leslie, trying to create a more serious, adult tone," I am more mature than you think I-I-." Leslie's face slowly turned a shade of red. Then, without her command, her eyes produced those wet traitors she so whole heartedly detested. Betrayed by her own tears! She couldn't believe it!

"Leslie don't cry, it can't be that serious. It's only a trip. Listen, you'll be turning eighteen in six months anyways, if you really want to go to the Caribbean, it can wait until you're not underage."

Bob studied his daughter's face. It was so hard to say no; after all, she was his little girl. But how could he just allow her to go away for a week, unsupervised? If something were to happen to her . . . . No, such thoughts are intolerable. But Bob knew better than anyone that all sorts of things can occur when teenagers go unsupervised. The drinking, the drugs, the sex. Bob couldn't wrap his head around it all. He knew everyone experienced it at one time or another, but he could not and would not bring himself to imagine his daughter, his little girl, involved in such actions.

"Leslie it's not that I don't trust you, it's everyone else I don't trust. If you want to leave when you're eighteen that's fine, but I don't' want to be liable for anything that can happen to you."

"Fine, I'll just go when I'm eighteen." Leslie's somber tone hinted that she had something in mind.

"Alright Les what gives," asked her dad.

"I have no idea what you're talking about. I just realized that you were right. Things will be much easier when I'm 18."

"What do you mean much easier?"

"Well you know I'll be eighteen, I pay for the consequences of my decisions, so I don't have to abide to anyone else's rules."

Bob's heart dropped. He hadn't thought of it that way. He knew that no matter what he did, his daughter would end up taking this trip. Now the difficult part was deciding when. Bob knew that if he didn't give her permission to go now, she would go right when she turned eighteen. And because she would be an adult by then he had no say in any of her decisions. And that killed him. He couldn't accept that his one and only little girl would soon be an adult.

"Leslie, I'll let you g—"

"Oh my God! Thank you Daddy, I KNEW you would come to your senses." Leslie tightly embraced her father. "See this is why I love you." She looked up at him, beaming her pearl white teeth. He couldn't help but smile in return, despite the tight knot he felt in his stomach.

It had been two days and Leslie had not called her father back. He paced his apartment anxiously.

"Well, it is the Caribbean and it's only twelve o'clock, she's probably out soaking up the sun. Yea, that's it: She's at the beach. Plus, it's not like she has nothing else to do. The Caribbean is a beautiful place, there's probably a lot of sightseeing to be done."

Bob knew that he tended to overreact. However, no matter what he said to himself, he could not alleviate the sick feeling he felt since he allowed her to go. As the days passed, this feeling continued to grow instead of fading.

"I have way too much time on my hands," he muttered. He started shuffling around his desk, searching for his keys. When he finally found them, he grabbed his keys and took for the door. As he was about to close the door behind him, his cell phone rang. He knew he was forgetting something at home. He quickly ran to the kitchen, trying to remember where he last put it. Perched right on top of his white refrigerator was his new Blackberry. Reaching for the phone, Bob realized that the caller was unknown. The sick feeling he had been experiencing for the past few days suddenly grew in magnitude.

"Hello?" said Bob in the least shaky voice he could procure.

"Alo. Alo?"

It must be an international call. "I think you have the wrong number."

Suddenly, there was a male voice screaming and giving orders to the woman on the other line. Bob tried to catch what they were saying but soon gave up when he realized they were speaking in what sounded like Creole. Suddenly the fighting ceased and a strong English accent dominated the now, too quiet, environment.

"Hello. Is this Robert Lawsin?" said the woman in a detached voice.

"Who is this?" Bob felt a chill climb up his spine. Not many people knew that his real name was Robert.

"Is this Robert Lawsin?" persisted the voice in a monotonous tone. The way she said it sounded more like a statement than an actual question.

"Yes. This is he. "Bob's caution caused his words to sound broken up.

"Robert. We have been watching you. Right now we are watching you. We know that you have a daughter Leslie Lawsin who is currently in the Caribbean. In fact, we now hold her hosta—"

"UNHAND HER! Don't harm her bastards. Who are you and what do you want! Who the hell are you?!"

The voice on the other line was eerily patient. Bob realized that she was not going to talk unless he was listening, so despite his fury he proceeded to close his mouth.

"Robert, we hold your daughter hostage and if you do not do as we say, you'll soon find her dead. Let me advise you to do exactly as we say; we are not afraid to kill a couple people in the process of obtaining what we want."

Bob took the deepest steadiest, "What is it that you want?" His voice was icy.

"We know you work for the CIA. We want exclusive information on the KULTRA project."

"I don't work for the CIA."

"We know you work for the CIA."

"I DON'T work for the CIA."

"Let us remind you to not lie, we have very intimate sources." A gunshot went off, a high girly scream followed.

"NO. Please. Please. Don't hurt her, I'll do anything else, but I don't work for the CIA. I used to, I'm retired now. I know nothing. I can be of no assistance to you."

"Fine. Mr. Lawsin, we'll make a deal. If you set us up with someone who will give us information, and hand us a total of half a million dollars, we will set your daughter free."

"No one's going to want to give you information. There's a reason we become part of the CIA."

"I know. That is why you won't be telling them."

Bob couldn't believe what he was hearing. He loved his daughter but to give up a teammate was unthinkable. But it was his daughter, his own flesh and blood. He had to do it. Unless there was a way to get around it all. Maybe if he informed his ex co-worker on what was going on he could find the kidnappers when the transaction was meant to take place. That way it would be a win-win situation.

"Fine I'll do it," he said finally.

"Let me remind you, do exactly as we say, do not inform anyone about anything. We will find out, and we won't hesitate to kill her. We'll be in touch." The line went dead.

Bob did not feel threatened by this, as a CIA member for more than 30 years he knew that no one handled better than them. There was no way they would ever find out.

Bob looked down at his lap. He was doing it again, shaking his leg uncontrollably. He felt such anxiety. He looked outside the airplane window and saw the vast blue Caribbean Sea. He had just boarded the plane half an hour ago, but it seemed like they had been flying for an eternity. He wondered about his daughter. About the risk this mission posed. And about the risk he was placing himself in. But if these people were as vigilant as they said to be they would have already known. Already killed his daughter. After all he had to tell his partner what was going on, neither of them could go into this mission blinded. These people, whoever these people are, would never send him two tickets if they knew that Bob and Stew had concocted some plan. In the end, though, he didn't blame them. After all, they were both once in the CIA. Bob and his co-worker were accustomed to dealing with secrets that would blow a normal person's mind. There was no way they could know.

"So Bob thanks for taking me on this trip. It has been a lifetime since I actually went on a vacation. You know I really do need time for myself. But try explaining that to Tess, she'll flip. She'll think I'm having an affair or something."

His former partner was very talkative and though talking too much usually showed signs of anxiety and uncertainty, the amount of talking his partner did was directly proportional to his certainty towards something.

"It's no problem Stew. I thought you could use a break, and there's really no one else I see myself going on vacation with."

Today was the day. He looked at his clock, paced back and forth, and looked at his clock again. It was two o'clock. The meeting was at two thirty, and he still didn't know where. They said they would get in touch with him. He couldn't wait to see his daughter, though it had only been a week since he last talked to her, knowing that she was in danger made it seem all the longer. Bob went to his bedroom balcony. The warm Caribbean breeze blew against his skin. The water sparkled against the highly positioned sun. Today the sun had an eerie glow to it. The sunlight was paler than usual, almost white. A sudden ring of his phone broke his concentration.

"Hello?" He said.

"Everything is ready; meet us at the downtown beach."

'Gee thanks for the directions, those were specific'

"Hey Stew want to go for a walk. It's a nice day to go to the beach, and I heard there are some real nice boutiques downtown. I kind of want to buy my daughter something."

Bob saw the recognition in Stew's eyes of what was going on after he mentioned his daughter. Stew barely said a word as he put his jacket on and was out the door faster than Bob could blink. Bob quickly followed. He checked his clicker, which, when his heartbeat elevated sufficiently, would indicate that it was time for the armed forces to intervene. He also made sure he had the money; they wouldn't even consider handing her over if he didn't show them some money.

When they finally arrived the sun was scorching. Though a trained professional, Bob still found it difficult to keep complete control of his body. He felt his palms begin to sweat, and tried to focus on something other than what he was about to do. Although he had been part of many missions, Bob never faced such high stakes before. Risking his life was one thing, but risking the life of his daughter and the life of his former partner was another deal. He felt a vibration, and tensed up right away. Realizing it was his phone, he read the incoming message. It was from an unknown number.

"Turn around, there is an alley behind you, the first door on your right is a super market. Enter it."

A supermarket? Wouldn't they want to do this transaction in a more discrete place? This sudden change of plans complicated things a little more. It meant that there was a higher possibility of civilian casualties.

"Uh Stew, let's get food to make dinner later. I'm sick of all this going out to dinner. I kind of want a homemade meal tonight."

Stew understood what was soon to occur, but his face expression did not mirror the confusion Bob felt on the chosen location.

Once they entered the supermarket Bob looked around. No one there seemed suspicious, and he was usually gifted at picking out that sort of thing. A man came up to him, asking him if he was a foreigner. Whether it was his heavy accent or the fact that Bob was not really listening, the local man had to repeat himself a couple of times. Bob felt dizzy and was having difficulty seeing. But at the same time, felt unusually calm. When he finally came to realize what was going on, the local man punched him in the gut and took control of him. Bob tried to escape, but he could not find himself to do so. He tried looking backwards, to see if his partner had also been captured and drugged. But the last he saw, as he hit the ground, was his partner looking over him with an unusual tranquility.

When he woke up he found himself strapped to a bed, in a dirty dim lit room. At first he thought it was all a bad dream, but then he looked around and felt the heaviness of his head from the drugs, and realized it was an unfortunate reality. Bob noticed a movement in the corner, and realized that it was a man who was trying to reach the door unnoticed. Not more than five seconds later, three men came in with a woman on one of their back. The girl looked as helpless as Bob felt. When he realized it was his daughter, his veins popped and his heartbeat rose, but he could not bring himself to move. His partner was amongst the three men.

"Hey Bob, how are you. They told you no funny business Bob, and the first thing you do is tell me. Now you don't leave us much of a choice Bob," said Stew.

Bob looked around, frantic; he noticed one of the three men was counting something. It was the money! They had gotten hold of the money.

"uheseeee. uheseeee." Bob tried to speak but he knew his speech was incomprehensible.

Stew leaned over him, "I'm sorry Bob I really am, but you shouldn't have been such a rebel." Stew had the girl set down on the bed beside him, and left the room.

Bob couldn't understand what was going on. Maybe they were letting her go. After all, they got the money, and that was all they wanted.

A couple of hours went by and Leslie finally woke up. She started crying when she saw her father.

"Daddy, you should have never came. They were never going to exchange me. You just risked your life. God you're so stupid. "Her words were slurred from her sobbing.

The three men came in again. But this time with a gun. Stew stayed in the back of the group this time.

"You know I really was gonna kill her a couple hours before, but I thought it would be better for you both to reunite first. You know, keeps the father—daughter relationship going," said the tallest man of the two.

The shorter, stubbier looking man on the right drew a gun and cocked it. Bob was frozen, he felt helpless, and there was nothing he could do but watch. Leslie shut her eyes, and right there and then, right next to her father she was shot cold, right in the chest.

Bob looked around the white walls. There was a certain numbness to him. He no longer had thoughts that he was able to call his own. He looked down at his hands, unable to move. It wasn't so bad when they drugged you. It took all the pain away. It did get lonely though, except for the occasional visitor. Bob couldn't remember too much about that night. Quite frankly he didn't like to. It wasn't healthy for him.

The betrayal he felt by Stew nearly drove him insane, and every time he thought of it he dwelled on how it was that Stew was ever able to deceive him.

A nurse came in. "Hello Mr. Lawsin, you have a visitor today. Your old friend came to visit you."

Bob looked around until he looked straight into those never ending blue eyes. It was twenty years later, and finally he had found his baby Leslie.

Afterword

I Wrote This Last Period

───ᵥₙₒₒₑₓₒₒₓₒₒᵥₙ───

The book you now hold in your hands is proof that teenagers have meaningful thoughts. Often, we are an age group looked upon negatively. Teenagers are obnoxious, wild, and think they know everything. However, as you have just learned, we are also inquisitive, thoughtful, and opinionated. When first given this task, the book did not bring us together, did not unite us, nor did it seem like anything more than an English assignment. But, now that it's written, put together, and in your hands, you can clearly see that this book brings our thoughts together, unites our experiences, and transcends all boundaries of an English assignment.

This book holds the ideas, beliefs, and feelings of fifty-five high school juniors. This is only one example of teenagers acting like young adults, not old children. Amid the pressures and stressors that students face on a daily basis, each one of us was able to put pen to paper. We wrote through our characters, but about ourselves. We wrote about our individual aspirations, beliefs, influences, and lives. And, yes, we wrote this last period. Our compilation should serve as a reminder to adults that even though we procrastinate, we've got the future under control.

Thanks for Reading,
Alex Libre and Michael O'Callaghan